P9-CDM-021

F
Coble

Coble, Colleen.

Lonestar angel.

DATE			

Seneca Falls Library
47 Cayuga Street
Seneca Falls, NY 13148

BAKER & TAYLOR

ALSO BY COLLEEN COBLE

Smitten

The Under Texas Skies series
Blue Moon Promise (Available February 2012)

The Lonestar Novels
Lonstar Sanctuary
Lonestar Secrets
Lonestar Homecoming

The Mercy Falls series
The Lightkeeper's Daughter
The Lightkeeper's Bride
The Lightkeeper's Ball

The Rock Harbor series
Without a Trace
Beyond a Doubt
Into the Deep
Cry in the Night

The Aloha Reef series
Distant Echoes
Black Sands
Dangerous Depths

Alaska Twilight
Fire Dancer
Midnight Sea
Abomination
Anathema

LONESTAR ANGEL

COLLEEN COBLE

THOMAS NELSON
Since 1798

NASHVILLE   DALLAS   MEXICO CITY   RIO DE JANEIRO

Seneca Falls Library
47 Cayuga Street
Seneca Falls, N. 13148

© 2011 by Colleen Coble

All rights reserved. No portion of this book may be reproduced, stored in a retrieval system, or transmitted in any form or by any means—electronic, mechanical, photocopy, recording, scanning, or other—except for brief quotations in critical reviews or articles, without the prior written permission of the publisher.

Published in Nashville, Tennessee, by Thomas Nelson. Thomas Nelson is a registered trademark of Thomas Nelson, Inc.

Thomas Nelson, Inc., titles may be purchased in bulk for educational, business, fund-raising, or sales promotional use. For information, please e-mail SpecialMarkets@ThomasNelson.com.

Scripture quotations are taken from THE NEW KING JAMES VERSION. © 1982 by Thomas Nelson, Inc. Used by permission. All rights reserved.

Publisher's Note: This novel is a work of fiction. Names, characters, places, and incidents are either products of the author's imagination or used fictitiously. All characters are fictional, and any similarity to people living or dead is purely coincidental.

Library of Congress Cataloging-in-Publication Data

Coble, Colleen.
   Lonestar angel / Colleen Coble.
      p. cm.
   ISBN 978-1-59554-269-4 (soft cover : alk. paper)
   1. Married people—Fiction. 2. Camp counselors—Fiction. 3. Missing children—Fiction. 4. Christian fiction. gsafd 5. Texas—Fiction. I. Title.
   PS3553.O2285L63 2011
   813'.54—dc22

                                                                2011030514

Printed in the United States of America
11 12 13 14 15 16 QG 6 5 4 3 2 1

Fic.

Seneca Falls Library
47 Cayuga Street
Seneca Falls, N.Y. 13148

For Alexa Coble
My perfect angel

1

SILVERWARE TINKLED IN THE DIMLY LIT DINING ROOM OF TWENTY, AN UPSCALE RESTAURANT located inside Charley Creek Inn, a classy boutique hotel. Eden Larson smiled over the top of her glass of water at Kent Huston. He was so intelligent and kind. His blue eyes were filled with intent tonight, and she had known what he had planned from the moment he suggested this place for dinner.

The piano player's voice rose above the music as he sang "Waiting for a Girl Like You." Kent had spoken that very phrase to her often in the year they'd been dating.

"Warm enough?" he asked.

"It's a perfect night."

"In every way," he agreed. "I want to—"

"Kent." She reached across the linen tablecloth and took his hand. "I need to tell you something."

Before he asked her to marry him, he needed to know what baggage she carried. She'd intended to tell him before now—long before. But every time she tried, the pain closed her throat. She wasn't ready to talk about it then, and maybe she wasn't ready now, but he deserved to know.

Kent smiled. "Are you finally going to tell me what brought you to town? I don't really care, Eden. I'm just thankful you're here. I love you."

She wetted her lips. It didn't matter that he said he didn't care. She owed it to him to tell him about her past and the demons that had driven her here to Wabash, Indiana. "Kent . . ." The sense of a presence behind her made her pause.

"Eden," a man said.

Her heart seized in her chest. She'd recognize the deep timbre anywhere. It haunted her dreams and its accusing tones punctuated her nightmares. The deep vibrancy of that voice would impress any woman before she ever saw him.

She turned slowly in her upholstered chair and stared up at Clay Larson, who stood under the crystal chandelier that was the centerpiece of the intimate dining room. "Clay."

How could he be here? He hadn't changed a bit. His hair was still just as dark and curly. His dark blue eyes were just as arresting. And her pulse galloped the way it had the first time she'd set eyes on him.

"I need to talk to you," he said, stepping toward her. "It's important."

Oh, she should have told Kent before now. This was the wrong way for him to discover her past. He was beginning to frown as he glanced from her to Clay, whose broad shoulders and vibrant presence loomed over their table. It was going to come out now. All of it. Her pretend life vanished into mist. What had made her think she could escape the past?

"Who are you?" Kent said. "And what right do you have to interrupt a private conversation?"

"The right of a husband," Clay said, his gaze holding her.

"Ex-husband," she managed to say past the tightness of her throat.

"No, Eden. *Husband*." He held up a sheaf of papers in his right hand.

"What are those?"

"I never signed the divorce papers," he said quietly, just to her. "You're still married to me."

She heard Kent gasp in the silence as the song in the background came to an end. "That's impossible." She stared at Clay, unable to take in what he'd said. "We were divorced over five years ago."

"You sent the papers over five years ago," he corrected. "I just never signed them."

She stared at the blank signature line he showed her. Why had she never followed up? Because she'd been too busy running. "Why not?"

He shook his head. "I had my reasons. Right now, there's something more important to discuss."

"What could be more important?" she asked. Fingers clutched her arm and she turned her head and stared into Kent's face. "I . . . I'm so sorry, Kent. I was just about to tell you."

"Tell me that you're married?" Kent's eyes held confusion and hurt. "I don't understand."

She shook her head. "I'm divorced. Or at least I thought I was. I haven't seen Clay in five years."

Kent's frown smoothed out. "I think you'd better leave," he said to Clay. He scooted back in his chair.

She laid a hand on his arm. "Let me handle this," she said. Anger was beginning to replace her stupor and shock. "Why are you here, Clay?"

"Would you like to step outside so we can continue this in private?" Clay asked, glancing around the room.

Heat flamed in her cheeks when she saw the interested stares from the two nearby tables. "Just go away. We can talk tomorrow."

His firm lips flattened but he stayed where he was. "I've found Brianna, Eden. She's alive."

She struggled to breathe. She searched his face for the hint of a lie but saw only implacable certainty. She shook her head. "That's impossible. She's dead."

Beside her Kent jerked, his eyes wide. She half rose.

"I never believed it," Clay said. "Her body was never found so I kept looking. She's alive, Eden."

She studied his expression. He returned her stare. His face was full of conviction, and she felt a tiny flutter that might be hope begin to stir. "You're serious?"

"I know she's alive. I can't retrieve her alone. I need you to come with me."

"How do you know these things? I don't understand anything."

"I'll explain all of it. But come with me now."

She wanted to believe him, but it was impossible. Had his grief made him delusional? Clay was the most logical, practical man she'd ever met. But what he was saying couldn't be true.

"I need to talk to Kent first," she said.

"I'll wait outside your apartment."

4

"How do you know where I live?"

"I know everything about you. I always have." He strode away through a gauntlet of interested stares.

She tore her gaze from Clay's broad back and directed her attention to Kent. There would be no tender proposal now. She hated the hurt in his eyes, hated that she'd put it there.

When she reached across the table to him, at least he didn't flinch away. His fingers gripped hers in the same confident way that had first attracted her. "I'm so sorry, Kent."

"You want to tell me about it?"

She didn't want to but she had to. "Clay and I didn't really know one another very well when we married. We met in Hawaii. He was on leave from the air force. He's a photojournalist. Our . . . our fling on vacation resulted in an unexpected blessing."

His brows lifted. "You got pregnant?"

"Yes. Clay wanted to do the right thing. And I wanted to provide the best upbringing for Brianna. I was in love with my daughter the first moment I laid eyes on her." Her eyes misted at the memory. "She was beautiful."

"I'll bet she was," Kent said, his voice soft. "She died?"

Eden nodded. "A kidnapping attempt that went wrong." Oh, she didn't want to talk about it. It hurt too much. Pain radiated from her chest to her throat. She swallowed hard. "Our marriage was all about her, not us. I ran away, unable to deal with his pain and my own." She managed a smile. "But I ended up here in Wabash, where I found Christ. And you. At least something good came of it."

They'd met at New Life, and she knew Kent understood the way her life had changed. He'd become a Christian a few weeks before they met.

Kent's eyes were troubled. "But now he's saying Brianna is alive."

She furrowed her brow. "I can't believe that's true."

Kent's expression grew calm. "Don't you think you'd better find out? If there's even a chance, you have to go with him."

She studied his dear face. While theirs had been no grand passion, they had a special relationship based on mutual respect, faith, and fondness. She'd had every intention of accepting his proposal when it came. His stability attracted her at the deepest level.

She pushed back her chair on the plush carpet. "You're right. Pray for me?"

"You know I will." He stood and walked her to the door, where he paused. "And if you come back to Wabash, we'll see what God has for us then. I think we both want his will."

She lifted her face for him to brush his lips across her cheek. "You're a good man, Kent Huston."

A slight smile tugged his lips upward. "Let me know what happens, okay?"

"I will." She left him at the restaurant and walked across the hotel lobby to the front doors.

Her cell phone rang before she reached the exit. She glanced at the caller ID. Daniel, her foster brother. He'd been in a snit ever since she told him she intended to accept Kent's proposal, and he hadn't answered any of her phone calls since. Well, he could wait himself now. Clay's revelation was too important to interrupt.

Through the glass door she saw Clay standing outside under the old-fashioned streetlight. He was staring at the marquee above the old Eagles Theater.

A forgotten emotion tugged at her heart. Memories vied for

possession of her mind, but she pushed them away and stepped outside. Brianna couldn't be alive. Could she?

❊

Clay stood outside the hotel on the brick sidewalk. Eden's apartment was just down the block, so he had time to admire this pretty town where she had ended up. Victorian-era buildings lined the downtown. Many had been renovated, even the old theater. The historic hotel that housed the restaurant also had a chocolate shop and other specialty stores. Too bad he wouldn't be here long enough to explore.

This was hardly Eden's type of place. He'd thought she would have fled to a big city where she could hide herself in the masses. She liked bright lights and nice clothes. At least she hadn't known he was a Larson when they first met. His family money had nothing to do with their instant attraction that day on the beach.

He reached into his pocket and his fingers touched smooth ceramic. He rolled the necklace around until his fingertips could trace the raised figure of a mother with a child. Clay had given the pendant to Eden when they married, and she had left it behind when she left him. An impulse had made him grab it today. Now that they knew Brianna was alive, maybe it wouldn't be as painful for her to wear again. She'd loved it once, a symbol of the family unit they wanted to build. Because the jewelry was from Colombia, it was a bridge between his two lives.

He heard a sound and turned to see Eden step through Charley Creek Inn's double glass doors. She wore a short skirt with heels and a rust-colored V-neck top that showed off her curves and made her auburn hair glimmer in the streetlight. The sleek glossy locks emphasized her high cheekbones and large turquoise eyes. She stared at him with a million questions in her expression.

"Ready?" he asked.

"I'm ready for some answers."

"Let's go to your place. You'll need to pack anyway." He fell into step beside her.

She stiffened but said nothing as they crossed with the light at Miami Street. He opened the double doors of her building and they entered a foyer dominated by a six-foot-wide staircase. Entering the place was like stepping back into the late eighteen hundreds.

"Nice," he said.

"I'm on the second floor." She led him to her apartment. The living room was spacious with gray-green walls and comfortable furniture. "I need coffee," she said.

He followed her into the kitchen and watched her measure water and coffee into her Cuisinart. When the aroma of coffee filled the kitchen, she leaned against the counter. "Tell me what you know about Brianna."

She seemed not to have considered that Clay might lie, which warmed him. He'd forgotten how beautiful she was, how she stirred his senses and made him forget everything but her.

Clay cleared his throat. "When her body was never found, I couldn't believe that she was dead. I hoped maybe someone had rescued her. I scoured orphanages, checked foster-care places in all the surrounding states, followed every lead. The trail went dead for over four years. Then I got this." He pulled the picture from his pocket and held it out to her.

Eden took it and held it under the wash of light. "Five little girls."

He'd studied it over and over. A row of little girls, all about five.

In the background was a ranch, and a sign beside them read Bluebird Ranch, Bluebird Crossing, Texas. "Look at the back."

She flipped it over. Her eyes widened as she read it aloud. "'Your daughter misses you. You'd better hurry if you want to see her.'" The color drained from her face, and she continued to study the picture. "What is this place?" she whispered.

"It's for kids in the foster-care system. They seem to do a good job with helping children."

Her eyes were pained. "She's been in foster care?"

"At least she's alive, Angel."

"I'm no angel, b-but maybe God has sent an angel to look over our daughter?" Her voice was breathless, just beginning to hold a tinge of hope.

He'd called her Angel the first time he met her in Hawaii. She'd thought it funny at the time. He'd been utterly serious. Her love had seemed so pure, so uplifting. Surely she was an ambassador of God to him. "I believe God has done just that."

She stared at him. "You're a believer now too?"

She'd become a Christian since he'd seen her last. That had been a constant worry for him. He nodded.

She stared at him. "Is it possible?" Her voice trembled and her gaze wandered back to the photo. "Where did you get this picture? How do you know it's not someone playing a nasty trick?"

He'd hoped she wouldn't ask. "I don't. Not for sure. It came in the mail, postmarked from El Paso. I took it to the police and they dismissed it as a joke. They never even discovered the name of the kidnapper, so I didn't expect them to have any leads. But look at the girls, Eden." He watched her study the picture again. "Something in my gut says she's there. Can we afford to ignore the possibility?"

"Who would send this?"

"I always thought the kidnapper who drowned had an accomplice. Maybe the partner sent it."

"Why? To taunt us? And why now?"

There was too much he didn't know. He couldn't let her see any weakness in him though, or she might not come. And he needed her. "I don't know the answer to those questions. Maybe it's a trap. It could be dangerous." He shrugged. "Maybe he wants his money after all. But can we afford to ignore even a slim chance of finding her?"

Eden's head snapped toward him. "I can't quite take it all in," she said.

Her eyes held a yearning that clutched at his throat. He'd felt the same way. "I don't understand what is happening either. Or why he's waited this long to get in touch again. But I have to go, and I need you to help me."

She stared back down at the picture. "Which one is she?"

Eden's beautiful face had haunted his dreams. He realized she was still waiting for an answer. "I don't know. Did her hair turn your shade or mine? We don't have any idea what color her eyes became. They were still blue when she was taken."

He knew the photograph by heart. There was a cute little blonde with blue eyes. Beside her sat a somber brunette with hazel eyes. The laughing one had auburn curls, a dimple, and green eyes. That was the one he was betting money on. A giggling girl with dark skin and large black eyes was next. The last one in the row of girls was a towhead with brown eyes. He'd been a towhead once, so she was a possibility too.

"I need to get a DNA sample from all the girls," he added. "We have Brianna's DNA on record."

"It will take ages to get the tests back," Eden said. She stared at the picture again. "I want to know now." She pushed the photograph back at him. "I'm happy here. Content. I don't know that I believe it, Clay. It might be the kidnapper's partner just trying to hurt us."

He had to make her see the truth. "You trusted me once, Eden. Can you put aside your doubts for a while and go with me on this?"

She glanced at her hands. "My peace has been hard won. I'm afraid."

Her admission made his chest squeeze. All he'd wanted was to protect her and build a home with her. But they'd barely started getting to know each other when their daughter was taken.

"I'm afraid too. But I know she's there. Still, let's say you're right—that someone's playing with us. This is the only shot we've got at finding out the truth. How can we ignore it?"

Eden's lips flattened. She took the picture again. "Where is this place?" She tapped a finger on the Bluebird sign.

"The ranch is near Big Bend National Park."

"I've never heard of it."

"It's in West Texas." He shrugged.

She turned back to pour cream into their coffee. "Why do you need me?"

"The ranch is looking for a married couple to serve as counselors. We'd be working directly with these girls."

She whirled back around to face him. "We'd be spending all our time with them?"

He nodded. "You'll come? I can't do it without you. They want a married couple."

He read the indecision in her eyes. Conflicting emotions of hope and fear flashed through them. "Eden?"

"All right. I'll come."

He closed his hand over her elbow and turned her toward the bedroom. "You need to pack. We'll be gone for several weeks at least. Maybe all summer."

She stopped and tugged her arm from his grasp. "What about my job?"

"Quit. Or take a leave of absence." If he had his way, she'd never come back here again.

She chewed on her lip. "I'll have to quit. They won't be able to get along without me for the summer. Do you have the job description?"

He nodded and dug the ad for the position out of his pocket, then handed it to her. "It's our perfect opportunity to slip in and find out the truth."

"Why can't we just go talk to these people—tell them what is going on?"

"If we waltz in there as strangers, the people who run the camp aren't going to give us the time of day. Their main goal is to protect the children. For all they know, we could be some nutso couple looking to make off with a child or two."

She read the ad, then handed it back. "But what about the police? Won't they help us find the truth?"

"They believe she's dead. The fellow in charge of the case blew me off when I showed him the picture. Once we get down there and assess the law enforcement, we can see if the sheriff is likely to listen."

"I still have a million questions," she said.

He took her arm and propelled her toward her bedroom to pack. "Ask me on the way."

2

CLAY'S "COWBOY CADILLAC" ATE UP THE MILES BETWEEN WABASH, INDIANA, AND BLUEBIRD Crossing, Texas. The last time Eden had been in a truck was the day she left Clay. The odors of horse, grease, and man took her back five years to a place and time she'd worked hard to forget.

She shifted as the memories tried to surface, staring out the window at the orange rocks and shimmering desert that went on for miles. They'd been on Interstate 10 for hours and had seen only one other vehicle. Sage and creosote bushes grew as far as the eye could see. "How far to Bluebird Crossing?"

"Almost there." Clay's voice was gravelly.

He hadn't slept in nearly twenty-four hours. Eden had offered to drive several times, but he'd kept his size-12 boot to the accelerator, stopping only for gas, grabbing food and bathroom breaks when they did. She'd hoped to find out more about his search for Brianna, but his first explanation had been the most complete.

"Why would the kidnapper's partner—if that's who's really behind this—contact you after all these years?" she asked. "I wish we knew that part."

"If we knew that, we might know who they were. And why they'd done it. The police always believed they were illegal immigrants."

"None of it makes any sense."

"No," he said, turning the wheel into a wide curve. "I always thought her kidnappers wanted revenge for that mission I'd been involved in down in Colombia. The money they demanded was the same amount that they claimed was stolen by the officers we got out of the compound."

As a photojournalist in the military, Clay sometimes got involved in dangerous things. During her pregnancy, after they'd been married only two weeks, he was sucked into the rescue operation of two Americans held captive by drug lords. Eden suspected his part was much more intensive than he'd ever told her.

"You've always said that, but the police found no evidence of it. And why would drug lords care about only ten grand?"

"They found no evidence of much of anything," he pointed out. "And I think wanting the money back was an honor thing. At least that's my theory. Besides, the money vanished from our SUV. Someone must have stolen it."

"There were kids hanging around watching."

He shrugged. "I still think an accessory took the money while we were occupied. And now I don't even believe Brianna was in that car that went under the water."

Without warning, images of the day they'd lost Brianna came flooding back. She'd been in her SUV that day, not Clay's truck.

THE SUV SURGED FORWARD WHEN SHE PRESSED HARD ON THE ACCELERATOR. SHE STRAINED to see through the rain sluicing down the windshield. Where was the river? Moisture gathered in her eyes and she blinked it away. Tears would solve nothing.

"Not so fast!" Clay leaned forward in the passenger seat, peering through the downpour. "I think the road turns any second. The pull-off by the riverbank is on the left."

Eden eased up on the pedal. "Do you really think they'll be here with Brianna?" Just saying her baby's name made her throat close and her breasts ache. Twenty-four terrible hours had passed since she last held her six-week-old daughter. Her empty arms twitched with the need to cuddle Brianna, who had given up her first smile the day before she was taken.

"They'd better be there." Her husband's voice was grim. His gun, a big, scary black one, was on his lap as well as the briefcase holding the ransom money. He pointed. "There's the turnoff."

She steered the vehicle onto the gravel path that led to the river. Her vision wavered again. Dratted rain. Opening her mouth to tell Clay she saw the rushing water, she shut it when she saw the other vehicle ahead. Her foot tromped the accelerator to catch the speeding car before she realized she was doing it. The tires spun on the gravel, then caught purchase and propelled the big vehicle toward the Taurus.

"Look out!" Clay yelled.

Too late she realized she was going to ram the Taurus. Her SUV slammed into the car's bumper, and it spun around as it slid down the embankment to the water. The sound of screeching metal filled her ears. The man behind the steering wheel had his mouth open in a scream she couldn't hear as her vehicle shoved the car into the swollen river. The Taurus hit the churning brown water and listed onto its side.

Shoving open her door, she staggered to the edge of the river. "Brianna!" she shrieked into the wind.

The driver pounded on the glass, his panicked face barely visible behind the window. His boot hit the pane and shattered it, and the man clambered through the opening. His head disappeared in the dirty foam. Eden started toward the water, but Clay dragged her back, then dived into the muddy river. She could barely see through the rain. Wading into the water, she tried to paddle after him, but she wasn't a strong swimmer, and the filthy water filled her throat and mouth. Her knees scraped gravel, and she came up gagging. She flung her wet hair out of her eyes. Where was Clay?

She caught a glimpse of his dark head. He'd reached the car, but the current had it as well, and the door handle rolled away from him. He kicked after it, and her heart rose as she saw him wrench open the back door. Water gushed in. He disappeared inside, and she watched with her heart pounding until he exited the rolling car.

He was empty-handed.

SOMETHING TOUCHED HER AND SHE JERKED BACK TO THE PRESENT. STUPIDLY, SHE STARED at Clay's big hand covering hers. The scar on his wrist was another stark reminder. He'd gotten it in the rescue attempt. She became aware that tears coursed down her cheeks, and she swiped her palm across her wet face.

The truck was stopped in a dirt drive. His steady gaze held hers.

"She didn't die in that water, Eden. Don't go there." He leaned over and thumbed away a tear.

She told herself not to react to the warmth of his hand or the gentleness of his touch. How did he know that's what she was thinking about? She could have been crying about anything. "It was my fault," she said.

"It was an accident. It wasn't your fault. It could have happened even if I'd been driving. But I wanted to be ready to play hero."

Her eyes burned and her vision blurred. The next thing she knew, she was sobbing against his chest, her tears dampening his shirt. His arms held her close, and he pressed a kiss against the top of her head. She'd forgotten how safe he always made her feel.

She drew away. Her shiver had nothing to do with his touch. The air conditioner was just too cold, she told herself, until a long-forgotten passion swelled in her. She pressed against him, and his embrace tightened. Would losing her pain in his arms be so terrible? His blue eyes darkened when she lifted her face toward him.

He lowered his head, and she realized what was happening. She couldn't go there again, where passion instead of careful thought ruled. Shoving against his chest with both hands, she tore herself from his embrace.

"I'm sorry," she said in a choked voice. "I'm all right. It's all a little overwhelming."

He gulped in a breath, then nodded and put the truck in drive. A few moments later he said, "We're here."

She leaned forward and drank in the two-story ranch house flanked by a big white barn. It had a hipped roof, and white paddocks stretched as far as she could see. She was surprised to notice a hangar that held a small plane.

A stucco bunkhouse was behind the main building and a newer similar building beside it. She smiled as a child shrieked with laughter, and children were playing jump rope in the grass. Her heart rebounded against her ribs.

Brianna was one of them. But which one?

※

His gaze on the children, Clay slammed the truck door and stretched out his muscles. He checked his impulse to go directly to the kids.

Eden came around the other side of the truck. She chewed on her bottom lip as she watched the children. She looked out of place in her high heels and short skirt. But very cute. He tore his gaze from her shapely legs.

Eden started toward them, and he caught her arm. "Not yet," he warned. "We're just here about the job, remember? Smile, be professional. We have to get hired first."

"I wish we could just tell them about the situation."

"There's no way they'd let us have access to the girls. Not without a court order. And the police aren't cooperating."

He turned her toward the wide porch attached to the front of the storybook farmhouse. The white stone gleamed in the sunshine. The red door stood partly open past the screen. He could hear a woman's voice on the other side but couldn't make out what she was saying. He put on a smile and rapped on the door.

A pretty brunette came to the door with a welcoming tilt to her lips. "Good afternoon! You must be the Larsons. I'm Allie Bailey." She opened the screen. "Come on in and don't mind the mess. We're still unpacking stuff. A group of older kids arrived this morning."

She led them down the hall, past suitcases disgorging their contents of brightly colored shorts and T-shirts onto the gleaming wood floor. In the living room, a small boy of about three sat in the middle of the chaos, and a girl of about nine with dark curls handed him a cookie.

"These are my two. Betsy and Matthew." Allie lifted the little boy from the middle of the clothes. "Sit here if you're eating a cookie," she said, placing him at the coffee table. She smiled at Clay and Eden. "Have a seat."

Clay glanced around the space and found a chair by the window. The wind blew the scent of hay and manure through the screen. He wiped his brow. "Please excuse our appearance. We drove all night to get here."

Allie's eyes widened. "You came straight from Indiana?"

"We didn't want to miss this opportunity. This is my wife, Eden." He saw Eden stiffen, but she said nothing. "We love kids, and this position is right up our alley."

Allie gestured to the other chair, and Eden settled on it. "Your résumés were pretty persuasive. I've seen some of your photos, Clay, and you can parachute, hang glide, dive, and find your way in any terrain." She laughed. "My husband, Rick, is eager to meet you. He used to be in the military himself and likes to talk about that kind of thing. Plus, we'd love to see you take the kids on some nature outings and teach them photography."

"Sounds great. Is Rick here?" Clay asked.

She shook her head. "He'll be back shortly. He had to run into Bluebird Crossing for supplies. You realize these are small children, though? The hiking trails you will be taking them on are pretty tame compared to what you're used to."

He grinned, already liking the petite brunette. "I'm ready for some tame."

She glanced at Eden. "You're a nurse?"

Eden nodded. "And I'm very organized. I look forward to the challenge and have a special place in my heart for foster kids. I was one myself."

Allie's blue eyes lightened in approval. "Some of these kids really need a woman with your compassion and experience. They've been in rough situations."

He exchanged a glance with Eden. Had their child been one in a tough situation? The thought shook him.

Eden's frozen face cracked into a commiserating smile. Finally. Clay was beginning to think she'd turned to stone where she sat in the chair. And he couldn't blame her. He'd thrown a lot at her in the last day.

"Tell me more about your program," Eden said, her voice surprisingly steady.

Allie nodded. "We get a variety of ages. You would have the five- and six-year-olds. Della and Zeke Rodriguez have the seven- and eight-year-olds that just came in this morning. These kids will be here a month. The group we have coming in after that is older. Teens."

Eden leaned forward. "Your ranch is pretty amazing. How does working with horses help disadvantaged children?"

Allie's smile held a shadow. "Most of the animals here are rescue animals. Some have been neglected and some actually abused. The kids look into the eyes of the horses and find the same misery they are experiencing. It creates a bond that helps them both."

"Amazing," Clay said. He didn't want to think about any child having misery. Especially his own. This was going to be a tough few weeks.

"The kids learn about responsibility and caring for another creature. They discover what giving of themselves is all about." Allie studied Clay's face, then switched her attention to Eden. "Your references had only glowing things to say about both of you. And our mutual friend Michael Wayne sang your praises to the heavens."

He leaned forward. "We really want this job. We brought our belongings with us and can start right away."

Allie blinked, as though taken aback by his forthrightness. "Rick usually makes the final decision, but he already liked what he saw from your résumé. You're hired!" She rose. "Let me show you where to put your things. I'll escort you around the ranch on the way."

Out in the yard, Clay's gaze went straight to the little girls. The redhead caught his eye at once. The color of her hair was like Eden's, gleaming like new copper. The child chased a ball that stopped by his feet.

She stopped and glanced up at him hesitantly. He stooped and picked up the ball, then offered it to her. "What's your name, honey?"

"Katie." She took the ball and stared at him.

"This is Mr. Clay and Miss Eden, Katie," Allie said. "They'll be sleeping in the bunkhouse with you. They're here to help you."

A lump formed in his throat, and he saw Eden take a step toward the girl. He grabbed his wife's forearm. "We'd better go. We'll be seeing you around, Katie."

The child's head dipped, and her gaze went back to the other children.

"Run along," Eden said, her tone brisk. "We'll get to know you all better tonight."

Clay clasped her hand and didn't let go when she tried to tug away. "We're eager to get started."

3

EDEN'S HEELS SANK INTO THE SANDY SOIL AS SHE FOLLOWED ALLIE ACROSS THE SCRUBBY
yard. She should have worn flats with her skirt, but when she'd chosen
the outfit back in Indiana, she'd needed the extra inches for courage
when facing Clay. A pungent odor hung in the air. Mesquite? Sage?

She sneezed and nearly stumbled, but Clay caught her hand and
she righted herself. He tried to clutch her fingers but she pulled them
free. His touch still ignited something inside her. The sensation was
nothing she was prepared to examine. Not now, not ever.

Allie pointed to the newer building. "The other bunkhouse was
just finished. Della and Zeke are housed there with the older girls."
She pushed open the wooden screen door. "Here we are. It's not a
Hyatt, but it's clean and functional."

She led them into a rectangular room that ran the width of the building. Easily forty feet long and fifteen feet wide, the space contained a kitchen and table with benches on one end and a living area on the other. The sofa and chairs had seen their fair share of bubble gum, Little Debbie cakes, and popcorn. An old-style projection TV took up one corner. But everything was spotless, even the plate-glass window that let sunlight stream onto the battered pine floors. The place smelled of lemon wax and an apple-scented candle.

Eden stepped onto the blue-and-white rag rug. "It's very homey."

"We do what we can to make the kids feel loved and wanted here. Let me show you the bedrooms." Allie pointed out the dorm on one side of the hall. Five bunk beds flanked by utilitarian dressers were scattered through the room. There was one queen bed back against the far wall. "We have only one gender here at time."

Eden glanced around and spotted hair ribbons and pink bows. A lump formed in her throat. She wanted to wander the room alone and examine all the little-girl items. Which bed belonged to Brianna? There was a stuffed bear on the closest bed. Its button nose was missing, and the little vest was ragged from the loving touch of small fingers.

She picked it up. "Whose is this?"

"That's Katie's."

The little redhead. The child she'd felt an immediate attraction to. Eden hugged the bear to her chest, then reluctantly placed it back on the corduroy coverlet.

Allie stepped to the door. "Your room is across the hall. There's a monitor so you can hear what's going on in here."

Room. As in one. Eden hadn't thought far enough ahead to consider sleeping arrangements. She stopped in the hall when she saw the king-size bed that dominated the room. Clay nearly ran into her, and his big hands came down on her shoulders to steady them both. She heard him inhale harshly at the same time she did.

She managed a smile at Allie, who had a raised brow. "Nice big room," she said awkwardly.

Their employer smiled. "There's a stereo and computer for your use. We've got satellite Internet too. Not the fastest high-speed, but better than dial-up. Oh, and cell phone coverage is terrible here. There are only a few hot spots in the county."

Eden walked the perimeter of the room, peeked into the massive closet, and nodded approval at the two big dressers. "We'll be fine here."

"I'll leave you to unpack, then," Allie said as a cowboy lugged their suitcases into the room. "This is Buzz. If you need anything, just ask." She gave a wave, then her sandals slapped against the floors as she exited.

The man's weathered face cracked into a smile. "Got iced tea in the fridge. Cheese and venison sausage there too if you're hungry."

"We're fine for now," Eden lied, eyeing the bed.

Buzz backed out of the room. "Just holler if you need anything." He shut the door behind him.

Eden exhaled. "Well, this is a nice mess you've gotten us into."

He lifted a brow and grinned. "What? It's a big bed. You stay on your side, and I'll stay on mine."

Her glare was lost on him because he turned away, grabbed the biggest suitcase, and heaved it onto the plaid bedspread. He lifted the lid and began to haul her belongings out.

"I'll do that myself." She elbowed him out of the way. That spicy cologne was the same one he'd always worn, and the familiarity made her want to lean against him for a moment. But she collected herself. She wouldn't be weak. She had to focus on her daughter.

She kicked off her heels and began to lift her things out. The braided rug was rough on her feet. "Okay with you if I take this dresser?" She pointed to the one on the left side of the bed.

He didn't look at her. "Whatever you want."

Fine. He could give her the cold shoulder if he wanted. She jammed her underwear into the top drawer, then began to hang up her slacks and tops. She glanced at Clay out of the corner of her eye. It would take all her strength to ignore the chemistry between them. And that's all it had ever been.

He turned and caught her staring, but he frowned when he saw her side of the closet. "Is that all you brought? No jeans?"

She wrinkled her nose. "Jeans?"

"I thought by now you would have unbent a little. Everyone wears jeans. It's not a sign of poverty."

What did he know of poverty? He'd never gone to school in jeans that were three inches shy of her ankles and riddled with holes. Not the stylish tears either, but gaping holes that made other girls giggle. When she had finally gotten a decent pair of slacks, she'd sworn never to wear jeans again. And she wasn't about to start now.

❋

An hour later Eden coughed as a cloud of dust kicked up by the horses' hooves enveloped her. The thick red dirt already coated her slacks, and she was sure it was in her hair as well. She sat on the top rail of the corral fence and watched Buzz lead the last horse into the barn. When were they bringing the girls out to meet them? Her insides felt as jittery as the grasshoppers she saw fleeing the cowboy's boots.

Clay touched her arm. "Here they come."

She turned and saw Allie leading the girls from the house toward the corral. The little redhead was first in the line. Clay put his big hands on Eden's waist and lifted her from the fence. She stepped away from him as soon as her flats hit the dirt.

The children reached the scrubby grass beside the corral, and Allie instructed them to sit in a circle. "This is Mr. Clay and Miss Eden, girls. They will be living with you in the bunkhouse. Can you tell them your names?"

The honey-skinned child with cornrows ducked her head. "I'm India," she said, twisting a braided lock around her finger. "I just turned six."

The redhead, Katie, stared directly at them with a curious expression in her green eyes. "I can do a somersault. Want to see?"

"In a little while," Eden said, taken by the child's spirit.

"Can I ride the horse?"

"Tell them your name," Allie said. "Then we'll see about the ride."

"I already did when they got here. I'm Katie," the child said. "I'm India's sister."

Allie smiled. "They've been inseparable since they arrived." She urged a brown-haired little girl forward. "And this is Lacie. She doesn't talk much, but all her shirts are red. Is that your favorite color, Lacie?"

Lacie nodded and puffed out her chest to show her Minnie Mouse shirt.

A blonde with huge brown eyes clung to Allie's leg. "Do you have a dog?" she asked. "My foster mom said I could have a puppy here."

"We have some puppies in the barn you can play with," Allie said. "And Jem is around here somewhere. He's a very nice dog. Can you tell your counselors your name?"

"Madeline," the little girl said. "I'm going to name my puppy Oscar."

Eden smiled at the last little girl. Smaller than the other children, she had her head down. Her mousy brown hair nearly hid her face. "What's your name, sweetheart?"

The child buried her head against Allie's leg. "Paige. I don't want to ride the horses. I'm 'lergic to them."

Allie smiled. "You're not allergic to them, honey. You're just scared. Give it a day or two and you'll find one you love."

"I want to see the puppies now," Madeline demanded. "Miss Casey told us they would be old enough today, and I still haven't seen them."

Allie grinned. "Casey was the previous counselor. She had to leave because her brother was in an accident. The kids are all yours." She pointed to the side barn door. "The puppies are right through there if you want to take the children to see them first. They just got their eyes open. Then you can do whatever activities with them you like. There's a jungle gym set up behind the barn as well as a swing in the hayloft."

Which one of these girls was Brianna? Eden studied each one in turn as they headed to see the pups. She jumped when Clay put his hand on her elbow and leaned toward her to whisper in her ear.

His breath stirred her hair. "Katie looks like you."

"She has red hair. That's all," she said. "Lacie and Paige both have brown hair like yours. Four of them could be Brianna." She'd so hoped one glimpse of the girls would tell her which one was their daughter, but it wasn't going to be that easy.

His hand dropped away and he yanked open the door to the barn. A border collie darted past him and raced toward the house. Eden peered past Clay to the dim interior of the barn. She sneezed at the scent of hay. Dust motes danced in a shaft of sunlight. Was that smell manure? The nauseating scent made her stop dead in the doorway.

Clay glanced at her feet. "I think we'd better get you some boots."

It *was* manure. A patty of brown lay between her and the closest stall. "Boots? I'm a city girl, not a cowboy."

"Alrighty then, city girl. Be careful of the rattlers and tarantulas."

She recoiled when he named the creatures. "You're kidding, right?"

"Dead serious." He pointed to something on the wall.

Peering closer, she realized it was the tail of a snake. The rattling part, she assumed. She shuddered.

"Puppies!" Madeline darted past them to where a border collie lay on a bed of hay. Six round-bellied puppies crawled around her.

"Ooh, too cute!" Eden squatted and scooped up an adorable black-and-white one that had one eye circled in black fur.

"Looks like they're about two weeks old," Clay said.

But he was watching her, not the puppy. Her face heated and she handed the puppy to Madeline. The little girl's wispy hair was so blond it was nearly as white as the little collie's pale fur. Eden resisted the urge to run her fingers through that fine fluff. She'd seen pictures of Clay, and he'd been a towhead as a child.

"This one is mine," Madeline said, cuddling the puppy close. "His name is Spot."

"What happened to naming him Oscar?" Clay asked.

The little girl stared at the puppy. "No, he's a Spot. Oscar is green."

Eden noticed Paige hanging back. "Want to hold a puppy?" she asked.

Paige backed away. "I can't have a dog. I'm 'lergic."

"Well, you can stay here with me, then. Maybe we can get you a fish or something." Eden smiled when the child leaned against her leg. Being around children again was awakening long-dormant feelings of warmth. She watched the other girls romp with the puppies. "Spot can be our group puppy. We'll come and see him often, okay? Because puppies need their mommies to grow up strong and healthy."

Her voice trailed off when the girls looked at her. None of them had mommies, poor kids.

4

EDEN WAS IN THE BATHROOM HELPING THE GIRLS WITH THEIR BATHS. CLAY SAT WITH HIS boots on the scarred coffee table in the TV room. Their first day was under their belt, but it had been too hectic to even think about getting DNA samples. They'd do that tomorrow for sure. He had brought a top-notch kit from a respected lab that law enforcement officers used.

A fist thumped the screen door, and he looked up to see a man in a cowboy hat on the stoop. "Come on in," Clay called.

The man pushed his hat to the back of his head and stepped through the doorway. "You two did a fine job today, Allie said." He held out his hand. "Rick Bailey."

Clay put his feet on the floor and stood, then gripped Rick's outstretched hand. "I've heard a lot about you from Michael Wayne.

And from Brendan Waddell. Michael is looking forward to seeing you again. I'm sure he'll be calling so you can meet Gracie and he can meet Eden."

"I'll track him down if he doesn't."

Rick dropped onto the sofa. "They both gave you a glowing recommendation." The man studied Clay. "Brendan says you helped him out in Colombia."

The awareness in the man's face was caused by more than information about Clay's past career. "Sounds like he's given you more than just my work stats."

Rick's eyes were kind. "He told me about your daughter. I'm sorry."

Clay couldn't hold the man's compassionate gaze. He sighed and glanced out the window. "Thanks." It was a relief to have that bit out in the open.

"Did you ever find out who was responsible?"

Clay shrugged. "Not really." He didn't know the man well enough to confide in him. He picked up the file on the table. "I've been reading about the girls in our bunkhouse. Rough stuff."

Rick nodded, his expression sober. "The things we see could break your heart. This batch of kids is sweet as all get-out, though."

Clay opened the folder. "Looks like Lacie was left outside a Catholic church when she was six months old. In February."

"A puzzle, that one. She'd been well taken care of. Had on a sleeper that came from Nordstrom's. That seemed odd. Her parents were well enough off to buy things at a fine department store but then abandoned her? Something weird about that."

"This was in Dallas?"

"Yep." Rick reached over to pull out a picture of a baby held by a nun. "This is Sister Marjo. She visits Lacie every month, so I hear. She's the woman who found Lacie."

Clay studied the woman's smiling face. "Does Lacie mention her?"

"All the time. The sister is coming here in two weeks while on vacation."

"That's dedication. Getting to this neck of West Texas is like visiting the moon." He flipped to the next child. "Madeline was taken from her mother when the mom was put in a mental hospital. Where is the mother now?"

"Evidently she was released two months ago. She's begun proceedings to regain custody."

Clay winced. "How well is she?"

"Probably not that great," Rick said. "Schizophrenia isn't easily cured. I'm doubtful she can get custody."

"We're quite taken with Katie," Clay said, picking up the picture of the smiling redhead.

"We all are. She lights up a room when she comes in. Her father was shot in a burglary. There were no other family members around to take her, so she ended up in foster care at age three."

"Was she home during the shooting?"

Rick nodded. "She has nightmares about it, though she says she doesn't remember. Several psychologists have tried to get details out of her. The murderer was never apprehended."

"Where's her mom?"

Rick shrugged. "Took off sometime before that and hasn't been in contact."

Clay picked up another paper. "From what I read, India's entire family was killed in a house fire?"

Rick winced. "Horrible situation. She was four. A meth lab explosion."

Clay's own plight began to feel less horrible, somehow, knowing the pain that innocent children endured every day. "Lot of heartache in these kids' lives."

"Too much." Rick leaned over and picked up a picture of Paige.

Clay's heart clenched at the somber expression on her face. Her mousy hair hadn't been washed. Too much misery stared out of those brown eyes. "What's her story?"

"No one really knows. She was a year old and found in a Walmart. There was a video that showed two men leaving her in the toy department."

"Was she—abused?" It was all he could do to force out the question. He wasn't sure he wanted to hear the answer.

Rick shook his head. "No. That was the first worry, but other than being dirty and uncared for, she was healthy."

"How did you know her name?"

"The foster home named her. She's been with the same couple for four years. In fact, they've started adoption procedures. Good family."

Which one was Brianna? Clay had no clue. He was drawn to Katie, but how much of that was simple charisma and personality? And the red hair, of course. His daughter could be any one of the girls except for India. He flipped back through the pictures. Why had he thought this would be so easy?

"Want to meet the other counselors?" Rick asked.

"Sure."

"They're coming here for devotions. We try to do that with all the kids together. I wanted to make sure you were up to it on your first night."

"I can use some of God's Word myself right about now. It's been a wild day. But fun."

Clay watched Rick step to the door and call across the yard. A few minutes later a couple trooped inside with eight girls. The kids were a little bigger than Clay and Eden's charges, calmer somehow, and a little warier.

The couple was in their late thirties. The man looked like a young James Earl Jones, burly and with an expressive face as he smiled and shook hands with Clay. "Glad to have some help here," the man said. "I'm Zeke, and this is my wife, Della."

His wife was beautiful with black hair and dark eyes that held love as she touched the head of a little girl near her. "I caught a glimpse of your pretty wife, Clay. Where is she?"

"She's getting the girls ready for bed." He heard them trooping down the hall. "Here they come." He drank in the sight of the freshly bathed girls. He was already beginning to think of them as his girls.

Eden paused in the doorway and smiled. "Hi. You must be the Rodriguez family."

"We're about to have devotions together," Clay put in.

The day she left him, she shouted that she wanted nothing to do with a God who would take her baby from her. She said she was a Christian now.

When her eager smile came, he wanted to know what had happened in the five years they'd spent apart that had brought her to Christ.

※

In the shaft of light through the open door, the children were clearly visible. Eden stared at each girl. They slept peacefully, curled together like puppies in the big bed. They'd begged to sleep together, but she doubted they'd stay like that all night. She pulled the door closed, squared her shoulders, and went to find her husband.

She stopped in the hall and gulped. Clay was still her husband. She hadn't allowed her thoughts to wander there much since this race to find their daughter had begun. Was it only yesterday at seven that he'd shown up in her life again? A few hours ago she'd been planning to accept Kent's proposal.

Forcing herself forward, she went down the hall and stood in the doorway to the gathering spaces. An old western starring John Wayne played on the television. The scent of popcorn teased her nose, and she saw Clay in the recliner with his boots off. A bowl was in his lap and a big glass of iced tea was on the table beside him. She knew without sipping it that there would be enough sugar in it to eat the spoon away.

He must have sensed her gaze on him because he jerked his head toward where she stood. Kernels bounced from his lap as he sprang to his feet. "Hey."

"The girls are asleep."

He held up the bowl. "Want some popcorn?"

The smell tantalized her, but the thought of cozying up to him on the couch to share the treat made her shake her head. She chose the chair the farthest away from him.

"Tea?" A grin tugged his lips as he held up his glass.

"I still have a gag reflex."

He took a gulp. "You'll be happy to know I've cut down on the amount of sugar."

"To what? Half a cup?"

His grin widened. "It's what keeps me so sweet-natured."

She squelched the desire to smile. During their very short and tempestuous marriage, he'd always had a way of coaxing her out of a bad mood. Picking up the remote, she shut off the TV. "We need to talk."

"I'm all ears."

"There's no way of knowing which of those girls is Brianna. We need that DNA test as soon as possible."

"I know." He picked up a manila file folder beside him. "I've poured through their histories and even talked to Rick. Any one of them could be our daughter, except India."

She reached for the folder and flipped it open. Katie's smiling face greeted her, and her gut clenched. "I think Katie is Brianna."

His gaze gentled. "She's a little cutie. But don't get your heart set on her. I'm betting Paige is our daughter." He moved out of the recliner and knelt beside her chair. Flipping through the pages, he pointed out Paige's stats. "Look here. She was left at Walmart by two men. Sounds like kidnappers to me."

The infant's photo tugged at Eden's heart. The baby's somber gaze held a light. "No one knows her real name?"

"Nope. But read the rest before you make a snap judgment."

She riffled through the other biographies, then finally closed the file. "You're right. Brianna could be any one of the four. So we really are going to have to wait for the DNA. How long will it take?"

His lips flattened. "Too long. Weeks after these kids leave here."

She desperately wanted to know which of these girls was their daughter. It had been all she could do while bathing them not to press her lips to their damp foreheads. She hadn't wanted to frighten them, though, so she'd been warm but kept an appropriate distance.

"I'll get hair samples from them over the next couple of days," she said. "Can you get them into a priority lab?"

"I can try."

And she knew he would. He had connections. She mentally prepared for what she had to say next. How did she even broach the subject of sleeping arrangements?

"Spill it, Eden," he said.

He grinned, and even though she wanted to glare at him, her lips twitched. She glanced away.

"I already know what's eating you, you know," he said. "But that bed is a king. We'll stuff pillows between us. I promise to stay on my side."

She let out a sigh. "I don't like it, Clay. Our marriage was over a long time ago. It feels—weird." Forcing her gaze up, she stared into his face. "It took me a long time to get over you."

"I never got over you," he said, his voice soft.

Heat flared in her cheeks. "See what I mean? This will never work if you remind me at every opportunity that we were once married."

His eyes narrowed. "We're *still* married."

"So it appears." She still couldn't believe her attorney hadn't made sure everything was final. She struggled to remember how things had happened five years ago. She'd rushed away when Brianna died, and her lawyer had said he'd take care of the details. Something had obviously fallen through the cracks.

But not for long.

"Why did you leave?" he asked. He looked down at his popcorn bowl. "You took off without a word."

She went cold. Admitting she left because his reason for marrying her was gone would only serve to show the chasm between them. But honesty was all that would do now. They had too much at stake to play games.

She held her head high. "Clay, you know perfectly well you only married me because I was pregnant. We barely knew each other. You were gone more than you were home. Once Brianna was gone, there was nothing to hold us together. I needed a clean break."

And she'd barely cauterized the wound. Or was it still oozing blood?

5

She couldn't stay in the bathroom forever. Eden eyed the peach-colored teddy she wore and shuddered. Why hadn't she checked her suitcase before rushing off on this search? What seemed fine in the privacy of her apartment was indecent here.

She let out a groan and leaned onto the sink. Surely there had to be another way to get to the truth. Why not just tell the Baileys that they thought Brianna was here? They had children. Any parent would be sympathetic to their cause.

But not if it impacted their business. Their mission.

How could she ask them to get involved? The Baileys had been entrusted with the children's welfare. Rick and Allie didn't know her and Clay. The Baileys might toss them out for fear they might kidnap one of the girls. She lifted her head and stared into her own frightened eyes.

She had to open that door and go into the bedroom. This wasn't some stranger she was sharing a room with. This was Clay. He wouldn't hurt her. The problem was, she didn't know how she felt about him. While he'd been absent, she could almost forget their marriage had ever happened. She could push aside the memories of a tiny body cuddled to her breast and the scent of her newborn baby.

The muscles in her throat worked at the memories that surged. Her eyes burned. She would not think about that day. Could not. Straightening, she twisted the doorknob and stepped into the hall and to the bedroom door.

The covers were turned back on the big bed. She focused on the picture above the bed of a tranquil mountain stream. Anything to calm the way her pulse jumped when Clay turned to look at her. His chest was bare and he wore blue pajama bottoms, a concession to her she was sure. In the old days he didn't wear—She cut off the mental image before it could form.

He let out a low whistle. "I assume Kent was to be the recipient of that getup."

She dived for the bed and covered herself with the sheet. "Our relationship was pure, and I'm in no mood for your tone."

He grinned and climbed into the bed beside her. "Want pillows between us?"

"If you promise to keep your distance, you can have the space."

He shrugged. "All I want is to find our daughter."

His words stung more than she'd expected. Not that she wanted him to be making a pass at her. "Why didn't you call?" she asked abruptly. "Rather than just show up. And how did you find me anyway?"

He put his hands behind his head and leaned back on the pillow. "I knew you'd never believe me without seeing the photograph. I've always known where you were. It's not hard to track someone."

He grinned and shrugged. "I tried to get up the nerve to call you when I got the divorce papers, but you'd made your wishes pretty clear."

"Why did you want to reach me then?"

"I wanted to talk you out of it."

She held his gaze. "Why? We were two dumb kids who got caught by our own foolishness. We didn't even know each other very well." They'd had passion between them but nothing more. He'd been in Hawaii on leave and she'd been mesmerized by his good looks and exotic occupation. At least that's what she'd told herself.

"It was more than that and you know it."

She turned away from the intensity in his eyes. "Was it? After Brianna was born, all we did was fight."

"I had to work."

It was a familiar argument. She hadn't wanted to be stuck at home by herself while he traveled the world.

"You blamed me for losing Brianna," he said.

"You blamed me too. You didn't say it, but I felt it."

He raised a brow. "It was my fault, not yours. And you can come up with a dozen other theories, but we both know the kidnappers wanted to punish me for something. So if anyone's to blame, it's me."

She was too tired to argue with him. "Maybe you're right about more than one person being involved." Her next thought chilled her. "What if he's lured us here for a reason?"

"It's a possibility, I admit, but I'm not about to let go of this opportunity to find my daughter. But, yeah, he wants something from us.
Money, something. I'm sure he'll make his demands known sooner or
later. In the meantime, we find Brianna."

She glanced at him in time to see the muscles in his jaw flex.
His determination had never wavered. Why was that? The baby had
been a part of their lives such a short time, but he'd never given up
hope of recovering Brianna. Against her will, the fact impressed her.

The sheet had slipped from her shoulder, and she tugged it into
place. "What could be in this place that would make it worth getting
us to come here? Bluebird Crossing is desolate."

"We're close to the Mexico border," he pointed out. "This area
is like an open door to the drug cartels. If the culprit who took
Brianna is associated with the drug lord I had a run-in with, this
would be a convenient place to get access to me. And there are few
people, so he wouldn't have to worry about interference."

"So he's got us isolated." She shuddered. "What if he's just saying one of the girls is Brianna? Maybe he wants revenge on you for
the man who drowned, and he knew you'd come if you thought our
daughter was alive." She didn't want to lose the thread of hope she
had, but common sense kept rearing its head.

Clay nodded. "It's possible. It's hard to figure when we don't
know who was behind Brianna's kidnapping."

"That envelope containing the picture. It was sent from El Paso.
It wouldn't be a problem for a drug lord to send one of his men across
the border to mail the letter."

"This whole area has been like a war zone with the violence
from Mexico spilling over the border. He'd have no trouble moving
around."

She turned off the light and rolled over, facing the window. After a moment, she said softly, "I want her back, Clay. I want to tell her everything and that I love her."

"So do I," he said in the darkness. "And I want to make the man who took her pay."

Though his words seared her, somehow they thrilled her too. And she found she believed every word.

※

The bunkhouse was quiet except for the crickets that chirped outside the screened windows. The high desert cooled down at night, and Clay had turned off the air to hear the night sounds. He offered to put pillows between them again, but Eden rolled over and offered her stiff back to him, a reminder that she didn't need a physical barrier to keep him in his place.

He shifted in the bed and turned his face toward the window on his side. The pungent odors from the outdoors were a reminder of what he used to be. He'd grown up in the Chihuahaun desert near Terlingua, a place he'd hoped never to see again. Big cities and bright lights were more to his liking now. And though he felt discomfited, he was sure Eden was a bird in the sea.

As he kicked off the sheet, he heard something. A soft slithering sound, like a rope being tugged over the wood. He went on high alert. A snake? His keys were on the nightstand. He threw them to the floor to see if he could elicit any different sound. Like a rattle. But all he heard was the clang of the keys hitting the rug, then a frantic slithering sound. Eden stirred beside him, then her breathing deepened again.

It was definitely a snake, but at least it wasn't a rattler. More likely a patchnose or a bull snake. It would be frightened, but he needed to get it out of the room before Eden saw it and freaked. Unfortunately, he couldn't do it in the dark. He sat up and put his feet on the floor, then flicked on the light. The warm glow chased the shadows from the room. He blinked and glanced around. A snake was coiled about six inches from his foot. He froze when he recognized the familiar markings. A rattler. It hadn't rattled, but then, they didn't always.

The snake was within striking distance, and Clay didn't move a muscle. If Eden moved or made a noise, the thing was likely to bite him. She sighed, and one hand stretched out. The snake's eyes didn't blink, but Clay could tell it had noticed the movement.

"Eden, don't move," he whispered. "Can you hear me? Don't move. There's a rattler by my foot."

She sighed again, and he knew she was sleeping too soundly to have heard his warning. She stirred again, and the snake showed signs of agitation. His best chance was to jerk back his foot, but he knew rattlers. They were lightning fast, and this was a big boy. It might even be able to reach him on the bed.

Wait. The pillow. Could he hit it with the pillow and knock it down? His mouth was dry. Keeping his gaze on the snake, he slowly moved his hand over to grasp the pillow. He threw the pillow and jerked his foot back at the same time. Everything happened so fast that he wasn't aware at first that he'd been bitten. Then a stinging pain radiated from his ankle.

"Eden!" he said, reaching over to grab her arm.

She fought him off. "Don't touch me!"

"Wake up. I need you." He wasn't sure if it was the poison or adrenaline, but his head spun.

She finally sat up in bed. "Clay? What's the matter?"

If he hadn't seen the drops of blood from the puncture wound, he wouldn't have believed it. His ankle stung. "A snake bit me. The phone is on your side of the bed. I need you to call Rick."

Her eyes widened, and the last of the sleepiness in her eyes disappeared. "You've been bitten?"

He nodded. "By a rattler. It's under the pillow on the floor. Don't get out of bed. Just call Rick and tell him what happened. I'm a little woozy. I have to lie down." He flopped onto his back.

She grabbed the phone on the bed stand and called the main house. He listened to her explain the situation to Rick. "He is coming over right away with some men." Her eyes were worried. "How do you feel?"

"My lips are numb," he said, struggling to talk.

"You might be having an allergic reaction. I think it's too soon for venom to be doing anything. I'll call Rick back. Maybe he has an EpiPen." She punched in the number again.

Clay struggled to draw in a breath. His chest felt tight, and his throat seemed to be swelling. Eden was right. The venom shouldn't be having an effect for half an hour, but allergic reactions happened sooner.

The pillow hid the snake, but he could see the reptile's tail sticking out from under it. The tail moved, but the rattle made no sound. So that's why he'd had no warning. He closed his eyes.

6

THE SNAKE'S HEAD EMERGED FROM UNDER THE PILLOW, FOLLOWED BY A LONG, SINUOUS BODY. Eden shuddered, unable to tear her gaze away as the beautiful creature slithered across the floor to curl in the back corner. She touched Clay's damp forehead.

His lids fluttered, then opened. His pupils were enormous. He licked his lips. "Where's Rick?"

"He's coming." A tourniquet wasn't advisable at this point, but she wanted to *do something*.

She heard feet pounding up the walk outside. A few moments later Rick and Buzz burst into the room. Rick wore his boots and jeans, but his shirt was half unbuttoned. He carried a pitchfork. Buzz was behind him with a shovel in his hand.

Rick stared around the room. "Where's the snake?"

She pointed. "There, in the corner. But what about Clay? Did you bring an EpiPen?"

He handed it to her. "You'd better give it to him while we take care of the snake."

Taking the pen, she opened the gray tab, then jammed the tip into Clay's thigh, holding it there for several seconds. Clay flinched but didn't open his eyes. His lips were blue.

Eden dropped the EpiPen and took his hand. It was cold and blue too. "Clay? Stay with me, Clay!" She clutched his fingers and watched the men approach the corner.

It took only moments for them to dispatch the snake. Mumbling under his breath, Buzz carried the snake out on the shovel.

Rick came to the edge of the bed. "He's got a little more color," he said. "What happened?"

"I'm not really sure. I woke up when he said he'd been bitten."

Clay coughed and opened his eyes. The scary whiteness was receding from his skin, and his pupils were looking more normal. His fingers tightened on hers, and he struggled to sit up. Something tight in her chest loosened, and she inhaled deeply, suddenly aware she'd been holding her breath.

"The snake," Clay whispered.

"Is gone," Rick said.

Eden stuffed some pillows behind his back. "You look like you're going to live."

"We still need to get that bite treated," Rick said, withdrawing another vial from his pocket. "I keep antivenom in the fridge."

"Where were you bitten?" Eden asked.

"My left ankle." Clay moved his foot out from where it had been entangled in the sheet. He closed his eyes. "It hurts."

She winced at the puncture wounds crusted over with blood. And even worse at the bruise beginning to travel up his leg. All thought left her. He couldn't die!

"Honey, you're crushing my hand," he said, lifting one lid.

She loosened her grip on him. "Where's the nearest hospital?" she asked Rick.

"Allie called the doctor. He'll come to us."

Eden injected the antivenom into Clay's other thigh. "IV is the best administration, but this will help for now. And the wound needs to be cleaned. I'll do it if you can get me some soap and water. Alcohol too."

Rick nodded and went to fetch the items.

Wheels crunched on gravel outside. "I think the doctor's here," she said to Clay, nearly giddy with relief.

Footsteps hurried toward the door, and Buzz ushered in an older man with hair that stood on end as if he'd gone from the bed straight to the car. He carried an IV bag and pushed a metal stand.

"This must be the patient," he said. Eden climbed out of the way while he got to work on Clay. She was suddenly self-conscious of her skimpy nightwear in the presence of these men, so she grabbed one of Clay's shirts from the closet and slipped into it while the doctor examined the wound. "One side looks dry. I don't think you got a full dose of venom, young man. You're very fortunate."

Rick touched her arm and motioned her back toward the door. "There's something weird about all this," he said.

She walked with him out of Clay's earshot."Weird? We're in the desert. Snakes get inside sometimes, don't they?"

"Not all that often. I've never had a rattler in the house." He put his hand in his shirt pocket and withdrew a piece of paper. "This was on the door."

She took it from his hand and stared at the letter. "'You shouldn't have brought her.'" Wrinkling her forehead, she glanced up at Rick. "What does that mean?"

"I have no idea."

"The kids are too little to do something like this."

He nodded. "Obviously."

"Did any of your other employees want this position?"

"Most of the cowboys have been with me for years, but I just hired Sam a couple of months ago. And I hired an assistant for the cook two weeks ago. There weren't any other applicants for counselor, if you want the truth. No one wants to live this far away from civilization."

The kidnapper. Had he wanted only Clay to come? As far as the kidnapper knew, she and Clay had divorced. "We have to tell Clay about the note."

"I will. But not until the morning, when he's got a clear head."

"Some kind of prank by a teenager from town, maybe?" She knew better, but maybe it would derail Rick's line of thinking. He was eyeing her with a speculative glint in his eyes.

Rick shrugged. "Maybe. It's a weird situation. I don't know what to make of it. Maybe the sheriff will have an idea."

"I hope so." But she mostly hoped Clay could call in some help from his special ops buddy, Brendan. If she had to go to bed every night and wonder what creepy crawlies would slither out to meet her, she wouldn't get a wink of sleep.

And if this had anything to do with Brianna's disappearance, could the children be in danger? She rushed down the hall to check on them.

❈

Clay felt as if he'd been hit by a truck. He blinked until his vision cleared. His leg felt encased in hot tar. When a cool hand touched his forehead, he turned his head toward Eden.

So beautiful. How had he ever let her go? He wanted to reach up and touch her cheek. It would be as soft as Brianna's skin had been.

"How do you feel?" she asked.

"Thirsty," he croaked. She helped him sit up and he practically inhaled the cool water that she offered him. "Where is everyone?" A vague memory of Rick and Allie as well as an older gentleman floated through his brain.

She backed away. "Looking around outside. The doctor had another emergency and had to leave once he was sure you were out of danger."

Her evasive manner sharpened his senses. "What aren't you telling me?"

She bit her lip. "They're looking for whoever put the snake in here."

"Put the snake in here? What do you mean?"

"There was a note on the door. It said, 'You shouldn't have brought her here.'"

His fatigue fell away. He set down the water glass. "It was deliberate?"

She nodded. "I'd bet he was trying to scare me away. I doubt he thought we'd be bitten. How did that happen anyway? A rattlesnake gives a warning."

"Its rattler didn't work." The room felt small and sinister to him now. "What does he want? There hasn't been another demand for money." She didn't have the answers for him, but it helped him to ruminate out loud. "Did anyone check for more snakes?"

"Rick did. The place was clean."

The bed moved as she sat on it. He resisted the urge to inhale deeply of the clean scent of the soap she'd used to bathe the girls. "Why would he care if you came with me? Seems odd."

"I wondered about that too." Her eyes glistened and she blinked rapidly. "I was thinking about what you said about revenge."

"We have no idea what he's planning. Whatever it is, it won't be pleasant."

"Maybe it's all a prank."

He held her gaze. "I wouldn't have interrupted your life for a trick."

The corners of her lips curved. "That leaves me with hope. You consider everything before you jump."

"Except when it came to you," he said, then winced. Had he actually said that? So much for protecting himself.

She looked away. "I always thought you examined what needed to be done and did your duty."

"My feelings for you had nothing to do with duty." Enough of this. He yanked the IV from his arm and swung his legs over the bed.

She grabbed at his arm. "You can't do that! Look at you, you're bleeding."

"The bag is empty. The bleeding will stop. Besides, the doc didn't think I got a full load of venom." He pressed his fingers to his arm. "Got a Band-Aid?"

She sighed but opened the first-aid box beside the bed and withdrew one. Her fingers were warm when she pressed them against his skin. She'd been cold a few minutes ago. He wished he could believe being around him had altered her temperature even one degree.

He jerked on his boots, though every muscle still hurt and his leg throbbed. "Did you check on the girls?"

"Yes, they're sleeping." She followed him into the hall.

He went to the door of the big dorm room and peeked in. The light from the hallway fell on their sleeping faces. He drank in the peaceful scene. Arms curled around dolls and stuffed animals. The air was scented with little girl. He stared until he saw each small chest rise and fall. Reassured, he turned and walked right into Eden.

She grabbed his shirt, and he steadied her. This close, the scent of soap was even stronger. He resisted the impulse to rest his chin on the top of her head. What would she do if he pulled her closer? Probably hit him. His hands dropped away.

"They're all okay."

Her gaze wandered past his shoulder, and she stepped back. "They're so beautiful."

He nodded. "I'm going to go outside with Rick. You keep watch over the girls."

"Do you think whoever tried to hurt us would hurt them?"

"Someone took Brianna once. We have no idea of his agenda."

She clenched her fists. "He won't touch these girls! Do you have a gun?"

"You won't need one. I'll be right outside." He pocketed his hands so he wouldn't touch her again.

Nausea roiled in his stomach. Probably a reaction to the venom. He steadied himself. This stunt wasn't going to keep him from protecting Eden and their daughter. Or the other girls.

7

A CHILL STILL HOVERED IN THE MORNING AIR WHEN EDEN WALKED ACROSS THE SPARSE YARD to the kitchen with five little girls in tow. The scent of maple syrup and pancakes made her steps quicken, and she smiled at the girls to see if they'd noticed. They giggled and skipped along beside her. She hadn't seen Clay the rest of the night, but she'd gotten little sleep. Coffee would wake her up.

India ran ahead of her and pushed open the screen door into the kitchen. "Rita, I'm here," she announced. "I saw some hummingbirds. Do you know they beat their wings fifty times a second?"

An attractive young woman turned with a smile on her face. "My goodness, so fast?" Her blond hair was in braids, as if she'd stepped from the pages of *Heidi*. She wore jeans and a blue blouse that matched the color of her eyes. When she spoke, her voice had a Southern accent that didn't match her appearance. The makeup she wore made her look like a Dresden doll.

"You must be Eden," she said. "Here's your coffee, strong and laced with lots of real cream, just as you like it."

Eden accepted the mug filled to the brim. "Who told you that?"

"Clay."

"He's here?"

"Was," the woman corrected. "He and Rick took off for town. Rick wanted the doctor to take another look at the snake wound."

Eden took a gulp of coffee. It was perfect. "Clay seemed okay? He and Rick were out all night looking for the intruder." She glanced around and made sure the girls were occupied.

"The sheriff came too." Rita turned back to the stove, a mammoth affair that had eight burners. Four of them held skillets with pancakes sizzling in them.

"You're the cook?"

The young woman nodded. "Rita Mitchell. I feed this wild bunch." She ruffled Lacie's hair, and the child hung on to her leg and looked up with clear adoration.

Eden could tell she and Rita were going to be friends. Was everyone in this area so welcoming? "Is Allie gone too?"

Rita nodded. "She had a planning meeting for a missions conference at church. The ladies are coming here for lunch, so you'll get a chance to meet everyone before Sunday."

Eden guided the girls to the table, then returned to seize plates of pancakes. "Is that real maple syrup?"

"Of course. I wouldn't feed my girls anything but the best." The young woman carried more plates to the table. "Eat up, honey. We need to get some meat on your bones. You a model or something?"

Eden's cheeks heated. "I'm a nurse."

Madeline touched Rita's braid when the young woman sat beside her. "Could you braid my hair like that? Then we would be twins."

"I sure can, honey. Or maybe Mrs. Larson can. She's probably better at it than me."

Eden smiled. "I'm not very good at braids. Maybe you could teach me as well."

"Where are you from, Mrs. Larson?"

"Please call me Eden. I'm from Indiana. A little town called Wabash."

"First electrically lighted city in the world."

"How'd you know that?"

Rita shrugged. "My cousin lives in Peru, just down the road a piece."

"Usually no one has ever heard of Wabash."

"The Wabash-Erie Canal. Wabash Cannonball. Lots of interesting things in the area."

Eden took a bite of pancake dripping with syrup. It was magnificent. "You're quite the history buff."

"I'm working on a historical romance set in Indiana. I've been reading up on the area."

"You're an author?"

"Well, not yet. Someday I'll be just as famous as Nora Roberts. Most folks think I'm just a dreamer, but they'll see when my first book is on the shelves."

Eden grinned. "Somehow I believe you can do anything you set your mind to do."

Rita's smile was brighter than the sunbeams gleaming on the

stainless sink. "We're going to get along swell, Eden. I'm glad you're here."

"So am I," Eden said, realizing she meant it. This place was so different from Indiana. The harsh landscape of red rocks and cacti. The sharp scent of creosote and sage in the air. The blue bowl of sky that went on forever. It was a little scary and exhilarating at the same time.

The girls finished breakfast and went off to watch their morning allotment of *Dora the Explorer* on TV. Eden helped Rita and her assistant, Tepin, a Hispanic woman of about thirty, clear the table.

"What do you know of the girls?" Eden asked Rita.

"They're sweethearts, aren't they?"

"They're wonderful. I love them already." Eden smiled. "Any of their families come to visit since they've been here?"

Rita turned on the hot water and dumped Dawn detergent into the sink. "Nope. We don't let them come until the kids have been here at least a week, preferably two. Visits too soon only make them more homesick."

Eden handed her a stack of dishes. "What did you think of that snake showing up last night?"

Rita dumped them into the soapy water. "I think it was blown out of proportion. Snakes get in all the time. One of the hazards of living in the desert." She shrugged. "I saw one in the bushes outside my window just two days ago."

Maybe no one had told her about the note. Eden opened her mouth to tell her, then closed it again. "Any new employees on the ranch right now?"

"Got several new ones. Tepin here. Sam's a new hand. You. I guess not everyone wants to live in the desert."

Before Eden could ask more questions, she saw Clay's truck pull up outside. "Clay's back. I think I'll go see how he's feeling," she said. "I'll be right back."

❋

He should have spent the night in bed, not roaming the rocky hilltops. Clay rubbed his bleary eyes and parked the truck. His leg ached, but he'd popped ibuprofen all night, and the pain was somewhat better this morning. He'd let Rick out down by the barn.

When Clay exited the truck, he turned toward the house and saw Eden running toward him. The sight of her brought him a surge of energy. The morning sun turned her auburn hair to fire. He had to grin at her pumps, so out of place with the jagged rocks of the landscape.

She stopped three feet from him and tucked her hair behind her ears to reveal gleaming diamond earrings. "Find anything?"

"Not much. Just some tire tracks behind the barn, but Rick had no idea how long they might have been there."

"You're pale. You should be in bed."

"I'm fine, really. How are the girls?"

"Watching cartoons. Then we're supposed to take them on a hike." She made a face. "But if you're not up to it . . ." Her eyes were hopeful.

He grinned. "I think we need to teach you to ride first. But you'd need to change into jeans and boots."

She lifted her chin. "Not going to happen."

"You look great in anything, you know."

She flushed. "Want some breakfast? I think there are pancakes left."

"Don't change the subject. What's it going to take to get past that

58

wall, Eden? When you left me, I didn't know you much better than the day we met."

Her eyes narrowed. "I don't know what you're talking about."

She turned toward the house, but he caught her arm. "I'd really like to know the woman past the pretty face and gorgeous hair. What do you want out of life? Who are you, really?"

Her green eyes flashed. "I'm exactly who I seem. It's not my fault if you wanted some kind of wife who hiked the mountains with you. I never pretended to be GI Jane."

"I don't want to change you, but I just want to know you. You were always this perfect woman at the pinnacle of her career. Intelligent and beautiful, but remote. Never rattled for a moment."

"Well, once we find Brianna, you never have to be disappointed in me," she said.

Did her voice quiver? He'd like to think that just once he'd gotten past her defenses. "I was never disappointed in you."

She met his gaze. "Our relationship is over, Clay. All I want is to find my daughter."

"When Brianna was born, I thought your guard was finally starting to slip," he said, tightening his grip on her arm when she tried to pull free. "You were crazy about her."

Tears filled her eyes. "I wish I hadn't given up on her."

"You're too hard on yourself. No one is perfect."

"Except you." Her tears vanished. "The protector and defender of the free world."

"You say that like it's an insult."

"You like being the tough guy who never sheds a tear."

Only because he had wanted to be strong for her. "You think I have no feelings?"

"Do you? You went off quite happily to South America when duty called."

If only she'd seen his internal struggle. But he hadn't allowed it. "The search here in the States was at a dead end." And he'd hoped to find some clue to their daughter's fate.

"I asked you not to go."

She'd done more than that. She'd said if he left, their marriage would be over. And she'd followed through. He received the divorce papers a month after he left. Why *had* he left? Without Brianna to hold them together, he wasn't sure how to make the marriage work. But was it because he couldn't bear to see her leave him? Just the way his mother had done when she left with her lover, without a backward glance at her kids.

He shied away at the thought of his mother. "I had to go, Angel."

She succeeded in pulling her arm free. "I hate that nickname!"

"It suits you." He lifted a brow rather than tell her what it meant to him. "I dare you to change into jeans and boots."

She brushed at an imaginary speck of dust on her shirt. "You know perfectly well I don't own any boots. Or jeans."

"I'll buy you some."

"I'd rather not be beholden to you."

"Where do we go from here?" he asked her. "We both want Brianna when we find her. We've carefully avoided the topic of what happens next."

She gave a shrug. "I suppose we act civilized like everyone else. I'll take custody of her and you can have her every other weekend."

Just what he didn't want. "I don't think so. I want her with me. You can have her every other weekend."

"I'm her mother!"

"And I'm the father who never gave up looking for her." The minute he spoke, he wished he could call back the words.

She swallowed hard. "How did you know, Clay? I'm her mother and I believed she was dead. Why didn't you give up too?"

"I can't explain it."

It had been an intuition deep inside. She thought he had no feelings. The truth was, he had more than he could handle most times. The older he got, the harder it became to maintain his tough-guy, careless facade. He'd accused her of hiding behind a mask. Wasn't he just as bad?

He turned her toward the house. "Let's get chow. My belly is gnawing on my backbone."

When they reached the kitchen, Rita turned with her smile increasing in wattage. "Clay, I kept some pancakes warm for you."

He blinked at the way she batted her lashes. Like she was a Southern belle. Who did she remind him of? That gal who played Heidi maybe. Beside him, he felt Eden tense. She'd always thought friendly women were coming on to him. He wasn't sure where her insecurity came from.

Putting his hand on Eden's shoulder, he guided her to the table. "I could eat a horse."

"I could make you some bacon too," Rita said. She set the stack in front of him, then turned toward the refrigerator.

"No need. These pancakes are plenty."

Rita pulled out a chair across from him and Eden. "Allie said you are a photojournalist. How romantic."

He glanced away from her sappy smile. "Don't let us interrupt your work," he told Rita.

"I can take a break. So you've been to lots of other countries?"

"A few." He shoveled in the food and passed the syrup to Eden.

Allie's voice came from the living room. "Rita, could you come here a moment?"

Rita heaved a sigh and got up. "Call if you want anything more to eat. I'll be happy to fix it." She directed one last smile his way, then stepped out of the kitchen.

"Before you say anything, she's just being friendly," Clay said.

"A little *too* friendly," Eden said. "But I think maybe it's just her way. She was friendly to me too."

He relaxed. "Glad you could see that."

"Besides, we're here only to find Brianna. I have no real hold on you."

That wasn't what he wanted to hear. As far as he was concerned, she could grab hold with both hands and never let go.

8

You shouldn't have brought her here. Eden had been puzzling over the cryptic message all day. What possible reason could the kidnapper—or anyone—have for not wanting her here? Was it possible someone intended to harm Clay but didn't want to hurt her? If that was the case, then could that person be someone she knew? Someone who cared about her? The police said a kidnapper was often someone known to the family. In fact, Clay and Eden were suspected for a time of harming Brianna. But detectives interrogated all their acquaintances at great length and filed charges against no one.

The bunkhouse held the scent of the baby powder she'd put on the girls after their baths last night. She settled onto the sofa and grabbed the landline. Daniel should be at home now. They'd grown up together in the same foster home, and he was a true friend and brother. Hearing his voice would calm her jitters. And he'd be happy to hear that her engagement to Kent didn't happen. Her heart hurt when she thought about Kent. She prayed he'd be able to get past the hurt she'd caused him. He deserved to find a woman with a whole heart.

But the phone rang until she was dumped into his voice mail. She left a message with the ranch number and hung up frowning. Would he really still be mad at her about Kent after all this time?

Glancing at her watch, she saw it was time to take the girls on a hike. The mountains were stark and forbidding. Cacti and who-knew-what creepy crawlies would be waiting at every turn. But by the time she retrieved the girls, found Clay, and started up the trail, she was enjoying herself.

India skipped along beside her. "Look, Miss Eden, a yucca. Did you know you can eat the flowers? Buzz told me. Can I taste one?"

"Um, I don't think so, India." Eden exchanged a rueful grin with Clay.

She held Katie and Madeline by the hand as they hiked up the desert mountain where they'd been told they could see into Mexico. The sun was bright and hot on her arms. The landscape was so different from Indiana.

"I'm hungry," Madeline said.

"I have a granola bar in my backpack," Eden said. She stopped and shrugged it off her back. None of the other girls wanted a snack yet, but Madeline scarfed hers down in six bites and asked for another. "I think you have hollow legs," Eden said, handing the little girl another one.

When they reached the peak, they stopped and stared at the

panorama. No people, just endless desert and, in the distance, a ribbon of blue that was the Rio Grande.

Clay set down the picnic basket he carried. She dug into her backpack and pulled out a tablecloth and spread it on the ground. He began to set out the sandwiches and chips Rita had packed for them. When the children finished eating, they began to collect wildflowers.

Clay leaned on his elbow on the tablecloth as he watched them. "They're all so different," he said. "It's fun watching them interact. I've been imagining first one then the other is Brianna."

"Me too," Eden admitted. "Just when I think I have it figured out, I change my mind."

His expression as he watched the girls filled her with warmth. She'd always thought he would be a good father, but he hadn't had the chance to show how good.

His gaze went from the girls to her face. "I don't like the note left on our door last night. There seemed to be animosity toward you in it."

She raised a brow. "I don't think so, Clay. I'm guessing someone wants me out of the way so I don't get hurt. You know how the police always said the kidnapper was likely someone close to the family. Maybe it's someone who likes me and hates you for some reason."

"That would mean he is likely a friend of yours. Or a relative." He shook his head. "I'm not convinced that was the intent of the note, though. I don't want you wandering off alone here. Stick close to me. I'll protect you."

"Just like you protected Brianna?" She wished she could call back the words when his eyes shuttered.

"You still blame me, don't you?" he asked, his voice soft.

She bit her lip. "You knew what you were doing in Colombia was dangerous."

"All my missions are dangerous. And I didn't know that one would be dangerous to my family! You're not without blame either, Eden. If you'd been paying attention that day . . ." He inhaled. "I'm sorry. I didn't mean that."

She blinked at the sting in her eyes. These same arguments were the ones that had sent her fleeing the moment he left the country. And she didn't really blame him. Not anymore. If losing Brianna was anyone's fault, it was hers.

She laid her hand on his. "I'm sorry. I shouldn't have said that. I didn't even mean it. I'd rather fight sometimes than admit the pain I feel."

He studied her expression. "Tell me what's been going on in your life."

Her face heated and it wasn't from the sun. "Just life," she said.

His smile vanished. "You lower the mask for a fleeting second, then slap it right back into place."

Maybe she did tend to be too secretive. She wished she could be more like Allie, laughing and open about her feelings. Maybe it came from being a foster kid. She ached for these five little girls.

"Earth to Eden."

She blinked and smiled. "Sorry, I was woolgathering." Could she let down a small corner of her veil with him? Maybe it was worth a try. "I'm working on being more open, but it's hard for me. Is there something in particular you want to know?"

"I'd like to know how you became a Christian."

"When Brianna . . . died, it was either go crazy or look for meaning. I chose to look for meaning."

His smile came. "And you found it?"

She nodded. "Well, as much as I could in such a horrible situation. I still don't know why he allowed it, but I came to realize we have no control over bad things. When I got to Wabash, a coworker invited me to church. I just held on to God a day at a time."

"What about Kent? How did he fit into all this?"

"He helped me start to live again. To begin to think I might do more than get through every day."

"I would like to have helped you do that."

She rubbed her head. "I saw the ruins of our hopes everywhere I looked, and it hurt too much."

"Now here we are." He smiled and nodded toward the girls. "She's here. We just have to find her."

"I hope so. One minute I'm clinging to hope, and the next minute I'm fearful this is a cruel joke. We don't know."

"I'm certain," he said. "Can't you feel her here, Eden?"

"Maybe it's wishful thinking."

He shook his head. "Trust me, Eden. Cling to that hope. We'll find her."

He had enough faith for both of them. "I'll try," she said.

※

Clay couldn't stop watching Eden. He should have seen it right away, that undercurrent of a changed soul. So much for the intuition he'd always thought he possessed. Now that he knew, it was clear to see.

He put his hand in his pocket, and his fingers touched his digital picture viewer. Had she looked at pictures of Brianna lately? Pulling it out, he turned it on, smiling when Brianna's chubby cheeks came into view.

"What's that?"

"I like to look at these," he said. He showed it to her. Brianna was cradled in his hand at the hospital. His hand was nearly as big as she was.

"Oh, Clay," she whispered, her voice full of tears. "I had that picture enlarged and hung it over my bed. On bad days, that's how I imagined her. Cradled in God's hands."

Her insight gave him pause. "And now we know that he's been taking care of her all this time."

She took the viewer and advanced to the next picture. The two of them were staring down at their baby with expressions of awe. In the next picture, they were gazing at one another with love in their faces. His breath caught. He'd forgotten about that one. He hardly dared glance at her, but she didn't go on to the next photo like he'd expected.

"We were so young," she said softly.

"Now we're old and decrepit?"

She shook her head and looked at him. "I didn't mean that. We didn't have any idea what life had in store for us. The pain that was coming our way in a few short weeks."

Tell her. He wanted to say that he'd never wanted her to leave. That he wished he'd been there to comfort her during those dark months after Brianna was taken. He opened his mouth.

"Look, Miss Eden, a tarantula!" India's voice was full of excitement.

Eden broke their eye contact. "Get away from it, India!"

"It won't hurt her," Clay said.

"I've heard those things jump."

"They don't usually bite. It's more afraid of her than you are of it." He pointed to the way the dark blob crawled under a yucca plant.

Eden shuddered and steered the little girl in another direction. "Let's play with the other girls."

But the children preferred to poke at the tarantula. Clay took a stick away from Katie and directed them to a rocky outcropping with a path that appeared safe. "Let's climb to the top."

The children squealed and raced for the top as he and Eden chased them. From the heights, the view of the Rio Grande was even more magnificent.

"People," Lacie said, pointing to about ten people, men and women, hurrying through the desert in single file.

Eden glanced at him with a question in her eyes. "Illegals," he mouthed to her. He could try to call them in, but by the time the Border Patrol arrived, they would be long gone.

"We'd better get back," he said, herding the group back down the trail. "It's almost time for our outing to Big Bend."

9

THE THERMOMETER STOOD NEAR NINETY, BUT THE DESERT BREEZE WAS DRY AND BRISK. THE girls were piled into the back of the Bluebird Ranch van, an older model that was neat and rust-free. Eden sat two seats back with one arm around Lacie and one arm around Katie. She relished the way the girls had taken to her.

Zeke rode shotgun with Clay driving, and Della and Rita were in the back with the older girls. Clay turned into the lot by the park headquarters. The girls chattered excitedly, showing one another their cameras. He'd bought an inexpensive digital camera for each of them.

"Everyone out," he said, opening the van door.

The girls squealed and jostled for the door. Eden counted heads.

Clay led them onto a trail that had vegetation marked. "Here we are. I want you to walk single file. Zeke, you bring up the rear and make sure no one wanders off," he said.

Eden reluctantly let go of the small hands she'd been holding. "Look, there's a roadrunner," she said, pointing to the bird by the agave plant.

The girls all shrieked, and before anyone could show them how to use a camera, the bird ran off into the desert. "I think we need a little lesson first," she told Clay.

He grinned and began instructions on the camera. Eden's eyes glazed over when he started talking about picture composition and where to aim the camera. Her gaze wandered to the high peaks around the park. Though stark, the place was beautiful, but she wouldn't want to be lost in the desert. It could be brutal. She saw something move by her foot and jumped out of the way as a tarantula lumbered by.

Shuddering, she went to stand by Clay. She glanced around, counting heads once more. Wait, there was one missing. She counted again and realized Katie's red hair was nowhere to be seen. "Clay, where's Katie?"

"I told her she could go to the bathroom." He jerked a thumb in the direction of the ranger building.

"Not by herself!" she scolded.

She jogged across the desert to the ladies' room, where she found Katie washing her hands. Eden realized she might have overreacted. This was a family park, and the girl had only gone twenty or thirty feet to the bathroom. But she wanted no snakebites, no run-ins with any of the scary creatures that inhabited this desert.

She took Katie's hand to go back, but the little girl stopped and tugged her fingers free. "I forgot Button!"

Button was the much-loved bear with the missing eye. "Where is he?" Eden asked.

"I left him in the stall." She pointed.

"I'll get him. Wait here." Eden walked to the back stall and pushed it open. The bear was on the floor. Ick. Not very sanitary. She'd have to wash him when they got home. When she returned to Katie, she handed her the bear. "Let's get back to taking pictures."

She pulled on the door handle but it seemed to be stuck. Frowning, she jerked on it again. What on earth?

"You're doing it wrong," Katie said. She grabbed the handle and pushed. It didn't budge.

"Hang on a minute." Eden stooped and peered through the crack in the door. "It appears to be locked. Maybe the janitor locked it accidentally."

But it was the middle of the afternoon. And they'd notified the rangers they were bringing a group of children today. She banged on the door. "Hello," she called. "Can someone let us out?"

She tried to keep panic out of her voice. Being locked in brought back too many memories from her childhood. Was there breathing on the other side of the door? The hair stood on the back of her neck as she listened. "Who's there?"

Silence. She was jumping at shadows. There was no one there. The faint stench of smoke came to her nose. She sniffed again. It was stronger now. Was the place on fire? It was all she could do not to beat on the door in panic.

Katie tugged on her blouse. "Miss Eden, are you all right? You're scaring me."

"I'm fine, honey." Eden picked her up and hugged her. "We'll call to Mr. Clay from the window. He'll come and unlock the door for us."

She retreated to the window and cranked it open. She could see Clay on the trail. He was showing Lacie how to use her camera. "Clay, I need help," she called. She had to raise her voice and repeat it.

His head came up and he turned toward the building. "Eden? Where are you?"

She waved, not sure he could see her in the window. "In the ladies' room. Someone locked the door. I . . . I smell smoke."

He jogged to the building. She heard him at the door, then it opened and he stuck his head in.

"It wasn't locked," he said.

"Well, I couldn't open it." Now that he was here, her courage came flooding back. "Go back out and let me try from in here."

He shrugged and complied. Once the door had closed, she pulled on it and it opened easily. "I know it was locked," she said. "I tried and tried to open it. I saw the lock thrown too." She gave Katie a pat on the behind. "Go join the other girls," she said.

After Katie ran off, Eden sniffed the air again. "Did you smell the smoke?"

"A cigarette." He pointed to a still-smoldering butt perched on the edge of the sidewalk.

"Did you see anyone out here?"

He shook his head. "Were you frightened?"

She hugged herself. "Clay, the door was locked. I know it was."

"A childish prank maybe. There's a group of teenage boys here." He frowned, his gaze intent on her face. "We can't discount it, though." He hugged her. "Stay close to me. I'll be on my guard. Don't be afraid."

Easier said than done, but she kept her mouth shut and followed him back to the children.

❉

Bluebird Crossing was a town with only one eye open. Or so it seemed to Eden that night as she peered through the café window at the sleepy town. She could almost imagine it was the West Texas version of Mayberry. Red-and-white-checkered tablecloths covered the tables, and the decor was vintage fifties. The aromas of enchiladas mingled with those of roast beef and fried potatoes.

"There they are," Clay said when a couple stepped into the café and came toward them. He rose and waved. "Over here."

Eden liked the looks of Gracie Wayne right off. Petite with fine blond hair and a dusting of freckles across her nose, she looked like the girl next door. Her husband, Michael, was military and had the erect posture to prove it. Good looking too. Eden liked the way he guided his wife with his hand at the small of her back. He clearly loved her.

The couple reached the table, and the men shook hands and introduced their wives before they were seated. "Good to get you back here," Michael said.

Back here? Eden glanced at Clay. She'd thought the men knew each other from the air force.

"Feels a little surreal to come home," Clay said. "Thanks for putting in a good word with the Baileys for me."

She should have asked him if the Waynes knew that Brianna was somewhere at the ranch. She'd assumed they didn't, but it was clear that the two men shared a special friendship. There was so much about her husband that she didn't know.

"I hear you have three children," she said to Gracie after the server brought their iced tea.

Gracie smiled. "Jordan, Evan, and Hope. We're a blended family."

Michael grinned. "About to be homogenized." He patted Gracie's belly.

The gentle swell told the tale. "Congratulations! When are you due?" Eden asked, trying to ignore the tiny stab of longing.

Gracie blushed. "Not for four months. The kids are so excited." She leaned her chin on her hand. "How did the two of you meet?"

Eden shrugged. "The usual kind of story. He was a handsome soldier on leave and I was on vacation."

Clay grinned. "Handsome? You thought I was handsome?" He nudged Michael. "I'll bet you can't say the same, buddy."

Michael nodded. "You're so right. She took one look at me and fainted."

"Stop it, Michael," Gracie said, shaking her finger at him.

He grinned and slipped his arm around her. "I'm a lucky man, and I know it."

"You two still act like newlyweds," Clay said. "I hear you're an EMT and own the only helicopter in the county. Rick says you're the go-to guy for everything."

The men started talking about work, and Gracie smiled and shook her head. Watching her and Michael, Eden wished she could feel so relaxed and free with Clay. What had they missed? She'd blamed their distance on his absence, but maybe it was more than that. Maybe it was some fundamental flaw in her. She knew she had walls. Over the years, she'd tried to tear them down, but her defense mechanisms were too strong.

After a pleasant evening, the couples walked outside together. As Eden waved good-bye to her new friends, she found herself tongue-tied with Clay. Did he ever think about what a marriage was supposed to look like?

"Ready to go home?" he asked.

"I need to walk off dinner a bit," she said. He offered his arm, and she took it hesitantly. They strolled the empty sidewalk along closed storefronts. When they stopped in front of the coffee shop, the only place except the café that was still open, she stopped. "Why didn't you tell me you were from around here?"

His easy smile vanished. "You never asked where I was from."

"You didn't think the fact that the kidnapper brought Brianna back to your home area was significant? I thought the location was just a random choice, but it seems it was personal."

"It couldn't get more personal."

"So we basically stepped into the lion's den?"

"I suppose so. But talking about it wouldn't have changed our minds. I'd face anything to get my daughter."

"Our daughter," she corrected.

His lips tightened. "Our daughter." He ran his hand through his hair. "Look, I just didn't want you to worry. It's my job to worry about the danger."

"This is exactly what broke up our marriage!" She turned and ran back toward the truck. She heard his footsteps behind her, but she didn't slow until his hand was on her arm and he pulled her around to face him.

"What do you mean by that?" he demanded.

She was so tired. Tired of fighting, tired of pretending, tired of the mask she always wore. "You always thought about what *you* should do. It was never *us*, what *we* should do. We were two separate people, never one unit. I realized that tonight watching the Waynes."

His hand dropped from her arm. "Maybe so. I wanted to take

my responsibilities seriously. A man isn't supposed to let his wife worry about anything."

"Who says? If they are one, they share everything. The good and the bad. At least that was always my dream. I didn't have the best role models, so I didn't have it all figured out."

"I hate fighting," he muttered. "That's all we seemed to do, and we're starting it again."

"At least we're talking when we're fighting."

He tipped his head and stared at her. "Do you start fights on purpose, then?"

She started to shake her head, then thought better of it. "Maybe I do. There's nothing worse than being ignored." As a child, she'd spent too many nights standing outside in the cold by herself. Or eating a peanut butter sandwich alone.

"I never wanted you to feel ignored. Just protected." He opened the truck door for her. She fastened her seat belt, but he didn't close the door. "Would you like to see where I lived?" he asked.

It was such a small thing, but she didn't miss the trepidation in his voice. She nodded. "Yes."

"It's on our way." He shut the door and went around to his side.

10

He'd driven this road a million times. Clay turned onto the dirt drive and wondered when the grader had last been down it. Darkness was falling quickly, but the moon was bright tonight.

"Are there any other houses back here but yours?" Eden asked.

"Nope. It's a dead end. Which is probably why the potholes are so bad." He hit one and the truck bottomed out and slewed in the road before he straightened it.

Why had he even suggested coming out here? The ghosts had long been laid to rest in his heart. Or had they? Maybe that was it. He needed to confirm this for himself. He turned the truck into the disused lane. Tumbleweeds were strewn around the yard and the drive. His headlamps illuminated several piled against the door, which was half open.

"Looks like vandals have been out here," he said. He parked the truck ten feet from the house and shut off the engine.

She glanced at him. "Are we getting out?"

"Sure." He shoved open his door, but the minute his boots hit the dirt, he wanted to climb back in. The ghosts still lived here.

Eden was beside him before he could change his mind and drive off. She craned her neck to look at the roof, which had a gaping hole in it. "You lived here all your life?"

"Until I was eighteen. I went to college in San Antonio, then joined the air force."

"Where are your parents now? You have two siblings, right?"

So strange that they were only now talking about these things. They'd barely skated the surface of their histories when they were together. "It's been several years since I've seen my sisters. One lives in Boston and the other in Oregon, so we are never together in one place."

"Do your parents live near one or the other?"

He shook his head and advanced to the door. It had once been a grand Santa Fe–style home. There was an interior courtyard that had probably been taken over by snakes and scorpions. It had all fallen into disrepair after being abandoned fifteen years ago.

"So where do they live now?" She followed him.

He kicked the tumbleweeds out of the way and pushed open the door. A frantic rustling noise warned him not to go in. He blocked the doorway with his arm. "Scorpions."

She shuddered and stepped away. "It was quite a place. Sad to see it in such a state."

"Things deteriorate quickly in the desert. By the time I inherited it, it was in sad shape."

"Why didn't your parents sell it?"

"My parents fought all the time and finally divorced. They tried to sell it, but the real estate market this far out is lousy, and my mom wasn't willing to let it go at a loss. So they finally gave up and gave it to us kids."

"Could it ever be brought back, or is it too far gone?"

"It's solid. Well built and stuccoed. The roof would need to be repaired, and some serious pest control done. It would take some time and money." He led her around to the side of the house and pointed. "There's a barn and paddock. A good spring in the back of the property where me and my sisters used to go swimming."

"Your parents?" she asked again. "Where are they?"

He shrugged. "My dad moved to Mexico and hangs out with all the senoritas. Mom remarried Dad's best friend and lives in Florida."

She winced. "I'm sorry. I'm sure that was painful."

"It was okay until I hit sixteen. Then everything was a battle."

"And we repeated that cycle," she said, a ghost of a smile touching her lips.

"There's that," he agreed.

"Do you like the house?"

She studied the house again. "It could be lovely. I imagine there are open beams inside, tile floors." He confirmed this with a nod. "I'd love to see it in the daylight. And without the scorpions, of course."

His fingers found the pendant in his pocket. He wanted to give it back to her, but only when the moment was right.

"Brianna would love it," she said, her gaze drifting back to the yard where a grove of trees surrounded the spring. "So this is your house now? You own it?"

"I do. My sisters signed off on it a couple of years ago. They said they were never coming back here."

"But you weren't so sure?"

"I loved this place once." He wished he'd brought her here in the daylight. But then maybe the mess would look worse. "I might renovate it."

"It would take a lot of money."

He stared at her in the moonlight. "I'm a rich man, Eden."

"You are? Soldiers make that much money?"

He grinned. "I had hazardous-duty pay, but I inherited a lot of money from my grandmother a couple of years ago that I've never touched." He frowned at a movement by the barn. "Who's there?" he called.

He heard rustling and rushed toward the barn. An engine roared to life and a small truck shot from the open door and careened away down the dirt drive. The Toyota barely missed sideswiping his truck. The bed held several people, but it was too dark to make out any features.

"Who could have been here?" Eden asked.

"Probably a coyote hauling illegals," he said.

"Those we saw from the hill?"

He shrugged. "I think I'll take a look."

He jogged back to the truck and got the flashlight out of the glove box. Eden followed close behind, and he could tell by her breathing that she was tense. If he'd had a gun, he would have brought it to reassure her. The beam from the flashlight illuminated discarded clothing, soda cans, and other debris. All the tack that had been hanging on the walls was gone, evidently stolen by the illegals and others who had passed through here.

For a moment he wished he'd kept this place up and never gone off to the military. Would his life have been any different? When he turned to go, he ran into Eden. Smelling the apple fragrance in her hair, he knew he would do it all over again, just for the chance to have met her.

※

Eden gave each of the girls new hairbrushes to make sure they had uncontaminated DNA samples for Clay to send in. On Wednesday Eden stood at the fence by the corral. Dust swirled in plumes from under the horses' hooves. She coughed and stepped out of the line of fire as best she could, steering the girls toward the fence.

"I want to ride that one." Lacie pointed to a paint horse that was rubbing against the barn siding.

"It's too big," Eden said, instantly regretting it when the little girl's face puckered. "How about the red one?" She pointed to a reddish pony with a sweet face.

The nearest cowboy, Buzz, shook his head. He was covered with red dust. "Don't let her fool you. She's a devil on hooves. She'll try to scrape the kids off her back when you're not looking."

Eden gulped. "I'm not sure this is a good idea."

"The kids love interacting with the horses. And the mares love it too. Don't you, girl?" Buzz patted the paint, which had moseyed over to take a lump of sugar from his palm.

She shuddered when she saw the mare's teeth. "Won't she bite you?"

"Naw. She's gentle." He gave her a final pat. "I'll saddle up the horses. We got two or three I trust with kids this young."

In a few minutes he'd saddled the horses and had them ready to go. She scurried out of the way as he and Clay had the girls take turns on the animals. Their animated faces made her smile.

"Look at me," Katie called. "I want to do a handstand."

Clay shook his head. "No way, kiddo. You stay right in that saddle."

Eden thought the child would cry, but instead she looked relieved. Paige, who never seemed to smile, squealed and waved grandly as she passed Eden's perch on the fence. The child was actually pretty when she was animated. Only Madeline had refused to get on a horse. She played outside the fence with Spot, her puppy.

Eden watched Clay as he interacted with the children. The man was a natural-born dad. He said he wanted Brianna with him all the time. He deserved it too. He'd always believed she was alive somewhere. That showed more faith and hope than she'd ever dreamed he could feel.

Her memory went back to that note on the door. *You shouldn't have brought her here.* Even now the ominous tone made her shiver. They'd heard nothing else. Not a problem in the bunkhouse, not a call. Nothing.

And what about Brianna? The only thing they could do would be to live close together so they could share their daughter. After all she'd been through, Brianna deserved having them both with her.

A family. The thing she thought she'd never have. Not now. What if they stayed together? Oh, the thought was ludicrous. Even if she were willing, Clay wouldn't be. The best they could hope for was an amicable relationship where they put Brianna first. Maybe that would be enough. It had to be, because she didn't have it in her to hope for more.

"Now you, Miss Eden," Lacie called. Her braids bounced on her shoulders as she came past on the horse. Rita had done a good job with the girl's fine hair.

"I don't think so, honey," Eden said.

Before she could react, Clay's big hands were on her waist. He lifted her down from the fence and turned her toward the paint. He smelled of man, dust, and the faint tinge of soap. He'd had a shower after breakfast, but stubble still darkened his chin.

"Smile," he said in her ear. "Don't show any fear. You can do this. The girls expect it."

The protest died on her lips when she saw the girls turn eager faces toward her. She was a role model even if she didn't want to be. "I'm not dressed for it." She glanced down at her shoes and expensive slacks.

"Your clothing will wash." He guided her to the side of the horse. "Put your left foot in the stirrup."

She so didn't want to do this. Her insides were shaky. *Coward. Weakling.* All the name-calling in the world didn't stop her hands from trembling. Dust coated her tongue and swirled around her feet. Her designer shoes wore a layer of red and the stuff tinged her pants as well. She might never get the stain out.

"You're game to try it?" His eyes warmed as they looked her over.

The man was entirely too handsome. And he likely knew the way his touch turned her insides to mush. "You've left me no choice."

Gritting her teeth, she hoisted her left foot into the air and stuck it through the stirrup. Clay's warm hands remained at her waist. They felt much too natural on her. It was as if five years had dropped away into the canyon behind the ranch.

"Now step up," he instructed.

She lifted herself with his help and threw her right leg over the saddle. "I should put the other foot in this stirrup?" she asked, looking down the mare's rounded side. From this vantage point, the horse seemed even bigger. The ground was much too far away. It would hurt if she fell.

"Yes. And take the reins."

"Don't turn me loose!"

"I've got a hold on the bridle." He beckoned Buzz. "Can you adjust the stirrup on that side? They're too long." His fingers brushed her ankle as he lengthened the strap.

The saddle was hard under her bottom and against her inner thighs. Could she even perch here without falling? It felt so precarious. But the girls' faces were avid with excitement and she couldn't disappoint them. Or Clay either, though she hated to admit she wanted to see admiration in his eyes.

He put the reins in her hands. "Hang on to the horn."

The horse took a step, and she lurched, then clutched at the saddle horn. Then the jarring ride smoothed out as Clay led the horse around the corral. The girls clapped as she passed by them. She was doing it! Actually riding a horse. Something she'd sworn never to do. And it wasn't so bad. Not if it made Clay's eyes glow with pride.

11

She needed a shower. Eden swiped dusty hair behind her ears and squinted into the noonday sun. A rumble came from the driveway, and she turned to see a line of cars and pickups pulling up to the house. Two pickups and two cars. She recognized Allie's red compact. Women got out of all the vehicles and started toward the house.

Allie saw her and waved. "Eden! Come join us for coffee," she called.

Though the last thing she wanted was to allow other women to see her in such a disheveled state, Eden could hardly refuse the imperative tone in her employer's voice. She glanced at Clay.

"I'll be here with the girls," he said. "Buzz is going to teach them some roping tricks."

She wished she could stay and watch. The thought of Clay's strong shoulders flexing as he roped a calf intrigued her. *Bad Eden.* That physical magnetism he possessed had gotten her into this trouble in the first place.

"Clay, I'm a mess! You could save me," she said.

He draped an arm around her shoulders. "You look great. The friendships will do you good."

It was as if he knew she needed a bit of encouragement. The embrace was brotherly, but her own reaction was anything but sisterly. She nearly stood on tiptoe and brushed a kiss on those firm lips. Too hastily she tore out of his embrace, then regretted it when she saw his eyes cloud. He thought he repelled her when the very opposite was true.

"I'll be back," she said, keeping her tone distant. She'd rather he didn't know of her attraction.

Everything felt different here. She walked across the sandy yard toward the house. Friendships were usually so superficial in Eden's world. Jealousy was quick to spring up, and coffee dates in Boston where she'd grown up were times of talking about other women, men, jobs, men again, and other women again. The raw land here seemed to inspire close confidences. Maybe it was because survival depended on others.

She already felt herself changing here. Letting down her guard in small ways. Reaching out and wanting to let the inner ice thaw. She heard laughter when she reached the screen door and immediately stiffened, thinking the others were laughing at her dusty appearance. Or were they mocking her designer shoes? Then she made out Allie's voice telling the women about how she'd put sugar in chili the first time she'd made it and Rick had eaten it anyway.

Not many women that Eden knew poked fun at themselves. She pasted on a smile and eased into the back of the living room.

A pretty blond woman with striking blue eyes saw her and smiled. "You must be Eden. I'm Shannon MacGowan. My husband, Jack, and I are next-door neighbors. My, how pretty you are."

"Thanks." Eden wasn't sure what to do with her hands. Or where to sit. When had another woman complimented her? Never in her memory.

These women made her realize how inadequate she was for this job. Their jeans were as natural to them as the sand outside. They'd be able to ride a horse like they drove a car. Facing the vast expanse of wilderness exhilarated them and left her feeling inadequate. They wouldn't have screamed at the sight of the snake the other night. They would have stomped it with their boots. And that tarantula on Tuesday at the park? They would have picked it up and put it in a safe place.

Allie patted the cushion beside her on the sofa. "Sit here and I'll introduce you. You just met Shannon. She's a vet, and her husband owns the biggest ranch in West Texas. And you know Gracie."

Gracie smiled. "I was looking forward to seeing you again."

The last woman was older, probably near sixty. A pair of wire-rimmed glasses perched on her nose, and her sharp eyes looked Eden over. "I'm Julia, also known as Judge Julia. You look familiar."

The woman was a judge. What if she'd seen the write-up in the papers when Brianna was taken? The kidnapping took place in San Antonio—not so far away, given how this area didn't even have its own newspaper.

Eden managed a smile. "I have one of those familiar faces."

"That's not it," Julia said, her eyes narrowing. "It will come to me."

Not if Eden had anything to do with it. She didn't want any law enforcement looking at her and Clay with suspicion again. "What's going on here?" she asked, glancing around the room at the excited faces.

Julia's focus wavered. "Planning the menu for our missions conference at church. We're doing an international dinner. Want to help?"

"I'm not much of a cook."

"I have the recipes for everyone. Pretty easy." The older woman handed her a paper titled "Thai Coconut Chicken."

Eden wanted to hand it back to her, but she didn't dare. The woman might start questioning her again. "Coconut chicken? I'll see what I can do." She glanced at Rita, who came into the room with a tray of coffee and cookies. "Rita might need to help me."

"If it's got coconut in it, you're on your own," the woman said, placing the tray on the table. "I can't even stand the smell." A small pill bottle rolled from her apron, and she quickly retrieved it. She looked a little pale.

"You okay?" Eden asked.

Rita grimaced. "Migraine."

Allie's smile faded. "Go lie down awhile. We can take care of ourselves."

"Thanks, I think I'll do that," Rita said.

Shannon poured herself a cup of coffee and glanced at Eden. "I saw that handsome husband of yours in the corral with the children. How long have you been married?"

Eden started to answer, then checked her initial response of a year. "Six years. We went out to see the house where he grew up. A Toyota went tearing out of the barn."

Julia lifted a brow. "Illegals?"

"That's what Clay thought."

"We've had a lot of problems with that lately," Gracie said. "Drug-lord wars have spilled across the border nearly every week. You're lucky they didn't shoot at you. Where is the house?"

Eden told her. "It was gorgeous once."

Gracie nodded. "I've seen it. Michael showed me when we found out you two were coming. Are you going to live there again?"

Eden glanced at her hands, wishing she hadn't brought up the house. "I don't know. It would take a lot of work to repair it."

"It would be worth it. Lots of room for kids, eventually," Shannon said.

"It was dark, so we didn't get a good look. It's very isolated. Is it safe?"

"With your big husband around, anywhere is safe," Allie said, smiling.

As the conversation went back to food, Eden leaned against the cushions and wondered if she would ever fit into this countryside as well as these women did.

⁂

The little girl was much too quiet. Eden glanced at Lacie sitting beside her, so composed. Her bare feet dangled off the edge of the truck seat, and she didn't tug at the seat belt the way so many children would have. Her hands were folded in her lap, and she stared straight ahead.

Eden had been glad Clay interrupted the women's planning with a child's chewed-up shoe in his hand. Their kind probing had left her uncomfortable. And she wanted to get away from Judge Julia's inquisitive stare.

"The dog didn't leave much of your shoe," Eden said to Lacie. "Shall we look for sneakers or sandals?"

Lacie glanced at her from the corner of her eye and tucked her chin before shrugging. Eden wasn't sure how to draw the little girl out. She'd hoped to learn more about Lacie this afternoon in a private outing to get more shoes.

"I heard Sister Marjo is coming next weekend to see you," Eden said.

Lacie lifted her head and her face brightened. "How many days is that?"

"Ten."

The animation vanished as if wiped away by a giant hand. Lacie dropped her chin again.

"You must really love Sister Marjo."

The little girl nodded, a bob so slight Eden nearly missed it. Lacie crossed her feet at the ankles and turned to stare out the window. The desert landscape rolled out as far as the eye could see. A gleam of white in the distance caught Eden's attention. The truck rounded a curve and she made out the tattered remains of a trailer park. Her gut tightened. She hated the reminder of the life she'd led until she was eight. Though she wanted to avert her gaze as they passed the decaying mobile homes, she had to look. She could almost hear her mother yelling at her.

"Go on out now. He'll be here any minute."

Eight-year-old Eden felt the sting of tears in her eyes and blinked. She was much too old to be whining, according to her mother. "It's cold, Mama."

Her mother lined her eyes with black liquid that made the skin look harsh and thin. "Put on your mittens. You can make a snowman."

"I want to play with my doll." A lady from church had given Eden the baby doll. It wasn't new and had ink marks on the cheeks, but it was the first doll she'd ever owned. And there were clothes to go with it. She could spend hours changing outfits on the doll she'd named Sally.

"Your silly games aren't going to change a thing. Get outside and take the stupid doll with you." Her mother wheeled to glare at her. "He'll be here any minute. Get going before I take a belt to your legs."

Her mother would do it too. Eden slowly went to the only closet in the trailer, a tiny, cramped space in her mother's bedroom. She barely managed to pull down her coat. There were holes in her mittens, and she had no boots, but she knew better than to complain again. When she turned back toward the room, she lost her balance and toppled to the floor. Her forehead thumped the footboard on the bed, and the force of the blow brought tears to her eyes. She pressed her fingers to the spot that was already beginning to bump out.

"Quit crying. You're not hurt." Her mother pulled her roughly to her feet and pushed her toward the door. "You're going to look ugly when your father comes to see you tonight."

The last thing Eden wanted was to be ugly, to see her father's face cloud with anger the way it had when she'd cut her bangs with scissors. Tears spilled down her cheeks. "I want to look pretty for Dad," she said.

"Another reason to go outside and put some snow on your forehead. Now get out of here."

Her mother was pulling on a blue filmy thing when Eden went to the door. "That's pretty, Mama."

Her mother smiled and pirouetted in front of the mirror. "If Mr. Smith thinks so, I might have enough money to get you some pizza tonight. If you're a good girl and stay outside. Now scoot."

Even the thought of pizza failed to lift Eden's spirits. It was scary out at the playground. The big kids threw rocks or made the swing go too high. But there was no persuading her mother, so she put on her coat and went outside.

Snow spit her in the face as she pulled the trailer door closed behind her. As she went down the cracked sidewalk, she saw the car drive up. It was shiny and black. Newer than Eden was used to seeing. The man didn't get out until she was across the street, and she got only a glimpse of his heavy coat and a hat pulled low on his head.

She still had that image of her mother twirling in the mirror when she returned three hours later to find her mother gone, with no trace other than the scent of her face powder still lingering in the bedroom.

EDEN BLINKED AND PUSHED THE MEMORY AWAY. SHE GLANCED AT LACIE AND SAW THE CHILD staring with rapt attention at a trailer near the road. Its green shutters hung askew. Through the gaping front doors, she glimpsed the tattered remains of an orange sofa.

"No one lives there," Eden said.

"It looks like the other one," Lacie said.

"Other one? Did you live in a mobile home once?"

Lacie shook her head. "Sister Marjo takes me to see her niece sometimes. But I'm not supposed to tell the other sisters."

"Why not?"

"Mother Superior doesn't like Sister Marjo's niece. She says she's loose. Does that mean her joints might fall apart?"

No way was Eden going to answer that one. "Where is this trailer park you visit? In Dallas?"

Lacie nodded. "By the park."

Seeing the mobile homes seemed to have unlocked Lacie's tongue. Whatever these visits were, they'd impacted her mightily. "How often do you go?"

Lacie twisted in the seat for one final glimpse of the trailer. "I don't know. Sometimes."

"What's the niece's name?"

"Taylor. She's nice. She kisses my cheek and calls me her little darling."

Was it possible that Lacie was this Taylor's child? "You don't live at the convent, do you?"

Lacie shook her head. "I visit lots. Sister Marjo saved me, so she's 'sponsible for me."

A strange situation. The nun had found her five years ago yet had stayed involved. So maybe Lacie wasn't Brianna.

12

THE SWEET SCENT OF HAY, VERY DIFFERENT FROM THE SMELLS OF EXHAUST AND SMOG CLAY was used to, filled his lungs as he showed the girls how to feed the horses. They giggled and threw flakes of hay at one another. Dust motes danced in the sunlight streaming through the window opening.

He glanced at his watch. Eden had been gone for an hour. Surely she'd be back with Lacie soon. When the horses were fed, he led the girls back to the house to wash up for the meal. He sniffed the air. "Chili for supper, I think."

"Yay!" Madeline said. When the other girls ran on ahead, she slipped her hand into his.

Her fingers closed around his in a confidential way that warmed his heart. Her blond hair bouncing, she skipped along beside him.

He thought she looked a little like the pictures he'd seen of Eden when she was a child, but maybe all little girls were similar.

Her fingers tightened on his when a dented Ford came rolling up the drive. The sun had turned the red paint to a rust color. The back window on the passenger side had been busted out, and a black plastic bag fluttered in the opening. He glimpsed a woman behind the wheel.

Madeline stood stock still, her smile gone. "It's my mother," she whispered. "She's not supposed to come here."

Clay searched his memory. Rick had said Madeline's mom was filing for custody. "She was in the hospital, right?"

Madeline nodded, watching as the car lumbered to a stop. "She was in the loony bin," she said in a confidential tone.

He winced. "She has some mental illness she's fighting," he said gently.

"She scares me. Mom doesn't like her."

"Your foster mom?" Clay watched a woman get out of the car. Even from here he heard the door screech. That old rust bucket was bound for the junk heap soon.

Madeline nodded and hid behind his leg. "Mom said I don't have to talk to her."

"You run ahead inside. I'll talk to her." He watched the little girl run up the porch steps like someone was chasing her. And maybe someone was. He didn't know all the background. Just that the woman had been diagnosed with schizophrenia. If the doctors deemed her well enough to function, there should be no real danger.

He intercepted her determined stride up the walk toward the house. "May I help you?"

About fifty and thin as the fence rail, the woman was dressed in jeans that were stained with what looked like blood but he assumed was red paint. Was that smear of red on her forehead a cross? Her fingers were stained too when she held out her hand to shake his. She was very blond, and it looked natural.

Her grip was strong, almost like a man's. "I am here to get my daughter, Madeline," she said. Her accent seemed to indicate she might be Scandinavian. Her gaze wandered over his shoulder toward the house.

He resisted the urge to step away from the unsavory stench that he thought emanated from her hair. "Get her? Camp won't be finished for another month."

She leaned in and stabbed at his chest with her forefinger. "She belongs to me. You can't stop me from taking her."

"Do you have a court order to allow you to take her? She's not in your custody."

A crafty expression flitted across her face before she hid it. "I am her mother. I have rights." She dug into her pocket. "And I have this." She handed him a wrinkled paper stained with smears of red, blue, and yellow.

Her name was Else Bjorn, so his impression of a Scandinavian accent was correct. He smoothed out the wadded document and scanned it before handing it back to her. "This just says you are filing for custody of Madeline. It doesn't say the custody is granted." Poor woman. He knew the pain of having a child being taken away.

"She is my daughter. You have no right to keep her from me." The woman attempted to brush past him.

He blocked her path. "I'm sorry. I can't allow you to see her. You don't have any visitation rights."

Large tears pooled in her eyes. "Just for a minute," she begged.

"She needs to know her mama loves her. I am fighting for her. Those people put me in jail and are trying to turn her against me."

Was that how she saw it? No way should this woman be out on her own. She couldn't take care of herself, let alone Madeline. Was there someone he could call about this? He'd have to ask Rick or Allie. And as he stared at her, he considered her age. Madeline was five. This woman was at least fifty, unless something other than years had aged her.

"I'm afraid you'll have to talk to the judge about this. You don't want to scare Madeline, do you?"

"Why would her own mother frighten her? She wants to see me. I know she does."

He might have to call the sheriff. Agitation came off the woman in waves. Her pupils were dilated too, and he wondered if she was on any kind of medication for her condition. "Not today," he said in a soothing murmur. "She's eating right now. Talk to the judge and come back when he says it's okay."

Her shoulders slumped and she turned back toward her car. She rummaged inside a moment. "I have something for you." She emerged and wheeled toward him.

A blade glittered in her hand, and her face twisted in a snarl. She leaped toward him with the knife raised over her head. The moment seemed poised in time, almost surreal, as the woman's blond hair flew out behind her and the knife arced toward his chest.

Almost too late, he gathered his wits and dodged to the left. The blade barely missed his shoulder, and he felt the wind of its passing. He twisted back toward her and seized her wrist. She fought back ferociously, baring her teeth and trying to bite his arm. He blocked her and forced the knife from her fingers. The anger drained from her face, and she went limp. He eased her to the ground and yelled for Rick.

While the other man called for the sheriff, Clay watched her, but she never raised her head from her knees as she sat curled in a ball.

※

Surreptitiously, Eden glanced at the time, then watched Lacie pick up first one shoe then the other. The child had been patient when Eden stopped at another store to buy pajamas that covered her more than the lace teddy she'd been sleeping in. Lacie's eyes had brightened when they stepped into the small shoe store.

"Where do you usually buy shoes?" Eden asked.

Lacie stopped with her hand poised above a pink sneaker. "My foster mom brings them home from Walmart."

"You don't try them on?"

The little girl shook her head. "She measures me. She says she won't take me to the store because all the kids ask for things. That's not fair, though. I've never asked for anything."

Lacie had an odd kind of maturity. Even her syntax seemed advanced to Eden. "Let's try these on," she said, picking up a pair of pink Nikes.

Lacie's eyes widened. "They have the swoosh on them. They cost too much."

"I can afford them." She resolved not to submit the bill to the ranch. "Sit there."

As Lacie clambered onto a nearby bench, Eden's cell phone played "The Voice" by Celtic Woman, which meant the caller wasn't in her contacts list. She clawed the phone from her purse, but it had already rung four times by the time she swiped it on and saw *Unknown* on the screen. For a moment she was tempted not to answer, but what if the caller was Clay and he had his number screened?

She touched *Answer Call* on the screen and put it to her ear. "This is Eden." An electronic noise filled her head. "Hello?"

"I know what you did," the man whispered. The sound of the voice gave her chills. Then she realized there was an electronic device distorting it.

She clutched the phone to her ear and turned her back to Lacie. "Who is this?" she demanded.

He knew what she did. What did that mean?

The voice vibrated with rage. "You'll pay and pay dearly. I took Brianna once. This time will be worse. Much worse. You shouldn't have come."

The kidnapper. The blow nearly doubled her over. "Don't you touch my baby!" she said fiercely.

"How will you stop me?" he sneered.

"What do you want from me? I'll do whatever you say. Just leave Brianna alone."

"Anything, Eden? Really? Would you walk away from Bluebird Ranch right now? Leave Clay behind? I've seen the way you look at him. You still love him, don't you?"

She glanced quickly around the store. Was he here somewhere? Watching her? "No, of course not. I haven't thought of him in five years."

"I didn't think you'd have the nerve to come here with Clay. You're going to wish you hadn't."

The past week had allowed her to put that nightmare behind. "I'm just here for Brianna. Nothing else."

Seneca Falls Library
47 Cayuga Street
Seneca Falls, N.Y. 13148

"Prove it. Leave today. Right now."

Everything in her rejected the demand. Not when she was so close. "I'm not abandoning Brianna."

"See? I knew you wouldn't do anything. Now you know too. And you'll have no one to blame but yourself."

She paced on the carpet in front of the shoes. "My daughter is here and I'm not leaving without her." No more trying to appease him. He wasn't going to intimidate her. "What do you want with me anyway?"

The man laughed. "Do you really know who you are, Eden? If you did, you wouldn't be so smug."

She shuddered at the venom in this voice, but no enemy came to mind. "I know who I am. Who are you?"

"Remember, whatever happens, you brought it on yourself."

The click in her ear told her he'd hung up. She put the phone back in her purse and composed herself. Pasting on a smile, she turned back to Lacie. "How do those shoes fit?" she asked in a fake bright tone.

"I think they are good." Lacie had slipped from the bench and was walking a few feet on the carpet. "Can I really have them?"

"Of course. Let me check the size." Eden knelt and pressed on the toes and arch, but her mind raced and her hands trembled. She needed to talk to Clay.

"Do they fit?" Lacie's voice was hopeful.

"They sure do. Let's go pay for them and get back to the ranch. We've already missed dinner."

"We can eat leftovers."

"I think we'll grab some chicken nuggets on the way home. How does that sound?"

The little girl's expression brightened. "We're eating out?"

"I think a little treat is in order," Eden said, forcing herself to be in the moment. The caller was a nightmare, but this time with Lacie was reality. After all, she might be her Brianna.

"I can't eat nuggets, though. I'm 'lergic to wheat. But can I have french fries? And chili?"

"Whatever you like." She paid for the shoes. "Want to wear them?" she asked Lacie.

The little girl nodded. Eden had her sit on a bench, and she slipped on socks, then the shoes. "Now for food," she said.

She ordered their meal to go from the café next door. While she was waiting, she and Lacie stepped next door and bought a large java from Desert Coffee, then returned to the café. When the order was ready, she took Lacie's hand and went out to the parking lot where she'd left the truck. The lot held only a small yellow car. She stared down the street but saw no big black truck.

Was she mistaken about where she'd parked? Maybe it was on the other side of the street? But no, she was sure it was right here.

Lacie ate a fry, then licked her fingers. "Where's our truck? It was parked there." She pointed to the spot where the car sat.

"I know."

Lacie was admiring her shoes. "Maybe Mr. Clay had to borrow it back."

"You might be right." Someone had stolen Clay's fancy truck. He'd be livid. Was it the man who had called her? A chill shuddered through her. He was here. Somewhere close. Watching, waiting to strike.

She pulled out her phone again, then realized she didn't know Clay's cell number. "Let's go see the sheriff while we wait," she said.

Lacie skipped along beside her as they crossed the deserted street to the sheriff's office. Only a receptionist was inside, and the woman told her she'd page the sheriff, who was out on a call. When

Eden stepped back outside, the yellow car was gone, and the truck was right where she'd left it. She saw a flash of yellow and turned to see the car driving away with a teenage boy behind the wheel. Had he taken the truck, or was it a coincidence that he'd parked there?

She took Lacie's hand and walked slowly across the street. When she opened it, a male cologne wafted to her nose, and it wasn't Clay's.

13

IT WAS MUCH LATER THAN CLAY HAD EXPECTED BY THE TIME THE TIRES OF HIS BLACK TRUCK crunched up the gravel drive. He left the girls watching a video in the main house with Rick and Allie's daughter, Betsy, and went out to meet Eden. A fiery sunset backlit the hulking peaks of the surrounding hills, and he glanced around, an odd chill on his spine.

Both doors on the truck opened, and Lacie ran to him. "See my shoes," she said, lifting one for his inspection. "Miss Eden bought them for me. And we had supper out!" Without waiting for his response, she took off for the house. "I have to show the girls!"

He grinned and watched her leap the steps and rush inside. When he turned back toward Eden, he sensed a wariness in her stance. "Something wrong?"

"Someone took your truck for a joy ride," she said. She came around the front of the truck and stopped two feet from him.

"Who?"

"I don't know. I went to report it to the sheriff, and when I came back out, it was back in the space."

He frowned. "You sure you looked in the right space?"

Her face went white. "Yes, I know exactly where I parked it. The spot was empty." She hesitated. "Maybe it was just a kid out for a joy ride. There was a yellow car in the lot too, and it belonged to a teenager."

"Is that it? You seem more upset than the incident would warrant." Even in the gloom, he could see her tremble. He curled his fingers into his palm to keep from reaching out to pull her close.

"I . . . I got a phone call." Her voice shook.

He straightened. "Kent?"

"No, no." Her voice became stronger as anger replaced fear. "It was the kidnapper."

"How do you know it was him?"

"He said he took Brianna once and he could do it again." Her voice began to shake again. "I think he took the truck. To rattle me."

Clay's hands clenched into fists. "He's not getting his hands on her," he said fiercely. "Or you."

"We have to protect our girls, Clay." Her voice was panicked.

"We'll protect them all." He couldn't help but reach out and hold her when he heard her choked voice. She collapsed against his chest. It had been so long, yet she fit there as if she'd never left.

How had he let her go? Fighting for her had seemed pointless at the time. Each of them had been full of recriminations and hurt, and neither had been willing to bend and listen. God forgive him, he'd blamed her too. It shamed him to admit it to himself. He'd been consumed with the what-ifs. What if she hadn't gunned the engine? What if he'd delivered the ransom money alone? What if he'd never gone back to South America? The blame he'd felt toward her had radiated from him, and their fragile relationship had splintered.

"Why is he doing this?" she whispered against his chest. "He seems to be intent on revenge against me."

"Against you, not me?" They'd both assumed the kidnapping had something to do with him. The drug money stolen during the bust. A piece he'd written that had offended someone. Some picture he'd taken that had humiliated a subject.

Sniffling, she pulled away. "He said that whatever happened, I'd brought it on myself."

"Brought what on yourself?"

"I don't know. He asked me if I knew who I really was. Almost as if he knew I'd grown up in a foster home."

"You've offended someone pretty badly. Who could it be?"

"I can't think of anyone."

Her foster brother would know everything. "I bet I know."

"It's not Kent. He's an honorable man. He sent me off without any strings. Besides, someone else sent you the picture. Kent didn't know about us until you showed up."

"I'm not talking about Kent. I'm talking about Daniel. Think about it. He was hanging around the whole time we were married. Commiserating with you about how terrible it was when I flew off to Colombia for that mission. Right there to help when you walked out."

She held his gaze. "Daniel's like a brother. There was never anything between us. We grew up together, for Pete's sake! That feels dirty for you to even say it."

"You're not biologically related."

"He's my brother in every way that counts."

Maybe *she* felt that way, but that didn't mean the slimeball hadn't reveled in their breakup. Clay hadn't trusted him one bit. "How did he take your romance with Kent?"

The flicker of her lids showed her uncertainty. "He didn't say much about it."

"I'm not surprised. You never noticed the way Daniel looked at you. Like you belonged to him. He objected to Kent too, didn't he?"

"What if he did? He was just looking out for me."

"Have you heard from Daniel since you've been here?"

Her frown held confusion. "He called the night you showed up but didn't leave a message. H-He hadn't been accepting my calls."

"What does that tell you?"

"That he would have gotten over it, just like he got over me marrying you. I'm all he has. I should call him again."

"Again? You've tried calling him?"

She frowned and nodded. "Before you showed up and since we've been here. He still hasn't returned my calls, though, which isn't like him."

His insides felt like they were twisted ropes of hot lead. Forbidding her to call the jerk would escalate the tension, but he wanted to tell her to open her eyes. The guy was way too possessive.

"He had the nerve to call me up after you left me," he said, unable to hold it in any longer.

Backing away, she shook her head. "Daniel called you in South America?"

"Sure did. Right in the middle of an interview. Told me you were through with me. Like I didn't know that already."

She batted her eyes and chewed on her lip. "He never told me."

"Of course he didn't. He thought with me out of the picture, he could move in on you. Why didn't he? Or did he try and you were too naive to see it?"

"Well, he tried to kiss me once," she admitted, almost to herself. "I told him it was sweet of him to try to comfort me, but I didn't need that kind of attention. I just assumed . . ."

"You guessed wrong. I bet he's fuming since he found out you ran off with me."

"He'd understand I have to find Brianna." But her lids flickered and she glanced away.

At least she had a few doubts. Crossing his arms across his chest, he glared at her. "If he's so understanding, why hasn't he called?"

"I'm sure he has a good reason."

She was blind where that guy was concerned. "Dinner's getting cold," he said. She walked behind him into the house.

When they stepped into the living room, Paige came rushing toward them. "Mr. Clay, look what I found!" She thrust a yellowed yearbook at him and pointed to a picture of the Spanish Club. "Is that your dad? India says that boy's name is Clyde Larson."

He stared at the photo. "No, it's my cousin." The boy beside his cousin made him squint and take a closer look. *It couldn't be.* "Eden, look here." He thrust the book under her nose. "Who does that look like?"

She leaned over the page and gasped. "It's the kidnapper who drowned!"

"I thought so too. Says here his name is Jose Santiago."

"We need to let the detectives who worked on the case know," she said.

He nodded. "Santiago is a common name, though. It may tell them nothing." But that man's identity might be the clue they needed to figure this all out.

⚜

Eden gave the sheriff a statement about the missing truck. She and Clay also showed him the picture of Jose Santiago, and he promised to call the detective about it. He already knew about the snake and the note on the door.

After he left, Eden flounced in the bed. She held the cotton quilt under her nose to blot out the alluring scent of Clay on the other side of the bed. Those moments in Clay's arms when she got home tonight replayed over and over in her head. How natural it had felt. How wonderful. It had taken all her strength to make herself back away. Had he felt anything at all? She doubted it. All he wanted was to find their daughter.

Which was her goal as well. Her only goal.

Clay's accusations against Daniel made her squirm. He'd been like a brother since she was ten. There wasn't anything between them but friendship. Both foster kids, they'd clung together through their growing-up years in the same foster home.

But why hadn't he called? She should call him again. Before she realized it, her bare feet were on the cool hardwood floors. She eased open the bedroom door. Clay's even breathing didn't stop, so she pulled the door shut noiselessly behind her and padded down the hall. The glow of the nightlight lit the path. She hesitated long enough to peek in on the girls. All sleeping.

The clock on the stove glowed the numbers 10:10. After eleven back in Indiana. She went to the sofa and picked up the phone. Sinking onto the cushion, she listened to the call go through. His phone rang five times, and she was trying to decide whether to leave a message or hang up when he finally answered.

"Hello, Eden."

His voice was odd. Cold, detached. Normally, he was happy to hear from her. This man seemed a stranger, not her best friend. "How did you know it was me?"

"I heard you went to Bluebird Ranch. That's what came up on the caller ID."

"Daniel? You sound—odd. Is something wrong?"

"What could be wrong?" Still that remoteness.

"You haven't called."

"You run off with a husband who deserted you and leave me without a word." The words ran together, faster and faster. "I finally got it, Eden. I might be stupid but I finally got it."

She paced in front of the sofa. "What are you talking about?"

"Good old Daniel was always there to pick up the pieces, wasn't he? Well, I'm through being your whipping boy." Passion finally sparked his voice. He was nearly shouting by the time he finished.

"You were never my whipping boy. You're my best friend."

"I showed you in so many ways I wanted to be more than that, Eden. When you decided to marry Kent, I thought I could deal with it. I'd start easing away so I didn't humiliate myself any more than I already had."

To her horror, she realized he was crying. Her throat tightened, and she wanted to weep with him. "I never knew, Daniel. Really. I love you like a brother."

"Brother! I don't want to be your brother. Lover, husband.

That's my role. But you never saw it. You've kicked me for the last time, Eden Davidson."

"Larson," she whispered. "My divorce from Clay was never finalized." Why hadn't she understood all this sooner?

"So I heard. How do you think I felt—to find out from rumors around town? Couldn't you at least have bothered to call me yourself? If I'm your best friend and all."

"I . . . I . . ." She gulped back the tears. "You're right. I should have. Clay told me Brianna was still alive, and everything else just flew from my mind." The strength ran out of her legs, and she sank onto the ground. What had she done to Daniel?

Silence echoed on the other end of the connection. "Brianna? I hadn't heard that one. What kind of trick is he pulling on you now?"

"No trick. She's here. We'll figure it out in just a few more days."

"Then what?" His voice softened, grew lower.

Was he hoping . . . ? Surely not. "Then we try to rebuild our lives. To help her get over whatever has happened to her."

"You're not coming home?" His voice was sharp again.

"Not now. Brianna is all that matters." The reminder of her priorities strengthened her. She rose and leaned against the wall, wrapping the cord around her arm.

"I see. Of course. I was never important. I keep trying to find some way around that truth."

The silence on the other end was so long she thought he'd hung up on her. "Daniel?"

"I'm here." He sighed, a long, drawn-out sound. "I went by your apartment. Doesn't look like you forwarded your mail. Your box was full so I took it inside."

"Thanks." Where was this going?

"There was a letter from the court. I opened it."

"You opened my mail?"

"It looked important."

She couldn't be angry. She'd always shared everything with Daniel. "What was it?"

"Your birth mother is trying to find you."

Of all the things she might have guessed, the thought wouldn't have crossed her mind. "What does the letter say?"

"Just what I told you."

"My birth mom." She couldn't take it in. "What if I don't want to see her?"

"Nothing will proceed unless you agree. I tried to call them to get more details, but the receptionist said you'd have to call yourself. I'll text you the phone number."

Eden couldn't think past the pain squeezing her chest. After all these years, her mother was trying to find her. Why? And did she even want to see the woman after all these years? What good would it do? But even as she tried to talk herself out of it, the desire to ask her mother why she'd been abandoned welled up.

"Send me the number," she said.

"I said I would. Then we're square. Good-bye, Eden. Don't call me again."

The connection broke in her ear. She stared at the phone stupidly. Her best friend was gone. Maybe it was for the best. She'd been so blind. What else was she wrong about? Everything?

14

THE MOON SPILLED IN THROUGH THE WINDOW AS EDEN TIPTOED BACK INTO THE BEDROOM. Her nose was still clogged with tears. As she reached her side of the mattress, the moon went behind a cloud and plunged the room into darkness. Feeling her way, she pulled back the sheet and quilt.

Clay's side of the bed was much too quiet when she eased between the sheets. The springs squeaked and she winced. She was cold, so cold. Mostly because she knew what she was going to do. Tomorrow she would call the office and say she wanted to see her mother. Then what? Did she expect her mother to rush to her with open arms? To ask for forgiveness? And could Eden even give it if her mother asked?

Shivering, she pulled the sheet up to her chin. It was hot outside, but the air-conditioning was too cold. Or else it was stress. Clay's warmth radiated out from him, and remembering how safe she'd felt in his arms earlier, she wished she could curl up against his back.

Clay's deep voice came out of the darkness. "Is your *brother* okay?" His voice was derisive. He rolled in the bed, and the springs protested.

"I . . . I don't know what to think," she said. To her horror, her voice shook. He wouldn't understand her quandary. He'd go see Eden's mom, tell her she was worthless, then never see her again. Good riddance. Eden should feel that way too, but she didn't.

"Hey, what's the matter?" He scooted closer, and his arm came around her. His breath stirred her hair. "Did you have to cover yourself from head to toe?" he asked, a smile in his voice. He didn't wait for an answer. "Tell me what's upset you."

The musky scent of his skin left her motionless when she should have moved away. His warmth seeped into her. He pulled her closer and she didn't protest, though every nerve shouted the danger to her emotions. "I don't want to talk about it."

His fingers tangled in her hair, and he pulled her so close there was no room down the full length of her body. *Danger!*

"It's dark. You can tell me your secrets and I can't see your face." His lips brushed her cheek.

The desire to talk to him swept over her. What could it hurt to unburden her soul? There'd been so few times in her life that she could tell anyone how she felt. Even when they were together before, she was always sure he'd married her because she was pregnant.

What was different now? She couldn't define the difference, but she knew it was there. There was a special bond now that had never existed before. The wariness that had held them apart was gone.

She turned her face against his neck and inhaled. "My mother wants to see me."

His hand smoothed her hair. "So tell her to come down. There's room here in the bunkhouse." His warm chuckle came from the darkness. "I'd like to see your foster mom sharing a bathroom with the kids. She'll be in there and one of them will come flying in yelling at her to get out of the way."

She should laugh, but nothing felt funny. "You don't understand. My real mother."

His arm seemed heavier across her midsection. His muscles hardened too. His hand quit petting her hair. "After all these years?"

She nodded her head, though she knew he couldn't see it. Her throat thickened. She hated to cry. Strength, not weakness, was admirable. "I want to ask her why she abandoned me. But I don't want to face that rejection all over again."

His lips brushed her brow in the darkness. "I'm sorry, sweetheart." His breath stirred her hair, then his lips trailed down the side of her face. "You don't have to see her if you don't want to."

She held her breath and nearly turned her head to press her lips against his. What was she thinking? This was much too dangerous. But she was too languorous to move, her muscles too heavy with desire. They'd always had this chemistry between them. She never should have agreed to this charade. But all her internal protests weren't enough to make her move.

She pulled away a fraction. "I think I want to see her. Is that crazy? She doesn't love me, but I still love her. She entertained men, and those were awful nights. But I also remember the evenings we watched TV and ate pizza together."

"It's perfectly understandable."

"Is it?" she whispered. "To love someone who doesn't love you back?"

"Maybe she realizes her error. She might have found God too."

Was that possible? She'd prayed for her mother. Somehow it made the pain of rejection better. Clay touched her cheek and turned her face toward him. She was helpless to resist him.

"I've missed you, Eden. So much."

His lips trailed across her face to her lips. She couldn't help the way her arms came up and pulled him closer. Why not? They were married. It was perfectly natural. But even as the thought crossed her mind, she heard a tap at the door.

"Miss Eden?" Madeline's voice. "Paige wet the bed and it got on my nightgown."

Clay groaned and his arm fell away. "I thought five was too old to be wetting the bed."

"They're still babies." She felt cold without his arms around her. "I'll be right there," she called, swinging her legs out of bed. It was just as well. Making love to him would have led to endless complications when the time came for their lives to separate.

❄

The bedding had been changed and the girls settled. Clay still detected the faint stench of urine, but the apple candle Eden lit was quickly chasing the odor from the room. The candle's flickering light illuminated five eager faces turned toward where they sat on the edge of the bed with Katie and Paige.

"Sing to us," Madeline demanded. "Do you know 'Amazing Grace'?"

Clay didn't want to look at Eden's expression, but he had to. He'd overheard her singing in the shower a time or two, but she never sang when she thought someone was listening. She was biting her lip as she tucked the blanket under Katie's chin. The air conditioner hummed.

"I know the song," Eden said. "But you need to go to sleep."

"I have to hear it," Madeline insisted. "I tried to play it on the CD tonight, but it's scratched." The other girls chimed in with their pleas as well.

Clay saw Eden physically wilt at the plaintive tones in the girls' voices. "I'll sing with you," he said.

"You can sing it by yourself," she said.

"He can't sing," Lacie said, over in the next bed. "I heard him in the barn today. He sounded like the cow."

Clay grinned. "Just for that, you might have to be tickled." He wiggled his fingers at her, and she squealed and huddled under the covers. He looked at Eden. "I don't think you can get out of it."

She sighed and stared at Madeline's determined face. "Then you have to promise to go to sleep. Mr. Clay and I are tired. It's nearly eleven."

"We will," the girls said in a chorus.

Tension radiated from Eden's slim shoulders, clad in pale blue cotton. He could still feel the texture of her pajamas under his palm from earlier. Probably just as well they were interrupted. She had no intention of working on the marriage. Any entanglement would make the ultimate breakup even more painful. He would not think about how right she had felt in his arms.

"You start," he said. "I'll chime in." He waggled his brows at Paige, who giggled and pulled the sheet up to her chin, then sneezed.

"'Amazing grace, how sweet the sound.'" Eden's voice was a little choked but sweet and even.

"'That saved a wretch like me.'" His raspy voice blended with hers.

"'I once was lost but now am found. Was blind but now I see.'" His eyes stung when he saw the way the girls listened. Did they feel lost as they went from foster home to foster home? Only a couple of them had stayed in the same place. The hunger in their eyes made him want to gather every one of them in his lap and never let go.

And Eden. She'd had the same experience they had. He saw the sheen of her eyes and the way she gulped down her emotion. What would have happened to them all but for God's grace? His gaze met Eden's across the bed as the song ended. The pathos in her eyes told him she saw it too. The hunger for love in these little girls.

"Time for sleep, kiddos," he said. He and Eden made the rounds, brushing kisses across every cheek. "Love you, honey," he told each little girl. The starved way they wrapped their arms around his neck brought a lump to his throat. Katie didn't want to let loose of Eden, and he watched her hold the child close.

He followed Eden back to the living room and dropped onto the sofa. "That was hard," he said. "They need love so badly. Every one of them."

Her eyes were moist when she turned to stare at him. "You love kids so much. Why didn't you just sign the divorce papers and remarry? You could have had two or three more by now."

"God hates divorce. So do I." His voice shook, and he tugged his boots off. There were so many things they'd never told each other about their past and how those things had shaped the person they'd become. "My parents divorced when I was seventeen," he said, wincing when his voice showed his pain. "I always thought it was my fault. They were always arguing about something, and usually it involved me.

Whether I would be allowed to stay out late the night of homecoming. Whether I should have a job. I realize now I was just a convenient excuse to show their dislike for each other."

He glanced up to see sympathy in her eyes. Was there any hope of tearing down the walls between them? He was willing to try.

She sat beside him on the sofa. "You're worried about Brianna and how growing up with us divorced would affect her."

"Aren't you?"

"Of course. She's been in a foster home, without the security and love of her own parents. We don't even know what kind of circumstances Brianna has been in, but looking at the girls' reports, not one has been in a place I'd want our daughter to experience."

He tried to read her expression, but she kept her gaze on the clasped hands in her lap. "Do you still have any hope left, Eden? Hope for that perfect little family we dreamed about once?"

She raised her eyes to his. "Sometimes. But I'm afraid, Clay."

His pulse leapt at her admission. "You think I'm not? I failed you and Brianna once. I want to be here for you both and never let you down again."

Something flickered in her eyes. He wanted to believe it was the beginning of a bit of trust and hope, but before he could nail it down, one of the girls let out a heart-stopping scream.

"Get away, get away!" the child's voice shrieked.

Clay leaped from the sofa and rushed for the bedroom. Eden was right behind him. They spent the next hour soothing Katie from her nightmare, but watching Eden's face, he wondered if she was thinking about what he'd said.

15

Eden's eyes were bleary from lack of sleep. She'd tossed and turned much of the night with the words of the old hymn echoing in her brain one minute and the thought of what she would say to her mother the next. She sat sipping her coffee with Allie and Della at the kitchen table while Rita bustled around clearing away the breakfast dishes. Beyond the window, Clay and the children were out with Rick and Zeke, headed to the corral for another riding lesson.

"I needed coffee this morning," Della said, taking another swig. "One of the girls was throwing up all night." She nibbled on a piece of toast.

"Eden, you're pensive," Allie said, dumping more Cheerios in Matthew's bowl.

Eden felt she didn't know Allie well enough to bare her soul about her mother. Or God. "Paige wet the bed last night. And Katie had a nightmare. By the time we got the bedding changed and all of them settled down again, it was one."

Allie winced. "That was one of our fears when we agreed to take kids this young. We had plastic mattress covers put on all the beds."

"Good decision. She soaked everything. I'll bring the laundry over after a while."

"Tepin will get it," Rita said. "Won't you, Tepin?" she asked the quiet worker who was washing the dishes.

Tepin nodded. "When breakfast is over, I get it."

"I hate to cause you more work," Eden said.

"It is my job," the woman said.

"I want to watch Barney," Matthew demanded. He banged his spoon onto the table and began to slide down from the chair.

"I'll turn on the video," Rita said. "Madeline will be sorry she missed it. And I made her some peanut butter fudge. I was hoping she'd hang around this morning."

"She's glued to Clay," Eden said. "All five girls think he's Superman."

Rita smiled. "I'm making him the hero of my novel. He's enough to make all my readers swoon."

The other woman's focus on her novel was cute. Eden took another sip of her coffee. "The girls have all had such a hard life. It's heartbreaking."

Allie's smile faded. "That was the hardest thing to get used to while running this camp. We love them for a little while and try to make as much difference as we can. Eventually we have to let them go, though. The only way I can get through it is to put them in God's hands."

"Why would he let them go through something so awful?" Eden asked. "I've never figured that out."

Allie's forehead wrinkled. "Life is hard, Eden. For everyone. We all have different challenges to face. All those hardships strengthen our faith and form us, though. I suspect God has great tasks in mind for some of these children. They'll need great grace to accomplish those tasks, so great trials are needed."

Eden frowned. "You believe trials change us?"

"Don't you? Have you ever had a trial that didn't?"

When it was put that way, Eden supposed she hadn't. "Some changes aren't always for the better."

Allie shrugged, then stood and picked up Matthew's bowl. "Only if we allow ourselves to be bitter and resentful over our lot in life. Sometimes we have to ask how we can allow this to make us a better person. There's always a choice in how we react."

Della sat listening quietly. "Was that you I heard singing late last night? I thought it was 'Amazing Grace.'"

Eden smiled. "Madeline insisted. It's her favorite song and she claimed she couldn't sleep without it."

"Sounded to me like you knew the song pretty well."

"I do." Something squeezed in Eden's chest. She stood and walked to the door. "You need me for anything, Allie? I have to make a call."

Allie shook her head. "I'm going to check on Matthew, then take Betsy over to play with Gracie's daughter, Hope."

Rita came back into the kitchen and called after Tepin, who had slipped out the back door. "Bring those soiled linens and don't dawdle. I'm doing laundry today."

Eden grabbed the portable phone from the wall and took it outside, where she settled onto the porch step. The breeze brought the scent of the desert to her nose. Some sweet smell from the wildflowers blooming on the hillside. The purple and yellow blooms fortified her for what lay ahead. She dug the number Daniel had given her out of her pocket and punched it into the phone. Her gut clenched as it began to ring on the other end. The pen in her fingers slipped to the ground and she picked it up.

The phone was answered by a woman with a gravelly voice that made Eden assume she was at least fifty. Or a smoker. Eden cleared her throat. "This is Eden . . . um . . ." Should she say Larson or Davidson? "Davidson," she said. "Eden Davidson. Someone from your office sent me a letter to tell me that my birth mother is asking for contact with me."

"Ah yes, Ms. Davidson. Your foster brother said you weren't interested. If you'll give me your social security number, I'll log in your refusal."

"Actually, I'd like to contact my birth mother."

There was a pause on the other end. The gruff voice softened. "I'm sure she'll be happy. She's been hounding my office for several days. Should I give her your number?"

"Could you give me her number? I'd like to be the one in control of when we talk. I want to make sure I'm alone."

"Of course." The woman rattled off the phone number. "Would you repeat it, please?"

Eden read the number back to her. "Where is the 214 area code?"

"That's right here in Dallas. I have her address as well if you'd like that."

"I would." It would take Eden some time to decide how she wanted her first contact with her mother to go. When she finished writing down the address, she read it back to the clerk as well. "Thank you for your time." She hung up and stared at the slip of paper. Why not call right now?

But she couldn't force herself to punch in the number. In her head, she heard her mother's voice. *"You're going to look ugly when your father comes by."*

Would her mother have changed? She'd always had beautiful skin. Her hair was red-blond. Men turned to look when she walked by. She'd be much older now.

Eden was afraid. That's what kept her hands in her lap. What if her mother wanted to see her but the mean-spirited comments continued? What possible reason could she have to be looking after all this time?

❊

The riding lesson was over, and Clay turned the girls over to the Rodriguez couple, who would be with them for about an hour as all the children did crafts together. Eden had never shown up, so he went in search of her. When he didn't find her in the bunkhouse, he started for the back door of the ranch house. As he neared, he saw her bright-blue blouse and walked toward her.

She sat on the porch step with her phone in one hand and a piece of paper in the other. Her hair was curled and perfect. She wore immaculate navy slacks and pumps. He'd been sure that she would drop that mask of perfection within a day of hitting the ranch. To find she still clung to her city-girl image confused him. Was there a real person under that smooth exterior? He'd thought so last night.

His boots crunched on a rock, and she looked up. Her eyes were swollen, as though she'd been crying. "You okay?" he asked. "What did your mother say?"

"I haven't been able to bring myself to call her." Her eyes darkened, and her voice trembled. "So many bad memories."

"Yesterday you remembered good ones too," he reminded her.

"In the night it seemed possible that she loved me. Missed me. In the daylight, it seems more likely she wants to yell at me more. Maybe she thinks I ruined her life."

"How could you ruin her life? You were a kid." He dropped beside her on the stoop.

She hunched her shoulders and clasped her knees. "I suppose it doesn't make sense. But nothing about this makes sense. Why would she even want to contact me after all these years?"

"Want me to call her?" The words were out before he stopped to think.

Her head came up to reveal eyes full of hope. "You'd do that? I don't know what to say."

"Give me the phone."

She put the phone into his outstretched hand. "Want me to read you the number?" He nodded, and she read the number slowly.

He listened to the ring on the other end and tried to think how to start the conversation. How old would she be? At least fifty, since Eden was thirty. Unless she'd had Eden as a teenager. Definitely a possibility based on what he'd heard about her.

After five rings, the call was picked up. "Hello." The voice on the other end was male. Pleasant enough, though. Sounded like a man in his fifties or sixties.

"My name is Clay Larson. Eden Davidson is my wife." It felt strange to say the word *wife* when they'd been apart so long. He glanced at the paper Eden held. "Does Nancy Santiago live there?" *Santiago?* He glanced at Eden and wondered if she'd made the connection in her own mind. It was a common name, but the kidnapper's name had been Santiago. Coincidence?

"Oh yes, yes, she does. She has been hoping for this call." The voice grew muffled. "Nancy, Eden's husband is on the phone."

Chills raced up his spine at the excitement in the man's voice. The woman made a smothered exclamation he couldn't make out, but it was clear she'd been hopeful to hear from her daughter. Maybe this wouldn't be a bad thing for Eden. He prayed her mother had changed, that this would bring healing and a new perspective to her.

"Hello?" The woman's voice was eager, almost girlish.

If he didn't know better, he'd think she was as young as Eden. "Hello, Mrs. Santiago. I'm Clay Larson, Eden's husband. She was given this number and told you were looking for her."

"Oh, I have been. For several years now. I'm so glad you called. Can I talk to her?"

He glanced at Eden and mouthed, "She wants to talk to you." When Eden shook her head violently, he spoke back into the phone. "I'm afraid that won't be possible right now. Is there a reason you're looking for her?"

"I'd think it was obvious." The animation was gone from the woman's voice. "She's my daughter. I . . . I didn't do right by her. I'd like to see if she needs anything. Tell her I'm sorry."

Praise God. "That's really good of you, ma'am."

"Can I see her? Maybe it would be better to say everything in person. I wasn't a good mother, Mr. Larson." Her voice broke.

"Call me Clay. And we all make mistakes." He saw Eden tense and look at him with a question in her eyes.

"I hope she can forgive me," the woman said, her voice trailing off.

"I think she will," he said. Eden was going to kill him, but he gripped the phone and made a decision. "Where could we meet?"

Eden shook her head but he ignored her. "We're in Texas too. How about Alpine?"

"That's about a day's drive." Nancy's voice was eager. "We could meet Saturday for dinner."

"That will be fine. I'll research where we might eat and call you back."

"I'll be waiting. Call my cell phone, because we might be on the road. I'll pack immediately."

She gave him her number, and he jotted it down, then hung up. Eden's fists were clenched when he looked at her. "We're meeting her Saturday in Alpine."

"I'm not ready, Clay." Her eyes flashed sparks. "Call her back."

"Some things you just need to face head-on. And this is one of those. I'll go with you."

"You won't leave me alone with her?"

He put his arm around her and she rested her head on his shoulder. "Not for a minute." He pressed his lips against her hair.

"Did she sound . . . eager? What did you think of her?"

"She sounded younger than I expected. How old is she?"

"Forty-nine, I think. She had me at nineteen."

"She seemed contrite over how she'd treated you. I think it will go well, honey. We'll face it together."

It might be the only thing she'd let him do for her.

⚹

After dinner, Eden looked at five eager faces, lips stained red from the Popsicles they were finishing. They had plenty of time before bed. "Let's build a tent house," she said.

"You mean we're going camping?" Katie asked, glancing at the darkening sky through the window.

"Sort of. We'll get blankets and build rooms out of them. Each tent can be for different things. You can make up what they're for."

"I want the red blanket!" Lacie said. She ran for the bedroom and returned dragging the red fuzzy blanket from her bed. "My room is for the stuffed animals to live in."

"I want to play," Madeline shouted.

"Hang on, let me get out the blankets," Eden said. She found a stack of linens in the hall closet and carried them to the living room.

In minutes every chair and sofa was draped with blankets, and the sound of giggles made her smile across the room at Clay.

"My room is for princesses," Madeline announced. "I must find a dress for the ball. Do you have one I can borrow?" she asked Eden. "Your pink nightgown would be lovely."

Eden smiled at her serious expression. "It's in my top drawer," she said. Madeline raced off to get her costume. "What's your room going to be for?" Eden asked Katie.

"For Olympic gymnasts. Would you like to see my floor show?" Katie pirouetted across the room, then did a cartwheel and came to a wobbly stop with her arms up.

"Good job!" Clay said. He lifted her to his shoulders and paraded through the room to her tent. "The winner gets to go in first." He set her in front of the opening to her tent room.

Grinning from ear to ear, Katie bowed grandly. "Thank you. I will do another show soon." She dropped to her hands and knees and disappeared inside.

"My room is a hospital," Paige said. "It's for patients with allergies.

No dust mites are allowed inside. I'm the nurse. I think I should take your temperature," she told Clay. "I need a thermometer."

"Use this," he said, offering her a Popsicle stick.

He opened his mouth and she stuck it in. A moment later she pulled it out. "Oh my, you have a temperature. We must put you to bed. Okay?"

"Whatever you say, my nurse." He winked at Eden, then crawled into Paige's tent.

Eden stared after them. Clay's and Paige's eyes looked so much alike, and Paige had that caregiving spirit she was seeing more and more in her husband.

Madeline returned with Eden's pink nightgown trailing around her bare feet. She had stuck bobby pins in her hair in an attempt to get her fine locks into an upsweep. Dark blue eye shadow made her eyes look bruised, but her dimples were flashing.

It was all Eden could do to keep from laughing. "You look lovely, Your Highness," she said. Madeline loved girlie things, just like Eden did.

Oh, which girl was theirs? It was so hard to know. She turned to India. "And what will we do in your room?"

"My room is a Sunday school," India said. "I'm going to teach my dolls about Jesus. Then we can all pray for God to send me a new mommy and daddy."

Eden's eyes filled. The faith of little children put her to shame. She hadn't even asked God what part she ought to play in this situation. All she'd done was follow Clay's lead and come here to find her daughter. What did God expect now that she realized she was still married to Clay?

16

Exhausted from the busy day, Eden sat on the porch of the bunkhouse and watched the storm approach. The night air held a hint of moisture. Lightning flickered off to the west, illuminating the jagged mountain peaks and leaving the scent of ozone in the wind. Storms exhilarated her. She felt alive with the thunder shaking the house and the flashes of lightning burning into her retinas. She was growing fond of this place of extremes.

The screen door slammed and Clay stepped out to join her on the porch. "Della and Zeke are helping with the games, then I told the girls to pick up their blankets and toys." He dropped into the rocker beside hers. "Storm's coming."

Another flash of lightning arced from the clouds to a tree atop a nearby peak. "I'd say it's here."

He straightened and peered up at the display that was nearly overhead. "We should go in. I don't want you struck."

"I love to watch it. We're safe here."

"I don't think so," he said, flinching when a bolt sizzled nearby. "Really, let's go in. It's bathtime anyway."

"In a few minutes." She lifted her face to the cooling breeze. "Thanks for calling my mother today." The generosity of his action still touched her. He'd seen her problem and had moved to help. She stared into the darkness. "I dread Saturday, though."

"I'll be with you. She sounded very nice, Eden. I'm not just saying that."

"Was that her husband who answered the phone?" It was too much to hope that the man was her father. She didn't even remember his name anymore, if she'd ever known it.

"I assume so. Seemed like a stand-up guy. He was as excited as she was."

Excited. Could they really want to see her that badly?

"What do you remember about your father?"

She glanced at him. Was he a mind reader too? "Not much. He came to see me about three or four times a year. They always fought, and he would slam out of the house without even telling me good-bye. I'm not sure why he ever bothered to come. He hardly noticed me."

Another light caught her eye. A car came up the drive, then stopped in front of the ranch house. A man and woman got out and approached the front door. The door to the house opened, and light framed Allie's figure. She gestured toward the bunkhouse. The man and woman turned to look, then started toward them.

"Looks like they're coming back here." Clay stood and stretched. "They'd better hurry. The rain is about to let loose any second."

He'd barely gotten the words out before the clouds opened up. The deluge was worthy of Noah's flood. Eden had never seen rain fall so hard and fast. The couple raced for the steps and arrived gasping and soaking wet.

"Let me get some towels," Eden said.

A basket of towels was just inside the door where she'd left them after dinner. She reached inside the screen door and snagged two. While the couple dried off, she took their measure. The woman had short dark hair in a stylishly layered cut. Large dark eyes. Dressed in Ann Taylor and a pair of red leather shoes. The man wore a navy suit and a crisp white shirt. His blond hair was plastered to his head. Both of them appeared to be in their late twenties.

The man handed the towel back to her. "Much obliged." He straightened his jacket and turned a smile on them. "I'm Tyler Rivers. This is my wife, Christine. We're here to see Paige."

"We're her parents."

"Her parents." It was clear from Christine's tone that she was laying claim to the little girl. And that she loved her.

"The camp prefers to let the girls adjust before visits with their foster parents," Clay put in. "We were told they needed to be here two weeks before there was a visit."

Tyler nodded. "Of course. But it's her birthday tomorrow, and we brought her a gift. Mr. Bailey said it would be all right to see her for a few minutes and give her the present. I have to fly out of town on business tomorrow, and we really wanted her to have her gift."

"If Rick said it was okay, then we're fine with it. Come inside." Clay held open the door for them.

The wave of protectiveness rising in Eden's chest alarmed her. These two were no threat. Was it because she didn't want any of the girls to be attached to someone other than herself? How totally selfish. If she had her way, none of the children would have to go through the abandonment issues she'd experienced. Of course she wanted Paige to be loved. She wanted them all to be cherished.

In the living room, the young girls looked up from their game of Chutes and Ladders. Zeke and Della had brought over their girls too, and there were several different games in progress. Della got up when the couple entered the room and lifted a brow in Eden's direction.

"Mommy!" Paige screamed. She leaped up and ran to throw her arms around Christine.

"Paige's foster parents," Eden said to Della and Zeke.

The woman knelt and picked her up. "I've missed you, honey. Are you having a good time?"

Paige nodded. "I peed the bed last night," she said with great solemnity.

"Oh dear."

"She peed on me!" India said, her voice indignant. "But she couldn't help it, I guess."

Christine's lips twitched. "I can see that would be upsetting," she said.

"How about a kiss for your daddy?" Tyler asked. When Paige reached for him, he took her into his arms and she kissed him with real affection.

Eden glanced at Clay and saw the same raw jealousy in his eyes that she felt. What if Paige was Brianna? Paige had been left by two men in a Walmart. It would rip this family apart to find out she didn't belong to them.

The living room still held the aroma of popped corn. Clay picked up the litter of Popsicle sticks and corn kernels.

"We can't let Paige's birthday go unnoticed tomorrow."

"What do you have in mind?"

Her dimples flashed. "Cupcakes. I'll bake them and you can ice them."

"I'm game if you are." Anything to keep that delight in her face.

He followed her to the kitchen, where she rummaged through the cupboards and found cake mix, a cupcake pan, and liners. Within minutes the cupcakes were in the oven and he put some decaf on to brew.

"I want to show you something," she said, exiting the room.

When she returned a few moments later, she held a tattered photo album. She sat at the table and he pulled out a chair and sat beside her. Even before she opened it, he knew it was pictures of Brianna. He'd probably seen them and, most likely, had copies himself. But when she flipped it open, he was faced with one he didn't remember. In the photo Brianna was peering over the top of his shoulder. She wore a pink ribbon in her thick blond hair.

"That was her first smile," Eden said. "Remember?"

He ran his fingers over the slick surface of the protective sheet. "I didn't see it. She wasn't facing me."

She pointed to Brianna's left cheek. "This is what I wanted to show you. See that dimple? Madeline has dimples."

"Do babies always keep their dimples?"

Her brow furrowed. "I don't know."

The next picture was one with Brianna and Eden. She wore the pendant he'd been carrying around in his pocket, and he put his fingers around it. Maybe now was the time to ask her to wear it again. To consider building their family unit new and fresh.

134

The phone rang, and she jumped to grab it. "This is Eden." Her smile faded and her fingers went white. "Who is this?"

He leaped up and grabbed the phone. "Who is this?"

An electronic hissing filled his ear, then the dial tone came on. He replaced the phone onto the hook. "Who was it?"

Her laugh was nervous. "I'm probably just skittish. It was likely a wrong number. No one answered."

But the fear in her eyes told him she didn't believe that. And he didn't either.

❋

In the morning Eden's vapors of the night before vanished with the scent of fresh coffee. She poured a cup, then eyed the components of her big project. The ingredients were assembled on the counter. She ticked them off her list: asparagus, chicken, curry powder, snow peas, coconut milk, carrots, onions, jasmine rice. This couldn't be too hard, could it? India and Madeline had begged to help—in fact, all five girls had wanted to help—so Eden compromised by allowing two to help with this trial recipe. The other three would get to help her bake cookies this afternoon.

She studied the recipe. What could she have the girls do that didn't involve a knife? "I need the water and rice measured," she said.

"Me, me!" India shouted, jumping up and down in her chair at the table.

"No, me!" Madeline said, shoving India off the chair.

The little girl hit the black-and-white tile floor but didn't cry. Madeline ran to Eden and snatched the plastic measuring cup from her hand before Eden could reprimand her.

Eden frowned at Madeline. "India gets to measure the rice because you pushed her, Madeline."

The little blonde's face puckered. "But I want to help," she wailed. "She always gets to do things instead of me."

"You can measure the water."

"That's just water." She folded her arms across her chest, and her lip stuck out. "You like India better than me."

"That's not true. I love you both equally. But you can't shove, honey." She put a bowl in front of India. "Measure out two cups of rice," she said. She helped the little girl hold the bag.

"Your turn, Madeline," she said, heading toward the faucet.

"I'm not going to help. She can do it." Madeline slid off the chair and rushed for the back door. Her tear-filled eyes glared at Eden before she focused on the door and began to yank on the knob.

Eden paused. Her first real challenge of discipline. What did she do? "Stop right there, Madeline," she said. She grabbed the little girl's arm and marched her back to the table. Madeline resisted, but Eden lifted her onto the chair. "Time-out. You sit there for five minutes." She walked back to the stove and set the timer. "When this timer goes off, you can get down."

"You're mean," Madeline said, her voice hiccupping in sobs. "I'm going to tell Mr. Clay."

"How do you think Mr. Clay will like the way you're acting?" Eden turned back in time to prevent India from spilling the rest of the rice onto the floor. She was beginning to wish she'd done this job by herself.

Clay stepped into the kitchen from the front room. "Did I hear my name?"

Madeline burst into noisy sobs. "She spanked me," she wailed.

Clay's gaze shot to Eden, and she shook her head. He walked to the table. "I don't think so, Madeline. Did you disobey Miss Eden?"

The little girl buried her face in her hands and sobbed. "You like India better too."

"What's this all about?" Clay asked.

"She knocked India off the chair in a dispute over who got to measure the rice. So I gave her a time-out."

He pulled out a chair beside Madeline. "You don't think you deserve a time-out for shoving India?"

Madeline raised her head. "I wanted to help." She swiped the back of her hand across her face.

"Did Miss Eden spank you? This is your chance to tell me the truth, Madeline. What did we learn in devotions the other night about lying?"

"That lying is as bad as murder," she whispered, staring at her hands.

"So what do you want to tell me?"

Madeline shot Eden a resentful glare. "She *wanted* to spank me."

Eden bit her lip to keep from smiling. Though the situation wasn't really funny, Madeline was determined not to take any blame. The situation was eye-opening. So this was what parenting was all about. It would have been easier to give in, to let her get by with rudeness and talking back. But it wouldn't have taught her anything.

"But Miss Eden didn't, did she?" Clay's voice was gentle.

Madeline looked at the table and not at Clay. "No."

"I'm proud of you for telling the truth. But you need to apologize to Miss Eden for lying about her. And you need to tell India you're sorry you shoved her."

"I won't!" The little girl folded her arms across her chest.

COLLEEN COBLE

Eden marveled at how well Clay was handling this. As if he'd dealt with five-year-old girls every day. Where did he get that calm firmness? She wanted to tell him not to press Madeline for an apology, but it wasn't the right thing to do. No child should talk back the way she'd done. Just because she was pained that the children had to be in foster care didn't relieve her of the duty to make sure the girls knew right from wrong.

"Then you'll have to go to your room and stay there all morning."

"What about lunch?"

"You can have it when you come out. That is, when you're ready to say you're sorry."

"I'm not ever saying sorry. I'm always the one who has to say sorry, even when it's not my fault!" Madeline's sobs grew wilder.

Eden took a step toward the child, but Clay held up a warning hand and shook his head. She couldn't help a flare of resentment even though she knew her compassion wasn't appropriate right now. How did he know when to be firm and when to back down? She could see where couples might have arguments over discipline, because she was ready to interfere. Madeline's sobs broke her heart. The little girl had been through so much.

She remembered feeling alone and unloved in foster care herself. And maybe just a bit of those feelings were what had catapulted her into full-blown anger with God when Brianna was taken. She thought she deserved better from him, to make up for the things she'd endured. But God hadn't given her any special favors. Just as Clay wasn't giving Madeline a license to disobey.

Eden gave a shake of her head. "No," she muttered.

Clay glanced up, a question in his eyes.

"Nothing," she said. "Just thinking aloud." She stepped to the

138

table and knelt by the little girl. "It's always easier just to get punishment over with, honey. Can't you tell India you're sorry? You could have hurt her."

Madeline's lip came out farther. "I'm sorry, India," she muttered. She glared at Eden. "But I'm not saying sorry to you. I'll stay in my room forever!"

"That's enough, young lady." Clay scooped her from the chair and carried her kicking and screaming out the back door.

Watching through the door's window, Eden saw them vanish inside the bunkhouse. She was so lucky God had forgiven her for her own stubbornness. Everyone had the same sin nature that deserved judgment.

17

THE HOUSE WAS QUIET EXCEPT FOR THE HUM OF THE AIR CONDITIONER. CLAY RAN A COMB through his hair, still damp from the shower. Eden had been quiet since they punished Madeline. The little girl had gone to bed without telling Eden she was sorry. Not even the thought of a cupcake for Paige's birthday had swayed her determination. He wasn't sure how to handle it next.

"That coconut chicken was pretty good," he said.

"I thought it was a little spicy," she said.

"Zeke ate his weight in it. So did I."

"Maybe it will be a hit at the international dinner." She was brushing her hair. Her hand paused before resuming the strokes. "How long before we get the DNA samples back?"

"Complete profiles will take about six weeks, but I had an idea." He tossed his comb into the drawer and sat on the edge of the bed beside her. "There are paternity and maternity DNA companies. In fact, I sent off a request for the kits and asked they be overnighted. I should have them soon. We could get those back in a few days."

"Days, not weeks? Would they be accurate?"

"I think so. They wouldn't provide a complete DNA strand, but they would tell us if we are the parents to any of the children. We'd have to send in our DNA along with the girls'."

Her eyes were bright. "Let's do it! I can't stand waiting. I'm growing to love all of them." She shook her head. "And that kidnapper is out there. Knowing which child is Brianna might help us figure out who did this. And why."

He nodded. "I dream about it most nights. About telling our daughter we're her parents."

She began to brush her hair again. "Can we do it tomorrow?"

He watched the hypnotic ripple of her hair through the brush. "It will take a couple of days to get it and a couple more for them to receive it. We should have the results within the week."

"And we'll know," she said slowly. "How amazing."

"Then what?"

"We can leave here and pick up our lives again."

He lifted a brow. "And leave the Baileys high and dry?"

Her forehead furrowed. "I didn't mean that. I wouldn't want to hurt anyone, especially not the other girls. We should stay at least until they go home."

"And we have separate lives, and a daughter to share. That's going to take some time to figure out."

She put down the brush, then stood. "I'm tired. We didn't get much sleep last night."

What was she thinking? Was there a chance she didn't want to live apart any more than he did? "No, we didn't."

When he went around to his side of the bed, she was already under the covers with her back to him. He clicked off the light and plunged the room into darkness. But even after he settled into the bed, he knew he'd never be able to sleep without talking to her about what he'd been thinking of.

"Eden?"

"What?" Her voice was sleepy but not impatient.

"I want us to stay married." There, he'd said it. Propping himself on his elbow, he rolled toward her. "Brianna will need all the stability we can give her." *Coward. Tell her you want her, not just Brianna.*

She still didn't answer and remained motionless on her side of the bed. He prayed for her to consider his plea, for her heart to be opened to another chance.

"What if we end up fighting again?" she said softly.

"We've been doing pretty well so far, don't you think? We never had the time to really get to know each other. Now we do."

"We don't know all the challenges yet. I don't want to go through . . ." Her voice trailed away.

What had she started to say? Go through losing him? He wished he could be sure of her feelings. She said nothing for a few minutes.

"Where did we go wrong, Eden?" he whispered. He wasn't sure if she was still awake, or if she'd even heard him.

The sheets rustled, and the line of her silhouette changed as she rolled over to face him. "We weren't suited."

"You think people have to be the same to be suited? What about complementing each other? You like schedules and I teach you to enjoy the moment. I like adventure and you show me the value of family and routine."

The silence lengthened. "We fought too much," she said. "I hated that."

"We were practically strangers." He reached out to touch her cheek. She didn't flinch. "I'll never forget the first time I saw you."

"At the beach in Kauai," she murmured. She leaned into his touch.

"You had on that gold tropical sundress and a killer tan. I thought redheads didn't tan." She'd seemed almost an angel, the way the sun lit her hair and skin.

"It was fake." There was a smile in her voice.

"I should have known."

"It was well done." She fell silent, then said, "You called me Angel."

"You saved me from a lonely life. Or so I'd hoped."

"I thought you were mocking me. I didn't know you thought—"

"You know what drew me first? You were sitting and talking to an old man." She hadn't seemed impatient at all. He'd stood and watched her chat with the old guy for fifteen minutes before he got up the nerve to talk to her.

"We were feeding the birds."

"You were so sweet to him. Not many people pay attention to the elderly."

"I always wanted grandparents."

"You had none? What about your foster mom's parents?"

"They lived in New York, and I saw them once a year. I was always afraid to touch anything in their home. My foster dad's parents died in a small plane crash when I was ten. I only met them once."

He rubbed his fingers over the silken texture of her cheek.

"When you said you'd have dinner with me, I thought I'd died and gone to heaven."

"You were cocky and full of yourself."

They'd packed a lifetime into two weeks. Or so it had seemed. And one night things got out of hand. He'd regretted his lapse of self-control, but when it came to her, he had no sense. It was a truth he'd accepted the minute he saw her again.

The faint glimmer in the room was her eyes. "What did you think when I called to tell you I was pregnant? You were so—cold. I was afraid to ask."

Something about the quiet of the night allowed him to admit it. "I was glad." *Glad.* Such a tame word for the rush of joy that had come over him.

She stiffened. "Glad! How can you say that?"

"I thought I'd lost you. You weren't returning my e-mails. Our phone calls seemed stilted."

"You didn't say anything for what seemed an eternity. Then you just said, 'Well, we'll get married. I'll be there as quickly as I can.'"

He heard the pain in her voice and regretted he'd been the cause. "I wasn't sure how you felt. I wanted to man up."

"Man up," she repeated. "I'd hoped you'd say you loved me. You came right away but you were all business."

How did he tell her he'd been overcome by his good fortune? The words seemed lame now. He should have realized. Why hadn't he? No wonder she'd been so prickly and aloof. It was the only protection she had.

"Then you went on assignment two weeks after we were married. What was I to think but that you were only doing your duty?"

"I had a wife and baby to provide for. I wanted to do right by you both. To be a better father and husband than my dad had been."

"But you told me out at the old house that you're wealthy. So why did you go if you didn't need the money?"

"I only inherited it a couple of years ago."

"I see." There was something in her voice. Panic, fear? He wanted to tell her she didn't have to be afraid.

"I'm sleepy," she said abruptly. She rolled over and presented her back to him again.

Just when he was about ready to tell her he still loved her.

⊰⊱

Eden couldn't sleep after that discussion. She lay still until Clay's breathing was deep and even, then rolled onto her back. He might be nostalgic now, but the day they'd set up house together, she'd been sure he blamed her for the pregnancy. There'd been no hiding the fact that he felt trapped.

Her eyes stung, and she threw her arm across them. Their short marriage hadn't had a chance. They'd been virtual strangers and hadn't connected except physically. There'd never been any question about their attraction to each other.

It has taken all this time to get over him. If I even am.

She pushed the insistent thought away. Of course she'd gotten over him. The month he left, she'd known it was over. She wanted to tell Clay why she'd left, but that would mean he would know she loved him. Her pride couldn't stand that.

And it didn't change anything. Not really. When they found Brianna, they would help her adjust, then they would split again. He hadn't uttered a single word of love since reentering her life. They'd been married nine months. And all but a few weeks of that time, he'd been gone. If he'd cared about her, he would have made spending time with her a priority.

She rolled to her side again, willing herself to sleep. Rest would stop this pounding in her chest, this nameless pain that radiated under her breastbone. Closing her eyes, she took a few deep breaths before they popped open again. Maybe warm milk would help.

She eased out of bed, then froze when she heard something at the window. *Scratch, scratch, scratch.* Probably a branch. Then she remembered she was in West Texas. There were few trees here, and none in the yard. The noise came again. Like a long fingernail on a chalkboard. The hair at her neck rippled. All she had to do was step to the window and look out to ease her mind. The cause of the noise had to be something very simple.

"Eden."

The whisper shuddered through her. Clay still slept. The voice came from the side of the house where the window was. For a moment she stood frozen in place. Then she wheeled and leaped back onto the bed.

She grabbed Clay's arm. "Clay!"

He sat up instantly. "What's wrong?"

"Someone is outside the window. He called my name."

He threw back the covers. "Go stay with the girls." He grabbed a flashlight from the top drawer in the chest beside the bed, then jumped up, jerked open the door, and ran into the hall.

She ran behind him and rushed to the girls' room. Her gaze went from bed to bed. They were all sleeping. Her knees went weak and she sagged against the door frame before she shut the door and locked it. She glanced around the room and saw a desk chair. After dragging it to the door, she propped its back under the knob.

She should have called the ranch house. Rick or one of the cowboys would have come running. There was no phone in this room. She went to the window and looked out onto the side of the house where she'd heard the intruder. The storm had passed except for a few stray clouds that shrouded the moon. Puddles glimmered in the few shafts of moonbeam. She didn't see Clay. That alone was worrisome. No intruder either.

She paced in front of the window, stopping occasionally to peer out. Nothing moved other than a jackrabbit that darted from the corner of the house toward the empty corral. No doubt it wished it could glance into the sky to see if an owl soared above. She knew the feeling of waiting for a predator to strike.

When the scratch came at the door, she froze. Had the intruder gained entrance? Had he hurt Clay? Then she heard Clay's soft whisper and ran to move the chair out of the way. When she unlocked the door, he opened it.

"All clear," he whispered. He drew her into the hall and led her to the kitchen, where a light chased away the shadows.

"Did you see anything?"

His jaw hardened. "Footprints outside our bedroom window. Fresh ones."

She closed her eyes and gripped the edge of the table. "So I wasn't dreaming. I didn't think so, but it was so surreal."

"What did you see and hear?"

She straightened and hugged herself. "First I heard scratching. Like a fingernail on the screen. Then someone whispered my name. That was it. I was too afraid to move the curtain and look out."

"Good." He rubbed his bristly chin. "I'm going to have to tell Rick tomorrow."

"Everything?"

"I think so. We have to protect the girls. And you seem to be a particular target."

"Should I call him tonight?"

"No use in disturbing him. There's no one out there now." He stared at her, his eyes intensely blue. "I want to investigate Daniel."

Her gratitude that he was taking this seriously vanished. "There's no need. He would never do anything to hurt me."

"I don't share your confidence."

"He was angry when I talked to him, but it's not him, Clay." She knew her lifelong friend. Her brother. Nothing Clay said would make her believe Daniel would harm her. "What about you?"

"What about me?"

"What if this person wants to hurt you through me?" As soon as she said the words, she realized how ludicrous they were. To hurt him through her would mean he cared. And he didn't.

He pulled out a chair and had her sit down. "I got some hate mail after that incident in Colombia. But this person seems very venomous toward you in particular. While hurting you would hurt me, you'd think he'd send me a warning too."

"Hurting you would hurt me." Did he really care that much? She watched him step to the refrigerator and pull out the milk. He poured her a glass before pouring one for himself. Why had she never noticed how giving he was? The answer came to her quickly. He hadn't been around enough.

18

Clay's eyes felt gritty. The bunkhouse was quiet for the first time in hours. Zeke and Della had taken the older girls on a hike. The younger girls were on an outing with the vet, Shannon MacGowan. She and her husband had two daughters a couple of years older than their girls.

He stopped short in his walk across the spindly grass between the sleeping quarters and the ranch house. *Their girls.* The children had crept into his heart already.

Eden glanced up at him. "What's wrong?"

"Nothing, really. I was just thinking about how often I think of the kids as *our* girls."

She smiled, her face tender. "Me too. I love them so much already."

"You ready to tell Rick and Allie about all this?"

"Do you think they'll kick us out?"

"They might, but I don't think we have a choice now. The girls' safety is too important." He held out his hand and she took it.

They found Allie and Rick in the kitchen still drinking coffee. Rita was nowhere to be seen. Tepin was doing the dishes, her face impassive, as though she were alone.

Rick pushed a chair out with his foot. "Have a seat, friends. You look like a mule dragged you both through a patch of cholla."

Clay pulled out another chair and let Eden take the one nearest Allie. "Didn't get much sleep last night."

"Another bed-wetting?" Allie's dark eyes were full of mischief. "You two are getting broken in right off." She rose and poured them each a cup of coffee.

"I wish it were that benign," Clay said.

Allie sobered and sat back down before glancing at Rick. "You're not quitting, are you?"

"Oh no! We love working with the children," Eden said.

Rick leaned back in the chair with his coffee in his hand. "Then what's up?"

"There was an intruder outside the bunkhouse last night."

Every trace of geniality vanished from Rick's face. He put his coffee down. "What happened? Who was it?"

Clay laced his fingers together. "We don't know, but there's more to our story than we've told you, and it's time we did."

Rick leaned forward in his chair. "What are you saying?" His voice was troubled.

"Five years ago our daughter, Brianna, was kidnapped. She was six weeks old, and we never saw her again." His voice quavered and he cleared his throat.

Allie put her hand to her mouth and her eyes welled. "Oh no! I can't imagine something so awful."

Rick nodded. "I knew that much."

"You never told me?" Allie asked.

"Brendan knows Clay, remember? He told me in confidence." Rick glanced back at Clay. "I can see how the experience would give you a heart for the hurting kids here at the ranch. Is the tragedy related somehow?"

Clay cleared the thickening in his throat and nodded. "Somehow I never believed she was dead."

"I did," Eden put in. "I gave up, tried to move on. Most of the time I thought I was doing a pretty good job of it. Then I'd see a mother with a baby or walk by a zoo and remember all the things I wanted to show Brianna but never got a chance."

Rick's gaze was sober. "So this intruder—?"

"I'm not quite to that part of the story yet. Hang on." This would be the tricky part, convincing Rick to let them stay when they hadn't revealed the real reason they were here. But the Baileys had children. Surely they could understand the lengths a dad would go to for his daughter. Clay glanced at Eden.

She gave a quick nod in his direction and took over the narration. "Clay got a picture a couple of weeks ago."

The wonder of it hit Clay again. He took a quick sip of coffee to swallow down the lump in his throat. "He sent me this." Taking the picture of the girls from his pocket, he slid it across the table to the Baileys.

Allie snatched it up first and stared at the smiling faces. "Our girls?"

Rick took it and studied it as well. "What do the girls have to do with this?"

"Look at the back," Clay said.

Rick flipped it over and looked even more grave. Allie's eyes widened. "So Brianna is alive!" Her voice trembled. She leaned over and took Eden's hand.

Eden squeezed her fingers and smiled. "She is." Her eyes were misty. "Truly a miracle."

Clay pointed at the picture. "One of those girls is our Brianna."

The Baileys froze in place. They exchanged a long glance with each other. Clay couldn't tell if they were judging his motives or the truthfulness of what he'd said.

Rick gave the photograph another stare, then handed it back. "No wonder you were interested in how they came to be here. Do you have any idea which one?"

"I called to get paternity DNA tests sent here. I had planned to wait on the results of full-profile tests, which I sent in after we arrived, but I realized we could get paternity and maternity tests done much more quickly. They would tell us all we needed to know."

Rick's scowl deepened as Clay spoke. "Are you even who you say you are?"

Clay had been expecting the question, and he didn't blame the other man. "I haven't lied about anything, Rick. Both Brendan and Michael vouched for me. I'm laying out everything now."

"The lie of omission is just as great." Rick didn't smile. "You only came here to find your daughter. I'm not okay with that. We're here to help these kids. Most of them have been through things we can't even imagine."

"Would you have hired us if I'd told you all of it?"

"No. I would have thought you were some kind of wackos."

Allie jumped to her feet. "Rick, we have to help them! I realize it would have been better if they'd told us, but—"

"But we wouldn't have hired them," Rick said, his mouth a grim line.

Allie put her hand on her husband's shoulder. "Maybe not. But they're doing a great job with the girls."

"There's more," Clay said. "And what else we have to tell you may convince you that you're right to throw us out. But I pray you won't. Our family's future is in your hands."

Eden clasped her hands together and leaned forward. "He's here. The kidnapper. He scratched on the window last night and whispered my name. In town the other day he called me on the phone and threatened to take her again."

Allie put her hand to her mouth. "Oh, Eden, no!"

"You expected him to be here, didn't you? That this was a trap?"

Clay nodded. "I'd thought he'd want money or something. Instead he seems to be taunting Eden."

Rick stared at Eden. "Is this true?"

Eden nodded. "He said I would have no one to blame but myself. Then he asked me if I knew who I really was. We don't know what that means. But we have to protect Brianna."

"You don't know which of the girls is Brianna," Allie said.

Clay nodded. "We need your help."

Rick rubbed his forehead. He stared at Clay, then Eden. "I'm inclined to make you leave. Your being here puts those kids in danger."

"Rick, no!" Allie cried. "Think how it would be if Matthew or Betsy had been taken. We have to help. Call the sheriff. We can protect them. With us all working together, we'll solve this and reunite a family."

"And if we leave, that leaves Brianna even more unprotected," Clay said.

Rick glanced at his wife and his brow furrowed. "I suppose you're right. And whichever girl is their daughter, she deserves to be with her parents and not in foster care. What can we do, Clay?"

"I think we need to talk to Brendan," he said. A surge of adrenaline hit him now that he had help.

✳

The Reata restaurant almost looked like a house except for the enormous R over the front door. A horseshoe dangled from the loop at the bottom of the R. Eden got out of the truck and walked on shaky legs to the entrance with Clay.

"We're a little early," he said as they stepped inside. He asked the hostess for as much privacy as they could get.

"It's pretty," Eden whispered when the hostess led them through the cowboy-decor room. The walls were painted in mottled warm browns and tans, and the doorway trim was a terra-cotta color. The hostess took them through the restaurant to the patio. Large cowboy murals decorated the side of the building. They were seated at a secluded table under a trellis on the patio. Grasses and yucca softened the surrounding buildings and made an oasis outside.

Eden toyed with her tableware. "Let's go, Clay. We don't have to stay."

"Calm down. It's not going to be as bad as you think." He gave the waitress, a smiling Hispanic woman, their drink order.

A couple stepped through the doors into the courtyard. Eden recognized the woman in an instant. The reddish hair. The slim build. Her mother hadn't even aged that much. She had the beautiful, unlined skin that Eden remembered so well. The peach suit she wore was impeccably fitted, and she wore it with style. The couple paused and scanned the courtyard. Eden sat frozen in place. She couldn't rise, couldn't speak.

Clay glanced at her. "That them?" When she nodded, he rose and beckoned to them.

Her mother's smile was tentative and didn't quite reach her eyes. She followed the man across the terra-cotta tile to the table. "Eden?"

Eden had heard that voice in her dreams. It was softer now, not as demanding. She found her tongue. "Hello, Mom." She cleared her throat and willed herself to stand, to embrace the older woman, who stood with her hands awkwardly in front of her.

Her mother glanced at the man beside her. Tall and distinguished, he appeared to be in his fifties, maybe ten years older than her mother. Or maybe it was the wings of gray at his temples that made him seem older. His mustache held a little gray as well. His genial smile revealed white teeth. Eden focused on his open grin rather than on her mother's pleading gaze. Something about him seemed familiar.

Clay pulled out a chair for her mother beside Eden. "Have a seat."

The breeze sent a familiar scent to Eden. Chanel No. 5. Instantly she was back in her mother's bedroom watching her spritz a liberal amount of the expensive perfume on her wrists and the back of her neck. Why had Eden agreed to this meeting? She should have run the other way. What good could come from this?

The server brought her ice water. She squeezed the lemon into her glass and took a sip. "I assume you're married to my mother?" she asked the man who'd accompanied Nancy.

"I'm sorry," her mother said before he could speak. "I never introduced Omar. We've been married ten years. This is Omar Santiago."

"Pleased to meet you," Eden said. What did she say now? Did she ask how they met or jump right into the reason for the meeting? But no, they should wait for any serious conversation until after they'd ordered their food.

A Don Edwards song played, his gravelly voice singing about cowboys. For a brief instant, Eden even imagined herself in cowboy boots. She shook the nasty image away. Once the server took their orders and left them in peace, she squared her shoulders and glanced at her mother, who smiled back.

"So, Eden," her mother said. "You look well. And your husband is so handsome. I'd like to know about your life."

"Since you walked away and left an eight-year-old by herself?" Eden couldn't help herself. It wasn't the best way to mend fences, but hadn't her mother even wondered what Eden had done when she came home to find her mother gone?

Her mother blanched and glanced at her husband, who took her hand. She lifted her chin. "I'm sorry about that, Eden. What did you do? I want to know the full extent of the damage I caused."

Was she gloating about it? Eden wished the encounter were over and she and Clay were headed home. "When the snowstorm hit, I came back to the house. It was dark. I'd been hiding out in the little playhouse at the park until I couldn't feel my fingers."

Her mother winced and tears pooled in her eyes. She took a sip of water. "I'm so sorry," she said, her voice choked. "Then what?"

Was her mother protecting Omar from the truth? "The trailer was dark. I called your name but stayed in the living room like I'd been told. When you didn't appear by ten, I went to bed. The next morning when I got up, I fixed you breakfast. Toast and jelly, the way you liked it. But your room was empty." Her throat closed and she swallowed hard, remembering the awful moment when she'd seen the empty closet.

She clung to Clay's hand. No good could come from replaying all this. The warmth of his fingers bolstered her courage.

"You saw my clothes were gone?" her mother asked.

Eden nodded. "I didn't know what to do. I didn't have my father's phone number, so I didn't do anything for a few days. I went to school and came home. Eventually I ran out of food, so I went to the neighbor's and asked for some bread. It all came out then. They called the welfare department, and a social worker came and took me away."

Her mother wept, dabbing at her eyes with a wadded-up tissue. Eden watched with a strange detachment. She should feel something, shouldn't she? At least sympathy? Or had all sensation been washed away as the emotions were dredged from her subconscious?

Her gaze caught Clay's, and she glimpsed compassion in the depths of his eyes. For the first time, she wondered how he felt when he realized she'd left him. She felt almost dizzy when she realized she wasn't that different from her mother. No, she hadn't abandoned a child, but she'd run away rather than face any unpleasantness. She looked down at her hands.

Omar motioned to the server. "Bring my wife some coffee, please," he said.

The server acted as though a woman sobbing at the table was an everyday occurrence. She grabbed a pot and a cup from a cart by the door and brought it to the table, then left.

Eden's mom poured half-and-half into the cup, then took a sip.

"I'm sorry. It breaks my heart to know what I did to you." Her eyes were red when she stared at Eden. "How long were you in foster care?"

"Until I turned eighteen." Eden dipped a chip in salsa so her mother couldn't see how upset she was.

Her mother took another gulp of coffee. "W-Were they good people?"

Eden decided she'd been pointed enough about her circumstances. Maybe her mother really was sorry. "Kind and loving." No need to say they had high expectations that had made her a perfectionist. No reason to mention they micromanaged every area of her life. At least she'd had a home and had always felt their love, even if it was conditional.

Her mother fished another tissue out of her purse, a Brighton that looked new. "I was so young."

"You were nearly my age," Eden said. "Hardly a child."

A flush stained her mother's cheeks. She glanced at her husband, who put his arm around the back of her chair and shot a disapproving glance Eden's way. Well, let him. He wasn't the one who'd been abandoned.

Her mother wetted her lips. "Looking back now, it seems the choices should have been easy. I got pregnant with you, but your father was already married. He promised to take care of us, but he seldom sent a check."

"So you became a prostitute." Even to her own ears, the statement was harsh.

Her mother winced. "Hardly a prostitute, my dear. I . . . I had some male friends."

"Who gave you money. I saw them leave it." Eden remembered

the rolls of cash left on the table or on her mother's pillow. Cash that bought them pizza or milk or electricity.

Her mother's eyes welled again, but Eden squelched her flash of sympathy. Her mother's actions might have been bearable if she had done it to keep them together or to feed her daughter. But too many times the cash had gone for pretty dresses or jewelry. Trips to get a manicure or a pedicure. Then she'd just walked away without caring if Eden had food or heat.

Her mother took another sip of coffee. "I thought I had no choice. That you'd be better off without me."

"Which makes no sense. How could an eight-year-old be better off alone, fending for herself?" Clay put in.

Eden glanced at him, heartened by his passionate defense. Did he see how inappropriate her mom's excuses were? But what about her own? She didn't want to see herself in her mother's behavior, but the notion kept popping up.

"Give Nancy a chance," Omar said. "She's trying to apologize for what she did."

The apology had seemed thin to Eden. Was that how Clay saw her own excuses?

When Eden said nothing, Omar rose. "Perhaps we should go," he said, putting his hand on his wife's shoulder.

Eden's mother took his hand. "Sit down, Omar." Her voice trembled. "I've gone about this all wrong. There is no excuse for what I did. All the rationalization in the world doesn't change the fact that I left my child to fend for herself. Without food. Without comfort. Without anything." She caught Eden's gaze. "I hope you can forgive me someday, Eden. I don't think I can ever forgive myself."

With no warning, tears flooded Eden's eyes. A simple, heartfelt apology. That's all she'd ever wanted.

Clay scooted his chair closer and put his arm around her. "You have a tissue?" he asked Nancy, who nodded and passed one to her daughter.

Eden took it and dabbed at the moisture in her eyes. How embarrassing to cry in front of them all. She never cried. She'd sworn never to let someone hurt her like that again. Now here she was, blubbering away.

"Why?" she asked. "What made you think it was okay to leave me? Did I do something?"

"What?" Her mother shook her head. "It was never about you. If I'd thought of you instead of myself, I wouldn't have left. I didn't think I could ever have a life saddled with a child. I was selfish, pure and simple. I rationalized to myself that you'd go to school and tell the teacher. Someone would come."

Eden mopped her streaming eyes again, willing herself to stop. "I never cry," she gulped. "What about my father? I don't even remember his name. It was all so long ago. I can't even remember what he looked like."

Her mother exchanged a glance with Omar. "It was Omar's brother, Hector."

Eden absorbed the news. Maybe that's why the man seemed vaguely familiar. "Where is he now?"

Omar shifted in his seat. "He's a drug dealer in Colombia."

19

SHE'D HANDLED IT BETTER THAN HE DID. THREE HOURS LATER CLAY STIRRED HALF-AND-half into Eden's coffee and slid it across the table to her. The coffee shop was deserted this late. Only a few customers plunked down money for a latte and hurried out into the sunset. The scent of cinnamon and yeast from a bakery down the street was tempting for dessert, but he didn't want to leave her long enough to buy a treat.

"Do you want to see her again?" he asked her.

She sipped her coffee. "No. Maybe." She gave a watery smile. "I don't know."

"You did good, honey. Handled it all with grace."

She dabbed at her eyes. "Hardly. I wish I could quit crying. I hate crying. And what was the point of this? To assuage her guilt?"

Had he ever seen her cry? He didn't think so. She'd screamed and hit things when Brianna was gone. Sobbed hysterically and hadn't slept for days, but her eyes had been dry. "I'd guess so. And to assure herself that you're all right. Maybe you can both move on now."

"Thank you for bringing me. I wouldn't have been able to get through it without you."

At her words, a curl of warmth encircled him. "I wanted to be here for you." He wanted to be there for her forever, not just for a day. Didn't she see that?

She sipped her coffee. "My father is a Santiago. The kidnapper who died was Jose Santiago. What does that mean?"

"A weird coincidence? Santiago is as common a name south of the border as Jones would be in the States." He shook his head. "But you're right, there might be a connection. But why would your father want to hurt his own daughter?"

"None of it has made any sense. Maybe your friend Brendan will have some insight. What time is he supposed to meet us here?"

He glanced at his watch. "Any minute. Rick was picking him up at the airport."

"Amazing that he was willing to come all this way as a favor."

"He saved my hide down in Colombia. I was taking pics of kids in a village along the river. A Jeep full of commandos rolled in and started firing rounds for fun. No good reason. They were laughing and joking while bullets flew. I confronted them. The kids got away and I got thrown in jail."

"Lucky you weren't killed," she said, her eyes huge.

"Actually, they were saving me for sport. My execution by firing squad was going to be in two days." He'd never told her all this. He hadn't wanted her to worry. "Brendan broke me out in the middle of the night."

"How did he know about it?"

"He's special ops. He knows everything." Clay grinned and took a drink of his Americano. "I guess he'd been at a neighboring village and heard about the gringo taking pictures."

"What happened to the pictures?"

"My camera and film were lost. I hated that. I had some really good shots that would have shown the lives these kids lead in drug towns. The only thing I got out with was that pendant I gave you when I got back."

Her eyes widened. "The one with the mother and baby?"

"That's the one."

"You told me a little girl gave it to you in exchange for a piece of hard candy."

"She did. I just didn't tell you the backdrop."

"I loved that pendant." Her voice was wistful. "Where is it now?"

"I've been carrying it around in my pocket."

She gave him a startled look. "How long?"

"Since I jumped in the truck to find you." He reached into his pocket and pulled it out.

Her eyes were soft as she plucked it from his palm. "It's always been special to me."

"I've been wanting to give it back to you, but I wasn't sure you'd take it."

She rubbed the pendant in her hands. "Did the child make it herself?"

"I don't think so. She was only five or six." He wanted to fasten it around her neck, but he waited for a cue from her. "I'm not sure what it's made of. I just like it because it reminds me of the little girl. The design looks pre-Colombian."

"Here, you keep it safe." She started to hand it back to him but he closed her fingers around it.

"It's yours."

She stared at him a moment, then lifted it to her neck and started to fasten the chain. It must have missed the clasp, because it slipped from her fingers and landed on the tile patio. He heard something crack, and when he looked down, the piece of jewelry lay in two pieces.

"Oh no!" She scooped up the nearest piece and it crumbled in her fingers. "I'm so sorry."

He looked at it in her hand and it was different now. Sparkly. "What's that?"

"Wait, it's not exactly broken. A covering has come off." She held out her open palm. Green and gold glittered in her hand.

"Wow." He scooped it up and examined it. "I bet this is worth money. Someone must have covered it over with the other stuff to hide it."

"How exciting!" Her eyes were shining. "Is that jade?"

He looked more closely at the baby. "I think so. And the gold is high quality."

"How would a peasant girl get something like this?"

"She probably didn't know what she had."

A truck maneuvered into a parking space across the street under the streetlight. Two men got out, and he recognized Rick and Brendan. "The reinforcements are here," he said. He stood and greeted the men.

Brendan hadn't changed much in five years. Broad shoulders filled out a casual blue shirt. His khaki pants were a little wrinkled and stained. His dark hair needed a trim, but those brown eyes that missed nothing were sharp and inquisitive.

"I've heard so much about you," Eden said, taking his hand.

"Same here." He squeezed her fingers, then glanced at the pendant on the table. Frowning, he pointed to it. "May I?"

"Sure." Clay handed it to him.

The other man examined it with care. When he turned it over, he inhaled sharply. "What are you doing with a Santiago heirloom? They'd kill to get this back."

Clay wrapped his fingers around the bauble. The trinket was worth so much more money than he'd dreamed, but even more than that, it was prized by a drug family connected to Eden. The cool weight of the jade in his hand convinced him it was real.

He held it up to the light. The veins and color of the jade were exceptional. "Are they looking for this?"

Brendan nodded, swiping a lock of hair out of his eyes. "I heard it was stolen by a rival about seven years ago."

"Stolen?"

Brendan leaned back in his chair. "The Santiago family is a rival of Juarez, that guy you had a run-in with in Colombia."

"Juarez stole it?"

"That's what Hector Santiago claims."

He heard Eden gasp beside him. "Hector Santiago?"

Brendan nodded. "Dangerous guy. He's blamed all the bad luck that's hit his family on its disappearance. Does he know you have it? It's worth more to him than the monetary value. Much more."

"I didn't even know I had it until Eden dropped it. It was covered with this." Clay stooped and pinched a sample of the material that had covered the jewelry.

"So why is it important?" Eden asked.

"It's been in his family for generations. Legend has it that the man who owns it will hold his wealth and power until death. Since it came up missing, his star has been waning." Brendan turned the stonelike substance over in his hands. "Someone took pains to disguise this. Tell me how you got it." He dug a plastic bag out of his pocket and dropped in the remains.

Clay told him how he'd come to have it in his possession. "It was in my pocket the night you busted me out of jail."

"I can tell you now that I'd been in the neighboring town investigating the shooting of someone Santiago thought had this thing. And you had it all along."

Rick came from the coffee shop with two cups in his hand. "Hazelnut latte, extra hot," he said, handing it to Brendan before sitting in the last chair. "What have you found out about the girls?"

"We haven't gotten that far yet." Clay brought him up to speed on the piece of jewelry.

"Is there any way this Santiago could know you have this? Maybe he took Brianna to get it back," Rick asked.

Eden plucked the pendant from Clay's hand. "The ransom demand was for money, not this. I think they're unrelated." Her voice was defiant, and she shot Clay a glance that warned him to say nothing about her father.

Clay held her gaze. "But I never thought money was the real issue. There are a lot of possibilities. I'd always thought they were luring us out into the open for some other reason."

"What about the camera?" she asked, wrinkling her forehead. "What pictures did you take?"

"Like I said, kids, the village." It had been so long ago. Though the trauma of the night in jail was burned into his memory, the village itself had faded into the mists of time.

"No pictures of this?" Rick asked.

"Nope." Clay tried to remember if there were any pictures of the pendant in existence. A dim memory tried to surface, but he couldn't quite grasp it.

"What?" Eden asked.

"Nothing. Let's talk about the girls."

She bit her lip. "Just a minute. We have to tell Brendan and Rick."

"Tell us what?" Rick asked, his face troubled.

"I just met my birth mother after twenty years. She's married to Hector's brother."

Brendan sat upright. "His brother?"

She nodded and exhaled harshly. "Omar. And my mother says Hector is my father."

"Holy cow," Brendan said softly. "This is a strange wrinkle. Where is your dad now?"

"I have no idea. The last time I saw him I was a little girl."

"And you have something he's been searching for a good six years," Brendan said. "That's ominous to me in light of your daughter's kidnapping."

"There's more. We found a picture of the dead kidnapper in an old yearbook at the ranch. His name was Jose Santiago."

"Hector's son."

Clay felt as though he'd been sucker punched. "Brianna's own uncle took her?"

"I . . . I killed my own brother?" Eden's voice trembled. She buried her face in her hands. "Oh, I can't bear it."

Clay scooted his chair closer and put his arm around her. "It was an accident, honey."

She raised a white face. "How could he do something like that? And why not just ask for the pendant back?"

Brendan shook his head. "Makes no sense, does it? I'll see what I can find out." He pulled the file toward him. "These the bios?"

"Yep," Rick said. Then to Clay: "And Brendan brought a copy of everything in the files about the kidnapping. We thought we could compare the two, see if there are any connections." Rick flipped open the file. "Let's look at Madeline."

"We know her mother was in a mental hospital. She showed up here," Clay said. "They look enough alike that I think we can rule her out. She has blond hair just like Madeline. Though she looked too old, it might just be that she's had a rough life."

Brendan pulled the file over to scan it. "In my line of work, you assume nothing." He began to read and his brow furrowed.

"What is it?" Eden asked.

"This makes no sense. The woman who claims to be Madeline's mother had a hysterectomy when she was fifteen, following a car accident. That seems to be what sent her over the edge. She's fifty now. So there's no way she could be Madeline's mother."

"But she came to the ranch," Clay protested.

"Maybe she's another relative, but she's not a mother. Has any-one talked to Madeline about her mother? Or the foster parents who have her? Maybe the mom contacted them and they know some-thing." Brendan made a note.

"I'll do that," Eden said. "She likes to chat with me while I brush her hair. Or rather, she did. She's a little miffed with me since I had to give her a time-out."

"What about the kidnapping?" Brendan asked. "How did this all go down?"

It was going to be painful for Eden to relive it. Clay took her hand. "Brianna was six weeks old. Eden was making cupcakes for my birthday. The baby was sleeping in her room."

"I had the baby monitor in the kitchen," Eden put in, her voice soft. "The dog needed to go out. I stepped outside to put him on his chain. When I came back in, I heard something bang. It almost sounded like the door, but I wanted to check on Brianna first so I ran up the stairs. Sh-She was gone. All that was in her crib was her blanket."

Brendan winced. So did Rick.

"Man, that had to have been hard," Rick said.

"You don't know the half of it," Clay said. "She called me hysterically. I started to dial the police, but before I could, my phone rang. It was the kidnapper demanding ten thousand dollars."

Brendan lifted a brow. "That was all?"

"My thoughts too. He said not to involve the police or we'd never see Brianna again. We had that much money in our account. We were saving to buy a house." He glanced at Eden, hating the pain he saw in her eyes.

"We were supposed to make the exchange at the river," Eden said. "It was all set. But I got in too big of a hurry on the wet roads and rammed into the vehicle. It fell into the water. That was the last time we ever heard from them."

"One body was found but never identified. Until we saw his picture—Jose."

"And then you got that picture of the girls at Bluebird Ranch," Brendan said.

Eden cleared her throat. "I tend to think Lacie might be Brianna," she said, shooting a glance at Clay. "She was left outside a church when she was six months old."

"Dressed in an expensive sleeper," Clay added. "So she came from a wealthy family. Or at least a family that could spend fifty dollars for a clothing item she would only wear a couple of weeks."

"Sounds possible," Brendan agreed. He studied the paperwork on the little girl. "What about this Sister Marjo? Has anyone talked to her?"

"There hasn't been time yet," Clay said. "She'll be at the ranch in a few days."

"You talk to her when she comes and I'll handle Madeline's so-called mother."

His friend knew his stuff. Clay felt empowered just having help. "Katie seems unlikely. Her father was killed in a burglary. The murderer never apprehended. So she had a family."

"Maybe. Let me check into it." Brendan made another note. "Hard to say how he got her. I'll check hospital records and nose around the neighborhood."

"Then there's Paige," Eden put in. "She's also rather likely. Two men left her in the toy department at Walmart." She looked down at her lap. "To be honest, I hope she's not our Brianna. I dearly love her, but her foster parents want to adopt her. She seems to adore them and they're crazy about her. It would hurt them all."

Brendan's gaze softened. "You're a good woman, Mrs. Larson." He read through the report. "I'll see if I can take a look at the Walmart security tape. We'll figure this out, friends. We'll find your girl."

20

THE STREETLIGHTS HUMMED AS CLAY AND EDEN STOOD BELOW THEIR GOLDEN GLOW. RICK would have Brendan in the air by now. Eden turned her face to the night sky, brilliant with stars. Alpine was quiet except for the occasional revving of a car engine on the main street that intersected with this one.

"Ready to go home?" Clay asked, his hand on the small of her back.

Home. How quickly they'd come to think of this starkly beautiful place as home. "Let's sit for a while in the park." She settled on a park bench and watched birds nesting on the trees, their heads tucked under wings. That's how she'd been going through life lately. With her eyes hidden to what was around her. She glanced at Clay. He sat leaning forward with his forearms on his knees. "Thanks for wait-ing until I was ready to tell them that my father is Hector Santiago. I know he's a bad man, but it somehow felt terrible to be ratting out my own father."

He straightened. "I'm proud of you for telling them. They needed to know. Brendan especially. Otherwise he'd be totally in the dark about what might be going on."

"I had a brother," she said, her voice trembling. "I always wanted a brother or sister."

"I'm sorry, honey. I don't understand why he didn't just ask for the pendant back. I would have given it to him when I found out it was stolen."

She held his gaze. "Would you, really? Knowing he was a drug dealer?"

He sighed. "Okay, maybe not. So if he ordered his son to take Brianna, why didn't he keep her? She was his granddaughter. And why not trade her for the pendant? If he's the kidnapper, he asked only for a paltry ten thousand. That's pennies to him."

"I don't know, but I think I need to talk to him."

"You?" He shook his head. "Way too dangerous. What if this has nothing to do with him but your call attracts his attention? And besides, why would he hate you? The kidnapper seems to have a per-sonal vendetta against you."

She didn't have an answer for him, but the truth he'd pointed out hurt. What could her father possibly have against her? She'd done nothing to him. "I don't even care about why he did it. I'll tell him he can have his pendant if he will go away and leave us in peace."

He chewed on his lip, and she could tell he wanted to believe it would work. And why not? Such a simple solution. He rose and walked the length of several sections of sidewalk before he came back and sat beside her.

"Okay," he said. "But I want to do some investigation first. See what he's up to. I'll have Brendan get Santiago's phone number for us."

"He might oppose our involvement."

"I don't think so. What's it to him if we manage to finally get this madman off our backs?" He pulled out his phone.

"He'll still be in the air."

"He'll have his phone on." Clay dialed the number.

She listened to him explain the situation. It was clear Brendan wasn't happy about it. Clay finally hung up.

"He was ticked," she said.

Clay nodded. "More than I thought he would be. He thinks it's dangerous to contact him."

"It's more dangerous if we don't," she pointed out. "Our daughter is still in danger. And maybe we can find out what he has against me."

"None of us likes it." He paused. "But Brendan is going to get the number. He'll have it for us within twenty-four hours."

And this nightmare might be over. They would identify their daughter and be able to move on with their lives. Clay's arm pressed against hers, and she suppressed a shiver. What would he say if she told him she'd never stopped loving him? He might chalk it all up to God's will. He didn't believe in divorce, he'd said.

Neither did she. But she wanted a man who loved her completely, for herself. Not for some misguided sense of duty. Yes, he'd said he wanted to marry her, that he missed her and was glad when he found out she was pregnant. But how many of his assurances were merely what he thought he was supposed to say?

"Eden?"

His mouth was near her ear, his breath on her neck. If she turned her head, her lips would graze his. But she didn't succumb to the passion burning through her veins. If she did, the heartbreak to come would be too great.

Tell him you want a future with him.

She turned her head and was lost when he slipped his arm around her and drew her close. His lips touched hers, moved to the curve of her jaw and to her ear.

"Tell me what you're thinking," he whispered into her hair.

She let herself mold to him. "I wish I'd had the courage to stay."

"I wish I'd never left you. Neither of us was thinking. What happened when you ran off?"

"Daniel was in Wabash, so I went there. I found a job." She didn't want him to be angry that she'd run to Daniel, so she blurted out the first thing that came to mind. "I spent weeks, months, dreaming that you found me. That you showed up at the door with Brianna in your arms. That was the only way I managed to get by, day by day."

"I should have followed you. Stupid pride got in the way. Then you were seeing Kent."

"That was no grand passion. It was survival."

"I don't think his emotions were heavily involved either."

"No, they weren't. He and I just seemed . . . suitable."

A train blew its horn a block over. A lonesome sound. "That whistle was like me, Clay. Sounding out a lonely note and hoping someone would hear me so I didn't have to be alone. Kent heard it and answered. But that's all it was."

He held her gaze. "I'm glad."

All the girls had freshly washed hair and smelled like Eden's lavender soap, which she'd brought with her. Every female liked fragrance. She'd dried five small heads, then tucked the girls into their beds with a book. Except for Madeline. She sat on the big bed against the wall, as far away from Eden as she could get.

Eden picked up a brush and went to join her. "Want me to brush your hair?" she asked. Madeline had loved having her hair brushed until the day Eden disciplined her. Maybe some cuddle time would end the tension. Eden longed to restore their good relationship. The pain in the child's eyes tore at her.

Madeline didn't look at her, but after a moment's hesitation, she nodded. "If you want." She presented her stiff back to Eden.

"Let's sit at the dressing table." Eden led her to the stool. She wanted to watch Madeline's expressions in the mirror.

Eden released the braids and ran her fingers through to loosen the strands before she began to run the brush through the long blond tresses. "You have such pretty hair. Why do you like so much to have it brushed?"

"Brushing makes it stay pretty."

"It's lovely. Brushing is good for it?"

"My mother used to do it."

Eden slowed the brush, then started again. "When did you see your mother last?"

"I don't know." Madeline closed her eyes, the expression of bliss on her face reflected in the mirror. "I guess I saw her for a minute the other day. She came when she wasn't supposed to. Mr. Clay made her go away."

"How old were you when she . . . went away?"

"I don't remember. Maybe three? I was little."

Eden nodded gravely, smothering her smile. "What do you remember about her?"

"She smelled good. Like flowers. And her hands were soft."

"What color was her hair?"

"It was blond. Like mine."

The blond hair on the woman who had visited the other day might have been dyed. And it wouldn't do any good to ask Madeline how old her mother was. A child had no concept of a parent's age. But Madeline had recognized her mother the other day—unless the person she thought was her mother really wasn't. It was all a muddle.

"She had a little spot right here." Madeline indicated a spot beside her mouth. "She said it was a beauty spot. I liked to touch it."

Eden would have to ask Clay if the woman claiming to be Madeline's mother had a mole by her mouth. "What else do you remember?"

"I had her eyes."

"So, blue eyes?"

Madeline nodded. "She used to sing to me too. She used to sing in the choir in Mexico."

"Mexico?"

Madeline nodded. "That's what she said."

The longer Eden brushed the little girl's hair, the more relaxed she became. Maybe things would be back to normal tomorrow. "Want me to braid your hair for sleep?" she asked, putting down the brush. When Madeline shook her head, Eden smiled. "Time for bed, then. Scoot."

Madeline slid from the chair and Eden patted her behind as she passed. Such darling girls. She felt fulfilled and necessary here. Like what she did mattered. She kissed each of the girls, turned on the

CD of hymns, then flipped off the light and shut the door, leaving a crack that let in a tiny sliver of light.

The heady scent of coffee hung in the air and she followed her nose to the kitchen. "Decaf?"

Clay turned from the pot with two cups in his hand. "Yep. I made it strong, though. And it's freshly ground."

"Smells good." Their hands touched when she took the coffee from him. "I talked to Madeline."

He led her to the living room and plopped onto the sofa. "And?"

She sank beside him on the cushion he'd patted invitingly. "She says her mother had a mole by her mouth. Did you notice a mole?"

He frowned silently for a moment, then shook his head. "No mole. I'm positive."

"She could've had it removed."

"Maybe. But I didn't see a scar either."

"She might have covered it with makeup."

"We can probably get a photo of her."

She took a sip of her coffee. Nice and strong. "I wondered if the woman she remembers from when she was little is different from the older one who came. Madeline seems fond of the memories but frightened of the woman in the yard."

He propped his feet on the battered coffee table. "The kits are on their way."

"It will be such a relief to know. Then we can begin to delve into the background of how Brianna came to be here. That might tell us who is terrorizing us now. I want that man behind bars."

"No more than I do," he said grimly.

She sipped her coffee and studied his expression over the rim of her cup. His comment last night had haunted her. He'd been glad she was pregnant. Glad! When the very thought had terrified her. And her misperception had set the tone of their entire marriage. She'd been sure he felt compelled to marry her, that if he'd had his choice, they never would have seen each other after Hawaii.

What if she hadn't seen anything right?

⁂

The DNA kits had been unpacked and spread out on the table. Clay eyed the swabs. "I guess we have to get the samples the way they want them. What do we tell the girls?" He glanced through the window at the children playing in the yard. They were catching lizards.

She took the pitcher of iced tea from the refrigerator and poured a glass over ice, then handed it to him. "We could just tell them we have tests we need to send in. I'm sure they've been to the doctor before. I doubt they'll think anything about it."

"I suppose. One at a time or bring them all in?"

"We'll make it a game with all of them." She shoved open the window. "Girls, would you come in here for a minute?"

The girls left the hapless lizard they'd been chasing and trooped into the kitchen.

"What's that?" Lacie eyed the swabs on the table.

"We're going to see who can do the best job with these swabs," Eden said. She picked one up and held it aloft. "We want you to stick it in your mouth and turn it against your cheek. Like this." She demonstrated, turning the swab against the inside of her cheek. "See if you can get it all wet without sucking on it. You need to push it against your cheek kind of hard but not hard enough to hurt." She finished the sample for herself and popped it into the plastic bag and labeled it with her name.

"I'm going to win!" Katie grabbed the first swab and worked it in her mouth.

The other girls were quick to follow her example. Five minutes later they had five carefully labeled samples. She sent the girls back out to play. "Now you," she told Clay.

He obliged. She labeled his, then slid the samples into the return bag. "Is this even legal?" she asked.

He hesitated. "I'm not sure, to tell you the truth. It wouldn't stand up in a court of law, but I don't think it's illegal. Any father could gather DNA and test a child he's been accused of fathering. I admit, I'd rather do it through the courts, but that will take too much time."

In a few days this nightmare would be over. They'd be able to tell Brianna that she had parents who loved her and wanted her to live with them forever. Eden's eyes misted at the thought.

"Have you thought about how we will tell her?" Clay asked as she sealed the envelope.

"I've thought of little else now that we'll know in a few days."

"And?"

"We have to be careful not to scare her. I'm not sure we should mention the kidnapping. Maybe just say we lost her for a while. Then, when the kidnapper is behind bars, we can tell her the truth."

He nodded. "I've been thinking the same. If Katie happens to be Brianna, she's already dealing with nightmares. We don't want to compound them." Clay's phone rang and he glanced at the screen. "It's Brendan."

She sat down. So much of her past was slamming into her. She wasn't sure she was ready for all of this.

Clay opened a kitchen drawer and rummaged, then produced a pen and paper. "Go ahead," he said.

Brendan must have gotten her father's phone number. Her insides were unsettled. What would she even say when she called? *Hi, I'm the daughter you never acknowledged.* That would go over really well.

Clay disconnected the call. "He got the number."

"I gathered that."

"You look nervous."

She clasped her shaking hands together. "I am."

"I can call for you."

She shook her head. "I need to do this. Maybe there is some sliver of compassion left in his soul for me. I can appeal to him to leave us alone." She didn't remember much about him—just that he was big with black hair and angry eyes.

Clay slid the paper across the table to her. "Tell him to send someone after that pendant and it's all his." He grimaced. "I hate to give it up, though. I liked seeing it on you."

"We'll find something similar," she said.

"All he has to do is leave us alone."

"And tell us which girl is ours," she said, picking up the paper.

"I doubt he knows." He held up the envelope. "This will tell us in a few more days."

She hoped he didn't notice the way her hands shook as she punched in the number. Her mouth was dry as she held the phone to her ear.

"Hola." The man's curt voice was gruff.

The voice turned her insides to pudding. "Is this Hector Santiago?"

"You should have known that before you called, *chica*."

"Don't hang up. Please." She wetted her lips. "Th-This is Eden

Davidson." When silence answered her statement, she thought he'd hung up. "Hello?"

"I am here. What do you want from me?"

"Nothing. I have information for you."

"Perhaps I do not want this information. Especially if there are strings attached. I gave your mother all the money she is getting from me."

"I have something you want."

"Which is?"

"Your missing pendant. The one with the woman and baby."

There was a thump on the other end as though his feet had hit the floor. "You have my pendant?"

A foreboding touched her spine and she shuddered. "I do."

"How is it that you are in possession of this item?"

She was tired of dancing around the truth. He had to know. "My husband has it. We didn't realize its significance in my daughter's kidnapping until yesterday."

The tinkle of ice in a glass came through the phone. "I do not understand."

"I . . . I suspect your son kidnapped my daughter, thinking to get this item back as a ransom once he lured us out for the switch."

"So you killed my son." Irony was in the undercurrent of his words.

"It was an accident." This wasn't going the way she'd thought it would. "Listen, you can have your pendant. We just want to be left alone now. Which child is my Brianna?"

"I know nothing of this matter other than that my son kidnapped a child and died. I never knew what his plan was."

Her hope deflated. Was he lying? "Maybe he wanted to bring the pendant to you as a surprise."

"Perhaps that is so. Thank you for your call. I will send someone to fetch my property."

The phone clicked in her ear. "He hung up." She swallowed hard. "He made no promise to leave us alone."

Clay's face was grim. "He claims to know nothing about Brianna?"

"So he says."

"I'm not sure I believe him."

She chewed her lip. "I don't know for sure, but he appeared to be telling the truth. His son could have been doing it on his own, hoping to gain some favor with Hector. He sounds like a tough and scary man."

"So we're back to square one. But if Hector is the one who has been targeting you, then the harassment will stop."

"Somehow I don't think he's been targeting me. Why scare me? Why not just come and get his property? Kill us if he has to. There is more going on than we know."

"I mean to find out what it is," Clay said. He rose. "I'm going to run these to Rita. She's going to town and can drop them at the post office."

"In a couple of days we'll know which girl is Brianna."

The waiting was almost over.

21

THE BED WELCOMED HER LIKE AN OLD FRIEND, THOUGH SHE DIDN'T EXPECT TO SLEEP WELL.
She was beginning to get used to Clay's presence on the other side of
the mattress. She waited subconsciously for another scratch on the
window or a sinister phone call, but all was quiet.

She was nearly asleep when a shriek tore through the air. She and
Clay leaped from the bed at the same time and collided in their haste
to get out of the room.

He yanked open the door. "Wait here."

"It's one of the girls!" She followed him down the hall.

When he thrust open the door to the girls' room, light spilled
from the hall onto the nearest bed. Katie was sitting upright with her
eyes open. Scream after scream tore from her throat.

"Check her."

Eden ran to pull the child into her arms while Clay stepped to the window and peered outside. "It's okay, honey," she said, smoothing the little girl's tangled hair from her face.

Like a monkey, Katie wrapped both arms and legs around Eden. She buried her sweaty face in Eden's neck and burst into tears. Eden rocked her back and forth, shushing her. "I've got you," she said against Katie's hair. "No one will hurt you."

When the child's sobs tapered off, Katie pulled away and a last shudder rippled through her. Eden glanced around to see all the girls sitting up with wide eyes. "Did you see something?" she asked Katie.

Katie shook her head. "I was dreaming. That man came."

"What man, honey?" A nightmare. Her gaze locked with Clay's over the top of Katie's head as he soothed the other girls and they settled back into bed.

"I don't know. Daddy hid me in the closet. But he never came back to get me. The policeman took me away."

"You didn't see the man?"

Katie put her thumb in her mouth and shook her head. She pulled it out shamefacedly, then put her hand in the pocket of her pajamas. "Just his back. I peeked through the keyhole. He had a blue jacket."

Eden hugged her. "It's okay. No one will hurt you."

Katie shivered. "What if he comes back? Maybe he thinks I saw him. But I didn't."

"I don't think he'll be back. Mr. Clay will protect you if he does. I bet he's bigger than that man."

A ghost of a smile lifted the little girl's lips, and she nodded. "He was skinny and not nearly as tall as my daddy."

A little more of a description but still not much. "Could you see his hair?"

She nodded. "It was red like mine. I only 'member because I never saw anyone with my color hair before. Daddy said it was because I came from the angels."

"The angels? What about your mommy?"

"I don't have a mommy." She nestled against Eden's chest. "I want a mommy!"

The words made something nameless swell in Eden's heart. Longing, regret, and pain all mixed to form some emotion that was harder to put her finger on. Maybe *helplessness* was the right word. She'd been caught in a maelstrom and was drowning in all the events that kept slamming her under the water.

"You're a sweet, sweet girl," she whispered against Katie's hair. She inhaled the fragrance of little girl and choked back the lump in her throat. She glanced at Clay. "Anything?"

He shook his head. "Guess it was just a nightmare."

Katie went limp against Eden, and her breathing evened out. Eden reluctantly let Clay lift the child from her arms. On the other side of the bed, Eden pulled back the covers, plumped the pillow, then covered Katie after Clay laid her down. When Eden kissed the soft cheek, she detected a slight smile on Katie's face. Even in sleep, she knew when she was loved.

The other girls were snuggled back in their pillows. She and Clay made another round, comforting each one and bestowing kisses on every face. She would miss this ritual when she was gone from here.

They backed out of the room. "Is that someone at the door?" Clay asked.

She heard the knock then. Not timid, but not loud either.

Authoritative. She followed Clay to the door. The man peering in the window was in his forties. His black hair curled over his collar. He looked dangerous to Eden.

"Are you sure you should open it?" she whispered. "He hasn't seen us yet." But as soon as the words were out of her mouth, Clay flipped on the light.

"Stay here," he said. He crossed the room in four strides and opened the door. "Can I help you?"

"Santiago sent me." The man didn't wait for an invitation but brushed past Clay to stand in the living room.

That was fast. "I'll get it," Eden said. Anything to get away. The man's gaze seemed to see through her cotton pajamas.

She rushed back to the bedroom and snatched up the pendant. Before she took it to the man, she pulled on a robe and tied it. One last time, she ran her fingers over the precious piece and allowed herself to regret that she had to give it up. It had been such a symbol of the family they wanted to build.

He and Clay were silent and tense by the door when she returned. The sooner they got this guy out of here, the happier she would be. "Here it is." She handed him the pendant.

He inspected it, then grunted. "You were telling the truth. I will tell Santiago."

What if they hadn't? Would her own father have murdered her?

❋

Clay could lie and watch her sleep for hours. He propped himself on his elbow and studied the even rise and fall of Eden's chest. So relaxed in sleep. All guards down. Every care eased from her face.

He could only pray turning over that pendant last night would make a difference in the attacks that had been directed at Eden, though she might be right to think there was no connection between the threats and the jewelry. He eased out of bed and went to the kitchen to make coffee. The girls all still slept as well. The late night had worn everyone out. Except for him. He was alert and eager to learn more today from Brendan.

The sun had just begun to peek over the mountain's jagged silhouette when he took his coffee out to the porch. He watched the sun chase the purple shadows from the peaks, exposing the cholla and prickly pear. A blooming cactus or two brought a little color to the hillside. Sipping his coffee, he rocked in the chair. The motion soothed him and let his mind wander. Only God could heal his relationship with Eden. The cracks went deep, and they needed the right foundation.

Boots crunched on gravel, and he saw Rick's familiar form. The other man mounted the steps and dropped into the chair beside Clay. "Want some coffee?" Clay asked him.

"Not that stuff you're drinking. A spoon could stand up in it by itself. I can smell how strong it is from here." Rick grinned and stretched out his legs. "Nothing like early morning for talking with God."

"My thoughts too." Clay felt a real connection with Rick. After rolling his suitcase around the world, Clay didn't have many close friends. His defenses were down with this guy. "Too early to hear from Brendan."

"Actually, I just got off the phone with him."

"That guy ever sleep?"

"He's a panther. Always on the prowl." Rick propped a booted ankle on his knee. "He watched that video from Walmart last night."

"And?"

"The two guys were Hispanic. Maybe Colombian, maybe not. But the interesting thing is that he thought he recognized one of them as a thug who works for Santiago."

Something kicked in Clay's chest. "So Paige is my daughter!"

"Whoa, don't go jumping to conclusions. We don't know that. For one thing, Brendan only thinks it might be him. He's going to run the tape through some programs and see if he can get a definite match."

Clay rubbed his eyes. "This is going to hurt that nice family. We'd hoped for one of the other girls."

"Like I said, don't assume anything." He stared at Clay. "The kidnapper lured you here. Why? He could have taken you out any-time and gotten that pendant, if that's what he's after. Good grief, man, you carried it in your pocket! All he had to do was knock you upside the head and take it."

"I know. Eden seems to be a personal target, which makes no sense. She wasn't even with me in Colombia. Or when I received the picture of the girls here at Bluebird."

"Any idea who might want to hurt her?"

"I had my suspects."

"Had? No longer?"

"Eden called Santiago. He sent a guy to pick up the pendant."

"And you're sure it's over?"

Clay sipped his coffee. "I don't know. Something still feels off about it. Look, there's something we haven't mentioned."

Rick sighed and put his boot back on the floor. "More danger?"

"No, nothing like that. But after Brianna was taken, our mar-riage fell apart."

Rick's eyes held sympathy. "It happens. Hard to endure so much pain."

"Eden blamed herself. I blamed myself. We blamed each other. Toxic combo. I headed out for a mission, and she wasted no time in ditching me." He hated the derision in his voice.

"I'm sorry."

"Eden filed for divorce. The papers came while I was overseas. I shoved them in a drawer and ignored them. Always thought eventually I'd come back and talk her into trying again."

"And you did."

"Only after I was shoved into it by the picture."

"Bet she was surprised."

Clay wished he could smile at the memory of her shock, but his own had been too great. There she was, about to accept another man's proposal. "I'd always known where she was, but my stupid pride wouldn't let me chase her. I found her in the middle of a marriage proposal."

"But she was still married to you?"

"Yep. But she didn't know it. She'd signed the papers and didn't realize the final decree hadn't been issued. Her attorney had a heart attack and never followed up after he got back to work."

"Hoo-ee, you mean this was one of those scenes like in the movies? You showed up and told her the happy news?"

"At least I got there before she actually said yes." Clay managed a weak smile.

"Bet that was a shock when she saw you."

"I thought she might faint. But I'll give her this—the minute she heard Brianna was still alive, she didn't hesitate. She walked away from the guy and never looked back."

Rick stretched out his legs. "What about him?"

"He let her go. Seemed to think finding Brianna was the best thing for her to focus on."

"So what's the problem? She's resistant to trying again?"

"Bull's-eye on your first guess, my friend. I'm working on it, though."

"My wife is pretty perceptive," Rick said. "She said the other day that it warmed her heart to see the way the two of you look at each other."

Clay wanted to cling to that encouragement, to hope Eden held some kind of feelings for him besides disappointment and betrayal. "I'm crazy about her," he said. "From the first time I saw her, I haven't looked at another woman."

"She'll find it hard to resist that kind of devotion."

"Well, that's the hope anyway."

Rick's stare was speculative. "Where will you go from here when that guy is behind bars and you have Brianna back?"

"Wish I knew. She's agreed to live together to give Brianna more stability."

"I don't know much about the problems in your relationship, but I know one thing," Rick said, his expression grave. "God can work miracles."

"That's what I'm going to need."

"And that's what I'll pray for with you."

When Rick bowed his head, Clay realized he meant now. God had sent him a prayer warrior right when he needed it.

22

After church and Sunday dinner, Eden went with Allie to take possession of a donated horse. The misery in the old mare's eyes clutched at Eden's heart. "Where'd she come from?" she asked Allie, who was coaxing the animal from the battered trailer with a sugar cube in her outstretched hand. "She doesn't look like she's been fed very well."

Allie's dark eyes flashed. "The way people mistreat their animals makes me furious. I'd like to put this girl's owner in a barn and feed him every three days and see how he likes it."

"Is that what happened?" The horse moseyed toward Eden, and she stepped back, even though she wished she had the courage to touch that rough fur.

"Yes. A neighbor turned him in. Rick talked the guy into letting us have her for a hundred dollars."

"You bought her?"

"It was the only way to save her." The mare finally nibbled at the sugar in Allie's hand, but she flinched when Allie touched her nose. "Easy," she murmured.

"Will she live?" Eden wanted to touch the poor, mistreated thing. She put out a timid hand, then withdrew it.

"I think so. Shannon seems optimistic. This old girl is malnourished, but the right food and some love will fix her right up. We have plenty of both."

"You seem to have an abundance of horses. Do you do this all the time?"

Allie stepped back when the horse meandered away. She wiped her hands on her jeans. "My grandfather had a dream. He saw how abused children responded to mistreated animals. A bond of love helped them both. So he opened this ranch to help children and horses."

"And you've run it ever since?"

"Well, Rick has. I came later." Allie smiled. "I love it here." She glanced at Eden's tan slacks. "There's a really great jeans store in town. Nice selection. We should go shopping."

She couldn't wear jeans any easier than she could shoot someone. Well, maybe she could. She'd been dreaming about jeans and boots. What did that mean? Was she changing? Being here had opened her eyes in some ways. But she wasn't quite ready for jeans.

"Maybe," she said. "I do love to shop. I need to make a call. Do you mind watching the girls a minute?"

"They're fine. Buzz and the guys have them under control. I'll sit right here and oversee." She hopped onto the top rung of the fence.

"Thanks." Eden went to the house, got the portable phone, then settled on the back step. Maybe she shouldn't, but she wanted to tell Daniel what had happened with her mother.

Glancing at her watch, she saw it would be two o'clock back in Indiana. Daniel would be working on his bills this afternoon, maybe watching sports on TV. Sometimes the two of them used to play Monopoly while they ate fudge and popcorn. She missed those days.

The phone rang and rang. She was about to hang up when he finally picked up on the other end. She knew he was on because she heard the TV in the background but he said nothing. "Daniel?"

"I told you not to call me, Eden."

"I know, but I thought you might want to know that I met with my mother," she said before he could hang up.

There was a long pause. "Oh? And why should that interest me?"

His voice was so cold. This was a mistake. "If you're not interested, that's all there is to say. Sorry I bothered you." She hesitated, but when he didn't say anything more, she clicked off the phone.

Her eyes burned. Daniel had been her brother in all the ways that counted. She must have hurt him terribly. Her chest heaved, quick little gasps of air. Daniel was so bitter, so angry. What had she done to him? It was as though she'd worn blinders all her life and didn't see anything clearly.

"Eden?"

She lifted her head at the sound of Clay's voice. "You were right," she said. "Daniel hates me. Hates me!"

He embraced her. "I'm sorry."

She leaned her head into his chest. "I'm not sure why this has hit me so hard."

"What did he say?"

"I called him to let him know I'd seen my mother. Since he gave me the agency's number and all."

"They say there's a fine line between love and hate. He crossed it?"

"It appears so." She leaned into him. His shirt smelled of Downy. She wished she could stay here all afternoon, sheltered by Clay's strength.

He dropped a kiss on her head. "We have that international dinner tonight, right? How about you go do your cooking and try not to worry. I'll look after the girls."

She knew he was right. There was no repairing the damage now. Daniel would get over it or he wouldn't. She went to the kitchen of the main house.

Rita had an apron for Eden and supplies laid out for her. And a pot of coffee on. "You know me too well," Eden told her.

Rita wrinkled her nose. "You'll need all the strength you can get to endure the coconut smell."

Eden grinned, then poured a cup of coffee. "You can leave if it's going to be too painful."

"I'm a big girl. I think you'll need some help." She glanced around. "Where's Clay? I made him some oatmeal-scotchie cookies."

"Those are his favorite!"

"The way to a man's heart is through his stomach."

"You'll have to give me the recipe." Eden turned to her ingredients. "The last batch I made turned out okay, but I have to double it for tonight." Fortified by coffee with cream, she set to work. The rice came out a little sticky, but the chicken mixture looked and smelled right.

She tasted it. "I think it's okay." What a relief. She hadn't wanted to let Allie down. She held up a spoonful. "You can't really taste the coconut."

Rita shook her head. "I'd be able to taste it."

"Are you going to the dinner tonight?" Eden asked.

Rita flipped a blond braid over her shoulder. "I should say! There's a cowboy who works for Jack MacGowan that I have my eye on. I'm not letting one of the other women get ahead of me." She smiled. "Besides, it's good fodder for my novel."

"How's that coming?" Eden had never known a writer.

"I'm halfway through. I got me a book on how to write a romance. I have one of those brooding heroes. One who sweeps the heroine off her feet. Like Clay." She sighed blissfully. "I bet I get a movie offer when it's done. Maybe Clay can land the lead role."

Rita had self-confidence at least. Eden chuckled. "He'd have all the girls after him."

She smiled and put the cover on the dish, then went to find Clay. They had to be at the community center in half an hour. He wasn't at the barn or at the ranch house. Rick told her Clay had asked about a handsaw and suggested she check the shed at the back edge of the property.

The building was on the west side of the back pasture, a dot in the distance from the backyard. Eden followed a crushed-stone path through knee-high scrub and sage to the building. Painted red like the barn, it appeared to be a fairly new addition to the property, about thirty feet square. The door was shut tight but the padlock hung loose. She opened the door and peered inside. It contained tools, a yard tractor, and various gardening items.

"Clay?" she called. The scent of oil and dust made her sneeze. She advanced into the building. "Are you in here?" There was no answer.

The gardening tools hanging on the wall reminded her of when she was a kid. Her foster mother had loved azaleas. There was a small plot of flowers at the edge of their house that held four plants, and her mother deadheaded them and mulched them all summer long. Eden touched a pruning shear, then turned to go.

Strange. She thought she'd left the door open. She twisted the handle and pushed, but it didn't move. Maybe she had to turn the knob the other way. She tried that, but the door still refused to budge. She yanked on it and tried everything she could before she admitted that she seemed to be locked in. Maybe there was another way out. She saw another door at the back and went to try it. It refused to open as well.

And what was that smell? She sniffed the air and the hair stood on the back of her neck. It was cologne, the same smell that had been in Clay's truck after it was taken. "Who's there?" she asked, hating the way her voice shook. "Show yourself."

Was that a scratching sound? Her skin crawled. She had to get out of here. Whirling, she ran to the window on the front of the building. She flipped the latch and tried to raise the sash. It seemed stuck. Maybe she needed to be taller to get better leverage. Grabbing a nearby bucket, she upended it and stepped on its bottom. She shoved the top of the window with all her might but it still wouldn't open. From her vantage point, she realized someone had locked the padlock on the door.

She hopped from the bucket and ran with it to the back window. The back door was padlocked too. She tried to lift the window there and managed to get it up a crack before it stuck again. She smelled gasoline, and the odor began to intensify. The shadows grew deeper too. Was someone hiding behind the tool bench or the yard tractor?

She shrank back against the wall. Would Clay miss her and come searching for her? Maybe Rick would tell him she was out here look-ing for him. She heard something else. A faint *whoosh*. Then another smell, acrid and noxious, began to overpower the gas. Smoke? Surely not. She sniffed the air again. It was stronger now. No mistaking it. Something was on fire.

A green hose was coiled on the wall. She rushed for it and grabbed it off the hook. Where was the faucet? She frantically looked around the space but saw no spigot. Maybe the hose was simply stored here. The smell was stronger now, and a haze hung in the air. She coughed at the burning in her lungs. There, on the workbench. A crowbar. She grabbed it and ran for the partially open window. With the hook of the crowbar on the bottom edge of the sill, she pried as hard as she could. It went up a bit but still not far enough to squeeze through.

The smoke swirled around her, obscuring her vision even more. The windows were small panes. Standing back a bit, she swung the crowbar at the window. The end of it smashed through the middle pane. The grids were part of the window, not removable. But maybe she could knock them out. She swung the heavy metal bar again and the thin wood popped out. Encouraged, she began to batter the win-dow as hard and fast as she could. Her vision swam and she coughed.

She wasn't going to make it.

23

CLAY WIPED HIS DAMP BROW. HE'D JUST FINISHED CLEANING OUT SOME STALLS. SOME ICED tea would be in order after he returned the saw. He found Buzz in the barn. "Thanks for the saw. Where's it go?"

The old cowboy glanced up from messing with a horse's hoof. "It belongs in the shed out yonder. I just had it up here to work on a fence."

"If you tell me where it goes, I'll put it back."

"Just inside the door to your left are hooks with other tools. Any of those hooks will do." Buzz went back to his chore.

"Be back shortly. The kids will be ready for their rides." Clay stepped outside the barn and squinted at the midday sun that glared down from a cloudless sky. Starting for the outbuilding, he saw a smudge against the sky. Almost simultaneously, he smelled something. *Smoke?* He stared and realized flames were licking at the roof of the building.

"Fire!" he shouted. "Buzz, Rick, the building is on fire!" He saw Buzz exit the barn and run toward him. The cowboy repeated the shout of "Fire!" and Clay put on a burst of speed and ran toward the building. Rick spurted out his door and raced toward him as well.

Clay reached the structure. It was padlocked. Buzz and Rick were only moments behind him.

Rick caught at his arm. "Did you see Eden? She was coming back here to look for you."

The men's gazes locked, and the fear in Rick's face kicked Clay in the gut. "I never came back here. Buzz had the saw." He yanked at the lock. "You have the key?" She couldn't be in there with it locked.

More help spilled toward them. Allie, Rita, Della, Zeke, the other hands. Most carried buckets of water. Rick dug his keys from his pocket and selected a small silver one. He thrust it in the keyhole and twisted. The lock fell open.

Allie reached him. "Where's Eden?" Clay asked her.

Her brows rose. "She was cooking, then came out here to find you. It's time for us to be leaving for the dinner."

Clay's pulse kicked. Then he heard a sound. A choked cry. He yanked the lock from the latch and pulled open the door. Black smoke roiled out. "Eden!" he yelled. He started to run inside, but Rick grabbed his arm.

"It's not safe!" Rick shouted.

Clay jerked out of Rick's grasp and plunged into the building. The smoke was like a living creature. Writhing and hot, it sucked all the oxygen from the air. Soot coated his tongue and throat, insinuated itself into his lungs and ears. The roar of the fire was so loud his own voice screaming Eden's name sounded muffled.

He stumbled over something and fell. Down here on the floor he could breathe a little better, so he crawled forward. "Eden!" he shouted.

His hand touched something yielding and inert. Cloth covering a leg. Eden? He touched a back, an arm, hair. It was her. But which way was out? In the blackness, he couldn't tell. His ears were ringing, and he began to pray for guidance. The fire flared off to his left. The roof screamed and groaned like someone in pain. The ringing in his ears grew louder, then a roof beam crashed down a few feet away. The fire flared higher, and he saw sunlight through the clouds of smoke.

Move, move! He couldn't stay here paralyzed. He needed to go where his toes were pointed. The answer should have been clear immediately. That was the way he'd come. Sliding backward, he dragged Eden's body with him. All he could do was pray he kept going in a straight line back toward the door. He laid his cheek on the hot concrete to rest a moment and try to draw in a bit of oxygen. He thought he heard shouts. Maybe they were close to being out of this nightmare.

Gathering his strength, he began to slide back again. His left foot hit resistance. The wall? "Rick," he croaked. His voice sounded weak and too soft. Rick would never hear him. He licked blistered lips and tried again. "Rick."

A hand grabbed his ankle and yanked. He had just enough strength to hang on to Eden's leg as someone hauled them from the inferno. Moments later he was lying on the hard ground, staring up into an impossibly bright and blue sky. His vision was blurry, but he recognized Rick bending over him.

"Eden," Clay croaked.

"She's out of the building. Allie is taking care of her."

Rick cupped water in his hand and trickled some over Clay's face. He'd never felt anything so wonderful. He opened his mouth and let a bit of the blessed moisture touch his parched tongue. "Does Eden have water?"

"Allie's giving her some."

Clay rolled onto his stomach and got to his hands and knees. "Where is she? Is she going to be okay?" He didn't wait for Rick to answer him but crawled forward a few feet to find his wife. She was lying on her back, but her eyes were open. Her face was wet too. The water Allie had given her had left rivulets in the soot marking her skin.

"Eden," he whispered.

She turned her head and saw him. "You look like you've been playing in mud," she said. Her voice was hoarse.

"How do you feel?"

"Alive." Her hand crept toward him. "You nearly died."

"So did you." Inexplicably, he wanted to laugh.

Her hand crept into his. "You nearly died with me."

"I wouldn't have wanted to live if you'd died." The words were out before he could stop them. And he'd never said anything he meant more.

✳

Clay's words had seared her heart. Could he possibly feel that way? Eden sipped the sweet tea Allie had pressed against her lips in the cool shade of the front porch. Clay was beside her. Her skin felt tight and hot. One spot on her leg was blistered, but not a large enough area to require hospitalization. The doctor had come and gone, leaving aloe cream to help with the burned areas.

Gracie Wayne had come over to take charge of the children and ease their fears while the adults tried to figure out what happened. Firefighters were pouring through the smoking ruins now.

Allie refilled the glass of tea. "Keep drinking," she ordered. "The doctor says we have to keep you both hydrated."

The warmth of Clay's arm against hers was almost painful against her reddened skin, but Eden didn't want to move away.

"What happened?" he asked, his voice hoarse from the smoke. "Do you remember?"

Eden was going to have to tell them about the locks and the cologne she smelled. Her sense of safety vanished. "Someone locked me in and set the fire."

His arm tightened painfully around her. "How do you know?"

"I left the padlock dangling when I went in. When I tried to leave, it was locked. I saw it through the window."

"It was locked when I got there," Rick concurred.

Allie shuddered. "Then what happened?"

"I smelled gasoline, then I heard a *whoosh*. The fire igniting, I suppose. Shortly after that the smoke came. I grabbed a crowbar and tried to bust out the window, but I couldn't get it done before the smoke got so bad that I couldn't breathe. I dropped to the floor so I could get air. That was the last thing I remember until you were giving me water."

Rick was frowning as he stared at her. "I don't think this has anything to do with Clay. You seem to be the only target. First he tried to scare you away, but you didn't go, so he's upped the stakes."

Her chest felt tight, and not just from smoke inhalation. Someone out there hated her so much that he wanted to burn her alive. "But why? I gave him back the pendant."

"Maybe I need to give your father a call," Clay said.

There was something deeper going on. Eden took another sip of tea, even though it was sweeter than she liked. "What if it's not him?"

"What if it is?" Clay countered, scowling.

"We need to investigate all possibilities. Check your background," Rick said. "What were you doing before you got here?"

"I've told you—working as a nurse," she said.

"Let's back up and take another look," Clay said. "How did you meet Kent?"

With their eyes on her, she hated to talk about Kent. "At church. You're on the wrong track there. Kent is a good guy. A friend at church introduced us."

"Was she interested in him?" Allie asked.

"I don't think so." Eden thought back to the church-wide dinner that Kent had come to. Had Molly been interested in him? What exactly had she said? Something about him being the prize sought by all the unattached women. "I suppose it's possible."

"How about hobbies or other activities?" Rick asked.

What could she say? That she collected shoes and purses like some women sought out fresh produce? That she was a professional window shopper? She shook her head.

"What about Daniel?" Clay asked, his voice quiet.

She'd been hoping Clay wouldn't bring him up. Shifting away from him, she straightened and shook her head. "I don't believe he'd try to hurt me."

"You just told me he hated you," Clay said, pulling his arm away.

"Not enough to kill me. I don't believe it."

"Who's Daniel?" Allie asked.

"My best friend. Well, he was. We grew up in the same foster home. He's like a brother."

"He wanted to be more to her, but she never saw it," Clay said, his voice hard.

Could Daniel want to harm her? She thought of his light blue eyes, his genial smile and slim build. "He's not the type. He might be mad at me right now, but he'd never do anything to hurt me. I'm sure of it."

"What's Daniel's last name?" Rick had his pen and paper out again.

Eden pressed her lips together, but Clay told him. She glared at Clay. "This is ridiculous. Daniel wouldn't do such a thing. It takes a really twisted mind to try to torch a building with a person inside."

The problem was, she didn't know anyone that sick.

⁂

Clay showered after the children were in bed, but the water on his tight skin was still an agony. He dressed in loose cotton sweats and went to find Eden. She was on the porch swing. Her knees were drawn to her chest and she sat in a ball and looked out toward the remains of the shed.

The swing creaked when he sat beside her. "You okay?"

She put her feet back on the floor. "The burns still hurt a little. I'm sure yours do too." When he nodded, she leaned back against his arm. "But we're still alive. Thanks to you."

Had she even noticed his slip of the tongue when he'd pulled her out? She hadn't said anything about it. He'd meant it, though. Life without her wouldn't be worth living. They swung in companionable silence for several minutes.

"I'm going to call your father," he said, holding up the portable phone.

She shook her head. "Not tonight. I can't take any more."

"I have to, honey. I've been thinking about it for two days. Someone hates you very much to try to burn you alive." His throat tightened and he couldn't say more.

She leaned her head back against his arm. "It is horrible to think about being hated that much."

"I tend to think it's not your dad who's behind this," he said. "But I want to verify it."

He plucked the phone number from his pocket and punched it into the phone. It would be much more pleasant to sit here and smell the apples in her hair, but he couldn't go through another day like this. Refused to go through it again. He'd nearly lost her.

The phone rang on the other end for so long that he thought he would have to leave a message. Then a gruff voice said, "Santiago."

"Mr. Santiago, this is Eden's husband, Clay Larson."

"I received my property back, if that is why you are calling."

"Glad to hear it, but I have something much more grave to discuss with you."

"Yes?"

"Someone tried to kill Eden today. She was locked in a shed and it was set on fire." He heard the guy gasp, then nothing for a moment. "Mr. Santiago? Are you there?"

"I am here. I gave instructions . . ." He went quiet.

Gave instructions to his henchman? So Hector Santiago *was* behind the attacks, even though he claimed to know nothing about

Brianna's kidnapping. "I'd appreciate it if you'd give those instructions again. I fear you have a rogue employee."

"It may be more than that, Mr. Larson. I will do what I can, but the risks to Eden are grave."

Clay's neck prickled. "What do you mean?"

"I can say no more. You will have to guard her carefully."

"At least you care a little about your daughter," Clay said.

"I doubt she is my daughter, but I can't have a rogue—"

"Of course she's your daughter!" Clay saw Eden's eyes widen, and he wished she hadn't heard that. Clay heard a click and stared at the phone. "He hung up on me."

She lifted her head. "He did that to me too. I think he likes the power. He says I'm not his daughter?"

"He didn't seem sure. It sounds like he told whoever was after you to lay off, but the guy disobeyed. I think your father isn't sure he can call him off."

Her eyes went wide. "So he *was* behind it? But why?"

If only he knew. It appeared this was far from over.

24

CLAY SCOOPED UP HAY WITH HIS PITCHFORK AND TOSSED SOME TO THE HORSE IN THE FIRST stall. The sweet scent of the grass blended with the earthy smell of the horse. He liked the combination for some reason. The barn was like a secret friend, living and breathing the odor and life of the horses and the cowboys. Living here on the ranch had changed him in some fundamental ways.

He wanted something different in his relationship with Eden too. He'd thought revealing his heart to her would bring about that sea change. If anything, she'd been a little more aloof the last two days. He'd tried to tell himself it was because she was hurting from her burns, but he wasn't sure that was the reason. Their talk the other night may have made her want to keep her distance.

A shadow fell on the haystack, and he glanced up to see India in the doorway. "Want to help?" he asked her.

She smiled and nodded, coming forward. "I brought Frost some sugar." She dug into the pocket of her jeans and produced two cubes covered with lint.

Her black hair was in cornrows tied with pink bows. Eden loved messing with the girls' hair, and they seemed to enjoy it as well. India's pink top had chocolate on it, and a smear of chocolate frosting dotted the corner of her mouth. Her jeans were getting too short, and he made a mental note to ask Eden to take her shopping.

He leaned on his tool and smiled. "The pitchfork is a little big for you, but you can feed Bluebird some hay when you're done spoiling Frost."

The little girl offered the sugar to the young gelding, then scampered back to where Clay stood. She seized a handful of hay, then held it up to Bluebird, Betsy's horse.

"Are you enjoying yourself here?" Clay asked.

India nodded. "I wish I could stay here forever with you and Miss Eden. I don't want to go back." She sounded forlorn.

The little girl had endeared herself to him in the past two weeks. Always cheerful, always smiling. But sometimes he caught her by herself with a pensive air and tear-filled eyes. She would never tell him the problem, though. He'd often wished she were Brianna, though her nutmeg skin made it impossible. His heart called her his, though.

She shuddered and clasped her arms around herself. "The fire was scary," she said. "I hate fire."

"I'm sure you do, honey. I'm sorry about your parents."

She hopped down from her perch on the fence where she'd been petting Bluebird. Two puppies raced to flop in her lap. "I can't remember my mama's voice anymore." Her voice was choked. "I never wanted to forget it."

He put his hand on her head. "I'm sure she loved you very much."

"Do you think she's looking down from heaven and watching me? The preacher says she is."

They were killed in a meth lab explosion. What were the chances that her parents were Christians? "Did your mama take you to church?"

India nodded. "We went every Sunday. Sometimes at night too. And Mama went to a Bible study across the street."

"How about your daddy?"

"I didn't see him much. He was always working. Sometimes he gave me horsey rides on his back." Her eyes were moist when she glanced up at him. "About heaven?"

"I think your mommy is there waiting for you."

"Mama threw my dad out, you know. She said he was doing bad things in the basement. I guess he was. He came back when she was at work. When she got back, she yelled at him and he slammed the door to the basement. Then she took me to bed and went back downstairs. The boom woke me up."

"How did you get out?" he asked.

"An angel," she said simply, her tone grave.

"An angel?"

She nodded. "He was dressed in a firefighter outfit, but when he carried me out, he disappeared and I never saw him again."

He could see she believed it. And who was he to say it wasn't real? When did he start thinking God would never do something miraculous for him? He brought about miracles every day. He'd saved Brianna when they all thought she was dead. What the kidnapper meant for evil, God had redeemed. Though danger was still out there somewhere, Clay had to trust God was going to see them through this. He'd done it so far.

"Mr. Clay?" India plucked at his shirtsleeve. "You have a funny look on your face."

"I was just thinking about how God takes care of things for us."

"Mama always said that too. And he let me come here. I prayed and prayed for him to take me out of that house."

"What's happening there, honey?" he asked, making sure to gentle his voice.

She was quiet a minute, her small face serious as she worked out what to say. He could see the indecision on her face, in the twist of her mouth and the darting of her gaze from him to the ground.

"There's five of us orphans," she said finally. "Cal and Wanda take their two kids to do fun stuff and leave us home. We usually have soup or peanut butter sandwiches for dinner." She lowered her voice to a whisper. "The older kids say they just took us in for the money."

Clay didn't doubt it. There were great foster parents out there but some stinkers too. The good and the bad mixed up together, as in all of life. He wanted to do something for this little girl. Did she have to go back to that situation? Could Rick make a recommendation that she be moved?

He'd never expected to be so embroiled in the lives of these kids.

※

Her burns had faded to darkened skin. Eden had avoided talking about anything personal with Clay. She didn't want to rush into anything, the way she had crashed into their marriage. Everything in her wanted to take his declaration of love at face value, but she hadn't been able to handle his frequent absences. What made her think she could endure them any more easily now?

India held Eden's left hand and Lacie held her right. Clay herded the other girls behind them as they hurried toward the store. Madeline wore her princess costume over her jeans. The girls stepped over the weeds sprouting through the cracks in the sidewalk, chanting, "Step on a crack, break your mother's back."

The morbid song brought an image of her birth mother's face to Eden. What was she going to do about her mother's desire to have a relationship? There was no animosity in Eden's heart, just caution. She didn't have the energy to focus on her mother when all she wanted to do was find Brianna and rebuild her life.

India yanked on the store door, and the cool rush of air hitting Eden's face brought her out of her thoughts. "Who's ready to buy jeans?" she asked.

"Me!" Madeline said, shuffling behind her in the plastic heels that went with her costume. "I don't want ones with holes. Can we get some with lace?"

"I'll see what I can do," Clay said, keeping a straight face.

Eden smiled and led the way to the stacks of girls' jeans. She pulled out sizes ranging from fives to sevens. "Let's try some on."

"I want red ones," Lacie said.

"How about a red top? I don't think they make red jeans," Eden said.

"Right here are some," the child said, pointing to a stack of colored jeans.

Sure enough, there were red ones in her size. Eden shrugged and draped two pairs over her arm. "Whatever you want," she said.

She found jeans for all the girls, then realized Clay was missing. When he reappeared, the smug expression on his face told her she wasn't going to like the reason he'd disappeared.

"What have you been up to?" she asked, narrowing her gaze at him.

His grin widened. "Who, me?"

Then she noticed the jeans on his arm. "Oh no."

"Oh yes. You need some too. And some boots." He held up what looked suspiciously like snakeskin boots.

Katie clapped her hands and jumped up and down. "Yeah, we can match!"

"I don't think so," Eden said. But when the girls' pleading faces turned her way, she began to relent. Surely she was adult enough not to care what people thought of her anymore. Who said she had to maintain that old image? She could re-create herself here. With Clay and the girls, she could be herself and not worry that someone might think she was poor white trash.

"It's hard to fit jeans, and I don't have time to try on half a dozen pair," she said.

Clay's smiled turned even more smug. "These will fit. Trust me." He held them out. She held his warm gaze as she took them. "If they don't fit, we'll forget them. I found some with lace for Madeline." He handed a pair of jeans with lace at the hem and on the pockets to the little girl, who squealed and clutched them to her chest.

Eden smiled and ushered the girls into the dressing room. The way he'd gone to the trouble to find them for her touched her in ways she hadn't expected. Clay surprised her at every turn.

After she got the girls fitted, she tried on her jeans. They fit perfectly. The boots fit too. She looked taller and even more slender in the dark jeans and heeled boots. All she needed was a saddle and he'd be putting her in the rodeo.

"I want a style show," Clay called from outside the dressing room. "You all have been in there long enough."

Her cheeks flared with heat when she stepped out of the dressing room and saw the appreciation in his eyes.

"Told you they'd fit," he said. "You look sensational."

A curtsy wasn't appropriate in these clothes, but she did one anyway. "Thank you. They're comfortable."

"Look at me, Mr. Clay," Katie said. She did a handspring across the floor. "Mine are stretchy."

"Very nice," Clay said. He complimented each girl in turn.

Eden marveled at his ability to say the most encouraging thing to each child. He was a born daddy.

25

A TRIP TO A BUFFALO RANCH. WHOSE IDEA WAS THIS? EDEN GESTURED TO THE GIRLS TO board the van. Zeke and Della already had their charges in the back and settled for the drive. Eden's girls were squealing and jumping up and down with excitement as she herded them onto the bus. Rita had come along as well. She wanted to research a buffalo ranch for one of her romance novels.

Allie waved to Eden from the porch. "Phone call," Allie said.

Eden stepped back off the van a moment and motioned for Clay to take over. Peering at the caller ID, she saw it was her mother's number. "Hello, Mom."

"Eden, dear, I wanted to check and see if I might stop by and see you."

"You're still in the area?"

"We've spent the past several nights here in Alpine. I . . . I wanted to give you a chance to adjust before I called again."

Eden found she wanted to see her mother, if only to find out if there was any chance that Hector Santiago wasn't her father. "We are going to Marathon today, to a buffalo ranch. It shouldn't be more than about thirty minutes from you." She gave her mother directions, then hung up and climbed into the van.

"Who was that?" Clay's eyes were shadowed. Neither of them had slept well last night because the girls were unusually wound up from their shopping adventure. "My mother. She's still in Alpine. She and Omar are meeting us at the ranch."

The bus was ready to leave, so there was no more time for a private conversation. As they traveled to the ranch, Eden thought about how to ask what she needed to know. Her mother was bound to be offended if Eden openly doubted her mother could know the identity of her father. The house had been a merry-go-round of men. How could Nancy be certain? Eden needed to know more.

"There they are!" Katie shouted, hopping up and down in her seat.

The buffalo grazed in a fenced meadow. The vanload of kids erupted into squeals. The animals were bigger than Eden expected. They lifted shaggy heads as the vehicle pulled into the driveway and stopped. Clay and Zeke guided the children out for the tour. Pen and paper in hand, Rita trailed behind taking notes.

"Are you all right?" Della asked Eden as she guided the last of her kids to the van door. "You look rather pale today. Are your burns still bothering you?"

"Not bad today. It was just a rough night. I could have taken another day before dealing with a buffalo tour."

"I've been here before. It's rather tame but the girls will enjoy it."

Della followed Eden out of the van, and they joined their husbands and the children at the fence. The girls were on the first rung of the fence, but Clay made them get down as the owner came toward them.

"They're not really buffalo," India said, tossing her black braids. "They're bison. Buffalo are water buffalo."

"How'd you know that?" Eden asked.

"I looked it up."

Though the little girl was only a year older than the others, she seemed much more mature. Eden hugged her and stared at the shaggy beasts.

"They're big and scary," Madeline said. "I don't like them."

Paige sneezed. "I think I'm 'llergic," she whispered. "Can I wait in the van?"

"You're not allergic. It will be fun." Eden pointed toward the sign that explained facts about the buffalo. Or bison, as India had insisted. One of the buffalo watched the girls climbing on the fence. The beast lowered its head and pawed. Eden frowned. "I think that one doesn't like your red shirt, Lacie. Come over here with me."

A man waved and joined them. As he began to tell them about the tour, Eden saw a car pull into the drive.

"They're here," she whispered to Clay. "Can you handle the girls by yourself?"

"Yeah. You'll be okay with her?"

"Of course. I'll catch up as soon as I can. Watch Lacie. That animal doesn't like the red." She walked down the drive to meet the car.

Her mother climbed out of the Lexus with a smile. She wore

a royal-blue sundress that showed her figure to advantage. Omar joined his wife before Eden reached them.

Her mother offered her cheek to Eden. The powder-scented skin brought back too many memories to Eden, and she stepped away as quickly as she could without causing offense.

"Eden, my dear, your face is red and blotchy. Rather unattractive. Did you forget your makeup this morning?"

Eden's cheeks heated. "I was in a fire recently, Mom."

Her mother gasped. "Fire? As in a building on fire?"

"The shed." Eden told her what happened.

Omar put his hand on Eden's shoulder. "Are you saying someone tried to kill you?"

"Yes. And would have succeeded if not for Clay."

Her mother went pale. "Oh my dear, I think I need to sit down."

She always did that. Made everything about her. Eden realized some things would never change even if her mother wanted them to. There was an outdoor patio area on the other side of the drive, and Eden pointed it out. Omar guided his wife to a chair, then went to get her a soda from a vending machine by the building.

"I talked to my father," Eden said as soon as he was out of earshot. "So did Clay."

"Your father? Hector?"

Eden nodded and held her mother's gaze. "He expressed doubts that he was my father."

"Of course he did. What did you expect?" Her mother dismissed Eden's concerns with an airy wave of her hand.

"Mother, I was eight when you left. I remember all the men. How do you know which one was my father?"

Angry spots of red bloomed in her mother's cheeks, but she looked down at her hands for a moment and the color faded. "I suppose I deserve that," she said quietly. She rubbed her hand over her forehead. "I wasn't always the woman you remember, Eden."

And yet, as far back as she could remember, Nancy had been exactly that woman. On Eden's fourth birthday, she'd been sent to her friend's house. She vaguely remembered her mother coming to get her smelling of an unpleasant odor. She later came to know that stench as beer.

When she didn't answer, her mother heaved another sigh. "I was a young girl, impressionable and naive, when I met your father. I didn't know he was married until you were on the way. He was my first real love. And I suppose I never really got over him. I went through a lot of men trying."

For the first time, Eden understood what it might have been like for her mother. "How did you meet him?"

"At a party." She glanced away. "I was young."

"So he knew you hadn't been with anyone else."

Her mother met her gaze. "He knew. Why did you call him?"

"I believe he was behind my daughter's kidnapping."

Her mother gasped. "He was behind Brianna's disappearance?"

Eden stared at her mother. "How do you know my daughter's name?"

"Well, I . . . I—you told me the other day."

Had she? Eden didn't think so.

Her mother smiled, though it was feeble. "What did your father say?"

"Not much. I'm going to try to see him." Eden only said this to see her reaction, and she wasn't surprised when her mother's eyes brightened.

"I'd like to say hello," her mother said. "When are you meeting him?"

"I'm not sure," Eden said. One thing she was certain of—her mother's interest was more than casual.

Clay joined them and draped his arm around Eden's shoulders. "What's going on over here?" he asked, his tone jocular.

"We were just talking about Brianna," Eden's mother said quickly. "Do you have a picture?"

"Sure." Clay dug a USB drive out of his pocket. It was still attached to the digital picture album. "There are some on there."

Her mother fiddled with the frame, then frowned. "These look like men in a jungle."

"Let me see." Clay took it. "You're in the wrong album." He pressed a few buttons, then handed it back. "There she is when she was a month old."

Eden watched her mother's face soften and wished she could believe the older woman really cared.

❊

"I think I'll sleep like the dead tonight," Clay said, yawning. "Neither of us slept worth a darn last night."

Eden had been quiet since the trip to the buffalo ranch. The expression on her face had warned him not to probe until she was ready to talk. Not that there had been much time. The girls had been wild all evening. All they'd talked about was the trip to see the buffalo.

She barely mm-hmmed in response as she got into bed and rolled onto her side with her back facing him. He shut out the light, but the faint moonlight through the window and the green glow from the clock let him see her silhouette. What would she do if he put his arm around her waist, spoon fashion? With every day that passed, he knew he never wanted her to leave him again. Wooing her would take all of his concentration.

Her voice spoke out of the darkness. "Clay?"

"I'm awake." He rolled onto his side, facing her. A mere six inches separated them.

"How much longer is your leave?"

Where had that come from? "Five weeks."

"Then what? Do you know where you'll be sent?"

He should tell her now, but what if it scared her off? When he placed his hand on her waist, she stiffened but didn't move away. "I don't know, Eden. I might not go back."

She rolled onto her back, then to her other side. They were practically nose to nose. "Not go back? What do you mean?"

She was close enough that he could smell her light fragrance. Close enough that he could kiss her if he wanted. "I'm tired of the travel. The excitement has grown old. And Brianna will need me." He wished she would say she needed him too, but he was afraid that was too much to hope for.

"B-But what will you do?"

"I have my inheritance. I could maybe use the money to start a business, but thought about applying for a job at the ranger station too, just to keep busy and do some wildlife photography. I think I'd like that. There's the ranch here we could fix up. It wouldn't cost much to live here."

"Just how much money is in this inheritance?"

He grinned. "Enough to keep you in any style you'd like."

"Really?"

Was she expressing doubt or hope? He couldn't tell without seeing her expression. His hand was still on her waist. He brought it up to cup her cheek. "Really. Think you could stand to have me home every night?"

"I'd like to try," she whispered.

His pulse leaped. He cupped the back of her head and drew her against him. His lips found hers. It was the sweetest kiss in his memory. He drank deep of the promise, hope, and longing in her lips.

She drew away. "You didn't ask me how it went with my mother."

He tried to keep the disappointment from his voice. "I thought you'd tell me when you were ready. You were both a little tense when I joined you."

She scooted a little farther away. "Clay, didn't you think it odd that she knew about Brianna? Did we mention we had a daughter or what happened?"

He thought back, then shook his head. "No. You both talked about the past, about your childhood. There was no mention of the kidnapping or anything. I assumed you didn't want to get into that with her."

"I didn't. But she even knew Brianna's name. I didn't tell her that."

He tensed. That didn't sound right. "What did she say?"

"I told her I suspected my father had something to do with my daughter's kidnapping. She gasped then and said, 'He was behind Brianna's disappearance?'"

He absorbed the information and looked for a logical explanation. "Maybe she looked us up online and ran into the story."

"She knew our name before we met her in Alpine. You introduced us to Omar. So they would have known that first evening. Wouldn't it have been the most natural thing in the world to ask about her granddaughter? To offer condolences?"

"Maybe. But things were awkward anyway. Maybe she didn't want to cause more emotional upheaval." Even to him, the excuse sounded lame.

He raised onto his elbow and stared through the darkness at her. "Eden, do you think it's possible she contacted you because of your father?"

"What do you mean?"

"What if she's involved in this too?" He shook his head. "No, I guess that's crazy."

"What's crazy is that she is married to my uncle. When she couldn't get my father, she settled for his brother. What if they are all in business together?" She bolted upright in the bed. "What if Omar is the one who has been trying to kill me?"

"But why?"

"I don't know." She flopped back onto the pillow. "It's all such a tangle. I have no idea what's going on. But all these things have to connect somehow. I want to know how she met Omar."

"Ask her. When are you going to see her again?"

"I don't know. They're not planning to leave Alpine until at least the weekend."

"I think we need to have another chat with them," he said.

His mind raced through the possibilities. Santiago had what he wanted, so why would anyone want to harm Eden now?

He opened his mouth to discuss it some more with Eden, but the steady rise and fall of her chest told him she'd fallen asleep. Flopping onto his back, he tried to do the same, but it was a long time before he succeeded.

26

CLAY SAT ON THE PORCH SWING WITH HIS ARM AROUND EDEN. "EVERY MUSCLE IN MY BODY aches," he said. "I thought tubing down the Rio Grande with the girls would be a piece of cake. That water was rough."

"I'm about ready for bed," she agreed.

Headlamps swept the front of the main house. A car light came on as the door opened, but he couldn't see who it was from here. Just that it was a woman. She came toward the bunkhouse with purposeful steps.

When she stepped into the glow of the porch light, Eden rose. "Judge Julia! I'm surprised to see you."

The older woman mounted the steps and dragged a rocker around to face them before settling in it. "I heard what happened out here the other night and came to see how you're faring." She looked them over with shrewd eyes in the wash of light. "You both look like something the coyotes fought over."

"Tubing with five little girls will do that to you." He rose and shook her hand. "Clay Larson."

"Judge Julia Thompson." She crossed her jean-clad legs and leaned back in the rocker, looking at Eden. "I remembered, you know. I knew it would come to me."

Clay heard Eden's sudden intake of breath but had no idea what was so upsetting about the judge's statement. "Remembered what?"

"Where I'd seen your pretty wife. And you too." She tapped her nose. "News has a smell to me. Especially crime."

"You know about our daughter?" He doubted the judge was going to go around talking about it.

"I do indeed. The last I heard, the two of you were split. Now here you are. In my county."

He glanced at Eden. How much should they tell this woman? "We're here because this is where our daughter is."

The suspicious glint in the judge's eyes dimmed. "She's alive? I figured the two of you . . ."

"Killed her and tried to cover our tracks?" He'd heard the accusations before, but they stung every time. "I think the investigating detective still believes it."

The judge shrugged. "It's usually a family member. Sad but true."

"I have been looking for Brianna for five years," Clay said. "I never believed she was dead."

"So what's she doing here?"

Clay told her what they knew, including Eden's father's involvement. When the judge heard the name Santiago, her expression grew more sober.

"Santiago's involvement is ominous," she said. "He's behind half the drugs that come through here every year. I sure would like to get him." She studied Eden's face. "Would you be willing to be a lure?"

Clay glanced at his wife. "I don't want her involved in anything dangerous. We have a daughter to raise."

Eden shook her head. "I won't put these kids in danger. If we rile up the situation any further, I don't know what might happen. If he thinks I'm a danger, he might go after all of us with real determination."

"Not if he's in jail," the judge said.

"He's escaped capture many times," Clay said. "I think the risk is too great."

The judge pressed her lips together. "If we can get Santiago and his crew, you'll all be safer."

Eden hesitated. "Maybe so."

He couldn't lose Eden. Not now. "No! I don't want her involved," Clay said.

"I'll have protection for you."

"I've heard that before." But what if Santiago couldn't stop the wheels he'd set in motion? What if the attacker struck again, or evaded capture and came back to avenge Santiago?

The judge steepled her fingers together. "Call your father. Ask to meet."

Eden shook her head. "What excuse can I give?"

"I wish you hadn't already given him that pendant," Julia muttered. "That was your best leverage." She studied Clay's face. "You've crossed tracks with Santiago before, on his turf. Do you have any photos linking him to the drug trafficking? He won't want anything in circulation."

"My camera was taken during that particular mission you're talking about." He shook his head, then an image came to mind. Car keys, flash drive. Eden's mother had mentioned pictures of a jungle, but he hadn't paid much attention. "You know, let me check an old flash drive I have. It's still on my key ring with pictures of Brianna, but there's another folder on it that I haven't looked at in a long time."

He left the women on the porch and went back to the bedroom, where he'd dropped his keys and change. He pulled the drive from the little digital photo album that he'd used to show Eden's mother the pictures of Brianna. He plugged it into the port on his MacBook, and two folders showed up seconds later. He clicked on the unnamed one, and the list of files came up.

Pictures. There were old pictures in the folder. He flipped through jungle scenes. Children playing in the dirt of a small town. These images had been taken the day before the commandos rolled in, firing on the kids, and he'd been thrown in jail for intervening. But was there anything incriminating?

The next picture was of a swarthy man scowling. He stood next to a truck loading stacks of white powder. Santiago? He printed off that picture and three more that clearly showed the contents of the truck. If it was Hector, Eden might recognize him.

❈

The swing swayed gently as Eden wondered what to say to the judge. The horrid accusations that had swirled around them after Brianna's disappearance brought a lump to her throat. Rumors traveled far. The first time a police officer had accused her of harming her daughter was seared into her memory. Only a lack of evidence had saved them from being arrested. Within a few days the ransom note proved genuine and the police backed off. But it was a painful time. No one stopped eyeing them with suspicion.

"You can stop brooding," the judge said. "If you'd seen what I have, you would have jumped to conclusions too. The way parents treat children is appalling."

Eden started to answer, then checked herself. Her childhood experiences were a confirmation that the judge was right. "I realize our situation wasn't typical. But when you're devastated by loss, then find you're a suspect, it's overwhelming."

The screen door screeched and Clay returned with a paper in his hand. "I hit pay dirt," he said. "You recognize this guy?" He thrust a printout into Eden's hand.

She held it under the porch light and was suddenly eight years old again. "It's my dad," she said.

"I thought so. Santiago is at a village with the drugs."

Julia held the photograph under the light. "It's him," she said. "Tell him you have these. He'll come for them."

Eden's memories crystallized, and she heard his gruff voice telling her to go outside and play while he talked with her mother. She'd always been an encumbrance to both of them. The day her mother left her had been a blessing. She just hadn't fully realized that until now.

The judge glanced at Eden. "Are you willing to try?"

"I don't want the girls in danger," Eden said. "Even if he's captured, what if his men come after us for revenge?"

"Hector's son is dead. His second in command has no interest in family squabbles."

"You don't know that."

Julia shut up and stared at Eden. "You're right—I don't. Not for sure. But don't you have any sense of justice? Don't you want to make sure others are not hurt by this man?"

The judge's questions stung. "Of course I do!" Eden said. "But I'm more concerned about my daughter and the other girls. And he's still my father, in spite of his despicable behavior. The Bible says to honor our parents. He wasn't much of a dad, but the thought of luring him into a trap makes me shudder."

Clay's warm fingers closed around hers. "That's a good point, honey."

"You would protect a man who had no compunction about ordering your death?" Julia demanded. "He would order those girls killed with as little thought. The safest thing is to lock him up where he can't hurt any of you."

"I don't trust that locking him up is the solution."

"We'll make sure the confrontation takes place far from the ranch," Julia promised.

Eden shook her head. "I'm sorry."

Clay's cell phone rang. He glanced at it and raised his brows. "Unknown," he said before he opened it. "Larson here."

She watched his face change, and he mouthed, "Your father." She went still and listened to his side of the conversation.

"I never tried to hide anything from you," Clay said. He listened, then said, "I see. Yes, you've made yourself perfectly clear. Just a minute." He handed the phone to Eden. "He wants to talk to you."

"What did he say?" Eden asked when he didn't explain immediately.

"He seems to know about these pictures. He wants them back."

Eden stared at the phone. "He has this place bugged?" She shuddered.

"He said your mother called him."

"My mother!" Eden collapsed back against the swing. "She would give him ammunition to hurt us more?"

"Apparently so." Clay's voice was dry.

She put the phone to her ear. What did she call him? Father? Mr. Santiago? "Hello," she said, settling for anonymity.

"I did not expect to have to speak with you again. You have been secretive with me."

"That's not true."

"Your mother tells me there are pictures of me. In the jungle. What do you intend to do with them?"

"We just found them. Clay had forgotten that they were on his drive."

"Somehow I doubt the *hombre* did not know this."

"It's true. My mother found them in an old folder. Why did she call you?"

"Money, of course. She does nothing without wishing for cash."

Eden's stomach churned with acid. Her mother had sold them out. "I assume you want the pictures."

"Of course. You will give them back and destroy any copies you have made."

"I told you—Clay just found them. There are no copies."

"See that it remains that way. And what is it you want in return for turning them over to me? I pay my debts."

"You owe me nothing." She glanced at Julia's hopeful face, then looked away. No, she couldn't risk the children. "You're my father."

"So your mother said. I was never certain."

He'd said the same thing to Clay, but was he trying to skirt his responsibilities? Or had her mother lied? Eden had learned never to trust what her mother said. Nancy appeared to have changed, but was it real? "Regardless, there is something I'd like."

"I thought so. Money, I suppose," he said, his voice bored.

"Of course not! I don't want tainted money. I want you to tell me which of these girls is our Brianna."

"Eden, I have not the least idea."

"So you lied to me? You lured us here with a picture and a false claim? You knew about the kidnapping all along, that she was your granddaughter!"

"I did not know everything," he said, his voice grudging. "I never saw the *niña*. Pictures only."

"Who has cared for her all this time?"

"I have no idea. It was not important enough for me to know a name."

Her fingers curled into her palms. His own granddaughter wasn't important. "What were the last pictures you saw?"

"I believe she was two."

Two lost years of Brianna's life. She had to have them. "The last photos I have were when she was six weeks old. So I'll trade you those pictures for these and the original flash drive."

"You are in no position to make demands." His voice held an icy edge.

"You asked what I wanted."

"Very well. I am coming to Texas next weekend. Have the drive ready and on your person at all times."

Her heart sank. She didn't want to see him face-to-face. "You're coming *here*?"

"Business, of course."

"I assumed you would send one of your minions."

"I wish to assure myself that there are no copies. I will be able to see if you are telling me the truth. You are very transparent."

"There's no need for that. I promise you that we will make no copies."

"We shall see."

This was not going as she'd expected. "Where should we meet?"

"I will call you. It is not safe to make prior arrangements."

The phone went dead in her ear. She put her phone down. "He hung up."

"It sounds like he is coming to see you in person?" Julia asked.

Eden nodded. "He's coming, but I don't know when." She may have made the situation worse. In truth, Eden would rather not set eyes on the man. The horror of the fire came to mind again. Her father had been unable to stop it. Would this meddling intensify the danger?

"I'll make sure you're protected," Julia said, her intent gaze on Eden's face.

Eden moved restlessly. "I don't want him anywhere around the girls."

"He won't be," Julia said. "We'll arrest him when he comes."

Eden couldn't see how it could work. "I have a feeling he's used to being careful."

"I don't think he'll be expecting his daughter to turn him over to the cops," Clay said. "The meeting was his idea."

Eden winced. "I'm still not crazy about it."

"He sicced a thug on you, honey," he said. "I don't think you owe him anything."

She stared at Julia. "I guess we have no choice but to go along with it. If I don't show up when he calls, he's liable to do anything." She shuddered at the thought and prayed that the Border Patrol would nab anyone who might be inclined to harm her girls.

※

The day felt oppressive. Thunderclouds built in the southwest, great banks of roiling clouds that looked like bruises. They were likely in for a big storm. Maybe even hail, according to Allie. The animals were restless too, stomping their hooves in the corral. Allie told Rick she didn't want the girls on the horses when they were so skittish.

Eden sniffed the moisture in the air as she saw the mail carrier stop at the end of the drive. *Please, please, let it be there.* The gravel slipped around under her boots as she rushed to get the mail. The huge box was filled with envelopes. She pulled all of it out and began to go through it as the wind kicked up around her.

Bits of sand pummeled her bare arms, but she barely noticed as her gaze fell on the return address of one of the envelopes. The lab results. There were three more pieces of mail just like it. She quickly sorted the envelopes. Four white rectangular pieces of paper. One of them would tell her which little girl was their Brianna.

She could barely think, barely breathe. Where was Clay? She had to do this with him. He deserved to see it first. He'd never lost hope, never given up. She started for the house as thunder rolled across the desert and hills. Light flickered in the depths of the cloud, and she smelled ozone. While she watched, a sliver of darkness reached down from a rotating cloud. For a moment, she didn't realize what she was seeing. Then it sank in. A tornado!

She started for the house at a run. The tornado was heading

straight for the ranch. "Clay!" she screamed over the sound that intensified around her. The wind howled so loudly it sounded like a train. She saw Allie point, then gather the children to her. They all ran toward the house, then disappeared inside. At least the girls were safe. Allie would take them to the cellar.

Eden struggled to run in the wind. It felt as though she was making no progress. It was these dratted boots. They were still stiff, and it would take too long to sit down and pull them off. Her epitaph would read DONE IN BY NEW BOOTS.

The horses were going berserk. Buzz and the other hands were trying to get them inside the barn, but she wondered if that would protect them. Where was Clay? She screamed his name again, but the wind snatched away the sound of her voice.

Then she saw him. He had a tripod set up at the side of the barn and was busy snapping pictures of the twister as it ripped up cactus and sucked sand into its mouth. Was it larger? She thought so. It roared toward them and she stood, mouth gaping at the destruction.

She glanced back to the barn to see that Clay had noticed her. He was shouting something but she couldn't make out what it was. He grabbed his camera from the tripod, then ran toward her waving his arms. She veered toward him, changing her original course of heading to the house.

They met in the side yard. "Get to shelter!" he shouted. He grabbed her arm and hustled her toward the barn, which was the nearest structure. The side door was shut, but he kicked it open and half dragged her inside as the tornado reached the end of the driveway.

"There's no basement in here!" she shouted above the din of screaming horses and high winds.

He paused and looked frantically around the space. "Under the feed trough!" He thrust her under a heavy wooden bin in the middle stall, then jumped on top of her.

His weight pressed the air from her lungs. Or was it the sudden closeness of the twister that sucked all the oxygen from her chest? She clung to him and listened to his ragged breathing in her ear. The wind roared all around them. She couldn't think, couldn't concentrate on anything but the thought that they were about to die before they found Brianna.

The pressure in her ears began to let up. The sound of a freight train about to run them over suddenly vanished. She drew in a lungful of oxygen. Then another. Breaths came more easily, or they would when Clay got off of her.

He lifted his head and stared into her face. "You okay?"

She nodded. "I think so. We need to get to the girls. They'll be frightened in the cellar."

He rolled off her and helped her to her feet. "We still have a roof on the barn."

She glanced up and saw he was right. "I can't even see any daylight through it."

A child called out, "Mr. Clay!" It sounded like Paige, their fearful one.

In unison, they rushed toward the door and stepped out into blue sky. The ominous cloud was to their northeast now. The twister's destruction stopped about twenty feet from the barn. Then the sparse grass was undisturbed.

"It must have lifted before it hit us," Clay said. "The house is fine too."

She could breathe again. The air was no longer close and thick.

Another miracle. Thankfulness welled in her heart. "God took care of us."

"He always does." Clay started toward the porch, but she caught his arm. "Clay, wait." She showed him the mail in her hands. "The results are here."

His eyes widened. "The DNA results?"

She nodded, watching his eyes brighten. He'd worked so hard for this moment. And she realized she loved him. Her love wasn't just physical attraction. His heart was as big as the sky overhead. He might not say things as well as he liked, but the emotion was there. He'd let nothing keep him from finding their daughter.

"I wanted you to open them. You deserve the honor after the way you never lost hope."

He swallowed hard. "Let's check on the girls, then go to our room."

27

FOUR WHITE ENVELOPES. THEY CONTAINED THE NEWS HE'D BEEN SEEKING FOR FIVE YEARS. Clay looked at them spread out on the coffee table. Which one would be theirs? He couldn't even say he had a favorite, that he hoped Brianna was a certain child.

His hand hovered over the first one to his left. "Start with this one?"

The skin on Eden's face was still a little reddened from the fire. Her green eyes widened and she nodded. "Do you have a guess?"

"I think Brianna is Katie."

"I think Paige is our girl."

He raised a brow. "Why Paige? That would cause some difficulties."

She nodded. "And that's why I think it's Paige. This has been so difficult that I can't see it suddenly becoming easy."

"Maybe it's not supposed to be. I'm stronger for the search. I think you are too."

He licked dry lips and picked up the first envelope. Turning it over in his hand, he ripped the flap open and pulled out the folded sheet inside.

Eden leaned over his arm to look. "Well?"

He stared at the probability figure: 0%. "This is Katie's. She's not ours." He showed her the paper.

She dropped the page and grabbed the next envelope. "Check this one."

He ripped it open and glanced at the heading. "This one is Madeline's." He skimmed to the results. "It's a zero too."

"So that leaves either Paige or Lacie. I told you it would be Paige." Her shoulders slumped. "How will we tell that sweet couple that they can't have her?"

He snatched up the next envelope and ripped into it. The waiting was killing him. The faces of the two little girls hung in his mind. He had no preference. They were both sweet kids. "This one is Lacie's."

The results suddenly appeared larger, almost bolded: a 99.97% match. "It's Lacie," he said slowly. "She's our Brianna."

"Lacie?" Eden took the paper from him and scanned it. "I thought it might be her. But she's so quiet. And what about that nun? I thought there would be some mystery to her background. That maybe Sister Marjo was her real mother or something." She clutched his arm. "Oh, Clay, she's our baby. Our Brianna. I want to see her now."

He hadn't dreamed it would be Lacie either. Of all the girls, she hadn't been very high on his list of possibilities. But her quiet strength and sweet nature would fit so well with them.

"When do we tell Lacie?" Her voice vibrated with longing, and when she locked gazes with Clay, pain flared in her eyes. "Can we do it now?"

She didn't seem to be aware she was wringing her hands. He put his hand over hers. "I think we have to wait, honey. We want to handle it right. And we need to talk to the sister."

"But she's ours. Doesn't she deserve to know that? I want to hold her." Her voice was thick.

"I want to tell her too. I'll talk to Rick and Allie about it. We'll let them guide us. Agreed?"

"All right," she said, her voice grudging. "I don't know how long I can hide my feelings. When can we talk to Sister Marjo?"

"She's coming to visit tomorrow. I'll arrange for a private meeting with her." He had hardly assimilated the news. "We've found her. Really and truly."

Something welled inside him—gratitude, disbelief, joy. The emotions swelled until they nearly smothered him. It seemed unbelievable that God would give them this incredible gift. "She's really alive, Eden." He pressed his burning eyes. "Sometimes I thought it was my stubbornness that wouldn't let me see reality. Then I'd get another whiff of hope and keep on looking."

Her touch was tentative on his arm. "You never gave up, Clay. That's the kind of man you are." She turned her head and looked out the window as if the intensity of his gaze bothered her. "It still seems a dream."

"Now what, Eden?" he asked softly.

At least she didn't pretend not to know what he was talking about, though she kept staring at the window. He glanced there himself to see nothing but the rocky hillside in the distance. The silence stretched out, but he wasn't going to say anything until she did. Maybe he was stubborn, but she needed to face the facts and make a decision.

He had to know. "Did you hear what I said after I pulled you out of the fire?"

She sighed and finally turned her head toward him. "I heard."

"I meant it. There's no life without you."

A tiny smile played at the corner of her lips, then she frowned. "We didn't make it before, Clay. What makes you think we can this time? I'm scared."

"You think I'm not?" He raised her hand to his lips and kissed the back of it. "For five years I've felt like a failure. There were so many things standing in our way—our youth, the short time we knew each other. Then losing Brianna. That would harm any marriage."

"Rebuilding from here isn't going to be easy either. Brianna will need a lot of love and support. There may not be a lot of time to focus on our relationship."

"There's always time. How do you think other parents handle it? All these kids want is a family that loves them."

She held his gaze. "I'm a little sad about that. I'd like to keep them all."

He winced. "Me too. It's going to be hard to let them go."

She chewed on her lip. "I hope Brianna will adjust."

"If we show her we love each other and she's an integral part of the family, she'll adjust quickly." There was a question in her eyes, and he knew he had to say the words. "I love you, Eden. I've always loved you. That's the real reason I wouldn't sign the divorce papers."

She inhaled but kept her eyes on him. "I thought I got over you, but I was just deceiving myself in order to get by."

He tried to squelch the leap of joy at her words. There was too much fear in her face. "So what are you saying about us? Are you willing to put doubt aside and forge a new future with me and Brianna? And any other kids who happen to come along?"

She brushed a lock of hair out of her eyes. "I'll try, Clay. That's all I can promise. But if I ever fail my daughter again, I . . . I . . ."

He put his finger to her lips. "We all mess up, honey. It wasn't your fault." He cupped her face in his palm. "I love you so much."

When he moved to take her in his arms, she put her hand on his chest. "Love wasn't enough before, Clay. What guarantee do we have that it will be enough this time?"

"There are no guarantees. We've both learned a lot, though. About each other, about patience, about give-and-take."

She nodded. "I want to try."

He couldn't hold back the grin. "Quit changing the subject. Say it, Angel."

A smile curved her lips, and she didn't pretend not to understand him. "I love you, Clay Larson. I will until the day I die."

The tension in her face drained, and she leaned over and offered him her lips. A gift he was happy to take.

⁂

Her eyes looked wide and aware. Eden glanced away from her image in the mirror and spit out the toothpaste. The mint taste cleared her head. She ran a brush through her hair. Her makeup was still on, but she didn't want to take it off. Not tonight.

When she stepped into the hall, she saw Clay through the open bedroom door. He was sitting on the edge of the bed with his Bible in his hand. "Ready?" she asked.

He nodded and put the Bible aside. "Remember, not a word yet."

"I know." Everything in her longed to tell Lacie the truth.

The girls were all on India's bed. It had taken awhile to calm them after the storm, though luckily they'd seen little of it from the cellar. The debris strewn around the yard had frightened them, so she and Clay had tried to make a game out of picking it up. They'd finally prayed with the girls, and the children began to lose their anxiety.

They had a stack of books scattered on the covers. Eden's attention went straight to Lacie. Her Brianna. She drank in the little girl's brown hair. Her light-brown eyes. They were blue the last time Eden had held her. Now that she knew, it seemed her daughter's identity should have been clear instantly. The straightness of her hair was like Clay's. The strength in her chin was her daddy's too. Those cheeks were like Eden's.

"Why are you staring, Miss Eden?" India asked. "Aren't you going to read to us?"

Eden collected her wits. "Of course, honey. You're all so pretty. I had to look, didn't I?"

India giggled. "No one ever calls me pretty."

When Eden sat on the edge of the bed, the little girl leaned her head against Eden's arm. "Want me to take your ribbons out?" she asked.

India nodded. "I like it when you do my hair. It feels good."

Eden exchanged a smile with Clay and saw his attention veer back to the child on her left. Brianna. It was going to be hard not to call Lacie by her real name. The amazement choked Eden. She took the ribbons out of India's hair and released the braids. The black hair sprang from her head in all directions, and Eden began to brush it out. India didn't complain at the tugging.

"What book are we reading tonight?" Clay asked, picking up the top one. "*The Cat in the Hat?*"

"We read that yesterday. Lacie wants *The Story of Ferdinand.*"

"Then that's what we'll read tonight. It is your turn, isn't it?" Eden asked, touching her daughter on the head.

Her daughter. Were two words ever more beautifully paired? She hoped Clay could find his voice to read because she wasn't sure she could. She finished India's hair, then Lacie scooted closer. "You want to be next?" she asked. The little girl nodded with a shy smile.

"I'll read," Clay said, his voice husky.

Eden listened to him read the story of a misunderstood bull. Everyone thought Ferdinand was mean, but he'd only been stung by a bee. She smiled as the children gasped and felt sorry for Ferdinand. The intensity in their eyes held her enthralled. When had she last entered into something as completely as they did? Making her marriage work and being a mommy to Brianna were going to take a similar commitment.

She ran her hand along the silken curtain of her daughter's hair. Though it wasn't red, the way she'd thought it would be, it was so beautiful. And hers. Hers and Clay's. They'd made this child together and she bore their imprint in her features. It was right and good that they picked up the pieces and went on. Brianna deserved a whole family. Clay deserved a wife who tried with all her heart. God was telling her what to do, but she was still so afraid.

"Time for prayers, then bed," Clay said, shutting the book.

They held hands in a circle on the bed. Eden clasped India's hand in her right and Madeline's in her left. The girls' eyes were closed and she took the moment to gaze at each one of them. All so individual. All so precious.

Clay shut his eyes. "God, thank you for keeping us safe from the tornado today. Thank you for each one of these girls. Thank you for bringing them into our lives. We love each and every one of them, as we know you do too. Keep them safely in your hands. In Jesus's name. Amen."

"Amen," she echoed. She kissed soft cheeks as she tucked them into bed. Clay shut off the light and closed the door partway behind them. It was too soon to go to bed.

"Want something to drink?" she asked Clay, heading to the kitchen.

"I'll take some tea," he said, following her. "Any of those chocolate chip cookies left?"

She nodded to the cabinet by the sink. "I hid some on the top shelf just for you."

"What a wife." He grinned and opened the door. "In this?" He indicated a plastic container.

"That's it." She took out glasses. "Maybe milk since we have cookies?"

"Sounds good."

Still not ready to face his eyes, she poured milk into the glasses.

"Honey, are you mad about something?"

Heat rushed to her face. "Of course not. I . . . I'm just feeling a little overwhelmed by everything that happened today."

He was smiling, oh so tenderly. She drank in the expression on his face. She wanted to believe his love, longed to put away all doubts. Dropping her gaze, she took a cookie from the container and bit into it. The chocolate hit her taste buds and the sugar gave her courage. She smiled back at him, daring to let her feelings show.

He stopped chewing. "I like that expression in your eyes. Could you look at me like that all the time?"

"Like what?" she asked, allowing her smile to widen.

"Like you might actually love me," he said softly. "I know you said it earlier, but I'm having trouble believing it."

She swallowed the last of her milk, then put down her glass. "I love you, Clay. So much it makes my chest hurt."

The light in his eyes intensified. He stood, reaching out his hand for her to take it. She did, and he drew her close. Before she could say a word, he swept her into his arms and carried her from the room.

28

THE AROMA OF STRONG COFFEE MINGLED WITH THAT OF BACON. EDEN SMILED AT CLAY ACROSS the kitchen table in the main house and prayed Allie and Rick didn't notice any difference. If only she and Clay didn't have things to do today, they could have spent the morning lying in bed and talking about the future. Last night had changed everything.

Rita dropped a skillet in the sink, and the bang roused Eden from her reverie. She rose and went to the coffeepot. "Thanks for making the coffee so strong this morning," she told Rita.

"It's your funeral," Rita said, softening her words with a smile. She pointed to the coffee. "That stuff is going to kill you." She gulped a pill down with water, carried a plate of bacon to Clay. Her smile widened, and she patted his shoulder.

"But what a way to go." Eden hid a smile at the way Clay shifted. She poured cream into the strong brew and carried it back to the table. "We have something to tell you," she said to the Baileys. She'd waited to bring it up until Zeke and Della were gone.

Allie pushed her empty plate away and dabbed at her mouth with the napkin. "What's up?"

"We got the DNA results yesterday." Goose bumps prickled the skin on Eden's arms. What a miracle.

Allie looked at Rick, who was finishing his scrambled eggs. He put down his fork. "Which one is Brianna?"

"Lacie," Clay said.

Allie exhaled. "I thought it would be Katie."

"So did I," Eden said. "But all the other girls were a zero. No chance of them being ours."

"What was the figure for Lacie?" Rick asked.

"It's 99.97 percent," Clay said.

"So, no doubt."

"No doubt," Eden said, nodding.

"Did you tell her yet?" Allie asked.

Eden took a sip of coffee, then shook her head. "We weren't sure how to do it. We don't want her upset. And how should we handle it? Talk to Child Protective Services first?"

Rick tossed his napkin onto the table. "I'll give them a call. I know the director."

Allie's eyes were moist. "Oh, Eden, such wonderful news! No wonder you're glowing this morning. I noticed it right off."

A blush heated Eden's cheeks, and she didn't dare look at Clay. "It feels too good to be true. I looked her over last night. I should have seen the resemblance to Clay right away. For some reason, we thought she'd look like me. But her eyes and chin are Clay's."

"And dark hair like him," Rita put in.

"Exactly. No red hair like mine." Eden tucked a lock behind her ear.

"A little Clay. How cute," Allie said.

"We don't know what the next step is," Clay said.

"I would imagine you'll have to petition the courts for custody and prove you're her parents," Rick said.

Clay frowned, his eyes clouding. "That will take a legal DNA test, I would imagine. We'll have to go to a collection place."

Eden's elation ebbed. "Is there any doubt?"

Clay slipped his arm around the back of her chair and smiled. "No, honey. No doubt. The test is the same, but for the court they want no doubt that the sample wasn't tampered with."

The ardor in his eyes warmed her. And she loved it when he called her *honey*. "When can we get the process in motion?"

"Let me find out." Rick went to the kitchen phone and dialed. He stepped from the room and his voice faded to a dull murmur.

"I really want to tell Lacie," Eden said.

"Maybe it will be allowed. Rick will find out," Allie said. She rose and began to collect the dirty dishes.

Eden stood to help her, though she would rather have stayed with Clay's arm around her. "Sister Marjo is coming today to see Lacie, right? Maybe we can find out more about the way she was found on the church steps."

"She's due here at noon," Allie said, stooping to load the dishwasher.

A crash made both women jump. Eden whirled to see Rita stooping to pick up glass shards on the floor.

"Wet hands," Rita said. "I should have dried them before I tried to carry the glasses." She glanced at Allie. "Have you met Sister Marjo? It's not common for the kids to get visitors. What's that all about?"

Allie stooped to help her pick up the glass. "I'm not sure. I guess she sees Lacie once a month and didn't want to let the tradition falter. The two seem very close."

"So you haven't met her?" Eden asked.

"No. But I feel as though I know her. Lacie talks about her all the time."

Eden turned when Rick stepped back into the kitchen. "Well?"

He went to pour another cup of coffee. "I was right. You'll need to petition the court. And provide the backstory of how your daughter was kidnapped. You'll need to submit to legal testing too."

"How long will all that take?" Clay asked.

"Several months is my best guess. The tests should come back fairly quickly, but you'll need to wait on a court date."

"Can we tell her before?" Eden longed to see Lacie's reaction when she found out she had a real home.

Rick took a sip of coffee. "I wouldn't. It might make the wait unbearable for her."

It was already unbearable for Eden. "She won't have to go back to her foster parents, will she?"

"Maybe. The director was unclear on that point. You can ask for a court date as quickly as possible. This will be an unusual case, so I'm guessing media attention will be strong. That might be enough to get them to move faster on it."

Eden felt like wringing her hands. "I can't bear to have her go back to her foster parents, Rick! Surely there's something we can do."

"Maybe Julia can expedite things," Clay said.

"Of course!" Eden glanced at Allie. "Remember when she said I looked familiar to her? She figured it out. She'd seen the newspaper stories."

"It wouldn't hurt to ask her for help," Allie said.

Eden rubbed her forehead. "We have to get this settled soon. We all deserve to be a family again."

"Let's get it done today," Clay said. "Call the judge."

Eden shrugged and pulled out her phone. "Okay." She placed the call and Julia agreed to help. She told them to come to the clinic and submit a DNA sample at eight thirty, an hour away. This would soon be over.

❈

Horses stomped their hooves in the red dirt. Their tack jingled and glittered in the hot sunshine. Clay squinted into the brilliant blue sky at the position of the sun. Nearly nine thirty. Sister Marjo would be coming soon.

He sensed someone behind him. Turning, he saw Eden moving toward the corral with Madeline by the hand. The little girl kept snatching her fingers from Eden's until finally Eden didn't try to grab them back. What was with the child? All the other girls adored Eden, but Madeline had never fully gotten over her pique of being disciplined. She would warm up for a few minutes, then fall back into her sullenness.

"Hi, girls," he said. "I'm surprised to see you here, Maddie. I thought you didn't like the horses."

"So did I," Eden said, stopping to catch her breath. "She decided she was going to try to pet one today."

Madeline went to grab Clay's hand. "But you have to come with me."

"I won't leave your side," he promised.

He exchanged a puzzled glance with Eden. She'd tried her best to get Madeline to make up with her, but the child refused to so much as smile in Eden's direction. He was a different story, though. She craved his attention.

He let her watch Allie's daughter, Betsy, and the horse Bluebird for a few minutes. Betsy was riding around the barrels in the corral as she practiced for the kids' rodeo coming up in two weeks. "She's good," he said.

Eden joined them at the fence. "Allie says she's even better than Allie was at that age."

Betsy cantered toward them when she completed the course. "Hi, Maddie," she said. "You want to ride Bluebird? He won't hurt you."

Madeline shook her head and buried her face in Clay's leg. He put his hand on her shoulder. "You said you were going to pet a horse today. How about I lift you up? I'll hold you while you do it. That way you won't be afraid."

"No," she said, her voice muffled. "I changed my mind."

It wouldn't do any good to try to force her. "Okay, honey. You can go with Miss Eden back to the ranch house."

"Don't want her. You take me."

Eden's eyes darkened, and he knew she was hurt by the child's behavior. "Okay. But Miss Eden is coming with us."

The three of them walked across the yard toward the house as an older blue truck hauling a horse trailer turned between the fence posts by the road. He stopped and watched the rust bucket approach. "There's a horse in the back," he said.

A young woman got out while the dust from the truck tires was still settling. She wore a petulant expression. Her boots were finely tooled leather, and the cowboy hat she wore looked new too. She stalked to the back of the trailer and threw open the door, then stood looking at them with her hands on her hips.

"Well?" she demanded. "Come get this old bag of bones."

He had to pry Madeline's hand loose from his. "Stay here," he said, nudging her toward Eden.

When he reached the woman, he saw an old horse inside the trailer. Black. The animal's head hung down and there were several sores on its legs. Flies buzzed around the broken skin. Poor thing. "Can I help you?" he asked the woman.

She gave him a haughty stare. "Isn't this the place that takes horses?"

"You're donating him to Bluebird?"

"It's either that or the rendering plant." She grabbed the animal's reins roughly.

"Let me," Clay said. When she shrugged and moved out of the way, he quieted the horse with a soft word and a gentle touch, then led it from the trailer to the gravel. People like this should never own an animal. He clamped his lips against the words he wanted to say.

"He's all yours," she said, striding toward the truck.

"You have a bill of sale or something?" he asked.

She stopped and turned. "You paying for him?"

"No, but I imagine Rick will need proof of ownership."

Her avaricious expression changed to boredom. "I'll sign off on him, then. Just don't expect me to pay for his keep or anything." She reached into the truck and pulled out a paper that she signed and handed over. "Been nice doing business with you."

Clay watched her climb in the truck and pull away. Eden and Madeline joined him. "What a piece of work," he said.

Eden hung back from the horse. "He's been mistreated?"

"Yeah. Looks half starved. And he's got welts on his back from a whip."

"Can we turn her in?"

"I'll have to ask Rick. She should be thrown in jail for cruelty to animals." He glanced down at Madeline and found her staring in fascination at the horse. "I need to name it." He checked the horse over.

Madeline kept her hands behind her back. "That lady was mean to him?"

"Yes. But he has a new home here. No one will be mean to him. We'll make sure he gets lots of food and love. He might like a pat to let him know you like him."

Tentatively, she held out her hand. The horse backed up a few steps, then put his head down. She gave his nose a quick pat. "He likes it!"

Clay grinned. "He sure does. I think you should name him. It's a boy horse."

"His name is Tornado," Madeline said. "He's the same color."

She had a point. The horse was as black as yesterday's storm. "Tornado it is. You're going to have to take charge of him, Maddie. He needs a friend."

She smiled and stepped closer. "Can I feed him?"

"I doubt he'd let anyone else do it. He knows a friend when he sees her." And the horse did seem to know Maddie meant him no harm. He bumped his nose on the little girl's shoulder, and she giggled, then patted him again.

She had a bright smile when she turned back toward the house. "I'm going to tell the other girls," she said.

Clay watched her run up the steps and disappear into the house. "Want to pet him?" he asked Eden.

She hesitated, then touched the horse's nose. Her eyes registered wonder. "It's so soft. Will he bite?"

He shook his head. "He's just glad someone cares." His heart swelled as she murmured soft words to the poor animal. There was so much tenderness in her now that she was dropping her guard.

29

Eden pulled the sheets from the beds in the bunkhouse. Though laundry wasn't normally her job, she liked to help out Tepin by at least getting the stuff into a pile. Nancy and Omar were supposed to show up sometime this morning. Too much to do today.

She paused and glanced at the phone. God had been prompting her to call Kent lately. He deserved that much. She picked up the phone and dialed Kent's cell phone number. When she got his secretary, she identified herself and was put through.

"Eden?"

Her stomach clenched at the eagerness in his voice. "I hope I'm not bothering you."

"Never," he said. "How's it going down there?"

She wetted her lips. "Good, really good. Um, that's why I'm calling. We've identified Brianna."

"Wonderful news." Caution entered his tone.

"The best," she said. "Clay and I have been talking . . ."

"And you're going to try to make it work," he finished for her.

"Well, yes." Would it be rubbing salt in the wound for her to tell him that she loved Clay?

"I could tell when you saw him that you still loved him. I've been expecting this, Eden. Don't feel bad, honey. My heart is only cracked a little. It's not broken."

Inexplicable tears burned her eyes. "You're a good man, Kent Huston."

"Too bad there's no demand for good men," he said with a chuckle. "If you ever need anything, let me know. I'll always be your friend."

It was all she could do to say good-bye and hang up. Though the call had been difficult, she felt lighter, freer, as she went back to her tasks.

Her iPhone dinged and she glanced at the screen to read her text message. *On my way. Meet me in 10 minutes at your husband's property. Be ready with the flash drive.*

Santiago was coming. He'd given her no time to prepare. Dropping the laundry, she called Julia and told her what was happening. The judge promised to mobilize the Border Patrol at the abandoned house as quickly as she could. Would it be enough? Eden suspected Santiago would show up with plenty of firepower.

She called his number. When he answered, she didn't wait for him to put her off. "I can't get to the property by then."

"Ten minutes, Eden. I'm bringing the last picture I had. Be there with that flash drive or you won't like the consequences."

He ended the call. She ran to the door and scanned the yard for Clay. He was watching Rick and Buzz working with the girls on their horseback riding. When she shouted his name and gestured, he jogged from the back paddock to the bunkhouse.

"What's wrong?" he asked when he reached her.

She tried to maintain her composure, but her pulse was knocking on her ribs. "Santiago wants to meet at your property. We only have ten minutes."

"My house? How did he even know about it?"

"I have a feeling he's much more powerful than we know. He'll be there in ten minutes!"

He fell into step beside her. "That's barely enough time to get there. Did you call Julia?"

She nodded and rushed toward the truck. "She's supposed to be getting Border Patrol out there, but I'm not sure they'll arrive in time to do anything."

She stopped when a familiar silver Lexus rolled up the drive. "Oh no, not now. Mom is here. We don't have time for this. You deal with her and I'll tell Allie what's going on." She rushed for the house and told Allie they had to run an errand and would be back.

Clay was waiting in the truck when she got back. The Lexus was rolling away down the drive. It turned left at the road and accelerated away. "What did you tell her?"

"That we had an errand to run. I suggested she go get coffee in town."

Eden climbed into the truck and fastened her seat belt. "I have a bad feeling about this. It's much too rushed. Something is going to go wrong. Why couldn't he just take the drive and leave us alone? He could trust us a little."

"Calm down, honey." He opened the compartment between them and withdrew a gun.

"Where'd you get that?" The sight of the black metal tightened her chest.

"I borrowed it from Rick."

"Does he know what's happening with my dad?"

"Yeah, I told him."

"I wish you wouldn't take that."

His expression went grim. "We're not going into this with no protection."

She said no more but clutched the grip on the door as they sped toward their destination. She prayed as the truck barreled over the potholes.

The turnoff to the dead-end road was just ahead. Clay pulled the truck to the side of the road. "See that house?" he said, indicating a low-slung ranch home. It was stucco and had a swing set in the side yard. "I want you to wait there for me."

She stared at him, unable to believe he would even ask her to leave. "I'm going with you."

"Eden, I don't have time to argue with you. I want you to wait here for me. Please. I can't have you walking into a dangerous situation. Brianna needs a mother."

"She needs a father too!"

He set his jaw. "And what happens to her if your father shows up with guns blazing and wipes us both out just to make sure we don't do something with any copies we've made? She'll stay in foster care, that's what. And I'm not ready for that to happen."

She wasn't either. "He's not going to shoot me."

"One of his thugs nearly burned you up."

She bit her lip, knowing he was right. The situation was fraught with uncertainty. There had been no time to negotiate a peaceful outcome. There would surely be bullets flying. "I'll call him back and tell him this won't work. That he can send his henchman to pick up the flash drive instead."

"I don't believe you'll be safe until he and his people are behind bars. There is more going on than we know. He's unable to control one of his guys."

"Escalating the situation won't change that."

"We might bring down an empire today." He leaned across and shoved open her door. "If I have to carry you to the porch kicking and screaming, I will."

She could tell by his face he was serious. Every cell in her body shouted for her to stay put, but she unbuckled her seat belt and slid out of the car. "I will never forgive you if you get yourself killed, Clay Larson."

"I'll try to stay alive, Angel. Pray for me."

She slammed the door with all her might and watched as he pulled away. She stayed where she was until he turned and disappeared in a cloud of dust around the curve. The derelict house wasn't far. She could walk there in ten minutes. But should she?

What if her father really was waiting with guns? She'd feel better if she knew the Border Patrol was stationed around the property. Julia would know. Pulling out her phone, she called the judge, who answered on the second ring.

"Eden, have you arrived?"

Eden paced along the side of the road. "Clay made me get out and he's gone on ahead. Is the Border Patrol there?"

"We got lucky. Two agents were in the area and hightailed it over to hide in the barn. As far as I know, they're there now."

Her stomach clenched. "Only two?"

"There are more coming. But they won't get there for another fifteen minutes. I'd hoped you'd be able to delay your father."

"Clay didn't want both of us in danger because of Brianna."

Julia grunted in agreement. "I didn't think about that. He's right. You stay put and let him handle it."

"Where are you?" Eden asked.

"At the courthouse, ready to throw them in jail."

"Call me when you hear anything," Eden said. She ended the call and dropped the phone back into her purse. She automatically stepped off the side of the road when a car approached.

Her heart sank when she recognized her father in the passenger seat. And three other men in the car with him. There was no chance to hide. They'd already seen her. The car slowed, then stopped beside her. The tinted passenger window rolled down.

Santiago's face was impassive as he looked her over. She could see her appearance here had thrown him off his expectations. "Father," she said.

"I told you that I doubt that relationship. Has your vehicle broken down?" He stared over her shoulder at the house behind her.

There was no car in the driveway so she couldn't confirm his guess. "No. My husband was unwilling to allow me to go. He was afraid you might harm me. He has the flash drive for you."

There was a flicker of his lids, then, "Get in."

The man on the passenger side behind her father opened the door, then slid over. She had no choice but to slide into the backseat. Her pulse throbbed in her throat. What was he going to do to her? The men all had guns. This didn't look good. If she'd just done what

Clay asked, she would have been up at the neighbor's house. Santiago wouldn't have seen her.

The car pulled back onto the road as soon as she shut the door. The thick silence weighed her down. She wondered how she could get a message to Clay or Julia, but the man beside her would take her phone the minute she dug it out.

The car turned onto the dirt road. Moments later Clay's old family house was in sight. His black truck was there. Behind it was a silver Lexus.

"Whose car is that?" Santiago asked, his voice sharp.

"My mother's," Eden admitted. "I don't know why she's here."

The man grunted. "What does she want?"

"I thought maybe you knew. She's married to your brother."

"I have seen neither one of them in ten years. I would have preferred to keep it that way. Though I did appreciate her call the other day."

Was that his teeth grinding? Did he hate them that much?

"Park here," Santiago said at the end of the driveway. "I do not like the smell of this. What did you see when you examined the property, Carlos?"

The man beside Eden shrugged. "It has been abandoned for many years. Other than squatters in the barn, there was no one here this morning."

"Very well. Drive in."

The driver turned into the lane and parked behind Clay's truck. Half expecting Carlos to forbid it, Eden opened her door and got out. Clay straightened from where he had been leaning at her mother's car. He froze when he saw Eden with her father.

Eden's mother climbed out of the car and stood watching Santiago. A moment later Omar did the same.

"Mom, what are you doing here?" Eden asked.

Nancy walked to the end of her car. "I knew something was going on so we followed Clay's truck. We suspected we would find Hector here."

"What's going on?" Clay asked.

"I think I should be asking that," Santiago said, slamming the door behind him. "I arrive for a friendly exchange and find this *puta* here."

Eden's mother didn't react to the derogatory term. She had eyes for no one but Hector. "Hello, Hector," she said. "It's good to see you."

He spat in the dirt, then glanced at his brother. "Omar, I would have expected you to have more sense than this."

"You owe us, Hector. Every other attempt to collect has failed. My wife didn't have to tell you that these two have incriminating pictures of you. You should show some gratitude and pay your debts."

"I owe you nothing." Hector motioned to his men. "Guard them while Eden and I conduct our business."

He walked back toward the barn. Eden and Clay followed. At the side of the house, Hector stopped and dug into his pocket. "This is the last photograph I have of your daughter." He held out a picture.

Eden took it and Clay peered over her shoulder. The little girl in the picture appeared to be about two years old. Blond hair. It had obviously darkened since then.

There was not much time to study it before Hector held out his hand. "My property, please."

Clay pulled the flash drive out of his pocket. He dropped the device into the older man's palm. "We're square now. Did you succeed in calling off the person who has been targeting Eden?"

Eden saw his lids flicker before he shuttered his expression. "I am working on it."

"Working on it? What does that mean?" Clay's voice rose.

"It has not been as easy as I had hoped."

Santiago turned to leave, but Clay caught his arm. "I need more assurances than that. Someone nearly killed her, tried to burn her alive! It takes a twisted monster to do something like that. Give me the name. If you can't handle the job, I'll do it myself."

Santiago stared at Clay's hand on his arm, then glanced at his face. "As I said, I am taking care of it. It is not your concern."

"Anything to do with my wife is my concern. You might be fine with walking away from your daughter, but she's my life. I won't let any harm come to her."

Santiago raised an eyebrow. "You persist in calling her my daughter. Perhaps you should ask my brother how he came to be married to her mother."

Eden gaped at him. Surely he didn't mean . . .

"You appear surprised, Eden. Did you not wonder when they came here together?" He pulled out his wallet and removed an old picture. It was creased and stained and showed two young men squinting into the sun. The backdrop was a small village. "Can you tell us apart?"

She studied the picture. "No."

"Neither could your mother. We shared her."

Eden recoiled. She wanted to clap her hands over her ears at such an ugly truth. "You've never had a paternity test?"

He shrugged. "He married her. To the victor go the spoils."

"Why are they here?" Clay asked.

Santiago's expression of annoyance deepened. "You should ask them." He walked away.

Eden glanced at Clay and mouthed, "Where is the Border Patrol?"

Clay shrugged and shook his head. They followed Hector back

to the front of the house, where they found Omar and Eden's mother surrounded by Santiago's henchmen.

Eden's mother clenched her fists. "This is ridiculous, Hector!"

He kept walking toward his car. "What is ridiculous is that you expect me to cave to your demands. I should dump you both in the desert."

Eden pressed forward to hear. She had to know what this was all about. It might explain why her mother had come back into her life after all this time.

Clay restrained her. "Don't get too close," he whispered.

"Half the business is mine," Omar yelled at Hector's departing back. "I demand an equal share. It's what our father wished."

Hector turned with a stony expression on his face. "Both of you destroyed my wife. When I washed my hands of you, it was for all time."

What did he mean? Eden doubted he meant that they had actually murdered her. She watched the way her mother took a step back and dropped her head. Omar seemed to bear no shame.

"She deserved to know the truth," Omar said.

"You sent her a photo of a child that may even be your own. All in a petty fit of revenge when you did not get your way."

"How was I to know she would go berserk?" Omar shot back.

"She was fragile, hurt. You knew this woman"—he pointed at Eden's mother—"meant nothing to me."

The history these three shared was becoming clear to Eden. Her picture as a child must have been the thing that had cost Hector his wife. No wonder he had so little regard for her. She should feel blessed that he had let her live. So far.

30

Where was the Border Patrol? Clay could only assume they were remaining hidden until reinforcements came. Eden looked shell-shocked. Hector was walking away. A few more seconds and it was going to be too late.

"Hey!" he shouted.

Hector stopped and turned back toward him. "What now, boy?"

"I want your word that no harm will come to my wife."

"We have been over that. I will do my best."

Was that a sound from the barn? Clay wanted to push Eden to safety somewhere, but there was no shelter. No tree, no lawn chair, nothing but open yard. The house was too far and there was no door on this side. The growl of an engine came in the distance, then an SUV came careening up the dirt road with clouds of dust spewing from its tires. A van was right behind it.

"Ambush!" Hector shouted. He grabbed Eden's mother and, using her as a shield, propelled her toward his car. "Go, go!" he shouted to his men.

But it was too late. The vehicles blocked the lane, and two agents brandishing guns erupted from the barn. Doors slammed as men poured from the SUV and the van. Santiago's men brought their guns up. When the first shots were fired, Clay dived for his wife. His weight bore her to the ground and he covered her with his body. She didn't struggle, and he could hear her breathing in his ear, a frantic gasping.

"Were you hit?" he asked.

"No." Her arms came around his waist as more gunfire rocketed around them. "Can you see if he's been shot? Or my mother?"

Clay raised his head cautiously as the shots tapered off. "I don't see anyone on the ground except the driver. They're handcuffing Hector. I don't see your mom or Omar."

When the men were all in custody, he rolled off Eden and got up, then helped her to her feet. Santiago's glare held menace when he spotted them. Clay's gut clenched at the hate in his face.

Hector's wrists were cuffed behind him, but he jerked away from the grip of the agent and took a couple of steps toward them. "You will pay for this. Enjoy your wife while you can. She will not be alive for long."

The agent grabbed his arm again and hustled him to the back of the waiting van. The other men were shoved into the vehicle as well. A Border Patrol agent walked toward Clay and Eden.

"Everyone okay?" he asked.

"We're uninjured," Clay said. "I wasn't sure you were going to get here in time. Good work." But he felt queasy when he remembered Santiago's words. "When you question him, see if you can get him to tell you who has made several attempts on my wife's life."

"I'll do that," the agent said. "These guys are snakes. Dispose of one and a dozen more show up." He tipped his hat. "Appreciate your help, ma'am. We've been trying to get him for a long time."

Clay glanced to where Eden's mother stood with Omar. "You got anything on Omar Santiago? That's him over there."

The agent frowned. "Santiago's brother?"

"Yeah, that's him."

"There is no warrant out for his arrest. If he's been involved in this, he's kept a low profile. We'll be sure to question him and Hector both, though."

Eden's mother came running up. "Eden, please tell me you had nothing to do with this ambush." Her mouth was twisted and tight, and angry tears stood in her eyes.

"He had to be taken off the streets, Mom," Eden said. "And he sent someone after me. Someone who has tried to kill me."

Her mother's eyes widened. "You did set this up! I can't believe it."

Clay stepped in. "What did you expect her to do? Look away while this guy destroyed lives and ruined kids?"

"But he's her father!"

Eden's chin came up. "He says it's more likely Omar is my father. Is that true?"

Her mother glanced away. "That's a lie," she said, but her voice lacked conviction. "How could you do this to your own family? I'm disappointed in you."

Eden laughed derisively. "My family. You used me to get to Hector. You didn't come back because you loved me and wanted to make amends. You thought Hector would agree to see me, and you could contact him that way."

Her mother met her gaze. "I did no such thing!"

But Clay saw the truth in her eyes. Eden was right. This pair had used his wife. "Haven't you put her through enough? Did you have to hurt her like this?"

"How has this hurt her? She's fine. Not a scratch."

"I was actually beginning to believe you," Eden said softly. "I thought you'd really had a change of heart, maybe even found God or something. I believed you weren't the same woman who left me on my own. Now I find that I was just a tool."

Clay pointed to the van. "And according to Hector, this isn't the first time you've used her. What was all that about his wife?"

Her mother started to walk away. "This is no concern of yours."

Clay caught her arm and turned her around to face them. "Let's have the truth."

In the harsh light her mother looked older, drained. "Hector broke off ties with Omar when Omar told him we were going to marry. They argued. Hector said some hateful things about me."

"Like maybe the fact you weren't welcome in the Santiago family?" Eden asked.

"Yes. He called me names. We were desperate, though. Neither of us had a job, and we needed money. I thought maybe his wife would make him support his daughter at least."

The woman's lies took Clay's breath away. "But you'd already abandoned Eden by then."

The woman had the decency to blush. "Else didn't know that. We thought she would make Hector do his duty."

Eden shook her head. "No, you wanted revenge. You wanted to hurt Hector."

Her mother pressed her lips together. "He's skated through life without a thought for other people. It's about time he paid for some of his sins."

There was no getting through to this woman. She was blind to her warped character. "So you told his wife. What happened?"

"The silly woman was hysterical. From what I heard, she took some pills and overdosed. To this day, no one knows if it was accidental or deliberate."

"She died?"

"I have heard she lived but went a little crazy. I'm not sure, though."

The poor woman. Destroyed by this pair. "I don't ever want you to contact us again," Clay said. "Let's go, Eden."

❄

The agents were gone, leaving only dust in their wake. The acrid taste of betrayal clung to Eden's tongue. She stood with Clay's arm around her in front of the abandoned house. The wind rolled two tumbleweeds past their feet.

"It's over, honey," Clay said. "We'll go on from here. We have each other and Brianna."

The love in his eyes brought a lump to her throat. "I'm clinging to that. It will take me a few minutes to come to grips with everything she's done." She glanced back at the house. "Can we look at it in the daylight?"

His grin came, tenderness in the curve of it. "Let me make sure there are no snakes in our path."

They went to the door. He kicked the pile of weeds out of the way, then shoved the door open. Sunlight streamed into the open courtyard between the outer entrance and the house. There were more tumbleweeds in the corners, but the hand-painted Mexican tiles on the ground were untouched. Their colors glowed in the sunshine.

"It's lovely!" She stepped onto the tile behind him. A mural was still intact on the back wall of the house. Eden studied the scene of cacti and distant mountains. Warm terra-cotta-colored paint on the other walls made her feel at home. Dead rose branches overran the trellis that covered a seating area. "Who painted this? I love it."

He stood examining the space with her. "I did. It was one of my early teenage attempts at art."

"It's really good." She pointed to the other walls. "You could do some other murals there. Ones of the mountains." She went to the French doors on the right wall. "Where does this lead?"

"Into the dining room." He opened the door and led her into the house. "Looks okay," he said.

She followed him into a huge room flanked with floor-to-ceiling windows. The light had a quality that lifted her spirits. She could see them living here. Brianna playing with her toys on a rug that warmed the tile. On one end of the room was the kitchen. It was still decked out in the eighties style, just like when it was built. Dust and cobwebs covered the counters and cabinets, but the layout and structure attracted her. There was a beehive chimney over the stove. In her mind's eye, she could see a new kitchen with granite counters and cherrywood cabinets.

"How many bedrooms?" she asked.

"You won't believe it. Six. And six bathrooms."

She gaped. "Why so many? There were only three of you kids, right?"

He nodded. "Mom wanted room for company, and she liked to

sew, so one room was set up as her craft space. It was a great house to grow up in." He took her hand. "Let me show you our room."

Our room. Eden liked the sound of that. They could make a home here with Brianna. She could hear her daughter's laughter in this place. And any other children who might come along too. She let Clay lead her to a wing that had several rooms sprouting off of it. She peeked in as she passed and saw two generous bedrooms and several bathrooms.

"The master is at the end of the hall," Clay said.

The door was closed, and he pushed it open to reveal a huge room with fifteen-foot-high ceilings. Clerestory windows illuminated the space. Eden wandered the room and exclaimed over the huge bathroom with a separate shower and soaking bathtub. The walk-in closet was as large as their bedroom back at the bunkhouse.

"I never expected anything so grand," she said.

His grin widened. "Only the best for the love of my life."

She realized the tension she'd felt was gone, washed away by dreaming of the future with this man she loved so much. "Let's see the rest."

By the time she'd seen the five bedrooms in the wing at the other end of the house, she was ready to move in. "How long do you think it would take to get it ready?"

"Depends on what all we want to do. We'll have to get it cleaned, a new roof for sure."

"A new kitchen," she said. "The bathrooms are fine. They just need to be cleaned." The expensive Mexican tile and hand-painted sinks were still in good condition in all the bathrooms. "This place is like a small village. The three of us will have trouble finding one another."

"I can find you anywhere," he said, taking her in his arms. "You can run and hide, but it will do you no good. You belong with me."

"It's the only place I want to be," she said, nestling against him.

They would fill this house with love and laughter again. "What time is it?" she asked. It felt like two days since they'd left the ranch.

He glanced at his watch. "Nearly noon. Sister Marjo should be getting to the ranch soon. We'd better go."

31

SITTING HERE WITH CLAY, IT WAS HARD FOR EDEN TO REMEMBER THAT A FEW HOURS AGO they feared for their lives. It was all over now. The judge had called to report that one of Santiago's lackeys was beginning to talk. Julia hoped to have several branches of Santiago's empire cleanly amputated in another day or two.

Eden glanced at her watch, then at Clay, who was on the porch swing with her. "She's late." She was enjoying resting in the circle of his arm. The girls played with Frisbees in the front yard.

He hugged her. "Only forty-five minutes. Be patient. We're in the boonies. It takes awhile to get here from Austin."

Allie stepped from the house. "Lunch, girls!" She held the door open while the children scampered inside. "Still not here?" she asked.

Eden nearly groaned. "Where is she?"

Allie's smile faded as she glanced at her watch. "She said she thought she'd be no later than noon. I hope her car didn't break down."

The phone rang from inside. Eden had a feeling it was going to be bad news. Her stomach muscles clenched when, a few moments later, Allie returned with a grim expression.

"What is it?"

"That was the sheriff. He found Sister Marjo's car abandoned off the road. There's no sign of her."

Clay lurched to his feet. "She had an accident and tried to walk for help?"

"Maybe. It appears that someone sideswiped her. The driver's door was hanging open like she got out in a hurry. He's got some deputies out looking for her now."

"We should help too," Clay said.

Allie nodded. "Maybe on horseback. Rick can decide. There's lots of desert to cover."

That plan ruled out Eden. No way she was getting in a saddle. "What else can we do?"

Allie glanced at her with an intent expression. "Pray."

"I have been." And God had been so faithful. Little by little, he had filled Eden's life with hope. She'd been afraid to allow herself to dream, but God had given her all she could possibly desire.

Clay rushed off to the barn to fetch Rick. Both men returned leading saddled horses. Eden watched them mount up.

"I want to go too," Allie said.

"It's brutally hot out there today," Rick said. "I'd rather you stay home. In your condition."

Eden glanced at Allie and saw a flush running up her neck. "Condition?"

"I'm pregnant," Allie said. "I suppose I'd better stay home. But I don't want to."

Rick dropped a kiss on her lips. "We'll find her. Try not to worry. And pray."

"We will."

The men mounted their horses and rode off down the drive. "Congratulations," Eden said. "When is the baby due?"

Allie smiled. "Not for five months yet. I'm not even showing. Betsy is hoping for a girl. Matthew wants a brother, of course."

Eden found her own hand had wandered to her belly. She remembered carrying Brianna. Then she'd been young and scared. What would it be like to have another baby with Clay now that the barriers between them were finally down?

She forced her thoughts back to the present. "We might as well make sure the girls are eating," Eden said.

Clay settled in his saddle. "Would you mind shutting the barn door?" he asked Eden. "I just realized we left it open."

"Sure." She glanced at Allie. "You want to check on the girls? I'll shut the door."

"Sure."

Allie headed toward the house. Eden had shut the door and turned to leave when a voice from inside the barn stopped her.

"Eden," the distorted voice whispered. "I have her."

She wanted to run, but she stepped closer to the barn. "You have who?" But she was afraid she knew. "Sister Marjo?" Who was on the other side of this wall?

"Only you can save her."

A window was nearly at eye level. She stared into the barn, but the brilliant sunlight turned the glass into a mirror and she could see nothing. "How?"

"Leave Bluebird. Today. Right now. Clay's truck is outside. His keys are in it. All you have to do is get in and drive away. I'll let the nun go."

"Did you hurt her?"

"Not yet."

The implied threat made her swallow hard. "She's done nothing to you."

"Oh, but she intended to. I had to stop her."

She doubted she could trust this guy. "How do I know that you'll turn her loose?"

"You have my word."

"The word of a kidnapper? That's hardly any guarantee."

"Brianna is next. Do you want their blood on your hands?"

She shuddered at the mental image. What could she do? If only she could summon help. Someone could sneak into the barn and find out who was threatening her. But even if she yelled for help, Allie wouldn't get here in time. Eden could run in the front of the barn, but the man was likely to escape out the back.

"What's it going to be, Eden? Your choice."

"Who are you?"

"You should know."

The voice was distant now, as though the man had moved away from the wall. Which way should she go to catch a glimpse of him as he fled? She paused a moment, then ran for the back of the barn. Nothing. She ran around the side to the front. No one there either. Did she dare go inside? She glanced at the corral and saw Buzz pulling a saddle from a horse.

"Buzz!" She waved frantically, and he dropped the saddle on the top rail of the fence and joined her.

"Yes, ma'am?"

"There's someone in the barn, threatening me. Will you go inside with me?"

He pushed his hat to the back of his head. "Ain't no one, Miss Eden. I was just in there."

She grabbed his arm and tugged him toward the barn door. "It's the person who tried to kill me, Buzz!"

He quit resisting her. "I'll get him, Miss Eden!" Detaching his arm from her grip, he stepped inside the barn's shadows.

She hesitated outside, then followed him. The darkness was an adjustment after the brilliance of the day outside. It took a moment to see clearly. She sniffed to see if the guy's cologne perfumed the air but smelled only hay and horse. Buzz was cautiously checking out the stalls. He shook his head when he saw her in the doorway.

"The haymow?" she asked.

He shrugged, then climbed the ladder to the haymow. While he searched there, she went to where the man must have stood while he was talking to her. The tack hung on nails, and metal cans of feed lined the area. Staring hard, she thought she saw the imprint of where he'd stood. But there was no other sign that he'd been here.

Buzz's feet appeared from the haymow as he backed down the ladder. He shook his head. "No one here, ma'am."

She shivered as she realized she was no closer to identifying the kidnapper. And Clay was out there looking too. He needed to be warned. Whoever this guy was, when he learned that Hector had been arrested, his venom would increase.

※

By dark the men had to give up. The moonless night was too black to see tracks or even the ground from their perches on their horses. Clay didn't want to admit defeat, but he had no choice. Eden would be worried as well. Lacie would have to have heard about it by now too, poor kid. Eden had left a message on his voice mail, but he'd been riding at the time and lost the signal before the message could play.

His spirits were dragging by the time he dismounted at the barn. One of the stable hands grabbed the reins of both horses and led them off to be curried. Clay's belly rumbled and he realized he hadn't eaten since breakfast. It was now nine.

"I reckon Allie will have something warm for us," Rick said.

Though he was hungry, Clay wanted to see Eden. "I think I'll have a peanut butter sandwich at the bunkhouse, then hit the hay. See you in the morning."

"Thanks for your help," Rick called, heading to the house.

Clay's steps dragged as he went back to the bunkhouse. The drone of the TV floated from the building. Canned laughter, then a man speaking. Andy Griffith. He stepped inside to the aroma of popcorn. It was like a welcome-home kiss.

He didn't call out Eden's name because he didn't want to wake the girls. After hanging his hat on the hook by the door, he kicked off his boots and padded in his stocking feet to the living room. Eden lay sprawled on the sofa, one arm flung over her head. Lacie was curled in the crook of Eden's arm. Their eyes were closed. So peaceful. When they heard the news that Sister Marjo was still missing, they'd be upset.

He thought about carrying Lacie to the bedroom, but he'd

probably wake them both that way. Rattling around in the kitchen would awaken them too. He grabbed an apple from a bowl on the table and went to the bedroom. Maybe there was something on the news about Sister Marjo.

He fired up his laptop and logged on to the Internet. Nothing on the news. Maybe a nun's disappearance in the desert wasn't newsworthy. Checking his e-mail would help him unwind. He was still wired. He launched Apple Mail and saw he had five messages, all from his superior officer. A new hot spot was breaking out in Africa. He wanted Clay to cut his leave short and come back. Clay's fingers poised on the keys. No time like the present.

He wrote an e-mail telling the captain that he would be on leave until his enlistment ran out.

Now he had to figure out what he wanted to do, but God had led him this far. There was something out there for him. He went to the national park site and studied the openings. Nothing in Big Bend yet, but it would come. He was sure of it.

His camera bag was beside his chair. He hadn't seen the pictures he took of the tornado yet. Plugging his camera into the laptop, he took a look at the shots he'd taken. The first one made him suck in his breath.

"I bet I can sell these," he said. He called up his list of publications and contacts, then returned to the Internet. It was satellite Internet, slow as molasses, but he got the best images sent off to his top-paying contact. He would go through every door the Lord opened. The future would be good as long as he had God and his family.

He shut down the computer, then went to check on Eden. She had rolled to her side. Before he decided what to do, she opened her eyes and gave a sleepy smile.

"Hi, beautiful," he said, sinking to his knees by the sofa.

"You're home," she murmured, stretching her hand toward him. He leaned over to kiss her, but before his lips touched hers, her eyes filled with alarm.

"What's wrong?"

"Did you get my message?" she whispered over Lacie's head.

He shook his head. "No signal most of the time. I saw you'd called, but I figured you were wondering when I was coming home."

She clasped her arms around their daughter. "He was here."

"Who?"

"The kidnapper."

He started to rise. "You saw him?"

"No, he was in the barn. Whispering to me through the wall." She shuddered.

His temper began to simmer. "Did you call for help?" He sat beside her and slipped his arm around his girls.

She nestled against him. "Buzz helped me look for him. I think he must have watched to see which door I went to first, then waited for me to go to the other one before darting out the back."

"What did he say?" As she told him the guy's claim that he had Sister Marjo, his gut twisted. "Did you tell Allie?"

"Of course. She called the sheriff, but there wasn't anything he could do. We have no idea who the guy is. If Hector would cooperate, we could get him. Julia said one of the other men is talking, though."

For the first time in a lot of years, Clay wanted to swear. He'd get his hands on the guy and make sure he never bothered Eden again. "I'm going to check out the barn. Maybe there's a clue you missed."

When he pulled his arm away, she grabbed it. "It's dark out there now, Clay. Buzz and I checked it out. There's nothing."

"I have to see for myself. I'll be right back." He shoved his feet back into his boots, grabbed the flashlight, then went across the yard to the barn.

When he flipped the wall switch, the lights pushed back the shadows but not enough. Eden was right, though he hated to admit it. Even the flashlight didn't help much. In the side of the barn where she said the man must have stood, Clay scuffed the loose straw on the floor with his boot. Nothing but floorboards under there.

He ran his hand along the sill and checked out the tack hanging on the walls. His fingers touched some kind of wire. He traced it up to a tiny speaker just over the window.

"What on earth?" he muttered.

The guy had rigged up some way to talk to her while she stood outside. No wonder she and Buzz hadn't seen him. He'd never been there in the first place.

32

E<small>DEN EXPECTED</small> C<small>LAY BACK FROM THE BARN ANY MINUTE.</small> S<small>HE'D RETURNED</small> L<small>ACIE TO BED</small> and gone into the kitchen to get Clay some dinner. Chili bubbled in the pan on the stove. She stirred it, then shut off the gas. She cut slices of homemade bread and got out the peanut butter.

"Miss Eden?"

She turned to see Madeline rubbing her eyes. "What are you doing up, sweetheart?"

"I heard a voice." The little girl leaned against her leg and moved restlessly. "I have to potty."

"It was just Mr. Clay. He got home. Let's get you back to bed." She took the girl to the bathroom, then tucked her back into her bed. "It's okay."

"Read me a story," Madeline said, pulling the sheet to her chin.

The night always brought a new softness to the child, but her underlying antagonism returned with the morning light.

"You've already had a story." Eden kissed her cheek. "I'll sing you a song, though." She sang the favorite "Amazing Grace" and realized how meaningful the words were to her tonight, how amazing it was that God had brought her daughter back to her.

Madeline was still awake, so Eden caressed her hair and sang two more verses. She could feel the little girl relaxing. Her gaze went to the bed where Lacie lay, but it was too dark to make out the child's features. Soon they'd be a family. The three of them could cuddle in a king-size bed and tell stories and sing songs.

"Mr. Clay was outside my window," Madeline muttered, her eyes already closing.

Eden didn't bother to explain that his voice had carried from the living room. She went back to the kitchen and glanced out the window but saw no sign of Clay. Maybe she could check her e-mail while she was waiting. She went to the bedroom and lifted the lid of Clay's MacBook. It opened to the mail program. She started to click out of it, but the message from Clay's commander was on the screen and she caught the words MIDDLE EAST ASSIGNMENT.

She felt sick as she read the captain's request for Clay to cut short his leave and head out on a new tour of duty. What had been his response? He'd talked about living here, but when it came down to actually walking away from the military, would he do it? She feared the answer was no.

No longer in the mood to check her e-mail, she shut the lid and went back to the kitchen. She picked up the plate of bread she'd cut. As she set the bread on the table, the lights in the kitchen went out.

Every muscle tensed. "Clay?" Did she hear breathing or was it her imagination? She felt along the top of the refrigerator. No flashlight. Of course, Clay had taken it. She didn't even know where to look for another. She stood in the middle of the kitchen with her heart pounding against her ribs.

She had to get help. Cautiously feeling her way, she eased toward the door. When she stepped onto the porch, a breeze lifted her hair. It was just as dark out here. There was no moon, and clouds hid the stars. She couldn't even see the steps to the yard. Her hand found the porch post, then her foot felt the steps drop off. If she didn't fear waking the girls, she'd call out to Clay from here. The thought of walking across the yard in her bare feet was daunting. There could be snakes, scorpions, or tarantulas.

After hesitating, she decided to go back and get her shoes. It wasn't as though the lights being out would awaken the girls. She retreated to the house and felt her way to the living room, where she found her shoes by the sofa. She slid her feet into them and went to the back door again. From here she should see the lights on in the barn. At least she had a direction to aim for. It was pitch black out here. She realized she still clutched the spoon she'd used to stir the chili.

She heard something behind her. "Clay?"

Half turning, she felt a hand on her arm. Then something sweet and moist pressed against her nose and mouth. Struggling, she tried to scream but only succeeded in sucking in more of the chemical on the rag pressed against her face.

Then she was falling into a darkness even more profound.

The flashlight beam probed the darkness only a few feet as Clay walked back toward the house that he knew had to be back here. But there were no lights to guide him. Surely Eden hadn't turned out the lights and gone to bed. Frowning, Clay strode in what he thought was the right direction. He stopped and shined the light higher, then saw the outline of the bunkhouse. Finally. He mounted the steps and poked his head inside.

"Eden?" He flipped the switch on the wall but nothing happened. He caught his breath. A thrown breaker or something deliberate? "Eden?" he called again.

Where was the breaker? He tried to remember. He'd seen it somewhere. In the kitchen maybe? He made his way to the kitchen. The scent of chili hung in the air. He hadn't smelled it when he came in the first time, so Eden must have been warming it for him. He touched the stove and found the pot warm. Where was she? Alarm bells were ringing in his head.

He shined the light around the room. No sign of the breaker box. Wait, wasn't it on the outside wall right here? Letting the flashlight guide his way, he shoved open the screen door and stepped onto the back porch. The electrical box was mounted on the siding. He aimed the light at the panel and opened the cover. All the breakers looked okay. Frowning, he studied them, then stared at the main. It was flipped off. His gut clenched.

He stepped back into the kitchen. "Eden?"

It didn't matter if he awakened the girls now. He had to find his wife. Room by room, he turned on lights and searched. The bright lights did nothing to lift his fear. Not in the living room. Not in the bathroom or their bedroom. In the children's room, they all slept in spite of his voice calling for Eden.

He had to get help from Rick. He went out to the living room and called her name once more, then stepped to the porch, pausing to turn on the porch light. The bulb pushed back the shadows, and he could see the swing and the chairs on the porch. No Eden.

Cupping his hands to his mouth, he called for her again. When there was no answer, he went down the steps to the yard, sweeping the flashlight beam over the area. Something glittered in the weeds. He focused the flashlight. A spoon covered with chili.

"Eden!" He raced to the main house and pounded on the door. When Allie opened it, he looked past her. "Get Rick. Eden's missing."

"Oh no!" She turned and called over her shoulder. "Rick, hurry!"

Rick came through the kitchen door still chewing on his dinner. He swallowed. "What's wrong?"

"I think someone has taken Eden." The words caused cold terror to curl in his belly. "Call the sheriff." He sagged against the door frame and wondered if he would ever see his wife again.

33

EVERY BREATH DRAGGED IN A SICKENINGLY SWEET TASTE. EDEN TRIED TO OPEN HER EYES and couldn't. Another odor penetrated the smell of chloroform. Mouse droppings. She managed to lift her lids and squinted in the dim light.

She lay on a dirty sofa littered with chewed paper and mouse dung. Every instinct told her to spring to her feet, but her muscles refused to obey. The most she could do was to lift her head away from the disgusting mess.

A soft hand touched her arm. "How do you feel, dear?"

She stared into the face of a woman in her late forties or early fifties. Dark hair, sweet smile, compassionate eyes behind wire-rimmed glasses.

286

Eden tried to smile back, but she was sure it was more of a gri-mace. "My head hurts."

The woman helped her sit. "You've been unconscious all night."

Eden's head throbbed so badly she found it hard to think. "Where am I?"

"I'm not sure. In a cabin somewhere in the desert. I can't make out much. The windows are boarded up and there are only tiny cracks to see out. The door is padlocked on the outside."

It all rushed back to Eden. The lights going out. The attack. She wobbled to her feet. "I have to get out of here!" Brianna and the other girls had to be okay. And Clay.

The woman grabbed her arm. "Settle down, honey. Neither of us is going anywhere."

"We're prisoners here?"

The woman shrugged. "The only power over us is what God has allowed. When he's ready to release us, nothing will stand in his way."

Her manner drew Eden. Such confidence and trust calmed her. She wished she was so quick to have faith. "Have you seen our captor?"

"Only vaguely. I could tell little through the windshield as I tried to escape being struck by the truck. I hit my head when I was forced off the road. When I awoke, I was here."

Eden eyed the woman, realizing who she was. The lady wore a black skirt and white blouse that was a little wrinkled. Where was the habit, the wimple? "Forced off the road. You're Sister Marjo?"

"Why, yes. How do you know of me?"

"We were expecting you at Bluebird Ranch. I'm Eden Larson. My husband and I are counselors for the girls."

She took off her glasses and polished them on her skirt. "Then you've been taking care of our Lacie."

"I have."

"What did you see when you were taken?"

"I was drugged in the dark and saw nothing." She could still smell the sickening odor of the chemical and wished she could have a sip of water. "Is there anything to drink?"

"Let me get you water." The nun went to a plastic jug by the door.

A sleeve of cups was beside it. There was also a loaf of bread, a jar of Jif peanut butter, and a can of nuts beside it, but Eden wasn't hungry. Her tongue wanted to stick to the roof of her mouth, so she drank the water greedily when the sister handed her the red cup.

"Did you see him bring me in?" Eden asked after she drained the last drop.

Sister Marjo shook her head. "I was sleeping, then heard the door shut. I found you on the floor just inside the door. I assume he dropped you inside."

"You carried me to the sofa?"

The nun shuddered. "I couldn't let you lie on the floor. Spiders and scorpions."

Eden shivered too. "Thank you."

She peered around the dim space. The one-room cabin held only a battered table, the shredded sofa, and a bank of open cabinets that were empty. The place smelled of dust and disuse. And mouse.

"Where did you sleep?"

"I curled up on the table."

"I'm sorry."

"It was nothing, my dear. I was quite comfortable."

Eden went to the boarded-up window on the wall by the door. She tried to slip her fingers under the board, but she couldn't even get her nail beneath it. "I think these haven't been up long."

Sister Marjo came to stand beside her. "I thought the same. They appear to be quite new."

Eden went to look into the old sink, layered with cobwebs. "If we only had something to pry them up with."

"I looked everywhere. There isn't so much as a spoon."

Eden glanced to the door. "What about the peanut butter? How are you spreading it?"

"I haven't so far. I assume he expects me to use my fingers, but there's no way to wash so I've had a handful of nuts only. I didn't want to contaminate the whole jar of peanut butter with my filthy hands."

No help there, then. "If there was even a stray nail," she said. "It's so dim in here. Can you tell what time of day it is?"

"I believe it's morning. It was still dark a couple of hours ago, then the room began to lighten a bit." She pointed to threads of sunshine coming in through cracks in the walls and the roof. "I don't have a watch."

Eden was already feeling a bit claustrophobic. She wanted out of here. If she had the nerve, she would crawl on her hands and feet along the floor and feel for anything that might be helpful. She slipped off her shoes and swept her stocking foot back and forth across the surface.

When she heard something roll across the floor, she pounced on it. "It's a nail!" she said, holding it aloft. Maybe they'd get out of here yet. She had to live, had to raise her daughter.

⁂

The first board held fast to the wall. Eden's initial high hopes began to fade when she couldn't pry the nail under the second board either. "I need something to hit it with," she said. "Maybe the nut can?"

Sister Marjo ran to get it. "Here you go." She handed it to Eden.

Wedging the tip of the nail under the lip of the board, Eden smacked the head of the nail with the can. "It's under!"

She knocked it again and it slipped a tiny bit more. Little by little she drove the nail under the edge.

"You need something to exert leverage now. The nail is too small to maneuver," Sister Marjo said. She glanced around the room. "Let me see if I can get the table leg off."

She flipped the table on its side and began to wiggle one of the legs. "It's loosening!" The leg clattered to the floor, and she brought it to Eden. "Push on the nail with this."

Eden wedged the edge of the nail into a crack in the end of the table leg and pushed on it. The board seemed to give a little. Patiently she repeated the movement so many times she lost track. "I've got it!" she said when the board came up far enough that she was able to get the table leg under it. One more hard shove and she was able to wrench the board from the window.

Sunlight streamed through the opening. There was no glass in the frame.

The nun peered outside. "Any idea where we are?"

Eden stared too. "Not really. I don't see any other houses or roads around." Even if they got out of here, which direction should they head? "I think I can get the rest of these boards off now."

She grabbed the board she'd removed and used it as a fulcrum to pop the next board loose. Once it was out, she and Sister Marjo might be able to squeeze through the window sideways. But once it was free, she decided to take another board out. Then the entire window was open to the elements. The heat poured in, and she wiped her brow.

"You're very inventive, young lady," the nun said. "Shall we get out of here?"

Eden smiled. "I'll go first so I can help you out." She put on her shoes. With one arm through the window, her shirt snagged on the rough wood, and she heard the material tear. Jerking it free, she managed to get outside the building. She could toss the blouse.

"This should be fun." The sister hiked up her skirt and put one leg through.

Eden grabbed her arm and helped her onto what was left of a front porch. They were free! She turned and stared at the barren hills. There was no sign of civilization in any direction. No sound of tires on pavement. Only the caw of a crow overhead. The wind rustled through the cacti and grasses and made her feel alone and vulnerable. A lone coyote cried somewhere in the distance and the sound raised the hair on the back of her head.

"I can see you're frightened," Sister Marjo said. "Don't be. God sees us."

Eden knew that too, but there was something in the nun's voice that was more confident than a platitude. "He talks to you?"

"Not in audible words, but with impressions." The nun put her hand on her chest. "I feel it here. And we should go that way." She pointed to a distant desert peak.

It wasn't the direction Eden would have picked. They would have to climb that peak. But somehow she trusted the other woman's instincts. "Okay."

She and Sister Marjo set off across the sand. The hillside was nearly covered with cholla cacti, and she knew enough to proceed carefully. Also known as the jumping cactus, just the slightest brush would have left their skin punctured with tiny needles. The sun beat down on their heads, and she hadn't been gone from the cabin more than five minutes before perspiration trickled down her back.

They reached the top of the peak and stopped to catch their breath. The vista from here didn't reveal any clearer idea of their location. "Now what?" she asked. Was she crazy for listening to a nun she didn't even know? One who had never been here before either?

Sister Marjo peered from behind her glasses. She took her time staring in all directions. "That way," she said, indicating they should continue west.

"You're the boss," Eden said.

They trudged down the slope and hit the flat desert, which seemed to stretch out for a hundred miles. Not a single cloud softened the brutality of the sun on their heads. Eden wished she had something to cover her arms. She was already beginning to burn.

"We should have brought our water and food," Sister Marjo said.

Eden nearly groaned. "That was dumb," she agreed. "I'm already getting thirsty. I guess I thought we couldn't be far from help, but I was wrong. There are no ranches, no nothing, as far as I can see."

"God knows where we are, dear girl. 'Where can I go from Your Spirit? Or where can I flee from Your presence? If I ascend into heaven, You are there; if I make my bed in hell, behold, You are there.'" Sister Marjo smiled. "I love the 139th Psalm, don't you?"

A pang of longing clutched Eden's heart. Such confidence, such trust. If the nun's faith were a bucket of water, Eden had only a drop of the same confidence. She wiped her forehead again and glanced around. This desert was similar to hell, but Eden kept the thought to herself. She set her sights on a patch of cactus in the far distance. If they saw nothing by the time they reached that vista, she was turning back for the water.

34

Eden had been gone all night and all day. Clay leaned back in the saddle as he reached the ranch and wiped his forehead with a handkerchief. They'd found no sign of her. The sheriff had everyone in four counties looking for her and the nun.

Allie came rushing down the steps from the porch. "Nothing?"

"Not a sign." He didn't even try to hide his discouragement. "Has anyone else reported in?"

"The sheriff called a few minutes ago. He's found nothing yet. Zeke is still out. Della is taking care of all the kids."

"Are the girls worried?"

"We haven't told them, but I think they suspect something is wrong. They're a little wild today," Allie said. "Brendan is here."

Clay dismounted, and Buzz took the reins, then led the lathered horse away. "Where is he?" Clay started toward the house.

"Getting a horse so he can help with the search. He and Rick are about to go out again. Rick came in half an hour ago to get a fresh mount."

Clay changed direction and followed Allie to the corral, where he found both men saddling horses. "Thanks for coming to help, Brendan," he said.

The other man pulled the cinch on the saddle. "I did some research on that Daniel character you mentioned," he said. "He's been gone from home for two days. No one seems to know where he is."

"You think he's around here, that he took Eden?" *The slimeball.* Clay wanted to strangle him.

"It's a possibility." Brendan stopped and glanced at Clay. "You look as scraggly as a coyote."

"I haven't slept." He'd tried for about an hour, but his eyes had refused to close. "Anything else you've uncovered?"

Brendan flipped the stirrup into place. "The ransom money in that suitcase. You put marked bills in it. Some of it surfaced."

Clay had checked for a while, but the money had never turned up. The last time he'd asked about it had been a year ago. "Where?"

"In Bluebird. About six months ago."

That was a shocker. "Well before we came. But how do you connect Daniel to the money? And Bluebird?"

Brendan finished saddling his horse. He put a boot in the stirrup and vaulted onto the horse. "I'm not. Just relaying what I found out."

Rick mounted his horse. "What about Santiago? Is he giving up any new leads?" He sneezed and the horse reared a bit, but he quieted the animal with a touch.

Brendan leaned back in the saddle. "Still not talking. But I'm sure he's connected, since you believe that his influence caused the attacks on Eden in the first place."

What about Daniel, though? Clay still thought Eden's foster brother had something to do with it.

Rick glanced at his wife. "Rita back from town yet?"

Allie pointed to the truck. "I just saw her pull into the drive. Why?"

"I sent her after cold meds, and I could use a dose before I go out again." He blew his nose, then put his hanky back.

Allie called the cook as she got out of the truck. "Could you bring the medicine, Rita?"

The young woman dug the box out of the bag, along with a bottle of water, and jogged toward them. "I was hoping you guys were here. There was a man asking about Bluebird Ranch when I got gas."

"What did he look like?" Clay asked. Maybe this was their break.

"Young, maybe thirty."

"What did he say?" Rick asked, downing his pills with a gulp of water.

"Asked the way to the ranch. He wanted to know if the Larsons were still here."

"What else can you tell us besides his age?" Clay asked. One of Santiago's henchmen?

Rita shifted the bag to her other hand. "Sandy brown hair. Horn-rimmed glasses. Snappy dresser. I can't remember the last time I saw a man with shoes that shiny."

A picture formed in Clay's mind. Daniel had been missing for two days. Long enough to get here. "Daniel," he said. "I'll bet it's him."

"But if he's just now asking how to get to the ranch, he can't have Eden," Allie said.

"Unless it's a ruse," Brendan said. "I'd better talk to him."

"I'm coming with you," Clay said.

"I don't think either of you will have to go anywhere," Rita said, staring at the drive. "There he is now. I thought he'd likely be right behind me." She started for the truck. "I'll let you handle this. I forgot milk after I heard this guy. I need to run back to town."

Clay watched the blue Chevy, obviously a rental, roll up the drive. He walked toward the vehicle as the door opened and Daniel got out. He hadn't changed any since Clay last saw him five years ago. He still wore his hair slicked back. The plaid button-down shirt and the pants with the sharp crease completed the image of a man consumed with his image.

Daniel's expression was wary as Clay stopped in front of him. "Clay," he said. "I came to see Eden. I . . . I started missing her and realized I don't want her out of my life."

Clay wanted to grab him by the neck. "Like you don't know where she is." He was vaguely aware that Rick, Allie, and Brendan had stopped just behind him.

Daniel's eyes widened. "What are you talking about?"

Clay took a step closer. "Where is she?" he yelled in the guy's face.

Comprehension dawned in Daniel's eyes and he grinned. "You mean she's left you already? I knew it would happen."

Clay clenched his fists. "She didn't leave me. Someone took her." He jabbed his finger in Daniel's chest. "I'm betting that someone is you. The sheriff has a few questions for you."

"What are you talking about?" Daniel held up his hands. "I just got to town." He reached into his pocket and drew out a boarding pass. "See here? I flew into El Paso four hours ago. When did she go missing?"

"Yesterday." He didn't trust anything this guy tried to say. Clay batted Daniel's hand away. "I want to know where she is."

The paper flew from Daniel's hand. Rick caught it in the air. He opened it and stared. "He's telling the truth, Clay. He just got to town. This is his flight information and the rental receipt for the car. There's no way he was here last night when Eden went missing."

"You're serious?" Daniel asked. "Someone really kidnapped Eden?" His voice rose. "What are you doing to find her? She's been gone a whole day!"

※

Her lips were as cracked as the dry riverbed they'd just crossed. Eden wasn't sure how much longer she could keep going. Squinting at the sky, she realized it was midafternoon. They had been out here at least six hours. The point she'd been heading toward was farther than it looked. They should have turned around, but by the time she realized it, they'd gone so far that they decided to keep on. They thought they would find civilization soon. She missed Clay and the girls. The thought they might be in danger haunted her.

"Let's rest a minute," she told Sister Marjo when they reached a spot where limestone cliffs streaked by erosion rose in the sky.

Several caves looked inviting, but she knew better than to crawl inside to escape the sun. They could harbor anything from bats to snakes. And scorpions and tarantulas were almost a given. She dropped onto a nearby stone and wiped her forehead. Her skin felt hot and tight.

Sister Marjo still appeared to be doing all right. Her face was red and her forehead moist, but she had retained her smile. She took off her glasses and polished them on her blouse, then perched them back on her nose before joining Eden on the rock.

"Are you doing all right, beloved?" she asked, putting her hand on Eden's arm.

"Why do you call me *beloved*?" Eden asked. The sun stripped her of the inhibition that had kept that question locked behind her teeth. "You barely know me."

The nun cupped Eden's cheek in her hand. "Because you are God's beloved." She smiled when Eden shook her head. "I see from the hurt in your eyes you don't believe it."

"I know he loves me, even though I don't deserve it. But he sometimes lets his children die." She hadn't meant to say what she was thinking. She didn't want to frighten Sister Marjo, though she was beginning to think the woman would face a saber-toothed tiger with equal equanimity.

The woman dropped her hand. "There is no death for a believer. Not really. There is only this life and eternity waiting."

Eden moved away from a lizard on the rock. "I want to raise my daughter. To love Clay. I don't want to die out here. I've been asking God to let me live." With every step, she'd pleaded with God for help to arrive.

"Jacob wrestled with God in the desert when he saw the ladder with angels ascending and descending. Perhaps he brought you out here to do the same."

"Clay calls me Angel," Eden said.

"Messenger of God," Sister Marjo said.

"I'm far from a messenger from God."

"We are all his messengers. We can choose to trust and let his love shine out of us, or we can let bitterness and disappointment steal our joy. It's your choice."

Eden turned her head to stare at the limestone jutting into the sky. *Choice.* She didn't have any choices. She hadn't chosen to be abandoned. She hadn't chosen to have her daughter kidnapped. And she certainly hadn't chosen to die out here under the blazing sun. In spite of it all, she clung to her trust in God, but fear still coiled in the pit of her stomach. God had her in his hands, but there was no telling whether he might choose to take her to heaven today.

The last time she'd been in church with Clay, the preacher had delivered a message about Job. The minister had said something about trusting God when all seemed lost, because he had a purpose in everything he allowed. She'd wondered what possible purpose God had for allowing them to be deprived of their daughter for five long years.

Her vision became distorted. Was she dehydrated? She blinked as she saw a bird overhead that appeared as large as a pterodactyl. She huddled into a ball, hoping the bird didn't see her. Her head spun as she seemed to shrink to the size of a mouse. It felt as though she were in a vortex, spinning faster and faster. She wanted to fling out her arms and grasp something solid, something she could trust to hold her steady.

I am here.

God's voice wasn't audible, not like the caw of the crow overhead, but she heard it in her heart. He had never gone anywhere. Who was she to question his ways, even if he let her die today? A verse came to mind. *"Where were you when I laid the foundations of the earth?"*

"I can choose to trust," she said aloud. Her voice seemed small and insignificant, but her chest expanded with the words. Trust was hard for her. It always had been, probably because of being abandoned by her mother. She wanted to have the kind of faith Sister Marjo had, the kind Clay had. Her own seemed anemic by comparison.

A hand pressed hers. God's? Or Sister Marjo's? She closed her eyes and toppled to the sand. The grit bit into her cheek, but she couldn't move. Was God looking at her? Seeing her distress the way he'd seen Hagar in the desert? Gradually her head quit spinning, and the nausea in her belly subsided.

She sat up. The sun had sunk a bit lower in the sky. Her sense of having met with God remained. Maybe she would die out here, but if she did, Clay and Brianna would be all right. She'd glimpsed a tiny bit of God's power.

Needing water desperately, she staggered to her feet. Sister Marjo was nowhere to be found. Had the nun wandered off?

"Sister Marjo!" she screamed. The steps in the sand led toward the limestone cliffs, and Eden followed.

She ducked under a rocky bridge and entered a small valley. The sound of water came to her ears. A small spring bubbled by a tall ocotillo. Sister Marjo crouched beside it with her hands cupped together.

"Sister?" Eden said.

The nun looked up. "You're better! I was about to bring you some water," she said.

This place was a tiny bit of paradise in the desert. Eden stumbled past green sage and a few desert wildflowers. "How did you find it?"

"I heard the water."

There'd been no sound out by the rocks, but Eden didn't argue. She knew the woman would claim God had told her. And maybe he had. She stooped and plunged her hands into the pool. Gulping the cool moisture greedily, she drank her fill, and her light-headedness began to subside.

"You're different," Sister Marjo said, her gaze fastened on Eden's face.

Eden met her gaze. Of all the people who would believe she'd had an encounter with God, it was this woman. "I can trust now."

Sister Marjo's face broadened. "You heard God's voice."

"Maybe. I just know I have no control and never have had. I have tried to control everything about my life after my mother abandoned me. I realize now that all I can do is trust God." Oh, how she wanted to see Clay's face again. To tell Lacie she had a mommy and daddy who loved her. But that was not for her to decide.

35

EDEN AND SISTER MARJO SAT BY THE STREAM AND RESTED. EDEN DANGLED HER HAND IN THE water. The only thing lacking was shade, but the cool water made up for it. It was tempting to stay here and wait for someone to find them, but it wasn't going to happen. They'd stumbled in here by accident, so the chances of someone else doing the same were remote. Once they rested, they had to decide what to do.

"Tell me about your family," Sister Marjo said.

Eden smiled. "My husband is an air force photojournalist. He's always off documenting stories of war and combat. He's won a lot of awards."

"Out of the country?"

"Yes, quite often. He loves what he does." That e-mail. Would

302

he leave again soon? "He's talked about getting out of the military and becoming a ranger, but I'm not sure he will do it. He loves the excitement."

"And you have a daughter?"

Eden stared into Sister Marjo's kind eyes. This woman knew her daughter better than anyone. "My daughter was kidnapped when she was six weeks old." She launched into the story and watched the nun's eyes widen and fill with tears.

The sister took a hankie from her sleeve and blew her nose. "I'm so sorry, beloved. You'll see her again someday."

"I already have." Eden leaned forward, unsure how much to tell her. Something about the nun inspired confidence. "We found out one of the girls at the ranch was our Brianna. But we didn't know which one, so we had DNA tests run. We just got the results. Lacie is our Brianna."

The nun gasped and put her hand to her chest. "M-My Lacie? You're saying my Lacie is your daughter?"

"Yes." Eden patted the nun's hand before she leaned back. "So you don't have to worry about her anymore. We want you to stay part of her life, but I'm sure you are happy to know she has a mother and father who love her very much."

Sister Marjo took off her glasses and cleaned them. Her smile didn't return. "I don't know much about DNA tests, Eden. But I do know that what you are saying is impossible."

Eden's eager smile faded. "I don't understand."

The sister replaced her glasses. "The story about her being left on the church steps? It's not the full story. My niece is Lacie's mother."

"Th-That's impossible. The DNA test was very specific. Lacie was the only match." Eden tried to think through how this could be. "Did you see your niece pregnant? Maybe she was involved in the kidnapping and passed Lacie off as her own child."

"No, dear. I delivered the child myself. I saw Lacie's birth with my own two eyes."

Eden shook her head violently. "This doesn't make any sense."

"No. No, it doesn't. But I can assure you that Lacie is no relation to you."

Eden's fatigue fell away. "I have to tell Clay. We must figure this out. I think you and I should go back to the cabin. We can hide and watch to make sure the guy isn't there. He's got to have a vehicle. We can see the direction he came from."

"I think we're close to finding the road," Sister Marjo said. "Just over the hill."

"We've been thinking that for hours." Eden took a last gulp of water and stood, drying her hands on her pants. "But we've just wandered farther and farther. I don't think we can keep that up. Right now we're not lost, but if a wind kicks up we could be. All we have to do is follow our tracks back."

She set off toward the limestone bridge, the exit from their piece of paradise. She headed toward the opening, but a figure ducked under the limestone. It was Rita.

Eden rushed toward her. "Rita! How did you find us?"

The cook was in jeans and a long-sleeved cotton blouse. She had a knapsack slung over one shoulder. "I saw your tracks at the cabin and followed them in the four-wheel drive."

"You went to the cabin first?"

Rita nodded. "I remembered it was out here. When no one could find you, I decided to check it out on my way back from town.

I saw the boards missing and your footprints out across the desert, so I followed."

Eden's hope that Clay was with her vanished. "Is Clay all right? And the girls?"

"Oh yes. Shannon took the girls with her. That big MacGowan place has enough employees to populate an army. Clay is out looking for you."

At least the girls were safe. "I don't suppose you have any food in that sack, do you?" Eden asked. "We're famished."

The young woman smiled. "I sure do." She dropped the satchel to the sand, then knelt and opened it. There was a jar of peanut butter and some bread inside. "This seemed the least likely to spoil," she said.

Jif peanut butter. Just like the food at the cabin. Eden told herself that millions of people used Jif. It meant nothing. "Thanks," she said, taking the jar. "Do you have a knife?"

Rita's smile faded. "I didn't think to bring a knife. Use your finger. Your hands have been in the water."

Eden turned her back to Rita and went toward Sister Marjo. She and the nun exchanged a long glance, and she knew the other woman was as uneasy as she was. Could it be just coincidence, or did Rita have something to do with all of this? She knelt and unscrewed the lid to the Jif, then smeared some on a piece of bread. The rich aroma made her mouth water. She handed the peanut butter and bag of bread to the nun, then licked her finger while Sister Marjo made a sandwich of her own.

Eden took her time eating the peanut butter and bread while she turned the facts around in her mind. The cabin was in the middle of nowhere, yet Rita had gone there to "check it out." It sounded fishy. She leaned over the spring and took a long drink.

She pasted a smile on her face, then stood and turned toward Rita. Her smile froze when Rita's hand came up with a gun in it. "What's this all about?" Eden asked.

"I knew you wouldn't buy the story for long," Rita said, her face calm. "Let's go."

"Where are we going?"

The other woman's smile was cold. "To a funeral. Yours."

❋

There were few hours of daylight left. Clay urged his horse toward the ranch. He had to find Eden before darkness fell again. If he had to endure another night wondering about her fate, he would go crazy. But this horse was done in. He had to have a fresh mount.

When he reached the corral, he dismounted and ran for the house. Maybe some news had come in while he was gone. His cell coverage had been nonexistent out in the desert. "Allie!" he called.

Allie stepped out onto the porch as he neared it. Her eager smile faded when she saw him. "I'd hoped you'd found her."

He sagged against the porch post. "No news?"

"Nothing. Rick and Brendan just went out again, and of course the sheriff and his men are out. Julia came by. She brought you this." She handed over an envelope. "I think it's the court-ordered results on the DNA test. She said they would normally have mailed it, but she knew you were eager so she took a look and ruled on it."

He ripped it open. If they had a court date, he could tell Eden when he saw her. And he would find her. He scanned the paper until a word brought him upright. DENIED. He read it again.

"What's wrong?" Allie asked.

"This says there was no familial match with Lacie."

"That can't be right!"

Clay glanced up at her. "I have a DNA test that says differently. What's the judge trying to pull here? Could she be blocking the proceedings for some reason?"

"The sample collection was supervised and observed," she said. "I don't see how that's possible. Could you have mixed up the samples you sent in?"

"Eden and I did it together. We were very careful."

"You took them to the post office yourself?"

He thought back, then shook his head. "No, Rita took them for me. She was going to town to buy stamps."

Allie frowned. "Speaking of Rita, she never came back from the store, and she left hours ago."

Something screamed for Clay's attention, but he couldn't put his finger on what had made him so uneasy. "Have you tried to call her?"

"Yes, but you know how spotty cell reception is out here."

"Wasn't she just going after milk?"

"So she said." Allie glanced at her watch. "It's been four hours. Something has to be wrong."

Rita had taken the samples to the post office. And it was clear someone had switched the samples. "Could we check out her room?"

"Check her room? I don't understand. She's just late."

"Maybe it's more than that, Allie. I want to see her room."

Allie frowned. "I hate to invade her privacy like that. Maybe she had a flat tire."

Clay wanted to know the truth. Now. "Think about it, Allie. It's clear someone switched those samples. She's the only one who had opportunity."

"But what could be the reason?"

"You tell me. How long has she been employed here?"

Allie's forehead wrinkled. "About six months I think. Yes, that's right. Six months."

"Six months!"

"Does that mean something to you?"

"Brendan said the marked money from the kidnapping attempt showed up in Bluebird six months ago."

She put her hand to her mouth. "Oh, that's right!" Her lips pressed into a straight line. "All right, let's check out her room."

He followed her into the house, nodding at Betsy and her little brother. "Where are the rest of the girls?"

"Shannon came and took them for me. She and Gracie are organizing a sleepover together."

"Good. They shouldn't be witnessing all of this."

Allie stopped at a closed door at the end of the hall. "This is her room." She tried the door and frowned. "It's locked. No one locks stuff here."

"Do you have a key?"

"Somewhere." She thought a moment. "There's a master on the ring by the back door. Wait here." She hurried back the way she'd come.

Clay twisted the knob, but it didn't budge. None of this made sense to him. Unless Rita was in cahoots with the kidnapper. Maybe his girlfriend?

Allie returned with the key ring in her hand, and he stepped out of the way. She fitted the key into the lock and twisted. "Got it." She flipped the switch inside the door.

He followed her into Rita's room. It was smallish, with a double bed covered by a quilt. A dresser and chest of drawers were on either side of the bed. "Let's start here," he said, stepping to the dresser. He rifled through neat stacks of T-shirts, shorts, and socks.

He held up a bottle of men's cologne. "Does she have a boyfriend?"

Allie sniffed it. "Not that I know of. Strange."

He dug farther into the drawer and pulled out a Cowboys T-shirt. "What the heck? I've been looking for this for over a week."

Allie's eyes went wide. "It's yours?"

"Sure is." He dropped the shirt and went to the last drawer. It held high school yearbooks and other documents.

A picture lay on top. He picked it up and stared. Rita looked to be about sixteen in the photo, but he was more interested in the boy who was beside her. "Holy cow, look at this. She's beside Jose Santiago." He flipped it over and read the back. "Rita and Jose Santiago." He stared at Allie, who was rummaging in the drawer. "She's related to Jose!"

Allie was reading something else. "Here's her birth certificate. And passport. It's not from the United States. She's foreign? She gave me citizen documentation before we hired her."

Clay opened the passport. "It's Colombian. It says here her name is Rita Santiago. Jose's sister?"

Allie glanced at the birth certificate. "Her mother was Else Björn. Her father was Hector Santiago!"

The strength went out of his knees and he sank onto a chair. "What if she blamed Eden for her mother's situation?"

Allie nodded. "It makes sense. And her mother was probably blond, so that's why she doesn't look Hispanic. Even if she colored her hair, her skin is fair."

He rubbed his head, then began to flip through the pile of

yearbooks. Rita seemed to have attended several different schools. "Whoa, this is where I went to school," he said when he reached the third one. "This is my senior yearbook."

Allie looked as puzzled as he felt. He flipped through the annual. "I don't even know what I'm looking for."

"There are a couple of sticky tabs." She took the yearbook from him and flipped to the yellow slips of paper. "Is this you?"

He stared at the photography club page. A very young version of himself stood proudly holding an award he'd received for a photo documentary at the zoo. "Sure is."

She squinted at the people in the background. "This young girl looks a little like Rita. Only she's got brown hair in this picture."

Clay studied the picture. "I vaguely remember her. She was three years behind me in school. I noticed her hanging around a lot. My friends said she had a crush on me, but I don't know if it was true or not. I never really spoke to her. She was just a kid. I never even knew her last name."

"Look here." Allie pointed to handwriting on the edge of the page. "'Your words are my food, your breath my wine. You are everything to me.—Sarah Bernhardt,'" she read aloud. "There's an arrow pointing to your face."

He wanted to shudder. "It's a little creepy."

"It's a lot creepy. You don't suppose she's followed you all these years, do you?"

"I think we'd better find out," he said grimly. He took the yearbook from her and tucked it under his arm. "I'd better call the sheriff."

36

THE STENCH OF MOUSE DROPPINGS AND DUST GREETED THEM WHEN RITA TOLD EDEN
to open the door of the cabin. Darkness had fallen by the time they
got back, but the truck headlamps kept them following the footsteps in the sand. Eden had tried to ask her questions, but the woman
had remained silent except for the occasional order to shut up.

Eden stopped just inside the door. "You can't kill me without
telling me why."

Rita grabbed a lantern by the door and thrust it into Sister
Marjo's hands. "Light it," she said, indicating a box of matches on
the floor.

Eden watched the nun fumble with the matches before managing
to get the lantern lit. Did Rita plan to leave them to die here in the

cabin? She seemed to like fire. Eden prayed the woman didn't intend to set the cabin afire.

Sister Marjo adjusted the wick, then held the lantern aloft. "Where shall I put it?"

Rita gestured with the gun. "The table is fine."

"Where are your cohorts?" Eden asked. "Are we waiting for them?"

"He's dead. All because of you." Hatred laced her words, and her eyes spit venom.

"The man in the car?" Eden couldn't figure out the connection.

"You've destroyed my life. First you took Clay. Then you made me lose my mother and my brother."

"The man who drowned in the car was your brother?"

"Yes." Rita shut the door behind her and gestured to the sofa. "Sit. Both of you."

Eden looked at the gun, then at the filthy sofa. There wasn't a lot of choice. Her discarded sweater was still here, so she laid it out and sat on it, perching gingerly on the cushion. Sister Marjo settled beside her as if she didn't even notice the mouse droppings and stains.

None of this made sense to her. Rita's mother and brother? "I don't understand."

"You will," Rita said.

"I'm not to blame for Jose's death," Eden said. "His greed was the cause of his death." It suddenly hit her—Rita had to be her sister unless she and Jose had different fathers.

"Shut up!" The other woman advanced two steps and waved the gun menacingly. "You knocked his car into the river. He didn't have a chance. I don't know what you were trying to do. Didn't you care that you could have drowned your own daughter?"

"It was an accident." Eden eyed the manic light in the woman's eyes. Was she even sane? "I misjudged the distance, and the car skidded."

Rita's eyes narrowed. "I was watching. It was deliberate."

"Why did you take my daughter? You didn't even ask for that much ransom."

"It was never about the money. She should have been mine."

"I don't understand."

"Clay belongs to me. With you out of the way, we can be the family we were meant to be."

Though nothing she'd said made sense, Eden decided to humor her. "Is that why you lured us here? To kill me?"

The woman smiled and stood taller, almost preening. "I've seen the way Clay looks at me, talks to me. You're blind if you haven't noticed he wants me and not you. He'll be glad when you're out of the way. You were never supposed to come with him."

Eden decided not to discuss the woman's delusions about Clay for now. "How is this my fault?"

The woman dug in her pocket and pulled out a tattered picture of a family. "We were so happy before you came into our lives." She held it under Eden's nose. "Now one is dead, the other is imprisoned in a mental hospital, and there is only me to avenge them all."

A much younger Hector Santiago stood with his arm around a beautiful blond woman. She had her hand on the shoulder of a girl of about ten with light-brown hair and solemn blue eyes. Rita. Beside her stood a boy about a year or two older. He looked more like his father.

"You're my sister?" Eden asked, unable to look away from the photo. No wonder Santiago had been unable to call Rita off. She was bent on revenge. "Why did you ask for money if you wanted revenge?"

"It was my brother's idea. To lure you out so he could eliminate you for me. But you killed him! I hate you!" Rita aimed the gun at Eden's head.

Sister Marjo leaped between Eden and the gun. "My dear girl, think about what you're doing. Clay is a good man. He'll be torn up with guilt if you do this. You'll lose him forever."

The gun in Rita's hand wavered. Her finger left the trigger. "Why did you have to get involved in this, Sister? This is not your concern."

The nun took a step closer. "I don't believe I had a choice. It was you who ran my car off the road and brought me here."

"Only so you wouldn't tell that Lacie wasn't Brianna. I had no choice." She narrowed her eyes as she stared at the nun. "You told her, didn't you?"

"Yes," Sister Marjo said, still blocking the path to Eden.

Eden tugged at the sister's hand, and the nun sat back down on the sofa. "Why didn't you want me to know?" she asked Rita.

"It was too soon. I needed more time. Once Clay realized the results were wrong, he would have remembered that I was the only one who could have switched the samples. I couldn't let that happen."

The results were wrong. "How do you know Clay? He didn't seem to recognize you." Eden held her breath. Maybe that was the wrong thing to say.

Rita shrugged but her lips tightened. "My hair is a different color. You know how men are. And I've changed since school. But he recognized me all right. That's why he talked to me so often. He didn't want to tell you, though. Not yet."

Rita must have generated these excuses when Clay didn't say anything about knowing her. Eden decided not to follow that train of thought any longer. "Where have you kept Brianna? If she should have belonged to you, why is she being raised by foster parents?"

"Her name is Madeline, not Brianna." Rita's eyes darkened. "It's all my mother's fault," she spat. "She had to go and take an overdose. When she was put in the mental institution, the state took Madeline before I could get out myself. Pushy, nosy people."

Madeline. Her Brianna was Madeline. Eden wanted to live long enough to hold her daughter, to breathe in the scent of her hair.

She soaked in what Rita had said about her mother. Hospitalized. Schizophrenia could run in families. This woman was obviously mentally ill, but Eden wasn't educated about the different illnesses. "Who was the woman who came to see Madeline? Clay met her."

"My mother. I had to stay in the house. She didn't know I was there."

"She called herself Madeline's mother."

Rita shrugged. "She had Madeline for three years while I was— away. She won't be back. I'm sure my father has her stashed somewhere again." She loaded the peanut butter and other items around the room into a sack. "Can't leave any evidence," she said.

Eden's stomach clenched. *Evidence.* Whatever Rita had planned wasn't going to be good.

Rita pointed the gun. "Enough talk. It's time to go."

Eden nodded, trying to maintain an open, interested expression free of condemnation. She had to save Sister Marjo somehow, but there was no reasoning with someone as delusional as Rita.

"Where are we going, dear?" Sister Marjo asked.

Rita smiled. "It has to look like an accident. I know just the place."

⚜

The helicopter rotors were so loud no one could hear a thing. Clay sat in the back with Shannon MacGowan's husband, Jack. Rick was in the front seat with Michael Wayne, who was piloting the bird. Friends of Bluebird Ranch had scoured the desert by land and air, but it was dark now. And they'd seen nothing. Clay had berated himself for hours as they searched for a sign of the truck. Why hadn't he recognized Rita? He'd thought she reminded him of someone but assumed it was an actor, that one who'd played Heidi.

Michael glanced at Rick and made a cutting motion across his throat. They were heading back. Clay wanted to protest, but the chopper was running out of fuel. The helicopter banked and began to circle back the other way.

Was his wife dead? He rejected the thought. She had to be all right. He had to find her. If they went back without her, he would get a horse and go back out. He couldn't rest until she was safe at home again.

Desperate for some clue, Clay pressed his forehead against the window and studied the dark landscape. Was that a light? He stared, willing it to come again. *There.* A dim glimmer, so faint it could have been a reflection of the moon off water. He tapped Michael's shoulder and motioned for him to go down to take a look.

The other man's glance was compassionate, but he held up two fingers, meaning he'd circle for no more than a couple of minutes. The chopper dropped down closer to the desert. All the men pressed their noses to the glass and stared at the dark ground beneath them. Clay knew the others had seen that glimmer when Rick pointed excitedly and Jack nodded.

"Set it down!" Rick yelled over the sound of the rotors.

Michael nodded and eased the helicopter onto its skids. The

tail boom spun around until the cabin faced the light. Clay opened the door and jumped out, keeping his head down. The pulsating air nearly knocked him over. He didn't wait for the other men but headed across the desert to a dark shape that appeared to be a cabin. The light came from an opening in one of the boarded-up windows.

As he neared, he heard the engine winding down on the chopper. The other men would be right behind him. He reached the front door in a few steps and shoved it open. A lantern was set on the table, its wick sputtering. His gaze swept the room, but it was empty. Whoever had been here hadn't been gone long or the lantern would have burned out.

Rick and the other men rushed into the cabin behind him. They stopped and no one said anything for a long moment. "Guess that's it," Michael said.

Clay stepped to the sofa. "I can't figure it out. If this place is inhabited, why does it look like no one has been here in decades?"

Rick snatched up the lantern and held it aloft. "You're right. No one has lived here in years. But this lantern was lit?"

"Yeah." What was that on the sofa? "Bring that light here," Clay said. As Rick neared with the lantern, he realized a navy sweater lay on the cushion. He snatched it up. "This is Eden's!"

"Are you sure?" Rick asked.

"She had it on last night after the sun went down and the air cooled." He held it to his nose. Beyond the smell of the sofa, he caught a whiff of Eden's cologne. "It's hers. She was here. And not long ago." He strode to the door. "Bring that light with you. Let's see if there are tire tracks."

Outside, the darkness was so vast that the lantern cast little light except in its immediate circle. Rick swept it back and forth. "There!" he said, pointing at his feet.

Clay saw it too. "Tread marks." He knelt and put his hand in one, as though it would make him nearer to Eden. "They have to be close. Can we get back in the air and look?"

Michael hesitated. "I've got only an hour's worth of fuel left. I have to head back to my place in no more than half an hour or I won't make it."

Clay stood and brushed the sand from his hands. "Deal."

The men ran for the helicopter. The engine coughed to life and the *whup-whup* of the rotors began to drown out the desert's night sounds. By the time they were airborne, Clay was ready to jump out of his skin. They'd missed Eden and her captor by mere minutes, he was sure. He peered through the window, but the landscape was dark.

He realized the chopper was heading for the road. Tapping Michael on the shoulder, he shook his head and screamed over the noise of the blades. "Go back over the desert. She won't risk driving on the road."

Michael nodded and the helicopter began to bank to the right. As the craft soared low over the desert, Clay saw a moving light. "There it is!" He jabbed at the window, then realized no one had noticed. He smacked Michael and Rick on their arms and pointed. "Down there!"

Rick pointed and the helicopter picked up speed to catch the vehicle. The twin beam headlights on the truck went out.

"She's seen us!" Clay shouted. How could they follow when the night was so black? Before he could ask the question, Rick flicked a switch and lights blazed down to the desert from the helicopter. "There it is!"

Michael nodded, and the chopper dropped lower and sped up

until it was right over the top of the truck. The lights shone into the cab, and he saw Eden's face pressed against the passenger window. Her face set and determined, Rita gripped the steering wheel with both hands. Her teeth were bared. He caught a glimpse of an older woman in the middle. Sister Marjo?

How could they get the truck to stop? There wasn't much fuel left in the helicopter. If Michael put it down in front of the truck, Rita would just go around it and keep on driving. They couldn't force the truck off the road because there was no road.

"Take it down!" he yelled, his mind made up. When Michael complied, Clay thrust open his door and jumped.

37

IF NOT FOR SISTER MARJO, EDEN WOULD HAVE LEAPED FROM THE TRUCK SPEEDING ACROSS
the desert. But she couldn't leave the nun behind. The sound of the
helicopter filled her head. It had to be Michael with Clay and the
other men. Rescue was in sight. She could have clung to that hope if
a madwoman wasn't behind the wheel.

A sudden thump jarred the truck. Eden whipped her head to look
out the back window and saw Clay lying in the bottom of the truck
bed. He got to his hands and feet and his gaze met hers. Seeing him
gave her fresh courage. She had to help, but how? The blinding light
from the helicopter grew dimmer as the chopper rose and fell back.

Rita glanced in the rearview mirror and smiled. "I knew he
couldn't stay away from me."

Eden glanced back and saw Clay crawling toward the window. She unlatched the window and slid it open before Rita could stop her.

"Stop the truck, Rita," he said through the open window. "Let's talk about this."

Rita smiled. "Not just yet, love. I have to take care of these women who are trying to keep us apart. Wait for me at the ranch. I'll be back soon."

"I can't go to the ranch unless you stop."

Rita frowned and shook her head, as though trying to think through the logic. "I guess that's right." She tromped on the brake, and Eden and the nun nearly went flying through the windshield. Eden grabbed the dash and hung on. The truck's rear end slewed in the sand before coming to a stop. Rita switched off the engine. The tick of the motor beginning to cool was loud in the sudden silence.

Eden whipped her head around to make sure Clay was all right. He lay crumpled at the front of the bed. "Clay!" She thrust open her door and jumped out in spite of Rita's grab at her arm.

He stirred when Eden called his name. She put her foot on the tailgate and climbed into the bed. He had to be all right. She reached him and knelt by his head. Her fingers came away wet when she touched his forehead. Blood? It was too dark to see the color of the moisture, but the coppery odor was enough evidence.

She looked up to see Rita bearing down on her. "He's hurt," Eden said.

"Get away from my Clay," Rita said through gritted teeth. "I'll take care of him. You've done enough." She pointed her gun at Eden.

"You nearly killed him!" Eden held her ground. She wasn't leaving her husband.

Clay stirred and moaned. He put his hand to his head, then struggled to sit. "What happened?"

Eden helped him. "I think you hit your head."

"I said get away from him," Rita ordered.

Eden flinched as a loud report came from the gun. A bullet slammed into the truck near her hand. "Okay, I'm leaving."

She scrambled away from Clay. At least Rita wasn't going to hurt him. Once the woman's back was turned, Eden might be able to wrestle the gun away from her.

Rita climbed into the truck and knelt beside Clay. "Can you stand, my darling?"

"I think I need your help," Clay said, his voice weak. "Can you lift me up, Rita? You'll need to put the gun down so I can take your hand."

Eden held her breath. Would the woman fall for it? She watched as Rita hesitated, then stuck the gun in her waistband. She put one arm around Clay's waist and with the other took his arm and draped it around her neck. In a quick movement, Clay reached for the butt of the gun with his free hand and plucked it from her. He wheeled away, and Rita staggered back, then fell against the window of the cab.

"Clay? What are you doing?" She got slowly to her feet.

The gun was in Clay's hand. He backed away, then jumped to the sand. "Get out of the truck, Rita."

She was sobbing. "What are you doing, Clay? I did all of this for you. We can be together, you and me with Madeline. A real family." She sank to her knees, holding herself. Rocking back and forth she began to keen, a noise filled with pain.

In spite of all the woman had done, Eden wanted to go to her and comfort her. She started forward, but Clay's arm shot out.

"Don't," he said. "She's like a venomous snake. The minute you get too close, she'll strike." He nodded to the cab. "How's Sister Marjo?"

"She's fine." Eden sidled along the truck to the cab and glanced into the open door. The lights on the dash were still on.

Sister Marjo sat placidly clutching a tiny New Testament in the wash of interior lights. "Finished, beloved? I didn't want to interfere as the three of you made peace. Though I was praying, of course. God assured me he didn't need my help on this one."

Eden held out her hand. "It's all over. We can go home now." Behind her she heard the sound of running feet. The rest of the rescuers had arrived.

The nun closed her Bible and slipped it into the pocket of her skirt. She accepted Eden's hand and slid off the seat to the sand. "This has been an experience I don't believe I'll ever forget," she said.

Eden hardly knew what to say to that. Kidnapped, imprisoned, lost in the desert, and nearly killed. It had been eventful all right, but not the kind of event she ever wanted to repeat. She and the nun walked to the back of the truck as Rick and Michael approached Rita. Michael spoke in a soothing voice and soon had Rita quieted. She wondered if he'd given her a sedative.

Clay opened his arms, and she ran into them. Home. All that was missing was Madeline.

❋

The small group sat in the main house with a pot of coffee and a partially demolished plate of chocolate chip cookies on the coffee table. The sheriff's eyes were puffy with dark circles, and Eden wondered when he'd last slept. Even Brendan looked a little rumpled and worse for the wear. Daniel sat by Clay as if he was making an attempt to accept what he couldn't change. Eden could hear Sister Marjo on the porch with Lacie. They were singing "Jesus Loves Me."

Eden needed a shower, but first she had to hear what Brendan had to say. "So Rita got out of the mental hospital six months ago," she said, "then planned to eliminate me so she could have Clay." She glanced at her husband sitting beside her on the sofa. "Has anyone talked to her mother?"

"She's in an expensive mental hospital in El Paso," Brendan said. "Paid for by Hector Santiago."

"But she was just here a week or so ago," Clay said.

Brendan nodded. "When Hector said he was working on fixing the problem, I believe he thought his wife was behind it all. He found out she'd been released and had his goons track her down and take her back to the hospital."

"What about Brianna?" Eden asked.

"I sent one of my men to talk to Else. She showed him pictures of Brianna when she was a baby. Rita was holding her like a proud mother. Hang on, I have the picture on my computer." He clicked a few keys, then turned it around for her to see.

Eden stared into the smiling face. No trace of the insanity in those blue eyes. Just proud motherly love. She shuddered. "Anyone seeing her with the baby wouldn't have doubted anything."

"Nope." Brendan shut the computer lid. "From what we can tell, she took good care of the baby, but she had an episode at the grocery store. She lost her temper and overturned a whole aisle of food, screaming and raving. They had her hospitalized for observation.

She was diagnosed as schizophrenic and committed until she was stabilized."

"How old was Brianna when this happened?" Clay asked.

"About two. Her mother cared for the baby after that until she had another episode herself."

"Where have they lived? Not with Hector?" Eden asked.

Brendan shook his head. "Else left him when your mother told her about you. Hector gave her plenty of money and set her up on a ranch just west of here. I think he thought if she lived in a secluded spot, she'd be all right. And she was for a while."

"How old was Rita then?"

"About fifteen. As near as I can tell, she went to school with Clay that one year and became obsessed. When she found out he married her half sister, she had her first episode of mental illness. She was committed for a year, then got out. It was then she decided to get revenge and took Brianna. She appears to have loved the girl. Then she had the episode I mentioned."

Eden leaned more tightly into the safety of Clay's embrace. "We have to talk to Madeline. We're certain, right?"

Brendan nodded. "The picture of Brianna at age two cinched it. I had it compared to pictures of Madeline and it was a match. No doubts at all. The courts will want to do the DNA matching probably, but you can be assured Madeline is your daughter."

"I want to tell her now," Eden said, staring up at Clay.

"All right." His arm dropped away and he rose, offering her his hand.

She took it and they walked to the door. "We'll be praying," Allie called after her.

Eden stopped and turned. "I'll take all the prayers we can get," she said, meaning it. "God is the only one who got me through this." She saw Clay beginning to smile. Her friends too.

"What happened out there in the desert?" Clay asked as they walked back toward the bunkhouse.

"I did a little wrestling," she said. "God won."

38

EDEN AND CLAY STEPPED INTO THE BUNKHOUSE. SHANNON GLANCED UP FROM A BOOK AND smiled. Madeline was settled in the crook of her arm. "The girls are asleep except for Madeline here. She and I have been reading stories. Bible stories."

"The story is finished," Madeline said. She closed the book.

"I'll leave you all alone now." Shannon winked at them, then planted a kiss on the little girl's hair. "Remember what we talked about," she whispered to the child. "Talk to you tomorrow."

When the screen door slammed behind her, Eden glanced at Clay. Who was going to break the news? They hadn't discussed it.

Madeline's eyes were big, as though she was picking up their tension. Eden wondered what Shannon had said to the little girl. There was a new softness in Madeline's face.

Clay cleared his throat. "Miss Eden and I have something to tell you." He sat on the sofa beside her and lifted her to his lap.

"Am I in trouble?"

"Of course not. Why would you think that?"

She shrugged. "Miss Shannon made me stay up. I thought I was going to be punished for being rude to Miss Eden." Her face puckered. "I'm sorry, Miss Eden." She began to cry. "Miss Shannon said God doesn't like me to be disrespectful."

"Honey, it's okay." Eden pulled her onto her lap, and the little girl buried her hot face against Eden's chest. "I thought you were still mad at me about something. Want to tell me about it?"

The child nodded, her face still buried. "I thought you liked India better. I wanted you to love me."

Eden pressed a kiss against Madeline's hair. "I love you so much, honey. We have something very special to tell you, sweetheart. Stop crying and look at me." She pushed Madeline's head away and wiped her face with her palms. "We came here to find you."

Madeline's eyes widened. She swiped at her face. "Find me? Was I lost?"

It amazed Eden that they were here in this place about to tell their daughter the story. *Thank you, God.* She swallowed the lump in her throat. "Yes. Yes, you were very lost. And we were lost without you."

"I'm going to tell you a story about a princess, honey," Clay put in. "Once upon a time there was a king and his queen. They had a baby girl they named Brianna."

"I like that name," Madeline said, her eyes fastened on his face.

"A wicked witch took the baby and told the king and queen that their baby had died."

Madeline's lip came out. "I don't like sad stories." She laid her head on Eden's chest.

"This story has the very best ending," he assured her. "Anyway, when the baby got bigger, the king found out that the wicked witch had lied. Their baby wasn't dead. She'd just been hidden away. All they had to do was find her and they would be a family again."

"Did they find her?"

"They did. We did. *You* are Brianna, Madeline." His voice thickened, and he swallowed hard before continuing. "A long time ago, someone took you away from us, but we found out where you were and came to find you. You are our very own little girl." His eyes were wet. "And we're here to take you home with us."

Madeline's mouth gaped. Eden couldn't stop the tears from flowing. She hugged her daughter to her and kissed her cheek. "We've found you, honey. You're ours and we're never letting you go again."

Madeline's arms crept around her neck. "Is this a real story?"

"It's very real." Eden glanced at Clay and saw his cheeks were wet too.

He embraced them both. "You are our daughter, honey. We've searched the whole earth for you."

"So you're going to adopt me?"

"We don't have to adopt you," Eden said. "I carried you in my tummy."

"For real?"

"Pinkie swear," Eden said, holding up her little finger.

Madeline's tears dried up. "Can I call you Mommy?" She glanced at Clay. "And Daddy?"

"Forever and ever," Clay said. He picked her up and danced around the room with her.

Eden's heart was so full she almost couldn't bear it. She joined Clay and Madeline. He put an arm around her, and the three of them stood in a tight embrace.

"Wait until the other girls hear this story," Madeline said. Her eyes were drooping, and she put her head on Clay's shoulder.

Clay grinned at Eden. "Too much excitement."

"I know the feeling," she whispered. "I'm tired too. But happy. So happy."

His eyes filled, and he kissed her, then walked around the room with Madeline. He hummed a few bars of "Amazing Grace."

The little girl's eyes closed, and her breathing deepened. Eden watched the perfect trust as their daughter slept in her daddy's arms.

"She's out," Eden whispered. She went before them down the hall and opened the bedroom door.

Clay placed the sleeping child into her bed, and they kissed her cheek, then stood in the doorway and watched the sleeping girls before backing out of the room. Eden's heart welled as she looked at the faces of "her" girls. How could she bear to leave them?

Clay put his finger to his lips and led her down the hall. When they reached their room, he shut the door and leaned on it. "There's something else, Eden," he said.

His tone filled her with dread. "I know. I saw the e-mail. You're going out again." She didn't want to be that old Eden. The one who pouted and cried at the thought of being left alone. She had changed. "As long as you come back, we'll be okay."

He shook his head. "That's not it. I already turned in my resignation."

She gasped. "Y-You're not going?"

"Nope. You have to put up with me."

"Then what's the problem?"

"What about the other girls?"

"What do you mean?" His voice was so intense, and she wondered if he felt the same way she did.

"How would you feel about adopting all of them? Except Paige, of course. It wouldn't be fair since she has a family who loves her."

"You mean, we'd have four little girls?" She struggled to wrap her mind around it. It had been a secret dream of hers. Whenever she thought about separating the girls, her mind closed down and all she could see was the six of them around the dinner table together. Playing Candyland. Laughing and loving.

"Could you do it?"

She leaped into his arms and smothered his face with kisses. He reeled around the room and they fell onto the bed. "Yes, yes, yes! I didn't think you'd even consider something this drastic. We'll have a very full house," she warned. "And it will be expensive to raise four kids."

He hugged her close. "Maybe more if the Lord blesses us with another child or two. Maybe a boy this time. Oh, and one other thing."

"You want to adopt the whole world?" She laughed and snuggled closer.

"I want to continue to work here at the ranch. They can't pay much, but we already have enough. Our place isn't far. I could build another dorm there and expand the work here."

Her vision swam as her eyes filled. "I can't think of anything I would like more."

He lowered his lips to hers, and Eden found all thought fleeing. God was giving her paradise.

ACKNOWLEDGMENTS

I JUST CELEBRATED EIGHT YEARS WITH MY THOMAS NELSON TEAM——TRULY MY DREAM team! Publisher Allen Arnold (I call him Superman) changed everything when he came on board. Everyone in the industry loves him—including me! Senior Acquisitions Editor Ami McConnell (my dear friend and cheerleader) has an eye for character and theme like no one I know. I crave her analytical eye and love her heart. She's truly like a daughter to me. Marketing Manager Eric Mullett brings fabulous ideas to the table. Publicist Katie Bond is always willing to listen to my harebrained ideas. Fabulous cover guru Kristen Vasgaard (you so rock!) works hard to create the perfect cover—and does it. And of course I can't forget my other friends who are all part of my amazing fiction family: Natalie Hanemann, Amanda Bostic, Becky Monds, Ashley Schneider, Jodi Hughes, Ruthie Dean, Heather McCulloch, Dean Arvidson, and Kathy Carabajal. I wish I could name all the great folks who work on selling my books through different venues at Thomas Nelson. Hearing "well done" from you all is my motivation every day.

Erin Healy has edited all of my Thomas Nelson books except

one, and she is such an integral part of the team. Her ideas always make the book better, and she's a fabulous writer in her own right. If you haven't read her yet, be sure to pick up *Never Let You Go*, *The Promises She Keeps*, and *The Baker's Wife*.

My agent, Karen Solem, has helped shape my career in many ways, and that includes kicking an idea to the curb when necessary. Thanks, Karen, you're the best!

Writing can be a lonely business, but God has blessed me with great writing friends and critique partners. Hannah Alexander (Cheryl Hodde), Kristin Billerbeck, Diann Hunt, and Denise Hunter make up the Girls Write Out squad (www.GirlsWriteOut.blogspot.com). I couldn't make it through a day without my peeps! Thanks to all of you for the work you do on my behalf, and for your friendship. I had great brainstorming help for this book in Robin Caroll. Thank you, friends!

I'm so grateful for my husband, Dave, who carts me around from city to city, washes towels, and chases down dinner without complaint. As I type this, today is the first day of his retirement. Now he will have more time for those things—and more. Thanks, honey! I couldn't do anything without you. My kids—Dave, Kara (and now Donna and Mark)—and my grandsons, James and Jorden Packer, love and support me in every way possible. Love you guys! Donna and Dave brought me the delight of my life—our little granddaughter, Alexa! This year at Christmas she was interested in watching her Mimi sign copies for her daddy to give away. When I told her that Mimi wrote the books, I'm sure I saw shock in her face. Okay, maybe I'm reading too much into her little two-year-old mind, but she will soon understand what her Mimi does for a living.

Most importantly, I give my thanks to God, who has opened such amazing doors for me and makes the journey a golden one.

READING GROUP GUIDE

1. It's said a child's early experiences shape their personality when they're grown. What experience do you think was most instrumental in shaping Eden?
2. Losing a child is one of the hardest things a marriage can suffer. What could Eden and Clay have done to have been able to get through the pain of losing Brianna?
3. Clay never gave up on finding Brianna. Why do you think he was so steadfast?
4. What was the base problem in Eden and Clay's marriage?
5. At first Eden was determined to preserve her perfect image. Why do you think what other people thought mattered so much to her?
6. Why do you think Clay never got rid of his childhood home?
7. Why do you think God allows pain in our lives?
8. Why does God allow bad things to happen to good people?

An excerpt from *The Lightkeeper's Ball*

THE NEW YORK BROWNSTONE WAS JUST HALF A BLOCK DOWN FROM THE ASTOR MANSION ON Fifth Avenue, the most prestigious address in the country. The carriage, monogrammed with the Stewart emblem, rattled through the iron gates and came to a halt in front of the ornate doors. Assisted by the doorman, Olivia Stewart descended and rushed for the steps of her home. She was late for tea, and her mother would be furious. Mrs. Astor herself had agreed to join them today.

Olivia handed her hat to the maid, who opened the door. "They're in the drawing room, Miss Olivia," Goldia whispered. "Your mama is ready to pace the floor."

Olivia patted at her hair, straightened her shoulders, and pinned a smile in place as she forced her stride to a ladylike stroll to join the other women. Two women turned to face her as she entered: her mother and Mrs. Astor. They wore identical expressions of disapproval.

"Olivia, there you are," her mother said. "Sit down before your tea gets cold."

Olivia pulled off her gloves as she settled into the Queen Anne chair beside Mrs. Astor. "I apologize for my tardiness," she said. "A lorry filled with tomatoes overturned in the street, and my driver couldn't get around it."

Mrs. Astor's face cleared. "Of course, my dear." She sipped her tea from the delicate blue-and-white china. "Your dear mother and I were just discussing your prospects. It's time you married."

Oh dear. She'd hoped to engage in light conversation that had nothing to do with the fact that she was twenty-five and still unmarried. Her unmarried state distressed her if she let it, but every man her father brought to her wanted only her status. She doubted any of them had ever looked into her soul. "I'm honored you would care about my marital status, Mrs. Astor," Olivia said.

"Mrs. Astor wants to hold a ball in your honor, Olivia," her mother gushed. "She has a distant cousin coming to town whom she wants you to meet."

Mrs. Astor nodded. "I believe you and Matthew would suit. He owns property just down the street."

Olivia didn't mistake the reference to the man's money. Wealth would be sure to impact her mother. She opened her mouth to ask if the man was her age, then closed it at the warning glint in her mother's eyes.

"He's been widowed for fifteen years and is long overdue for a suitable wife," Mrs. Astor said.

Olivia barely suppressed a sigh. So he was another of the decrepit gentlemen who showed up from time to time. "You're very kind," she said.

"He's most suitable," her mother said. "*Most* suitable."

Olivia caught the implication. They spent the next half hour discussing the date and the location. She tried to enter into the conversation with interest, but all she could do was imagine some gray-whiskered blue blood dancing her around the ballroom. She stifled a sigh of relief when Mrs. Astor took her leave and called for her carriage.

"I'll be happy when you're settled, Olivia," her mother said when they returned to the drawing room. "Mrs. Astor is most kind."

"She is indeed." Olivia pleated her skirt with her fingers. "Do you ever wish you could go somewhere incognito, Mother? Where no one has expectations of you because you are a Stewart?"

Her mother put down her saucer with a clatter. "Whatever are you babbling about, my dear?"

"Haven't you noticed that people look at us differently because we're Stewarts? How is a man ever to love me for myself when all he sees is what my name can gain him? Men never see inside to the real me. They notice only that I'm a Stewart."

"Have you been reading those novels again?" Her mother sniffed and narrowed her gaze on Olivia. "Marriage is about making suitable connections. You owe it to your future children to consider the life you give them. Love comes from respect. I would find it quite difficult to respect someone who didn't have the gumption to make his way in the world. Besides, we *need* you to marry well. You're twenty-five years old and I've indulged your romantic notions long enough. Heaven knows your sister's marriage isn't what I had in mind, essential though it may be. Someone has to keep the family name in good standing."

Olivia knew what her duty demanded, but she didn't have to like it. "Do all the suitable men have to be in their dotage?"

Her mother's eyes sparked fire, but before she spoke, Goldia appeared in the doorway. "Mr. Bennett is here, Mrs. Stewart."

Olivia straightened in her chair. "Show him in. He'll have news of Eleanor."

Bennett appeared in the doorway moments later. He shouldn't have been imposing. He stood only five foot three in his shoes, which were always freshly polished. He was slim, nearly gaunt, with a patrician nose and obsidian eyes. He'd always reminded Olivia of a snake about to strike. His expression never betrayed any emotion, and today was no exception. She'd never understood why her father entertained an acquaintance with the man, let alone desired their families to be joined.

"Mr. Bennett." She rose and extended her hand and tried not to flinch as he brushed his lips across it.

"Miss Olivia," he said, releasing her hand. He moved to her mother's chair and bowed over her extended hand.

Olivia sank back into her chair. "What do you hear of my sister? I have received no answer to any of my letters."

He took a seat, steepled his fingers, and leaned forward. "That's the reason for our meeting today. I fear I have bad news to impart."

Her pulse thumped erratically against her rib cage. She wet her lips and drew in a deep breath. "What news of Eleanor?" How bad could it be? Eleanor had gone to marry Harrison, a man she hardly knew. But she was in love with the idea of the Wild West, and therefore more than happy to marry the son of her father's business partner.

He never blinked. "I shall just have to blurt it out then. I'm sorry to inform you that Eleanor is dead."

Her mother moaned. Olivia stared at him. "I don't believe it," she said.

"I know, it's a shock."

There must have been some mistake. She searched his face for some clue that this was a jest. "What happened?"

He didn't hold her gaze. "She drowned."

"How?"

"No one knows. I'm sorry."

Her mother stood and swayed. "What are you saying?" Her voice rose in a shriek. "Eleanor can't be dead! Are you quite mad?"

He stood and took her arm. "I suggest you lie down, Mrs. Stewart. You're quite pale."

Her mother put her hands to her cheeks. "Tell me it isn't true," she begged. Then she keeled over in a dead faint.

An excerpt from *Smitten*

NATALIE MANSFIELD'S HEART SWELLED AS SHE STOOD ON THE PERIMETER OF THE TOWN square and watched her niece and the other children decorate the town for Easter. A gigantic smile stretched across five-year-old Mia's face as her Sunday school teacher lifted her to place the lavender wreath at the top of the clock.

Mia saw her and waved. "Aunt Nat, look at me!"

Natalie waved back, her smile broadening. "She's growing so fast," she told her aunt, Rose Garner. "I love her so much."

Black threaded Rose's silver hair, and her smooth skin made her look twenty years younger than her sixty-two years. "I still remember the first day I laid eyes on you."

"How could you forget? I was a morose ten-year-old who snapped your head off every time you spoke to me."

Her aunt pressed her hand. "You changed our lives, honey. We were three lonely spinsters until you showed up. Now here you are providing a home for your niece. A full circle, just like that wreath. I'm so proud of you."

Her aunt's words made Natalie's heart fill to bursting. "You gave me the only stability I'd ever known. I want to do the same for Mia."

Aunt Rose wasn't listening. A small frown creased her brow. "Something's wrong."

Natalie looked at the men standing a few feet away in front of the hardware store. Their heads were down and their shoulders slumped. The dejection in their stances sent her pulse racing.

She recognized one of her coffee shop patrons, Murphy Clinton, and grabbed his arm as he walked past. "What's happened, Murphy?" she asked.

He stopped and stared down at her with a grave expression. "The mill's closing."

"That's not possible," she mumbled. Her thoughts raced. The mill was an institution and the main employer in Smitten. If it closed . . .

He finished her thought. "This town is finished."

❄

The aroma of the freshly brewed coffee overpowered the less appetizing smell from the drum roaster in the back room. Natalie let her employee Zoe handle the customers at the bar, as Natalie took the hot beverages to the seating area by the window where she and her friends could see white-topped Sugarcreek Mountain. Spring had come to their part of Vermont, and the sight of the wildflowers on the lower slopes would give her strength.

"So what are we going to do?" she asked, sinking onto the overstuffed leather sofa beside Reese Mackenzie.

"Do? What *can* we do?" Reese asked. Her blond ponytail gleamed in the shaft of sunlight through the window. She was the practical one in the group. Reese was never afraid of hard work, but while Natalie saw only the end goal, Reese saw the pitfalls right on the path. "We can't *make* them keep the mill open."

While rumors about the mill had been floating for months, no one had really believed it would fold. The ramifications would be enormous. Natalie's business had been struggling enough without this added blow.

She took a sip of her mocha java. A little bitter. She'd have to tweak the roast a bit next time. "If the mill closes, the town will dry up and blow away. We can't let that happen." If Mountain Perks closed, she didn't know how she would provide for Mia.

And she wasn't leaving Smitten. Not ever. After being yanked from pillar to post with an alcoholic mother until she was ten, Natalie craved the stability she had found here with her aunts and her friends.

Julia Bourne tossed her long hair away from her face, revealing flawless skin that never needed makeup. "This is one of those things outside your control, Nat. I guess we'd all better be looking for jobs in Stowe."

Shelby Evans took a sip of her tea and shivered. Her Shih-poo, Penelope, dressed in a fashionable blue-and-white polka-dotted shirt, turned around in Shelby's lap and lay down on her navy slacks. "I don't know about you all," Shelby said, "but I wanted my kids to grow up here."

The women had no children of their own—and none of them was even close to thinking about settling down—but that was a moot point for Shelby. She had a storybook ending in mind that included a loving husband and two-point-five children for each of them. Natalie was sure her friend would find that life too.

Natalie moved restlessly. "There has to be something we can do. Some new export. Maple syrup, maybe? We have lots of trees." She glanced at Julia. "What about your New York friends? Maybe you could ask some of your business friends for advice?"

Julia shrugged her slim shoulders. "They know spas. I hardly think a spa is going to save us."

Reese had those thoughtful lines on her forehead. A tiny smile hovered on her full lips, and her hazel eyes showed a plan was forming. "We don't have time for exports, but what about imports? Tourists would love us if they'd come visit. We have heart." She took out her ever-present notebook and pen and began to jot down ideas.

"They come to ski in Stowe anyway," Shelby said. "All we have to do is get them here."

Natalie rubbed her forehead where it had begun to ache. "But what do we have to offer that's different from any other town?"

Julia crossed her shapely ankles. "Smitten is cute with its church and all, but cute doesn't bring tourists. I can't even get a decent manicure in this dinky town. People aren't going to pay for ambience. We need some kind of gimmick."

Reese tapped her pen against her chin. "I have an idea," she said. "Everyone jokes about the town name. Why not capitalize on it?"

"How do you capitalize on a name like Smitten?"

"What does Smitten make you think of?" Reese asked. "Love, right? What if we turn the town into a place for honeymooners?"

Shelby adjusted the bow on Penelope's head. "I went to Santa Claus, Indiana, once. Tons of people, even in July."

Natalie swallowed a groan. They'd all heard about Santa Claus too many times to count. She needed to derail Shelby before she broke into a rendition of "Jingle Bells." "We could have love songs playing as people strolled the streets."

Julia snickered and nodded toward the man striding past outside the window. "I have a feeling Carson would have something to say about that. He hated all the jokes about his name in high school."

Natalie followed the angle of Julia's nod. Her gut clenched the way it always did when she saw Carson Smitten. He was a man who attracted female attention wherever he went. He looked like his lumberjack great-grandfather, with his broad shoulders and closely-cropped dark hair.

He had all the single women in town drooling over him. Except for Natalie, of course. If the other girls knew what she knew about him, they wouldn't think he was so great.

"I'm still thinking about my idea," Reese said. "This will mean new businesses, new jobs, lots of revenue pouring in. We'd have to get the entire town on board."

Natalie's excitement level went up a notch as she imagined the town transformed with its new mission. "The town meeting is coming up. I can present the idea there."

"It's a good thing you're a selectperson," Shelby said. "People listen to you."

Natalie dug paper and a pen from her purse, a Brighton that Julia had given her for her last birthday. "There needs to be a cohesive plan. What would this love town look like? Besides romantic songs playing over speakers around town." She peered at Reese's list and copied down the items.

Shelby retied Penelope's bow. "We need a lingerie shop that sells perfume," she said. "Chocolates. Some plush hotels and bed-and-breakfasts with tubs for two." Her smile grew larger. "Maybe old-fashioned lampposts along the path around the lake. You could put outside tables on the street and white lights in the trees. Flower boxes all around town."

"And we'll need more restaurants," Julia added.

Natalie eyed her. "You said a good manicure was impossible to find. What if you started a spa?"

Julia's perfectly plucked brows lifted. She grabbed the tablet and pen from Natalie. "I don't know. I'd like to move back to New York eventually."

"The honeymooners won't spend *all* their time in their rooms," Reese said, her eyes gleaming. "We offer great outdoor activities. The skiing here is as good as anywhere in the country. People just don't know about us." She gestured toward the mountain. "And look at that view."

Natalie groaned. "The last thing I'd want to do on my honeymoon is go skiing. I'd rather sit holding hands across a linen tablecloth with a lobster in front of me."

"But I'd go skiing in a heartbeat," Reese said. "Our big draw is our outdoor beauty. We don't have an outfitters shop. We'd need that." She jotted it down on her paper. "You know how I've been saving for a shop like that for years. Maybe now is the time."

"Now *is* the time," Natalie said. "Sometimes you have to take a leap of faith. We're going to push you until you do it."

"I love it!" Shelby stood and paced by the window. "Maybe my etiquette school can be part of it too. I can coach women on how to put on the best parties and cater to the society women who come to town. Maybe teach ballroom dancing."

"And your designs," Natalie said, unable to keep her voice from rising. "Those cute outfits you make for Penelope would sell like hot cakes." She glanced at the picture of herself with Mia hanging on the wall. "I have to do what I can to save the town. I want Mia to have the security I've never had. A-And I've been thinking. I want to be Mia's real mother. I'm going to see about adopting her."

Her announcement left her friends with mouths gaping. She glanced at Shelby, whose soft heart she knew would be the first to agree with her.

Shelby's dark eyes glistened. "Oh, Nat, that's just like you! You have so much love to give. Mia's a very lucky girl."

A lump formed in Natalie's throat. "Starting the adoption is going to be my birthday present to myself. Every day I wake up and wonder if Lisa is going to take her away from me someday. I can't live with that fear."

Julia grimaced. "Lisa is never going to own up to her responsibilities, but I'm glad you're going to make sure Mia is safe."

"I'll be praying for you," Reese said softly. "There will be lots of frustrating paperwork. Let me help you with that." She flipped the page on her notebook. "And it's all the more reason for us to get this idea sold to the residents. You don't want Mountain Perks to go under."

This was not going to be an easy sell to Carson Smitten. Natalie stared out the window again and watched the man yank on the door to his hardware store in his usual confident way. She had no doubt she could convince the rest of the town over his objections. After all, what did they have to lose?

P9-CDM-023

Acclaim for Colleen Coble

"Colleen is a master storyteller."

—Karen Kingsbury, best-selling author
of *Unlocked* and *Learning*

"Suspense, action, mystery, spiritual victory—Colleen Coble has woven them all into a compelling novel that will keep you flipping pages until the very end. I highly recommend *Without a Trace*."

—James Scott Bell, author of
Deadlock and *A Higher Justice*

"Coble's books have it all, romance, sass, suspense, action. I'm content to read a book that has any one of those but to find an author like Coble who does all four so well is my definition of bliss."

—Mary Connealy, author of
Doctor in Petticoats

"Coble captivates readers with her compelling characters. Action-packed . . . highly recommended!"

—Dianne Burnett,
Christianbook.com

"[*The Lightkeeper's Ball*] has romance, mystery, secrets and a bad guy. Coble wows the reader with a fresh storyline. Readers will enjoy peeling back the layers and discovering this is more than your average romance book. The characters are strong not only in themselves but also in their faith."

—Romantic Times, 4 stars

"Coble's historical series (*The Lightkeeper's Daughter*; *The Lightkeeper's Bride*) just keeps getting better with each entry. Coble has a strong feel for the time period (in this case, 1910) and has scripted believable characters in suspenseful situations."

—Library Journal, starred review

WHAT READERS ARE SAYING

"I have always been a hopeless romantic . . . When I began reading your books I couldn't put them down. I love not just the romance but the connection I feel with God when I read your books. It really is incredible!"

—JENNIFER

"I just finished *Blue Moon Promise* and it was outstanding! I am so looking forward to *Safe in His Arms*! Thank you for sharing your God-given talent with us."

—NANCY

"I love your books! I am a big fan :) You are by far my favorite author."

—KATELYN

"I wanted to let you know that I am reading *Blue Moon Promise* and I can't put it down. I love the way you write! I've read your Lonestar series and I can't wait to read *Tidewater Inn*."

—JEAN

"You are such an amazing writer and person. I've been dealing with lots of health issues, and on my 'bad days' I turn to your books to keep me inspired, to keep me thinking positive thoughts, and to help get me through the tough times. Thanks for being an inspiration and for all that you do to include your reader friends in your life."

—BECKY

"I just read *The Lightkeeper's Daughter*, *The Lightkeeper's Bride* and *The Lightkeeper's Ball*. I could not put them down. I also read the first two books of the Lonestar series and I can't wait to get my hands on the next two. I loved them all!!"

—ADELE

"I finished *Lonestar Angel* and just loved it!! Sure would love for that series to go on and on, keeps getting better and better."

—TERESA

"I just finished the Rock Harbor Series . . . I loved it. You should see my house, laundry, dishes, etc. I haven't done a thing in days. I literally couldn't put the books down. I am off to find *Alaska Twilight*. You are by far my new favorite author. I am from Indiana too, and have visited the UP before. I could almost smell the woods, feel the wind and hear the waves. Thanks for a truly amazing series."

—TANYA

"I just wanted to say thank you for writing the Rock Harbor series. I lost my son in a car accident 12 years ago this month. They waited to bury him when I woke from a coma. I don't remember the accident or barely the funeral. It felt like a nightmare, very unreal and out of body. In your book, she got her little boy back, but she also learned to not be so angry with God. That is something I will always have to work on. I feel very guilty for that, but I am angry. Your book has helped me with that some. I look forward to more in the series, strangely it gave me a peace."

—TIFFANY

"I am so very excited about your new books coming out! I have read almost everything you have put out in the last five years! I am counting down the days till the next Harbor Rock book comes out, and I am pre-ordering *Cry In The Night* this weekend! Thank you so much for all you do! Not only have I enjoyed the story lines, I feel like it's a daily devotional as well!"

—BESS

"I just finished your *Lonestar Sanctuary* novel & LOVED IT! I am a HUGE cowgirl/rodeo fan at heart and worked with troubled children so it really spoke to my heart. I am so glad I have discovered such a wonderful author and will highly recommend your books to my friends and book club!"

—KIM

"The number one gift on my wish list was *The Lightkeeper's Ball*. I read the first two of the Mercy Falls Novels and I LOVED THEM! I'm a huge history nut and I thought that these books were FANTASTIC!!"

—EM

"I just love your books! Rock Harbor is my favorite series. That series has rich plot, deep characterization, gorgeous backdrop, engaging dialogue. And I can't help hoping Bree keeps whispering secrets and suggestions to you about keeping the series going. There's still more to be told!"

—MARY

TIDEWATER INN

Also by Colleen Coble

A novella included in *Smitten*

Under Texas Stars novels
Blue Moon Promise

The Lonestar Novels
Lonstar Sanctuary
Lonestar Secrets
Lonestar Homecoming
Lonestar Angel

The Mercy Falls series
The Lightkeeper's Daughter
The Lightkeeper's Bride
The Lightkeeper's Ball

The Rock Harbor series
Without a Trace
Beyond a Doubt
Into the Deep
Cry in the Night

The Aloha Reef series
Distant Echoes
Black Sands
Dangerous Depths

Alaska Twilight
Fire Dancer
Midnight Sea
Abomination
Anathema

TIDEWATER INN

A HOPE BEACH NOVEL

By Colleen Coble

THOMAS NELSON
Since 1798

NASHVILLE   DALLAS   MEXICO CITY   RIO DE JANEIRO

Seneca Falls Library
47 Cayuga Street
Seneca Falls, N.Y. 13148

For Erin Healy
Editor extraordinaire and friend

© 2012 by Colleen Coble

All rights reserved. No portion of this book may be reproduced, stored in a retrieval system, or transmitted in any form or by any means—electronic, mechanical, photocopy, recording, scanning, or other—except for brief quotations in critical reviews or articles, without the prior written permission of the publisher.

Published in Nashville, Tennessee, by Thomas Nelson. Thomas Nelson is a registered trademark of Thomas Nelson, Inc.

Thomas Nelson, Inc., titles may be purchased in bulk for educational, business, fund-raising, or sales promotional use. For information, please e-mail SpecialMarkets@ThomasNelson.com.

Scripture quotations are taken from THE NEW KING JAMES VERSION. Copyright © 1982 by Thomas Nelson, Inc. Used by permission. All rights reserved.

Publisher's Note: This novel is a work of fiction. Names, characters, places, and incidents are either products of the author's imagination or used fictitiously. All characters are fictional, and any similarity to people living or dead is purely coincidental.

Library of Congress Cataloging-in-Publication Data

Coble, Colleen.
  Tidewater Inn / by Colleen Coble.
    p. cm. -- (A Hope Beach novel ; 1)
  ISBN 978-1-59554-781-1 (trade paper)
  1. Hotels--Conservation and restoration--Fiction. 2. Kidnapping--Fiction. I. Title.
  PS3553.O2285T53 2012
  813'.54--dc23
                     2012012625

Fic.

Printed in the United States of America
12 13 14 15 16 17 QG 6 5 4 3 2 1

Seneca Falls Library
47 Cayuga Street
Seneca Falls, N.Y. 13148

ONE

Libby Holladay fought her way through the brambles to the overgrown garden. She paused to wave a swarm of gnats away from her face. The house was definitely in the Federal style, as she'd been told. Palladian windows flanked a centered door, or rather the opening for a door. The structure was in serious disrepair. Moss grew on the roof, and fingers of vine pried through the brick mortar. The aroma of honeysuckle vied with that of mildew.

She stepped closer to the house and jotted a few impressions in her notebook before moving inside to the domed living room. The floorboards were missing in places and rotted in others, so she planted her tan flats carefully. She could almost see the original occupants in this place. She imagined her own furniture grouped around the gorgeous fireplace. She'd love to have this place, but something so grand that needed this much repair would never be hers. The best she could do would be to preserve it for someone else who would love it. She itched to get started.

Her cell phone rang, and she groped in her canvas bag for it. Glancing at the display, she saw her partner's name. "Hey, Nicole," she said. "You should see this place. A gorgeous Federal-style mansion. I think it was built in 1830. And the setting by the river is beautiful. Or

1

it will be once the vegetation is tamed." Perching on the window seat, she made another note about the fireplace. "Nicole? Are you there?"

There was a long pause, then Nicole finally spoke. "I'm here."

"You sound funny. What's wrong?" Nicole was usually talkative, and Libby couldn't remember the last time she'd heard strain in her friend's voice. "Are you still in the Outer Banks? Listen, I heard there might be a hurricane heading that way." She dug into her purse for her jalapeño jellybeans and popped one in her mouth.

"I'm here," Nicole said. "The residents are sure the storm will miss Hope Island. The investor is really interested in this little town. And we have the chance to make a boatload of money on it. It's all in your hands."

"My hands? You're the one with the money smarts."

Nicole was the mover and shaker in Holladay Renovations. She convinced owners to dramatically increase the value of their historic properties by entrusting them to Libby's expertise. Libby had little to do with the money side of the business, and that was how she liked it.

"I think I'd better go back to the beginning," Nicole said. "Rooney sent me here to see about renovating some buildings in the small downtown area. He's working on getting a ferry to the island. It will bring in a lot more tourism for the hotel he's planning, but the buildings need to be restored to draw new business."

"I know that much. But what do you mean 'it's in my hands'?" Libby glanced at her notes, then around the room again. This was taking up her time, and she wanted to get back to work. "We're doing the lifesaving station for sure, right?"

"Yes, I've already seen it. We were right to buy that sweet building outright. After you get your hands on it, we'll make a bundle *and* have instant credibility here. I've started making notes of the materials and crew we'll need. But I'm not calling about the renovations. I'm talking a lot of money, Libby. Millions."

That got Libby's attention. "Millions?"

"I stopped by the local attorney's office to see about having him handle the paperwork for our purchase of the lifesaving station. Horace Whittaker. He's got both our names on the paperwork now."

"So?"

"The secretary gasped when she heard your name."

"She knew me?"

"The attorney has been looking for a Libby Holladay. Daughter of Ray Mitchell."

"That's my dad's name."

"I thought it might be. I'd heard you mention the name Ray, but I wasn't sure of the last name."

Libby rubbed her head. "Why is he looking for me? My father has been dead a long time—since I was five."

"He died a month ago, Libby. And he left you some valuable land. In fact, it's the land Rooney thought he had agreed to purchase. So we're in the driver's seat on this deal." Nicole's voice rose.

Libby gasped, then she swallowed hard. "It's a hoax. I bet the attorney asked for a fee, right?"

"No, it's real. According to the secretary, your father was living in the Outer Banks all this time. And Horace has a box of letters Ray wrote to you that were all marked *Return to Sender*. It appears your mother refused them."

Libby's midsection plunged. Throughout her childhood she'd asked her mother about her father. There were never any answers. Surely her mother wouldn't have *lied*. Libby stared out the window at two hummingbirds buzzing near the overgrown flowers.

"Do you have any idea how much money this land is worth?" Nicole's voice quivered. "It's right along the ocean. There's a charming little inn."

It sounded darling. "What's the area like?"

"Beautiful but remote." Nicole paused. "Um, listen, there's something else. I met a woman who looked like you a couple days ago."

3

Libby eased off the window ledge. "Who is she?"

"Your half sister, Vanessa. You also have a brother, Brent. He's twenty-two."

"My father married again?" Libby couldn't take it all in. This morning she had no family but a younger stepbrother, whom she rarely saw. Why had her mother kept all this from her? "What about my father's wife?"

"She doesn't seem to be around. But there's an aunt too."

Family. For as long as she could remember, Libby had longed for a large extended family. Her free-spirited mother was always wanting to see some new and exciting place. They had never lived at the same address for more than two years at a time.

"You need to get here right away," Nicole said. "There are a million details to take care of. This is the big deal we've been praying for, Libby. You will never want for anything again, and you'll have plenty of money to help your stepbrother. He can get out of that trailer with his family."

The thought of buying her stepbrother's love held some appeal. They weren't close, but not because she hadn't tried. "I can't get away until tomorrow, Nicole. I have to finish up here first. We have other clients."

How much of her reluctance was rooted in the thought of facing a future that was about to change radically? She never had been good with change. In her experience, change was something that generally made things worse, not better.

Her partner's sigh was heavy in Libby's ear. "Okay. Hey, want to see Vanessa? She'll be here in a few minutes. There's a beach cam out by the lifesaving station, and I'm supposed to meet her there. I'll send you a link to it. You can see her before you meet her."

Libby glanced through the window toward her car. "I have my computer in the car." She tucked her long hair behind her ear and gathered her things. "What does Vanessa think about our father

leaving prime real estate to me?" She left the house and started for her vehicle.

Nicole cleared her throat. "Um, she's pretty upset."

"I would imagine. What did you tell her about me?"

"As little as possible."

"I don't know if that's good or bad."

"I wouldn't worry about them. She and her brother are fishing for info though. She mentioned lighthouse ruins and I asked for directions. She offered to show me, but I went out there by myself yesterday. I'm still meeting her today because I knew you'd want to know more about her."

It sounded like a disaster in the making. "I have so many questions."

"Then come down as soon as you can and get them answered. Wait until you see Tidewater Inn, Libby! It's really old. It's on the eastern edge of the island with tons of land along the beach. The inn was a house once, and it is a little run-down but very quaint. It's hard to get out here. Until Rooney gets the ferry approved, you'll have to hire a boat. You're going to love it though. I love this island. It's like stepping back in time. And I've even seen some caves to explore."

"No road to it from the mainland?" Libby couldn't fathom a place that remote.

"Nope. Boat access only."

Her phone still to her ear, Libby opened her car door and slid in. The computer was on the floor, and she opened it. "I'm going to have to get off a minute to tether my phone to the computer. Send me the link to the harbor cam. Don't tell Vanessa I'm watching."

"When can you get here tomorrow?"

"It's about two hours from Virginia Beach?"

"Yes."

Libby doubted she'd sleep tonight. It would be no problem to be in the shower by six. "I'll be there by nine."

5

She ended the call, then attached the cord that tethered the phone to the computer. She would use the cell signal to watch Nicole's video feed on the larger screen. Then she could watch and still take any calls that came in. Her skin itched from the brambles. She established the connection, then logged on to the Internet. No e-mail yet.

She owned property. The thought was mind boggling. No matter what condition it was in, it was a resource to fall back on, something she hadn't possessed yesterday. The thought lightened her heart. She stared at the grand old home beside her. What if there was enough money from the sale of the inn to allow her to buy a historic house and restore it? It would be a dream come true. She could help her stepbrother. She could buy some Allston paintings too, something she'd never dreamed she could afford.

A woman pecked on Libby's car window, and Libby turned on the key and ran down the window. "Hello. I'm not an intruder. I'm evaluating this gorgeous old place for the historic registry."

The woman smiled. "I thought maybe you were buying it. Someone should restore it."

"Someone plans to," Libby said. What if it could be her instead of her client?

The woman pointed. "I'm taking up a collection for the Warders, who live on the corner. They had a fire in the kitchen and no insurance."

Libby had only two hundred dollars in her checking account, and she had to get to the Outer Banks. "I wish I could help," she said with real regret. "I don't have anything to spare right now."

"Thanks anyway." The woman smiled and moved to the next house.

Libby ran the window back up and clicked on her in-box. An e-mail from Nicole appeared. She stared at the link. All she had to do was click and she'd catch a glimpse of a sister she had no

6

idea even existed. Her hands shook as she maneuvered the pointer over the link and clicked. The page opened, and she was staring at a boardwalk over deep sand dunes that were heaped like snow-drifts. In the distance was a brilliant blue ocean. A pier extended into the pristine water. The scene was like something out of a magazine. She could almost feel the sea breeze.

She clicked to enlarge the video and turned up the speakers so she could hear the roar of the surf. Where was Nicole? The pier was empty, and so was the sea. A dilapidated building stood to the right of the screen, and she could just make out a sign over the door. Hope Beach Lifesaving Station.

Then there was a movement on the boardwalk. Nicole appeared. She smiled and waved. "Hi, Libby," she said. The sound quality was surprisingly good. The sound of the ocean in the background was a pleasant lull.

Libby had to resist the impulse to wave back. Her partner's blond hair was pulled back in a ponytail under a sun hat, and she wore a hot-pink cover-up over her brown bathing suit.

Nicole glanced at her watch and frowned. "Vanessa is late. Like I started to say earlier, I didn't want to wait on her to see the lighthouse ruins, so I went out there alone. I have to show it to you. Wait until you see what I found. You'll seriously freak! Hey, give me a call. This pier is one of the few places where my phone works. Isn't that crazy—an entire island without cell ser-vice. Almost, anyway."

Libby picked up her cell phone, still connected to the com-puter. They could talk a few minutes. Before she could call, a small boat pulled up to the shore. Two men jumped out and pulled the boat aground. Nicole turned toward them. The men walked toward her. There was no one else in sight, and Libby tensed when Nicole took a step back. Libby punched in Nicole's number. She watched her friend dig in her bag when it rang.

When Nicole answered the phone, Libby leaped to her feet and yelled, "Get out of there. Go to your car!"

Nicole was still watching the men walk toward her. "It's just a couple of tourists, Libby," she said. "You worry too much." She smiled and waved at the men.

Libby leaned closer to the laptop. "There's something wrong." She gasped at the intention in their faces. "Please, Nicole, run!"

But it was the men who broke into a run as they drew closer to the boardwalk. As they neared the cam, Libby could see them more clearly. One was in his forties with a cap pulled low over his eyes. He sported a beard. The other was in his late twenties. He had blond hair and hadn't shaved in a couple of days.

Nicole took another step back as the older man in the lead smiled at her. The man said, "Hang up." He grabbed her arm.

"Let go of her!" Libby shouted into the phone.

The man knocked the phone from Nicole's hand and the connection was broken. The other man reached the two, and he plunged a needle into Nicole's arm. Both men began dragging Nicole toward the boat. She was struggling and shouting for help, then went limp. Her hat fell to the ground.

Barely aware that she was screaming, Libby dialed 9-1-1. "Oh God, oh God, help her!"

The dispatcher answered and Libby babbled about her friend being abducted right in front of her. "It's in the Outer Banks." She couldn't take her eyes off the boat motoring away from the pier. "Wait, wait, they're taking her away! Do something!"

"Where?"

"I told you, the Outer Banks." Libby looked at the heading above the video stream. "Hope Beach. It's Hope Beach. Get someone out there."

"Another dispatcher is calling the sheriff. I have an officer on his way to you."

"I'm going to Hope Beach now."

"Stay where you are," the dispatcher said. "We've got the sheriff on the line there. He's on his way to the site. Don't hang up until an officer arrives."

She had to do something. Anything but run screaming into the street. Libby looked at the computer. She could call up the video, save it for evidence. But the stream had no rewind, no way to save it. If she could hack into the site, she could get to the file. The police could save time and get the pictures of those men circulating. With a few keystrokes, she broke through the firewall and was in the code.

Then her computer blinked and went black. And when she called up the site again, the entire code was gone. What had she done?

Two

Smog hung over the New York skyline and matched Lawrence Rooney's mood. He studied the expansive view from his penthouse office on Fifth Avenue. The senator sitting in the chair on the other side of the gleaming walnut desk had better come through with the promised plum after all Lawrence had done for him.

Lawrence kept his attention away from the senator long enough to make sure the other man knew who was in charge, then turned from his perusal of his domain and settled in his chair. "You have news for me?"

Senator Troy Bassett tugged on his tie, then pulled a handkerchief from his pocket and blotted his damp forehead. "The city is like an oven today," he muttered.

In his fifties now, he had once been handsome, but his blond good looks had been replaced by flab and gray hair. Lawrence had known him since they went to Harvard together. They knew each other's weaknesses all too well. Lawrence had funneled a fortune into getting Bassett elected. But the rewards were coming—now.

"The vote?" Lawrence prodded.

The senator nodded. "Came through. The ferry system will be added next year."

"Excellent." Lawrence sat back in his leather chair. "I will have possession of the land by the end of the summer."

"I thought the old man refused to sell it."

"Luckily for us, he died." How he wished he could have seen Ray Mitchell take his last breath.

Bassett lifted a brow. "Natural causes?"

Lawrence laughed. "Of course. We both know I like to have my own way, but I've never stooped to murder. I've found money talks well enough that it's not necessary." A smile tugged at his lips. "Though there's always a first time for everything."

"You'd met your match in Mitchell though. He was adamant."

"True enough. But his son has no such scruples. He knows when to take a good offer and run with it."

"So he's agreed to your price?"

Lawrence nodded. "He has. I was willing to go up another five million if I had to, but he didn't know that. I got a bargain."

"You always do."

The door opened and Lawrence's secretary stuck her head in. "Mr. Rooney, Mr. Poe is here to see you."

"Excellent. Send him in," Lawrence said. "Stay," he told the senator, who had started to rise. "Poe will bring us both up to date."

Kenneth Poe, in a navy suit and red tie, strolled into the office. Every dark strand of hair perfectly coiffed, he was the epitome of a gentleman. His usefulness to Lawrence had grown in the past year. If Lawrence had been blessed with a son, he would have wanted the boy to be like Poe. Smart, ruthless, and handsome. He was nearly thirty now and still unmarried. Perhaps it was time to introduce him to Katelyn. Lawrence couldn't imagine a better son-in-law.

"Sir," Poe said, extending his hand. "Senator."

The men shook hands, and Lawrence ticked another box in Poe's favor. He knew how to act around power and had made sure

to show respect to Lawrence first. The boy must have taken a class on sucking up. Lawrence liked it.

"I hope you have a signed bill of sale for me," Lawrence said.

Poe settled into the other chair and casually propped one foot on the opposite knee. "Unfortunately, we've hit a snag."

Lawrence frowned at Poe's grave tone. "What kind of snag?"

"It's serious."

When Poe said something was serious, Lawrence paid attention. "How serious?"

"A young woman came to town. Very smart and nosy. She found the cave. I'm not sure if she saw the contents." He glanced at the senator.

Lawrence pursed his lips. "We just need her out of the way long enough for us to get the land signed over. Can you put her in a safe place until we accomplish that?"

"It's already done. But what if that causes even more problems?"

"If it does, we'll deal with it later. I have a great deal of money riding on this, Kenneth. I won't allow my plans to be derailed by a spelunker. Fix it."

"Yes, sir. I'll do my best."

Poe's best was usually spectacular. Lawrence dismissed his concerns and began to think about what he would do with the money that would come pouring in when he turned Hope Island into the next Myrtle Beach.

The sailboat was sinking fast, and so was the sun. Two people flailed about in the water below. Chief Petty Officer Alec Bourne sat on the floor of the Dolphin helicopter with his feet dangling over the edge. "Take it lower," he shouted over the roar of the rotors. His

Coast Guard team received the call for help twenty minutes ago, and he'd prayed all the way out that they'd be in time.

The hurricane had veered and was going to miss them, but its outer band stirred up fifteen-foot seas, and the small craft below had floundered in the wind and waves. It heeled to the port by about forty-five degrees. This distress call was likely to be the first of several for the day.

Aircraft Commander Josh Holman nodded, and the helicopter hovered closer to the waves pounding at the boat. Alec leaned into the wind. The stinging rain struck his face, and he smelled the salty air as he waited for the signal from Curtis Ireland, his flight mechanic and best friend.

"Stand by to deploy swimmer," Josh barked.

"Roger, checking swimmer." Curtis slapped Alec's chest.

Alec inhaled, then flipped the hinged buckle and released his gunner's belt, the last piece of gear that held him in the helicopter. He shoved off the aircraft. The wind buffeted him on the way down. The waves slapped the air from his lungs and he submerged, then popped to the surface and struck out for the first of the people in the water.

A woman in the sea struggled toward him. When she reached him, she grabbed his neck and nearly took him under the water. "Calm down!" He pushed her away, then grabbed her from behind in the traditional rescue hold. She stiffened, then relaxed in his grip. He gave Curtis a thumbs-up, and the rescue basket began to descend toward them.

"You're going to be okay," he assured the woman.

"We hit a shoal," she gasped, her lips blue. "We've been in the water for two hours."

"It's almost over." He grabbed the basket and got her inside, then signaled to Curtis to lift her to the helicopter while he went after her husband.

Five minutes later he was back aboard the Dolphin too. Mission accomplished. The health service technician, Sara Kavanagh, began to check out the woman's pulse and blood pressure. Both patients were swathed in blankets. They thanked Alec and his crew several times as the chopper veered back to the Coast Guard station, where medical personnel waited to attend the capsized sailors.

On days like this Alec knew he was right where God wanted him. There were other days when nothing went right, or when they lost someone they were trying to save.

He was smiling when he walked to the grassy picnic area of the station with his friends. Alec and Curtis had gone through training together. They were as different as two best friends could be. Curtis was the quiet, thoughtful one of the group. Though he came from money, he never flaunted it. Sara Kavanagh was the only female on their team. Her reserve kept the men at the station from making any inappropriate remarks, and she had earned their trust with her skills. He sometimes wondered if she and Josh Holman would end up a couple. Josh was a jokester and kept the rest of them laughing, but sometimes Alec thought he saw a special spark when Josh looked at Sara.

"You've got three days off, Alec," Josh said. "Gonna leave the island and head for the casino so you can win big and buy me a Jaguar?"

"I think you'll have to settle for a bicycle on what I have," Alec said. "Me and Zach will go crabbing. I hear there have been some good hauls. Maybe I'll make enough to build that back deck."

Sara was pulling food from a sack. "How is Zach?"

Alec's smile faded. He shrugged. "It's only been two weeks. You know how it is with a teenager. One minute he's got a head on his shoulders and the next he's doing something so stupid you think he was raised under a rock. He's sure glad to be back on the island though. He hated Richmond."

"There are bound to be challenges. You've never raised a kid before," Sara said.

"Darrell did most of the raising and I'll figure out the rest. He's all I have left of Darrell."

The small plane crash had been only six months ago, and Alec still missed his older brother with a painful ache. Zach was the spitting image of Darrell at that age too. The kid was a handful for his grandparents, though, and Alec had taken custody two weeks ago. He should have taken him right from the start, but Alec's mother had been adamant that the boy's place was with them. And Darrell had named his parents as guardians.

His cell phone rang and he grabbed it. The station was one of the few places on the island where his cell worked. The call was from his cousin Tom, who also happened to be the sheriff on this rock. "Hey, Tom."

"Sorry to bother you, buddy, but I've got Zach here in jail."

Alec's stomach plummeted. "What's he done?"

"He and some of his friends took it into their heads to spray-paint graffiti on the school. I caught him with the paint. I think you should leave him here overnight. Might teach him a lesson."

The thought of his nephew in jail pained Alec, but he knew his cousin was right. "Whatever you think is best."

"While I've got you on the phone, I need your help. A woman named Nicole Ingram was abducted out at Tidewater Pier."

"Abducted?"

"The Virginia Beach police called me. Her business partner saw it all on the cam."

Alec winced. "That had to have been rough."

"She was hysterical, according to the officer who called me. She's on her way here. Can I get your team to keep your eyes open on this one? The kidnappers took her in a boat."

"Sure thing. You got a description of the woman?"

Tom gave it to him. "Oops, got another call. Don't come until lunch tomorrow to spring your nephew."

Alec ended the call and put his phone away. The others were looking at him with curiosity. "Zach's in jail."

"So we gathered," Curtis said. "What'd he do?"

"Spray-painted graffiti on the school."

"I did that once," Josh said. "It's a rite of passage to adulthood."

"I never did," Alec said.

"Yeah, but you walk on water."

Alec grinned at the familiar joke. Just because he didn't drink or smoke, most of the other men thought he was some kind of saint. The truth was far different.

THREE

The trip to the Outer Banks was a blur, and Libby barely noticed the landscape, though she'd often wanted to go to the Outer Banks. She crossed the Chesapeake Bay Bridge. Route 168 turned into US 158 when she reached the Outer Banks. On her left was the Atlantic Ocean, and on the right she saw Albemarle Sound. The place felt like another world. She ran down her window to drink in the atmosphere of squawking gulls and murmuring surf.

By the time she reached Kitty Hawk, the sun had set. She parked in the Dock of the Bay lot and rushed out. Motorboats and sailboats gleamed in the moonlight where they bobbed in the dark water. There were few people on the dock at this hour, but they were tourists. She stopped everyone she met, but no one had a boat they were willing to use to get her out to Hope Island.

She found herself examining every man she saw, but none looked like either of the men who had taken Nicole. She saw a Coast Guard cutter in the distance and waved her arms, shouting for it, but it cruised on past without noticing her. How was she going to get to Hope Island tonight?

Now that she was here, her driving-induced fatigue fell away. When her stomach rumbled, she realized she hadn't eaten since

lunch. She was going to be here all night, so she got a bag of chocolate-covered peanuts from a vending machine and a cup of coffee. Both left her more jittery than before. She eyed the long stretch of water. Maybe a walk along the shore would calm her down. She sat on a rock and took off her shoes, then walked along the soft sand. The salty air cleansed her head, and she prayed for God to be with Nicole wherever she was. Who could have taken Nicole and why?

A boat horn sounded out in the water and the running lights flashed. She wandered out onto the pier and sat down with her bare feet dangling over the water. A fish splashed off to her right, and the sound of the waves rolling onto shore soothed her. God saw Nicole. He was in charge here. Libby had to try to cling to that fact.

With the adrenaline draining out of her, she yawned. Maybe she could sleep for a little while, then she'd find someplace to take a shower. But she sat with her eyes open through the long night. When the sun came up, she got up again and went in search of a charter.

She reached the top of the pier and smiled at a man and woman walking their dog along the beach. The dog sniffed her leg, and Libby stooped to pet it, a cute Yorkie. "You're a sweetheart."

The woman appeared to be in her forties. Her smile lines and straw hat made her look approachable. She wore khaki walking shorts and a red top. She smiled. "It's a surprise to see you here, Vanessa."

Vanessa. Her sister's name. "I'm not Vanessa. My name is Libby Holladay."

The woman's smile faded. "Oh my dear, I'm so sorry. You look so much like a young woman I know on Hope Beach. Pardon me."

"Someone else told me that. Are you from Hope Beach?"

The woman brushed a strand of hair from her eyes. "I used

to be. I taught school there for four years. Vanessa was one of my students. It's amazing how much you two look alike."

"I'm trying to find a charter out to Hope Island. Do you know where I might ask?"

"My husband and I are going there in a few minutes. We'd be happy to give you a ride." She put out her hand. "I'm Naomi Franklin, and this is my husband, Earl."

Libby shook hands with them. "That would be wonderful!" She'd been afraid of how much the charter might cost. "What time?"

"Right now," Earl said around a toothpick in his mouth. "Our boat is the *Blue Mermaid*. It's there." He pointed to a big sailboat. I just have to fill the tank and pack the supplies we brought for our summer house."

"She's beautiful," Libby said.

He beamed. "We've only had her a month." He took his wife's hand. "You can take her aboard, honey, and I'll get the supplies."

"What about my car?"

"It's safe here. Just leave it in the lot. You can rent a car on the island. Pricey, but maybe you won't need it for long," he said.

Libby rushed back to her car and grabbed her suitcase, then locked the vehicle and joined them at the dock. Earl helped the women aboard, and moments later the sea spray struck her arms and was dried off by the hot sun.

She stared at the horizon. "How far to the island?"

"About half an hour. You have business in Hope Beach?" Naomi asked.

Libby hesitated. "My partner and I restore historical buildings and sell them. She's been on the island investigating the idea of helping to restore the downtown area."

"There are some beautiful old properties on the island. Many

of them have fallen into disrepair, so you'll have your work cut out for you." Naomi tipped her head to the side. "You really do look like Vanessa Mitchell in a most astonishing way."

Libby managed a smile. "They say everyone has a twin somewhere in the world. Have the Mitchells been there a long time?"

"Oh yes. The old Tidewater Inn is the matriarch of the place. Make sure you see it. Since you are into historical buildings, I'm sure you'll be fascinated. It's lovely. Ray Mitchell's dad bought it in the thirties and raised a big family there. Ray bought out his siblings after their father died and turned it into an inn. Not that there are many tourists on the island, but he hoped he could entice families who wanted a quiet getaway."

"Are his siblings still around?" Aunts, uncles, cousins. The idea tightened Libby's chest.

"Just his sister. The rest moved to the mainland." Naomi opened the ice chest. "Water?"

"Sure." Libby accepted the cold, wet bottle and uncapped it. "Is that Hope Island?" she asked when she saw a speck of land in the distance.

"That's it," Earl said.

Libby almost forgot to breathe as the island neared. Why did the island appeal to her so much? She'd never been here, had she? Charming houses lined a small bay with a well-maintained dock. Most of the houses could use a coat of paint and some repair to the gutters, but the village was like something out of a painting from the eighteen hundreds.

"Where can I rent a car?" she asked.

"No need for one, really," Earl said. "Not if you're staying in town. You have a room?"

"Not yet." She ignored the lift of his brow. "Can you recommend a hotel?"

"Tidewater Inn would be your best bet. If you call them, they'll

fetch you," Naomi said. "Stop at the general store. They'll give you the number. We don't have a car on the island or we'd run you out there ourselves."

"There's a small lot by the harbor where you can rent a car though," Earl said. "Some people like to explore."

Home. The place felt like home. That was the sensation in her chest.

———

The sheriff's office felt deserted when Libby stepped onto the worn wooden floor. "Hello?" she called.

A man in a uniform came down the hallway. He was in his late thirties with dark hair just beginning to get salty. His tanned face was good-natured. "Can I help you?"

"I'd like to see the sheriff."

"That would be me. Sheriff Tom Bourne. Come on back." He led the way to a small office that held a battered desk and a metal filing cabinet, both overflowing with stacks of paper. He lifted a batch of files from the chair opposite the desk. "Have a seat and tell me what I can do for you."

She settled onto the hard chair. "My business partner was kidnapped yesterday."

His gaze sharpened. "You're Libby Holladay, the one who witnessed the kidnapping?"

"Yes. Is there any news?" Surely they had found Nicole by now. Alive, she prayed.

He shook his head. "Nothing. All I found when I got to the lifesaving station was her car. No sign of her. I've called in the Coasties, but they've seen nothing."

"Coasties?"

"Coast Guard. What can you tell me about your conversation?

You rushed off before the Virginia Beach police arrived to take your statement."

"I wanted to get here and find her." She described the men she saw, and he took notes. "One man gave her an injection."

"It would help if we could call up the video, but it seems to have been erased from the server."

She bit her lip. Should she admit what she'd done? How much trouble could she get into for that? It was an accident, after all. But didn't the police tend to blame the person closest to the victim?

The phone on his desk rang, and she sat back in the chair while he talked. He rose when he hung up. "I have to go. There's a problem at the jail. Where are you staying? Tidewater?"

She nodded. "I hope to. I haven't called yet."

He reached for some keys and tossed them to her. "I've got an old car I loan out sometimes. Go ahead and take it out to Tidewater. I'll catch up with you there and get it back. Just follow Oyster Road to the end. You can't miss it."

She took the keys and followed him out the door. There would be time to tell him about the video later. Maybe she could find the file and restore it. Then she wouldn't be in trouble.

The old truck reeked of fish, but it was the smell of money to Alec. The morning's excellent haul would fetch a premium price at the restaurants. But he needed to get to the jail and pick up his nephew. As he maneuvered the truck along Oyster Road just outside of town, he noticed Tom's red Honda along the shoulder. A woman crouched beside a flat tire. Tourist, from the looks of her.

He parked his truck behind the car and got out. "Need some help?"

Her sun-streaked light-brown hair framed a striking face with

bold brows and large brown eyes. In her early thirties, he guessed. There was an air of tension around her as if she were about to explode.

She held up the tire iron. "I'm not quite sure how to use this."

"Let me see if I can help." Alec took the tool from her. "Everything okay?" He knelt by the tire and began to remove the lug bolts. "You're driving the sheriff's spare car."

"My business partner is missing." Her voice trembled. "I was watching on a beach cam, and two men kidnapped her right in front of me."

His hands stilled, and he looked up at her. "Nicole Ingram?" He'd gone out last night on the search for the missing woman. All they'd found was her cell phone on the sand, a chilling sight.

She nodded. "She'd told me when she would be at the cam, so I got on the computer. Two guys came ashore in a small boat and took her away. I called 9-1-1, but by the time the sheriff got there, all he found was her car parked along the side of the road. No sign of Nicole."

"No sign of her in any boats that were stopped yesterday either."

She studied him as she fidgeted with her large leather bag. "How do you know that?"

He rose and stuck out his hand. "Alec Bourne. Part-time fisherman and full-time captain in the Coast Guard. The sheriff is my cousin, and he told me about your friend. My crew did a run through the area on one of the boats, but we didn't see anything suspicious."

She grasped his hand in a tight grip. "I'm Libby Holladay. You have to find her."

He checked the spare. "This spare tire is flat too. Tom needs to take better care of this vehicle. Hop in. I'll take you anywhere you need to go. Tom can collect the car later."

She studied his face. "I'm sorry, but I don't know you."

He couldn't blame her for being cautious, especially considering what had happened to her friend. He dug out his Coast Guard ID and held it out. Her fingers grazed his when she took it, and the bolt of adrenaline he experienced nearly made him snatch his hand back. She was beautiful, but he'd seen beautiful women before.

She returned his ID. "Thank you. I'm sorry if I offended you."

"No offense taken," he said while he fetched her belongings from Tom's car. "It's always wise to be cautious." He jerked his head toward the passenger side of the truck. "The door sticks. Give it a jerk." He put her suitcase in the truck bed, then slid behind the wheel of his truck and quickly moved some nets and tackle off the seat.

She yanked on the door, then climbed in. She wrinkled her nose as she shut the door. "I guess you *have* been fishing. The truck reeks of it." She smiled. "Sorry, I don't like fish much."

"You just haven't had the right fish. I went crabbing this morning. Nice haul." He started the engine. "The smell grows on you. Where you headed?"

She hesitated. "I was going to go to the Tidewater Inn, but you can just take me back to town and I'll call them."

"You live in the Outer Banks?"

She shook her head. "Near Virginia Beach."

"Your friend was here on vacation or something?"

She stared out the window. "Or something."

He didn't like the way she didn't look at him. Like she was hiding something. "By herself? She didn't say anything about being worried about someone? No one was following her?"

She shook her head and rested her cheek on the window.

"I get the feeling you're not telling me everything," he said. "I have a nose for deception. Comes with the job."

She finally lifted her head and turned to face him. Her dark eyes were anxious and strained. "It's personal."

He turned the truck into Dead Man's Curve and headed for downtown. "Might have something to do with your friend's disappearance though."

Her face was pale. "Do you know Horace Whittaker?"

Was she in some kind of trouble? "Sure. He was born and raised here on the island. Good man, good attorney."

"His secretary gave Nicole some interesting news. She said my father has left me some property out here."

He tried to think who had died lately. "Who's your father?"

"Ray Mitchell."

Alec raised his brows. "You're Ray's daughter? I never knew he had any other kids except for Brent and Vanessa. You never visited him here. I would have seen you."

"I *thought* he died when I was five." She pressed her lips together and looked down at her hands.

He absorbed the news. So the information that Ray had only died a month ago would have come as a shock. "Who told you that?"

"My mother."

"Your mom lied to you?"

She gave a barely perceptible nod.

He made a quick decision as he parked in front of the jail. "Give me Tom's keys. I'll have a couple of deputies handle the car situation, and we'll go see Horace."

She handed him the keys. "You think he knows what happened to Nicole?"

"He can tell us what he knows of her visit here. Maybe something will point to whatever happened. Though I doubt it's related to your inheritance, I could be wrong. Do your brother and sister know you're here?"

She shook her head. "Seems crazy that I have a brother and

sister I didn't know about until yesterday." She stared at him. "Did you see any boats out yesterday at all?"

He shrugged. "Fishing boats. Like I said, we stopped a couple but found nothing suspicious." He got out of the truck. "I'll be right back," he told her through the open window. He'd spring Zach while he was at it and tell the kid to go home and stay there.

FOUR

Libby craned her neck to take in the village of Hope Beach. The main street, Oyster Road, ran straight through to the harbor. Small shops lined the road and displayed wares ranging from beads to beach gear to driftwood furniture. Alec drove the truck past a restaurant with tables on a terrace. There was an ice-cream shop and a coffee shop across the street.

It was a town unlike anything she'd ever seen. She almost felt like she had stepped into a movie about a beach town in the fifties. There were very few cars but a lot of bicycles. So quaint and charming. What a wonderful place to grow up. Live oaks lined the sidewalks, and the street itself was cobblestone. The shop fronts were mostly clapboard. Libby loved it already.

She eyed a Victorian home with decorative siding in the gables. "Why isn't this place on the historic registry? It's like stepping back in time."

"You sound like an expert or something," Alec said.

She stared up at the fretwork on the next house. "I'm an archaeological historian. I work in historic preservation. Some of these places are real treasures."

She glanced back at the man beside her. Alec was a handsome guy, about six-two with sun-streaked brown hair. His blue eyes

were startling in his tanned face, and his muscular frame was from either hauling in nets or working out.

He parked in front of a clapboard house that appeared to be freshly painted. "It's expensive to renovate out here. Material has to be ferried over, and workmen are at a premium. So most make do with what they have or what they can accomplish by themselves."

She continued to stare at the buildings. "That's why they're still intact, then. In college I did my thesis on historic homes in Charleston. I compared contemporary photos that I'd taken to historic pictures I found in the archives. I wanted to show the progress over the years. What I set out to prove was that, historically, homes in Charleston were owned by folks who were too poor to paint but too proud to whitewash. So those places stayed the same."

He nodded. "You might be right about that. Happened here for sure."

She got out of the truck and shut the door behind her. "Why hasn't the charm been destroyed by tourism?"

"Your father gets the credit for that. He owned most of the town, and he refused to sell to outsiders. Some called him a genius and others said he blocked progress."

A rustic sign proclaimed the building to be that of Horace Whittaker, Attorney-at-Law. The place had so much gingerbread in the gables and on the porch that it looked like a fairytale cottage. She followed Alec through the entry and into the foyer, which was surprisingly dim. A young woman in jeans sat behind the counter.

Alec glanced around. "Hi, Mindy. Why are you sitting in here with no lights?"

She rolled her eyes. "Horace forgot to pay the electric bill again. And his bill at the dive shop. That man is so forgetful."

Or so irresponsible. Libby was quite familiar with irresponsibility. Her mother always wanted to play and let the bills take care of themselves. Except they never did.

"They're supposed to turn it on any minute. I don't mind." Mindy held up a romance novel. "I get to read instead of work. At least I have a window." The woman's eyes were sparkling. "You hear about the hurricane? The first one missed us but there's another heading this way."

Alec shrugged. "It's only a category 1. We'll be fine. Listen, is Horace busy?"

The secretary shook her head and picked up the phone. "Horace, Alec is here with a lady to see you." She listened a moment, then replaced the receiver. "You can go on back."

Libby saw the speculation in the woman's eyes. "I'm Libby Holladay."

The woman's eyes widened. "I'm Mindy Jackson. I met your business partner." She put down her book. "I got into so much trouble for telling her Horace was looking for you. He hates to appear incompetent. I was just trying to help though." She tipped her head and stared. "You look a lot like Vanessa."

"So Nicole said."

Mindy winced. "I heard on the radio this morning about her kidnapping. You're the friend who saw the men take her via the cam?"

"Yes."

"I see. Well, welcome to Hope Island, Ms. Holladay. I'm sorry about your friend. Hopefully the sheriff will find her soon."

Libby tensed at the doubt in the secretary's voice. "I'm sure they will," she said. "Did Nicole mention what she'd been doing? Did she seem afraid of anyone?"

Mindy shook her head. "She came in to have Horace help her with some paperwork. But she seemed more interested in the inheritance when she heard about it." She pointed down the hall. "You know the way to his office, Alec." Her tone dismissed them, and she stuck her nose back in her book.

Libby followed Alec down the wide hall. The woodwork was

quarter-sawn oak and appeared to be original. The plaster walls were painted an accurate period gray-green. She was sure there were original hardwood floors under the carpet. Alec pushed open a door at the end of the hall, and she glimpsed a man in his fifties behind a massive cherry desk. He looked like Burl Ives with his round face and belly and his pointed beard.

When he spoke, even his voice had that rich Ives timbre. "Alec, can't say I was expecting to see you in need of an attorney." His gaze went to Libby. "Or is it your friend in need of my help?" He rose and extended his hand. "Horace Whittaker."

She put her hand in his. It was warm. "Libby Holladay."

His fingers tightened on hers. His white brows rose. He pointed to the overstuffed leather chairs. "Have a seat. Let me save my work. I'm updating my website and I don't want to lose it."

Libby sat. "You saw my friend two days ago, Mr. Whittaker?"

He nodded. "Call me Horace. It was rather embarrassing that my secretary was so unprofessional." He smiled. "Still, it allowed me to finally track you down."

"You'd had trouble?"

He nodded. "The last address Ray had for you was in Indiana. Your friend said you're in Virginia Beach now?"

"Yes. For the past year." Libby leaned forward. "About my father . . ."

Horace's round head bobbed. "Ray. The town misses him already. He was a great philanthropist, always contributing to those in need. You would have passed the school on the way in. The playground equipment was bought by your father. He's been a driving force in the village for the past twenty-five years."

A lump formed in Libby's throat and she blinked rapidly, determined not to let these men see the emotion that threatened to overwhelm her. If he was so generous to everyone else, why had he ignored her all these years?

Horace wheeled his chair around. "In addition to the old letters, Ray gave me a package for you. It's in my safe." He leaned over a safe behind him, twirled the dial a few times, then popped it open. He reached inside, then shut and locked it again. "Here we are." He held out an irregularly shaped envelope. When she took it, he reached into a drawer and pulled out a shoe box. "Here are the letters."

"What's in this?" She felt the package and couldn't tell what it contained.

"I have no idea. He gave it to me shortly before he died and asked me to put it away."

Libby tucked the envelope into her large bag and put the box of letters on the floor beside it. She wasn't ready to read anything from her father in front of spectators. "Thank you." She leaned forward. "What about my father's second family? They all live here?"

The attorney nodded. "His sister, Pearl, too. She's the town postmistress. She moved into the big house to take care of him before he died."

"What did he die from?" she asked.

"He had a heart attack a year ago and went downhill afterward. He knew his time was short, so he transferred all of his cash to a trust fund for Brent and Vanessa."

"Do my siblings know that I've inherited something?"

"I just informed them last week. Brent was on a trip to England, so I delayed the reading of Ray's will until he got back." Horace nodded. "He's a young hothead, and he demanded that we break the bequest. I told him he didn't have any legal grounds."

She didn't want to admit to herself that her brother's objection hurt. "Is the inheritance so valuable?"

The attorney retrieved a file from his drawer and slid it across the desk to her. "The entire west side of the island as well as an

old inn is all yours. Now, it's not as valuable as if it were on the mainland, because progress has passed us by for now. But if tourists ever start flocking here, it could be worth a lot of money. Even in its current state, it's valuable."

She flipped open the folder. The first page was a photograph of a lovely Georgian hotel with porches and balconies. The second was of sand dunes and rolling whitecaps. "My siblings also have an inheritance? A trust fund, you said?"

"Oh yes, they're well taken care of. They each have more than a million dollars in the bank." He steepled his fingers together. "You really should draw up a will. The property is worth well over a million dollars," Horace said. "More if progress ever finds us."

No more money worries for her stepbrother. And that lovely old house she was in yesterday could be hers. She could create a foundation to help preserve the neighborhood. "I think I'd like to set up a foundation after it's sold," she said slowly. "For historic preservation." She sat back in her chair and exhaled. "I suppose I'll need a will too."

"I can draft something simple for you," Horace offered. "So you have something in place for starters."

"That would be nice. Thank you. I can't even think straight right now. I just want to find Nicole. The rest can wait."

⌒

Wind-tossed sand stung Libby's cheeks and arms as she stood on the boardwalk staring out to sea. Gulls swooped low over the water, and a crab scuttled across the wet sand. A few clouds floated on an impossibly blue sky. It should have been paradise.

"It's so beautiful," she said, then shivered. "And so deserted. This is the spot. I recognize the lifesaving station." She pointed to the lone building, a low-slung clapboard structure with a hole in the roof. "You say this belongs to me?"

Alec gestured to the west. "Not the station. That belongs to the town. Just over the hill is Tidewater Inn. You own this stretch clear to the inlet."

"Nicole was here to finalize the purchase of the station. We're going to restore it as a museum for the island." She scanned the area and saw what she was looking for. "There's the cam." It was mounted on one of the posts. She walked directly to it and stopped a few feet away. "Whoever you are, if you have my friend, please don't hurt her," she said. "Her name is Nicole."

Alec's eyes were warm with sympathy when she turned toward him and brushed moisture from her cheeks. "I thought they might be watching. They say an attacker usually goes back to the scene of the crime. And professionals say friends and investigators should try to personalize the victim."

Alec stood with his hands in the pockets of his denim shorts. "It's possible someone's watching. A plea doesn't hurt." He pointed to the final landing before the sand. "Her cell phone was found there. Her rental car was parked along the road with the keys in the ignition."

She winced. "I saw one of the men toss the phone. Would his prints be on it? And what about her hat? I saw it fall off."

"I'm sure Tom is checking that out. I'll do what I can to find her," he promised. "The first thing we have to figure out is where she was staying. My cousin may know." He pulled out his phone and placed a call. "Hey, Tom, I'm with Libby Holladay. Have you found out where Nicole Ingram was staying?"

His voice faded to a drone as she stepped away and stared down the deserted beach. Not a house was in sight of where she stood. No wonder the men had taken Nicole from this location. Gooseflesh pebbled her arms at the thought of what they might be doing to her friend. She swallowed down the wave of nausea that rose in her throat. She had to find Nicole. The most likely reason

she was taken was too horrible to contemplate, so she considered whether there might be another reason. Nicole had been poking around about Libby's inheritance. Could there be any connection?

Libby took off her sandals and dug her toes into the warm sand. The sound of the surf washed over her in a rhythm that would have been soothing in other circumstances. Carrying her shoes, she stepped back to find out what Alec had learned. He was just finishing his call.

"Uh-huh. Okay. I'll tell her, thanks." He dropped the phone back into his pocket. "She was staying at the small inn you own. Tom was just about to head out there. We can meet him there and see what is in her room."

Libby glanced around one final time, but there was still nothing pointing her to Nicole's whereabouts. This search was already beginning to feel hopeless.

FIVE

Filtered light struck her eyelids. Nicole groaned and threw her hand over her eyes. The brightness pierced her skull like a knife. She licked dry lips, then pried one lid open, wincing when the brilliance intensified. She rolled to her back, then sat up.

Where was she? The sound of the surf rolled through the small window covered by a grimy curtain. Her head pounded, and she staggered to her feet. Her eyes were beginning to adjust to the light, and she glanced around. She seemed to be in a small building. Overhead were wooden planks, and she could see thatching through the boards. Her sandals and hat were missing, and so was her pink cover-up. She wore only her swimsuit. The dirt floor under her bare feet was cool and damp.

When she put her hand on the door, a rough wooden one, it moved. Surprised it wasn't locked, she stepped out of the shack and onto a mixture of sand and grass. A small beach began twenty feet away. She glanced around and realized she was on a tiny island, barely as big as her yard at home. No other land in the distance as far as she could see. Trying not to panic, she walked along the shore, straining to see something—anything—in the distance. There was nothing but seagulls and waves.

She was incredibly thirsty. Maybe there were provisions in the

shack. And what was she doing here? The last thing she could remember was talking to Libby about the inheritance she'd discovered.

She fingered the soreness on her jaw. Ducking into the shack, she circled the perimeter of the space, about sixteen feet square. There was no kitchen, just the small cot and a camp chair. No food or water. Maybe there was a stream on the little island that she'd missed.

She went back into the sunshine and cut behind the shack. No cistern, no stream. Her head spun, and she fought back the rising panic. She'd better get out of the heat and inside. As she skirted the side of the shack, she heard a boat's motor *putt-putt*ing along. Maybe she could get help! She ran to the beach and shaded her eyes with her hand. A small craft rode the waves. Maybe a fisherman?

She shouted and waved. "Help! I need help!"

The bow of the boat headed for the beach where she stood. As it neared, she saw that it held a young man about seventeen or eighteen. The wind whipped his dark hair, and he waved back. When the boat was just offshore, he shut off the motor and threw an anchor overboard. He jumped into the water, and the waves came to midthigh, barely dampening the hem of his black shorts. He reached back into the boat and extracted a box.

She waded out to meet him. When he reached her, she grabbed his arm. "I'm so glad you came this way. I need help. I don't remember how I got here, but I'll pay you to take me back to Hope Island."

Frowning, he shook off her grip. "I brought you some food and water."

She took a step back. "You knew I was here?" She struggled to make sense of it.

He brushed past her and walked toward the shack. "The water should last a couple days and the food is stuff like bread and peanut butter. Your brother will come get you when the room at the mental facility is ready."

She followed him inside. "I don't understand. I don't have a brother. You're not making any sense."

He set the box on the dirt floor by the cot and opened it. "Like I said, this should last you a few days. I'll be back then with more."

He was going to leave her. She grabbed his forearm and squeezed. "Listen to me! I don't have a brother. You can't leave me here."

He glanced at her, then backed away as if she frightened him. "He said you'd say that. It's only for a little while, until he can get you in. You tried to stick him with a knife, and he can't trust you around people. The mental hospital will have an opening in a couple of weeks. It's for your own good."

His expression was closed. She bolted for the door, slamming it shut behind her to slow him down. If she could get to the boat first, she could get away. She ran to the water and struggled through the waves to the craft, where she threw herself into the bottom of it. Sitting up, she saw him running toward her. She grabbed the rope with the anchor and yanked it up, then scrambled back to try to start the motor.

He reached the water and plunged toward her. She tugged on the rope to start the engine, but she didn't pull it hard enough. Before she could try again, he was at the side of the vessel. She kicked at his hands with her bare feet, but he hauled himself aboard. He grabbed her arm, and she bit his hand. Tasting blood, she bit harder and clawed at him with her nails. He grabbed her hair, tearing the dangling ponytail holder free before he finally seized her.

He shoved her overboard, and she came up spitting salt water. "Please, you have to help me," she panted.

"You are one crazy chick," he said. Using an oar, he pushed the boat away, then turned and started the engine.

She screamed and shouted for him to come back, but he didn't even look at her. Sobbing, she collapsed onto the beach.

———

Alec cruised by his house on the way to the hotel. Zach's bike was parked in front of the house, but Alec's gut clenched when he saw Zach tying off to the piling. He'd obviously been out in the old boat in spite of having been grounded. What was he going to do with that kid? Alec couldn't be here 24/7 when he had to work. And Zach was old enough to start taking responsibility for himself.

"I need to stop here at the house for a minute if you don't mind," Alec said.

"Of course. Is that your son?"

Alec parked the truck by the garage just off the street. "My nephew. My brother and his wife are dead, and I've got custody. As of two weeks ago." He shoved open his door.

"I'm so sorry," she said.

"I am too." He led the way to the house.

"Do you mind if I use your restroom?"

"Help yourself." He should have thought to offer. He got out of the truck and led the way to the house.

"Cute," she said, pausing on the stoop. "Built in the fifties?"

He nodded and took a glance at the all-too-familiar two-story. It was white clapboard with gray shutters and a red door. "You're good. I bought it from my parents when they moved to Richmond." He held the door open for her and pointed down the hall to the bathroom. The place was fairly clean. "I'm going to go down to talk to Zach."

His house was right on the harbor, and his fishing boats were docked just offshore. He stepped around to the back by the upper deck, which was anchored into the sand with pilings. Zach climbed down into the rubber boat and rowed to the small dock by the house. The boy had to have seen him standing on the pier, but Zach didn't wave. He probably knew he was in trouble. Alec

waited until the raft reached the dock. Tight-lipped, he tied up the rope Zach tossed to him.

Zach stepped over the side of the boat and onto the pier. He tossed a cheeky grin Alec's way. "I got a job, Uncle Alec!"

Alec's lecture died on his lips. "What kind of job?"

"I'm delivering some supplies." Zach glanced at him from under a lock of dark hair. "I know I was grounded, but Grandpa has been on me to get a job, and this was too good to pass up."

He wanted to ask how the job had come Zach's way while he was supposed to be staying home, but Alec bit back the words. "School is starting again soon. Will the hours be okay?"

Zach shook his head. "It will be over before school starts. It's supposed to last from two to four weeks."

"You should have called me."

"I tried. You didn't answer your phone."

Alec lifted a brow and pulled out his phone. Sure enough, it showed a missed call. Maybe when he and Libby had been in transit to the beach. It hardly paid to have a phone on the island. "Okay, but when you're not working, you still need to be at the house."

Zach brushed past him. "I know, I know. Sheesh, give me a break. I'm doing the best I can."

Maybe he was. The boy was so much like Alec was at that age. Always pushing the boundaries, impatient to be his own man, looking at anyone in authority with derision. At least Zach had a job. That was progress.

"Okay," Alec called after him. "I'm proud of you for getting a job."

Zach just hunched his shoulders and bounded up the stairs to the deck overlooking the water. He plopped down in a chair and pulled an electronic game out of his pocket. The back door opened, and Libby stepped out onto the deck. Alec jogged to intercept her. She'd take one look at Zach and think the kid was a

hoodlum. Alec reached the top of the deck as she stepped to where Zach sat.

"You must be Zach," Libby said.

Zach didn't look up from his game. "Yeah."

"Ready?" Alec said. "Your place is about two miles out of town."

Zach looked up then. "The old Mitchell place?"

Libby nodded.

"You're staying there?"

"I own it," Libby said. "I'm Ray Mitchell's oldest daughter."

Zach looked her up and down. "Boy, is Brent ticked. He had plans for that place."

"He's twenty-two," Alec pointed out. "What kind of plans could he have?"

Zach slouched into his chair. "Forget it."

Suppressing a sigh, Alec touched Libby's elbow. "Tom should be there any minute."

She resisted the pull on her arm. "I'd really like to hear what Zach has to say," she said. "You probably already know this, Zach, but I didn't even know I had a brother and sister until yesterday."

His head came up and his eyes widened. "No kidding? Brent didn't say anything about that in the ice-cream shop. Just that some woman he'd never met was going to have the property. Said it was his sister."

"Did he know about me before our father died?"

Zach shrugged. "I don't know."

"I'd like to meet him. And Vanessa. Do they know I'm here?"

"I don't think so. He figures you'll sell the place. There's an investor after it hot and heavy."

"Oh?" There was interest in her voice.

Alec had heard the rumors. Now that the land was out of Ray's hands, everything was liable to change. He didn't know if that was good or bad.

SIX

Sand drifted across the pavement in places. The island was unlike any place Libby had ever seen. Wild, remote, and unbelievably beautiful with whitecaps rolling to dunes on one side and tangled maritime forest on the other.

She leaned forward as Alec's truck crested the hill. She caught her breath when she saw the inn standing guard over the empty beach that stretched in both directions. A small but inviting dock jutted over the water. Her chest was so tight she couldn't breathe, couldn't do more than take in the lovely Georgian mansion overlooking the Atlantic. Large trees sheltered it, and it looked as if it had been in that place forever. In a moment, she felt she knew the spot as if it had always been a part of her.

She could almost hear the voices of previous owners in her head. Pioneers, business owners, statesmen. The inn was alive with the history of its past. She couldn't wait to explore, to touch the woodwork and plaster walls.

"Th-This is mine?" she asked, getting out the truck when it rolled to a stop.

"So I hear."

The place clearly needed work, but she didn't care. She stared at the front of the building. "You said it was an inn." She eyed its

41

elegant lines. "It looks like a mansion. It's Georgian. Built in the late seventeen hundreds or early eighteen hundreds."

"It's an inn now. Small, I know. About fifteen suites, I think."

There were two curving staircases up to the porch, one on each side. There had to be two thousand square feet of balconies and porches. Great arched windows looked out on the waves. The place was in serious need of paint, but her mind's eye could see it restored to its earlier glory. How could she bear to sell it? But she had to. For her stepbrother. For Holladay Renovations.

He took her elbow and guided her up the nearest steps. "It used to be a single-family home. There should be some stuff about it in the attic."

No wonder Nicole had said she would love it. Libby took in every angle, every graceful line. "It's so large. Who would build such a magnificent place clear out here?"

"I don't remember all the history, but the builder had some kind of role in early government, and I guess he wanted to impress everyone. Though there weren't many to impress out here but Hatteras Indians. This place is really the beginning of our history as we know it, so it's in the school book about our island."

The porch was expansive, but the floor needed paint. Now that she was closer, Libby saw the signs of decay in the peeling shutters and rotting fretwork. It would take a lot of money to restore this place. Money she didn't have. But oh, how she wanted to keep it.

Alec opened the oversized front entrance. "The lobby is the room to the right."

Sand and salt had scoured the wood floors. Libby ran her fingertips along blistered paint on the plaster walls. She could repair it. She went down through the foyer to what would have been a parlor on the right. Ceilings soared to twelve feet. She glanced up and saw that the plaster drooped in places. It needed to be put back in place with plaster washers and screws. Or replastered altogether.

The reception counter was made of driftwood and marble. The woman behind the counter was in her early thirties. Her dark hair was up in a ponytail that curled down her back. She wore no makeup, and her strikingly beautiful skin didn't need any help. She smiled when Alec introduced Libby.

"I'm Delilah Carter, Ms. Holladay," she said. "I'm so sorry about your trouble. If there's anything I can do to help, just let me know." She rose with a key in her hand. "Let me show you to your friend's room."

"I see Tom outside," Alec said. "I'll join you upstairs in a minute." He walked back the way they'd come.

Libby fell into step beside Delilah. "Did you get a chance to talk to Nicole?"

The woman stepped into the foyer and started up the steps, easily six feet wide. "Oh yes. Lovely girl."

Libby mounted the steps with her. "Did she tell you why she was here?"

"For business, so she said." Delilah inserted the key into the lock and turned it. She opened the door and stepped aside for Libby to enter. At the first sight of her friend's familiar pink suitcase, Libby's eyes burned. Nicole's pajamas were in a heap on the floor. Her clothes spilled from the top of the suitcase. In the bathroom, her makeup littered the sink counter. Libby picked up her friend's hairbrush and caught a scent of the shampoo Nicole used.

She swiped fiercely at the moisture on her face. Crying wouldn't find Nicole.

———

Alec intercepted Tom on the porch. "Any news?"

Tom's lips flattened. "Not about Nicole."

"What's that mean?"

"Ms. Holladay hasn't been truthful with us." Tom took off his hat and wiped his brow with the back of his sleeve. "The reason I can't view the video of the abduction is because it was wiped off the server. The computer's IP address was traced. Libby did it."

Alec's gut clenched. Though he'd known her only a few hours, he would have sworn her innocence and concern were genuine. "So there is no proof her story is even true. The cell phone could have been planted. The car could have been left out there by anyone. We know she only came to town today though, right?"

Tom nodded. "I talked to Earl Franklin and his wife. They met her this morning. But I'm questioning all the charters I know of to make sure she didn't get here a few days ago to lay out her plan."

Alec marshaled all his objectivity. Since when had a pretty face blinded him? "When was Nicole last seen?"

"I was about to question Delilah. No one in town saw her yesterday."

"What about Vanessa? Libby claims she was meeting Nicole."

Tom returned his hat to his head. "I haven't spoken to her yet, but I will. Right now I want to look through Nicole's room and talk to Delilah."

"You haven't gone through her belongings yet?"

Tom shook his head. "My first priority was to find her."

"Delilah just let Libby into the suite."

"Great, just great." Tom jerked open the door and rushed into the house.

Alec followed. He'd sure botched that one.

———

"Libby?"

Libby put the hairbrush back onto the sink when Alec called to her from the bedroom. "In here."

When she stepped into the bedroom, she found identical expressions on the faces of the two men in the doorway. Alec was making an obvious attempt to mask his suspicion, but the sheriff's gaze bored through her. She took a step back.

"What have you touched?" the sheriff demanded.

"Nothing but the things in the bathroom." She stepped out of the doorway so he could brush past her. "What are you looking for?"

He glanced around the small bathroom. "You had no business coming in here until I had a chance to clear the scene."

"It's not a crime scene," she said.

"There may still be clues to what happened to her."

He hadn't been nearly so unfriendly at his office. And even Alec was tense. "H-Have you found her?"

The sheriff whirled and glared at her. "You mean her body? Is there something you want to tell us?"

The kidnapping had changed into a murder, and she was a suspect. That was the only possible reason for his change of demeanor. "You found her body, didn't you?"

"What was on that video that you were so eager to make sure no one saw?" the sheriff asked.

His accusing tone made her swallow hard. He knew she'd erased the video. "It was an accident. I was trying to save it so I could show it to the police. The screen went blank and it was gone."

"I might have believed you if you'd admitted it from the first. But you said nothing about it when you were in my office."

"I was going to, but—"

"Right." He turned around and stared at the room. "Delilah, did she touch anything in here?"

"No, sir," Delilah said. "I could see her when she was in the bathroom too. She didn't do anything." The phone rang in the distance. "I'll be right back." She dashed out of the room.

"Alec, take a look in the suitcase. I'll go through the drawers."

Libby curled her fingers into her palms and prayed that he would find something that would lead them to Nicole and those two men. "Just so you know, I did touch the hairbrush."

Tom looked her over. "Thanks."

Alec pulled shorts and tops out, then dumped out a bag with suntan lotion, sunglasses, and other sundries in it. The sheriff was opening the furniture's drawers and looking through them.

Libby spied Nicole's laptop on the desk and picked it up. "Maybe there's something on this."

The men glanced up. Tom scowled. "I told you not to touch anything. Alec, you know more about computers than I do. Have a look."

Alec lifted a brow and reached out his hand. "May I?"

Surprised he was gentlemanly enough to ask in spite of the suspicion in his expression, she handed it over. "You know anything about Macs?"

"I have one myself." He set the laptop on the desk and opened the lid. Pulling out the chair, he sat down and began to peruse the files. "She has a lot of files on this."

Libby stood behind him and watched over his shoulder. "Sort by date," she said.

He did as she suggested, then leaned forward and read through the sorted files. "What's this one?" He clicked on a file titled "Hope Beach."

The file opened with the picture of a woman. "Who is that?" Libby asked.

"Your sister, Vanessa. Definitely a family resemblance," Alec said, his voice distracted.

Libby drank in the woman's photo before the sheriff blocked her view.

He bent down to read the document. "It's kind of a diary.

46

Ms. Ingram is talking about everything she saw and did since she came. Scroll to the bottom first. Maybe there's an entry for yesterday."

Libby peered over his shoulder and read the entry.

Someone was outside my door last night. He whispered my name. I think it was Brent trying to scare me into doing what he wants. I'll have a talk with him tomorrow.

Libby drew in a breath. "Would Brent have hurt her?"

Tom straightened and stared at her. "Let me handle the investigation."

She clasped her hands together. "Look, Sheriff, I know it looks bad that I didn't tell you about the file, but you're wasting precious time by investigating me. I didn't have anything to do with her disappearance. I can prove where I was when she went missing."

He said nothing at first and continued to stare at her with those accusing eyes. "What kind of proof?"

"For one thing, you can track the time on my cell phone when I called in the abduction."

"You could have disposed of her and gone back to Virginia Beach before you made the call. It's not that far."

Delilah poked her head into the room. "Hurricane warning just came through. That smaller one has veered this way. We need to get the hurricane shutters in place."

"Is the Tidewater in danger?" Libby asked.

"We're on higher ground here so we're safe from the surge," Delilah said, "but we don't know how much wind we're going to get."

"I'd better check in at the station," Alec said. "I'm off duty, but they may need me to begin evacuations. How long do we have?"

"Twenty-four hours or so," Delilah said.

This was her place now. Libby roused herself. "I'll help with the shutters."

The wind had freshened, but it was far from gale strength yet. The hurricane wouldn't be here for hours, if it even hit. Storms were notoriously capricious. Alec strained to see any sign of movement on the tiny strip of land below as the helicopter powered toward it. He'd already helped evacuate several families to the mainland.

"What's wrong with McEwan?" he asked Curtis.

"Said he thought he might be having a heart attack. The boat is too far away, so they called us."

Alec winced. "We're nearly there. We'll have Sara check him out." She had a manner that generally soothed patients.

The chopper reached an open field just past the pier on the small island below. Though the island had no official name, those in the Banks referred to it as Oyster Island, because some of the best oyster beds were found a few hundred feet offshore. Five families lived on it, all related in some way. McEwan lived in a shanty on the north side. He'd built the place when he was forty and hadn't left the island since. He had to be in his eighties now. He relied on his son to go for supplies. Alec had always liked the old fellow's stories about life in the old days. Alec suspected McEwan had been a rumrunner back in the day.

The rotors were still whirring when he ducked out of the helicopter with Curtis and Sara. They ran through the pelting rain toward the small cabin. The three of them rushed with the stretcher into the building, where they found McEwan moaning on his cot.

"Took you long enough," he gasped. "Ticker's acting up." He hadn't shaved in several days, and the gray stubble added to his pallor. He wore a dirty T-shirt and cotton pajama bottoms that looked like they hadn't been washed in a month.

Sara brushed past the men and knelt by the bed. "Let me take a peek." She pulled out her stethoscope and listened to his heart.

"I'm going to give you a shot to relax your arteries," she said. "We'll get you to the mainland where the doctor can look at you, but I don't think it's a heart attack. Might be indigestion or gall bladder."

"I knew I shouldn't have had those raw oysters," the old man said. "They smelled a little nasty."

Alec grimaced. Oysters could contain dangerous bacteria when eaten raw, though oysters found offshore here were generally safe. It was hard to say what the old man had consumed. "We'll get you taken care of."

Once Sara administered the shot, the pain lines around the old man's face eased. Curtis and Sara got him onto the stretcher while Alec gathered a few items from the battered dresser by the bed. "Anything else you need?" Alec asked.

"My gun." McEwan pointed to a shotgun leaning by the door. "And the old suitcase under my bed."

Alec grabbed the gun, then reached under the bed for the battered old metal case. "Here, Sara, you take this stuff and I'll help Curtis carry the stretcher."

"I'm perfectly capable of doing my job." Sara grabbed the bottom of the stretcher.

Touchy. Alec raised his hands. "Suit yourself." Sara leaned in to whisper in his ear. "We'd better take him to the doctor at Hope Island first. I don't think there's time to get him clear to the mainland. I don't like the sound of his chest." Carrying the old man's belongings, Alec led the way back to the helicopter.

"Did that boat get back okay?" McEwan's voice was slurred and his lids droopy.

"What boat?"

McEwan waved his hand to the east. "Saw two men motor by yesterday. They didn't look like no watermen to me. One was yelling at the other one about how to steer. Didn't seem to bother the woman who was sleeping though."

Alec exchanged a glance with Curtis. Two men and a woman? Could it possibly be Nicole Ingram? Or was the old man out of his head? "Where were they headed?"

McEwan's eyes fluttered, then closed. "Out to sea. East."

Alec wanted to ignore the information, but what if the men were heading out to dump Nicole?

———

The inn was dark and gloomy with the hurricane shutters closed. Libby had never been in a hurricane before, and the breathless quality of the air added to her unease. "I think I'll sit on the porch and give my stepbrother a call," she told Delilah, who was instructing the housekeeping staff to ready some extra rooms.

Delilah nodded and Libby stepped out into the twilight air with the inn's portable phone in her hand. The sun was almost down and the sound of the cicadas enveloped her as she settled on the swing at the end of the porch. Could the police seriously think she might have hurt Nicole?

Libby put down the phone and clasped her knees to her chest. She had to figure out a way to prove her innocence. As long as the sheriff was investigating her, his attention wasn't on the right person. She should have told him about her mess-up with the computer. Everything was spiraling out of control because of her lapse of judgment. She could kick herself.

She still hadn't opened the items from her father. There hadn't been time, and she wanted no interruptions when she took a peek at the letters and the contents of the envelope.

The sand glimmered in the moonlight. The scene reminded her of when she was a little girl. She and her mom usually spent two weeks along a beach. One year it was California, another year the Texas Gulf, and yet another the cold water of the Pacific

Northwest. The various vacations were a kaleidoscope of memories, all slightly hazy with an aura of warmth and love.

That zany woman with the long braid and beads who had been her mother was hard to reconcile with a parent who would lie and deprive her daughter of all contact with her father. Yet that was the situation, if everything she'd learned today was true. But was it?

Libby stood and walked restlessly to the other side of the large porch. No matter what, she knew her mother had loved her. In spite of their constant travels and the many men in her mother's life, Libby's well-being had always been primary. She would cling to that fact for now.

Headlamps pierced the gloom and tires crunched on gravel. Her pulse jumped when she recognized Alec's truck in the glow of the security light. His door slammed, and he went around to the passenger side and helped an old man out.

Libby met them at the foot of the steps. Alec was assisting the man to the inn. "Is he all right?"

"This is Mr. McEwan. He lives on one of the unnamed islands. He had a little bit of angina, but the doctor says he's going to be okay. We generally bring people to the inn during a big blow. I assume that's still okay?"

Libby swallowed her disappointment at his distant tone. "Of course. Let me get the door." She jogged up the steps and held open the front door. "Delilah, we have a guest."

Delilah appeared in the entry. "I'll put him in one of our three downstairs rooms. This way." She led Alec and Mr. McEwan down the hall.

Libby wanted to rush to her room and eat a whole bag of jalapeño jelly beans, but she forced herself to walk back to the swing. Hiding away would make her look guilty.

SEVEN

The windows in Alec's house were boarded, and all they could do was wait. Few of the Hope Beach residents had left for the mainland. Too many times they'd evacuated and then been refused entry to their homes for weeks.

He paced the wood floor in his living room and listened to the wind beginning to pick up outside. The house was on stilts to deal with storm surges, so he and Zach should be okay. It still stood after Hurricane Helene's visit in 1958, a category 3. This was only a 1. Other 3s over the years, Gloria and Emily, had left the house fairly unscathed as well, so he wasn't worried, but he couldn't say the same for Zach.

Zach put down his game, then picked it up again and glanced toward the boarded windows. "You think we'll take a direct hit? And what about the smaller islands offshore? Will they flood?"

The boy's eyes were wide. Alec still remembered the first hurricane he'd gone through. He was just as nervous as Zach.

"We'll be all right," he assured his nephew. "It's supposed to give a glancing blow to this side of the island. That's all. And God is here with us."

The boy blinked. He got up and paced to the other side of the living room. "That's the thing, Uncle Alec. I've heard that my whole

life, but where was God when my parents went down in that plane? If God loves me, then how could he let them die like that?"

At least Zach was talking. "He was with your dad in the cockpit. They are with him now. Being a Christian doesn't mean trouble never comes our way, Zach. It just means God is here, and he gives us the grace to get through the heartache."

Zach hunched his shoulders. Alec could feel the boy's pain. He was an adult, but he'd wrestled with his brother's death too. Why do bad things happen to good people? It was an age-old question, and every Christian dealt with it sooner or later. Poor Zach had been faced with it much too soon.

The phone on the end table rang. Alec glanced at the screen. It was Frank Bowden, Zach's maternal grandfather. Alec's gut tightened the way it always did when he had to speak with the man.

"Hey, Frank," he said. Zach's head came up when he heard his grandfather's first name. Alec shot the boy a reassuring smile.

"Alec." Frank's voice boomed in his ear. "I hear there's a hurricane headed your way. Why haven't you evacuated?"

"I'm needed here to help. We're riding it out."

"We?" Frank demanded. "My grandson is there too?"

"He's fine."

"You have a boat. You could have taken it to the mainland! Or that fancy helicopter you're so fond of hotdogging in."

Alec pulled the phone away from his ear a bit. Frank's voice had nearly deafened him. "Yes, I could have, but it's only a category 1. We'll be fine."

"That's the problem with your family, Alec. None of you ever gives any thought to what's best for everyone. You think things will automatically be all right."

Alec clutched the phone almost tight enough to break it. He couldn't lose his temper. Frank had his own view of the world. It was varnished tightly in place, and no one was going to change it.

When Alec made no comment, Frank huffed. "I want to talk to my grandson."

Without another word, Alec took the phone from his ear and handed it to Zach. His nephew took it hesitantly. He had an uneasy relationship with his mother's dad. No one could live up to Frank's high standards, and Zach had given up trying by the time he was five.

"Hi, Grandpa," Zach said. "No, we're fine. I'm not scared. I want to see what a hurricane is like. It's only a category 1. We'll be fine."

Alec hid a grin and went out to the back deck. The gray waves crashed over the pier and rolled dirty white foam onto the sand. The tide left flotsam behind as it receded for another attack. A dark sheet of rain that was the first outer band of the hurricane was just offshore and would be on him in a few minutes, but he lifted his face to the wind and exulted in God's power.

Such an awesome display. God could choose to spare this little spot or wipe it out. It was all in his control. Alec stared another minute, then the first drops of cold rain struck his face. He returned to the house and got inside just as the deluge hit. The rain thundered on the metal roof. It sounded as though the house was coming in on them, and he began to wonder if he'd made the right decision to ride out the storm. Even a storm this weak could kill.

Zach's eyes were wide and fearful. "Uncle Alec!" His nephew swallowed hard and handed the phone back to Alec. "It's Tom."

Alec took the phone. "Trouble?" he asked his cousin.

"We just got word that high tide is going to hit at the same time in the morning as the storm surge." Tom's voice was tense and clipped. "And Mr. Carter called. Can you evacuate him to the Tidewater Inn?"

It was going to be a long night.

"On my way." Alec hung up the phone. "I need to help some of the shut-ins. You can wait upstairs in case there's a storm surge."

Zach shook his head. "No way! I'm a man now, Uncle Alec. Let me come along and help."

Alec grabbed a yellow slicker and boots. "Get dressed, then." He tossed Zach's gear at him. "Hurry."

He prayed for those caught in this storm. That no lives would be lost. Property could be replaced, but lives were much more precious.

⌒

The storm would be on them soon. Libby sat in a swing on the expansive porch with her father's package in her hands. Bob Marley was crooning to her through her iPod earbuds, and the reggae soothed her ragged nerves as she waited for the rain to hit. The windows were shuttered and ready. The generator was gassed up, and the house hunkered down before the coming storm.

She stared out at the sea. The waves were high, and a few surfers were out braving the massive rollers. Crazy. She watched them for a few minutes, but her task couldn't be delayed forever. Libby pressed the envelope between her hands and felt something hard inside. A small locket with a photo? A bracelet? She couldn't tell. She flipped the envelope over and slipped her finger under the flap. It opened easily. She inhaled, then upended the envelope so the contents slipped out onto her lap. A necklace, a notebook, and a letter fell out.

She picked up the necklace first. There were beads strung on jute. It was quite worn. She rolled one bead over to see an engraved letter on the other side. She could barely make out a J. The letters on the other beads had worn off, and she had no idea what it was supposed to spell. The paper might explain, but she

found herself a little reluctant to unfold it and read it—almost frightened, though there was no reason for the pounding in her chest. Who was this man Ray? And why had he deserted her?

She laid the necklace on her lap, unfolded the letter, and glanced at the greeting. *Elizabeth*. No one called her Elizabeth. That made the letter even more special in a strange way. Had he called her by her full name when she was a baby? No matter how hard she tried, she couldn't dredge up a memory of the man who had fathered her. Her gut tightened again, and she pressed her lips together. He was dead and gone, unable to hurt her any longer. These were just words on a page. She moved so the porch light shone on the letter and she forced herself to read.

My dear Elizabeth,

So here you are in my home. Finally, you are where I've longed for you to be these past twenty-five years. My biggest regret in life is that I was not part of your formation, but God assures me he has kept you safe under his wings. I have prayed for you every day of your life, and even now as I face my final days, I desperately pray that you will walk with the Lord. I want to fold you in my arms when you step onto heaven's golden streets.

I know there is so much you don't understand. I trust my sister, Pearl, will fill you in on many of the circumstances that forced me to abdicate my responsibilities. Just know that I have loved you so much even when I've been unable to contact you. I hope the inheritance can make up in some small way for my neglect. I know Brent and Vanessa have never really cared for the inn. Somehow, I believe you will love it as I have loved it. Do with it as you will though. It's yours.

Perhaps you are wondering what this old necklace means. My wife made it for me in 1992, and it never left my neck until

I took it off to give to Horace for you. "What Would Jesus Do?" has been the guiding mantra of my life. As you try to acclimatize yourself to the island and to your siblings, I want you to think about those words in all the challenges you face. Every day, I'd like you to jot down when you succeeded in the right responses and when you didn't.

I realize I have no right to ask anything of you. Any rights I might have had were destroyed when I walked away. I make no excuses for my failures. But if you'll wear this necklace and heed its reminder, it would be the greatest of all the possible legacies I might leave you. Much more valuable than the inn and the land.

I pray my God keeps and protects you all the days of your life. That you will walk humbly before him and serve him always. Your siblings will take this very hard, so I ask you to be generous in grace toward them. Extend them as much mercy as you can. The transition into the family will be challenging, and I wish I could be here to help with that. But even though I am absent in the body, I'm rooting for you from heaven. I love you, my dear girl, and always have.

Dad

Libby's face was wet, and she choked back the sobs building in her chest. He'd loved her. All these years when she thought he didn't care, he'd loved her and prayed for her. And had God *really* assured him that he'd kept her safe? She didn't understand any of it. Her father said to talk to her aunt, and tomorrow she would ask Alec to introduce them. Pearl. She liked the name and only hoped she could learn to love this unknown aunt—and even more importantly, that her aunt Pearl would love her.

The jute was rough in her hands. The necklace took on special meaning. Her father had worn it for twenty years. The worn beads had been smoothed by his skin. It was so loved that his fingers

had worn off all but one of the letters. But now she knew what they were. *WWJD.*

She lifted it to her neck and fastened it. The beads felt warm, almost alive. She'd become a Christian two years ago, but there was so much about faith that she didn't understand. And she didn't know if she'd ever stopped to consider what a godly response to any tough situation might be. Too often she reacted without thinking. She fingered the beads. What would Jesus do about this place? How was she supposed to know?

EIGHT

Nicole waited in vain for rescue as the wind rose through the afternoon. When the wind had first started to freshen, she was sure someone would be along any minute. But the hurricane was upon her. And she had nowhere to go for safety.

She peered through the single window of the shack. The sea was much too rough for anyone to come now. She was on her own. She opened the door. The sky was downright scary with black clouds blocking the sun. Tossing waves that left her breathless with fear crowded the shack. The flashes of lightning and rolls of thunder were terrifying, but not as frightening as the thought of drowning. If she didn't get higher, she was going to die. The surge was already swirling around her feet. The best she could do with her food and water was put it on the cot, but she feared it would soon be underwater.

She swiped the rivulets of water from her eyes and clung to the door as she stared at the small island. Through the driving storm, she could see a lone palm tree, but the wind had nearly bent it double. No sense in climbing that. More surges of water would be coming through. She had to get on top of the shack. It was her only hope. The sides of the building were rough-sawn boards, but there was a small window ledge that might help her climb. She grabbed hold of the top window frame and hoisted

herself up, planting one bare foot on the window ledge. The wind buffeted her back to the ground, and she splashed face-first into the seawater. She came up spitting salt and sand.

Maybe around back she would be protected from the wind enough to climb. Sloshing through the flood, she hurried to the rear. A plastic five-gallon bucket floated in the water. She upended it, then stepped on its bottom and managed to grasp the low roof. As she hauled herself up, the wind hit her again, driving stinging water into her face.

She wasn't going to survive this. Pushing the thought away, she swung one leg onto the roof. She got the other leg up too and lay gasping on the splintered surface with the wind trying to dislodge her. She forced her fingers and toes into every crevice she could find, but it took every bit of strength she possessed to stay atop the shack.

She pressed her face into the shingles and held on. If she fell again, she didn't think she would have the strength to climb, or to survive the night in the water.

Tidewater Inn seemed to shrug off the effects of the wind, though the storm howled mightily in rage at the way the inn withstood its power. Libby huddled under an afghan on the armchair in the parlor. Mr. McEwan seemed oblivious to the danger as he sat drinking his coffee and eating Delilah's fresh-baked cookies. The roar outside made her shudder. Where was Nicole in all this? Libby could only hope and pray she was all right.

Delilah flipped off the television. "The rain has messed up the satellite signal," she said. "Would you like some cookies, Libby?"

"No thanks."

"I'm always hungry when I'm nervous." Delilah headed toward the kitchen.

Libby rose and paced the Oriental rug that covered the oak

floor. *Please, God, don't let Nicole be in any danger from this storm. Let us find her alive and unharmed.*

A thunderous pounding came on the front door. She rushed to answer it. Alec stumbled in with a deluge of rain and wet, salty wind. Libby caught a glimpse over his shoulder of the stormy sky and ocean. Scary. Alec was supporting a wizened old man. Zach was behind him with an older lady almost as round as she was tall.

Alec slammed the door behind them. "I have two more guests for you. I hope that's still all right."

"Of course. We have plenty of empty rooms. Let me fetch some towels." She raced to the laundry room and grabbed a stack of fluffy towels, then hurried back to the parlor where she helped the elderly couple dry off. A thought flickered through her head. What would taking in people cost her? Could these people afford to pay for the room?

"Alec arrived just in time," the lady said. "But I'm worried about my angels."

Alec put his hand on her shoulder. "I had Zach load them in the back of the SUV."

She patted his hand. "Oh, Alec, did you really? You're a darling young man. Could you bring them in?"

"I'll get them." He glanced at Libby and motioned for her to follow him. At the entry, he stopped and folded his arms across his chest. "The lady is Pearl Chilton. Your aunt."

Her pulse kicked. "My father's sister?"

He nodded. "She's a sweetheart. I think you'll love her."

He was still staring at her with a wary expression. "Did you tell her I was here?" she asked.

He shook his head. "I thought I'd leave that up to you."

"Who's the older gentleman? I thought they were married."

"Her neighbor, Thomas Carter. Their houses were both flooded. He was at her house when I got there. Pearl still works as the town postmistress. She's done that for thirty years."

"She's been looking in on my brother and sister since my father died, correct?"

He nodded. "She should have been at your dad's house in town, but she was at her cottage trying to get her angels."

"Angels?"

"Collectible angels. The living room is stuffed with them."

"I can help you bring them in."

"I can handle it. I'll be back in a few minutes." He opened the door and stepped into the driving rain.

Thunder boomed overhead, and Libby shut her eyes against the brilliant flash of lightning. She slammed the door, then took a deep breath and went back to the parlor. Pearl had taken her long hair out of its bun, and the salt-and-pepper tresses lay drying on her shoulders and down onto her huge bosom. Barely five feet tall, she was round as an egg except for the shapely legs revealed by her skirt.

Pearl seemed to realize Libby was staring at her. "Is something wrong, young lady? I have a smudge on my nose?"

Family. She had an aunt, siblings, probably cousins here. Libby couldn't take it all in. If only she knew Nicole was all right, the moment would be perfect.

She shook her head. "I . . . I'm sorry for staring." She walked nearer to the fireplace where Pearl sat combing out her hair. "I'm Libby. Libby Holladay."

Pearl put the comb down. Her gaze searched Libby's face as she heaved herself out of the chair. "Ray's Libby?"

Libby's throat locked, and she nodded.

"Oh, my dear," Pearl said softly. She held out her arms.

Libby leaned forward and was enfolded in soft arms and an immense hug that smelled of lavender and mint. It was all she could do not to break down. Had her father ever held her like this? Once the fervency of Pearl's embrace lessened, Libby pulled away and swiped the back of her hand across her damp eyes.

Pearl's faded green eyes studied Libby's face. "I see your father in you," she said. "You have his dark eyes. I wish he were still alive to see you. Not raising you was his greatest sorrow in life."

Libby couldn't stop the tears that welled then. "I never knew he cared," she choked out. "My mother said he didn't."

Pearl pressed her lips together. "I don't like to speak ill of anyone, but your mother was determined to be free."

Libby sank onto the rug by Pearl's feet and struggled to keep her expression neutral. Just listening didn't mean she was betraying her mother's memory. There were two sides to every story.

Pearl settled back on the chair. Clasping her knees to her chest, Libby watched her aunt's face in the firelight. "What was he like, my father?"

Pearl smiled. "Generous as the day is long. He was always helping other people. I think that's why God blessed him so with material things. He knew Ray would let them run through his hands to other people."

"I—I hear my siblings are not too pleased to learn about me."

Pearl's lips flattened. "Oh, they always knew about you. Ray never made a secret of it. He spoiled them too much though, and they think the world owes them a living. This will be good for them."

Libby's growing impression of her siblings wasn't flattering. How long before she met them? The wind rattled the door. Did her aunt realize that Nicole was her friend? "I'm here to find my business partner, Nicole."

Pearl gasped. "The girl who was taken—she's your friend?"

The compassion in her aunt's voice nearly broke Libby's composure. She nodded and swallowed hard. "I saw them take her on the beach cam."

"Oh, my dear girl." Her aunt leaned over and hugged her again. "I've been praying for that young woman. Somehow, I think she's all right."

63

"You do?"

Pearl nodded. "When I pray, I have a sense of peace. You're going to find her."

"I hope so. It's so scary."

Pearl pursed her lips. "What about your mother? Where is she now?"

Libby shook her head. "She's gone. She died a year ago."

Pearl's lips flattened. "She was always a bit of a hippie. I imagine you took care of her—made sure she ate and took care of the house. You have that competent air about you."

Her aunt was perceptive. Libby nodded. "Mom always had a childlike way about her, but she was a good mother. Our house was always fun." *Until it was time to move on to the next town.* "I got a job in a museum when I was sixteen. That's where I learned to love history. I got a scholarship to college and got to follow my dream."

"What are you doing these days?"

"Nicole and I restore historic houses, then sell them. I love preserving part of the past."

Pearl stared at her. "Your father would have been proud of you. I wish he'd gotten to meet you."

Libby was forming a picture of her father that was very different from all she'd been told. But which was right?

NINE

The wind howled and Libby paced through the night. With every rattle of the storm against the windowpane in her bedroom, she prayed for Nicole, then for herself and the siblings she had yet to meet. Where was Nicole riding out the storm? Was she hurt? Would her siblings like her when they got to know her? The questions battered her.

The clock said it should be daybreak, but the black clouds outside blocked the sunrise. She might as well get up. The bedroom door creaked when she opened it, but she doubted the sound would carry above the pounding of the rain against the house. She slipped down the hall to the back stairway that led down to the kitchen. The house shuddered, and she grabbed the doorjamb, then felt along the wall for the switch. The bulb in the stairwell was dim, but its comforting glow lit the rubber-covered stairs.

In the kitchen she fixed some tea, then carried the hot mug to the parlor, where she curled on the sofa with just one light on to push back the dark. The storm still raged outside, but she felt safe and snug surrounded by the possessions of her father.

A shadow loomed in the hall, then Alec spoke her name. "You okay?"

She set her tea on the coffee table. "Did I wake you?"

COLLEEN COBLE

He shook his head and stepped into the room. "I wasn't sleeping. You had the same idea as me." He held up a Pepsi. "Only mine was easier."

Once he was settled into the armchair, she leaned her head back against the sofa. "I know you're wondering if I did something to Nicole," she said. "I didn't."

"I didn't say you did."

"Your cousin thinks I did. And you're acting differently now. Wary."

He took a gulp of his soda. "You have to admit it looks bad."

"I agree." She held his gaze. At least he wasn't afraid to look at her. "I care about Nicole. That's why I'm here. Will you give me the benefit of the doubt?"

"Okay, I can do that much."

She exhaled when his expression went from cold to lukewarm. "Good." Better to move on to another topic. "I like Pearl."

He wiped the moisture from the soda can. "I knew you would. She's an institution in town. Everyone loves her, even though she knows everyone else's business."

"I noticed that. She already knew my life story."

"She won't repeat it either."

"I didn't think she would." Libby paused, uncertain how much he knew. "She said my mother was adamant about no contact. My father didn't want it that way."

"I'm sure that's true. Ray loved his kids. Sometimes to a fault."

"Did he ever speak of me?" She held her breath, hoping to hear some small snippet of her father's love for her.

He shook his head. "Not to me."

Libby picked up an enameled egg from the table and rolled it in her palms. "According to Pearl, my siblings knew about me. She said my father made no secret of my existence."

"Pearl would know."

She put down the egg and pressed her hand against her forehead. "So much coming at me so fast. I just want to find Nicole, but there's all this other information clamoring to be absorbed. I can't even think."

"You saw the cam late in the afternoon?"

She nodded. "I came right away, but I couldn't find a boat to bring me across the sound until yesterday morning."

"What did you do all night?"

"I sat on the pier. I paced the dock and prayed."

He smiled. "So you're a believer too."

She glanced at him, surprised at the approval in his voice. "Not a very good one. I make it to church about once a month. Maybe that's why this has happened. God is punishing me."

"Forget that idea. Bad things happen even to good people. Life is hard. God never said it wouldn't be. And he's with us in the hard times."

"I feel very alone," she admitted.

"I know Tom will do all he can to find her."

"I might believe that if he will look somewhere other than at me." She finally spoke her greatest fear. "What if they dumped her at sea and she's fighting the waves out there?" He didn't have to answer that. If that was Nicole's fate, she'd be dead by now.

"There's no reason to think that."

She stared at him, caught by a certain tone in his voice. Almost a hesitancy. "Do you know something you're not telling me?"

There was a long silence before he spoke. "Mr. McEwan said he saw two men go past his little island in a boat. He mentioned a sleeping woman."

She sprang to her feet. "Nicole! Did he see Nicole?"

He held up his hand. "We don't know that. I'm going to take a run out there in my boat though. Once the storm subsides."

"Can I come?"

"If you like."

She bit her lip. "Everyone thinks she's dead. I can sense it. I just can't believe that. We have to find her." She willed him to agree with her, but he looked down at his hands.

He rose from the armchair. "I think I'll call into the office and see if I'm needed."

It was clear that he thought Nicole was dead.

———

The storm had finally died. Though it was still early, Libby took her mug of tea to the porch. The jute necklace was warm at her neck. She touched it, then opened the notebook her father left. What would Jesus have done yesterday? She grimaced when she realized money had been her first thought when Alec brought in people escaping the storm. Jesus would have been concerned about people, not money. She wrote down yesterday's date and jotted down how she'd failed. Today she would try to do better. She closed the notebook and tucked it into the cloth bag at her feet, then went down the steps to the beach.

Debris littered the lawn, but the old house had withstood the blow like the proud matriarch she was. Libby studied the stately lines of the house. It was so beautiful. Someone would pay handsomely to own this. She walked down the sloping sand. The boardwalk and cam where Nicole had been taken were about a mile down the beach. This stretch of sand seemed to go on forever. Did she dare walk along the shore alone?

Then a figure caught her eye. A man strode along the beach with a clipboard in his hand. Strikingly handsome, he had almost-black hair and broad shoulders. Muscular legs extended from walking shorts. As he neared, she realized his eyes were a vivid blue. He put her in mind of a young Elvis Presley. The breeze lifted his dark hair from his forehead.

She lifted a smile in the man's direction when she saw him looking at the inn and writing in his notebook. "Can I help you?"

He smiled and stopped about four feet from her. "I'm looking over the property for a client who is going to buy it."

Her hackles went up. "Oh? I think you should make sure the owner wants to sell it."

"Oh, it's a done deal," he assured her. "Are you a guest?"

"No, I'm Libby Holladay. The owner."

His smile vanished. "That's not possible. Mr. Brent Mitchell agreed to sell it to me." His eyes narrowed. "What kind of scam is this?"

The proprietary way she felt about the house already was a shock. This was *her* house. "He was unaware until recently that I inherited the house, not him."

He smiled, an obvious attempt to regain his composure. "Then I will direct my client's interest to you." He held out a card. "I'm Kenneth Poe. I have a client who would like to purchase this property."

She couldn't afford to reject his offer. "Why does your client want the property? It's not really a moneymaking venture at the moment. Tourists have to rent a boat to get here. I had a hard time getting here myself." She decided not to tell him about Nicole's disappearance. It was none of his business.

He shifted his clipboard to the other hand. "I'm sure you see that the place is a monstrosity. It's going to take a lot of money to fix it up. Better just to tear it down."

She gasped. "Tear it down? You have to be joking."

He held up his hand. "Look at the place. Rotting wood, peeling paint, outdated rooms and baths. It would be cheaper to bulldoze it and start over."

"The mansion should be on the historic registry. It will be if I have my way. I've spent my life protecting historic property. I'd die before I saw this place bulldozed."

His smile was entirely too smug. "Come now, Ms. Holladay. I think we can persuade you. My client is willing to pay you ten million dollars for this property."

The blood drained from her head, and she felt dizzy. *Ten million dollars.* The amount was outside her comprehension. She could buy a house outright, two houses, one for her and one for her stepbrother, here in town if she wanted. She could get a new car before her old clunker died for good. The future stretched out in an enticing way. But to follow that path, she would have to sacrifice an important piece of history. Could she turn her back on her convictions?

She wetted her lips. "I'll think about it."

"You do that. I think you'll see it our way. And my client might be persuaded to give you other incentives, such as a parcel elsewhere to build your own place. I'm sure we can come to an agreement. He's very eager to have this property."

Hope Beach would be just like the rest of the beach towns. There wouldn't be anything unique about this little bit of paradise any longer. Libby couldn't bear the thought, but she couldn't afford to reject it out of hand either. Any other investor would have the same idea, and this one seemed eager to move now.

"Like I said, I'll think about it."

"The offer won't be extended for long. If you don't wish to sell, he'll go after something else. I'd advise you to accept his offer before he loses interest. There are other properties he can purchase."

She bit her lip. "Could I meet with him? See what his plans are?"

Poe shook his head. "I doubt he'd have the time. He would tell me to say take it or leave it."

"I'll let you know next week," she said.

She watched him walk away and chewed her lip. What should she do? That was a lot of money.

What would Jesus do?

TEN

The expansive lawn had been meticulously groomed. The flower beds were in perfect condition for the garden party, and Lawrence smiled with satisfaction. His wife wouldn't be able to complain that he hadn't taken care of his duties as a host.

"How do I look, Daddy?" Katelyn twirled in a gauzy white dress.

His daughter might not be the most beautiful young woman he'd ever seen, but she was elegant and well bred. With her by his side, Poe could go far. Someone needed to be groomed to take over the Rooney businesses. Poe was the first man to come along who Lawrence felt might fill the ticket.

"Like a princess," Lawrence said, kissing her cheek. "There's someone I want you to meet today."

A dimple appeared in her cheek. "Your amazing Kenneth Poe?" she said. "I saw a picture. He's quite handsome."

When she blushed, Katelyn was downright pretty. Lawrence hoped Poe could see her attractions. "There he is now," Lawrence said, waving to Poe, who stood at the edge of the lawn looking around.

"Oh my," Katelyn said. "H-He's like Elvis."

Like Elvis. Lawrence hid his amusement. The girl was already halfway in love. Poe acknowledged the wave with an answering smile and strode across the green carpet of grass with a confident

air. Lawrence liked arrogance in a man. Poe had the strength to tame Katelyn. And he'd dressed nicely for the occasion. The suit he wore was an Armani, if Lawrence was any judge—and he was. Poe's tie was silk, and he'd had a fresh haircut.

Lawrence put his arm around his daughter as Poe reached them. "You just flew in, Kenneth?"

He nodded. "My chopper landed an hour ago."

Lawrence put his arm around Katelyn. "Kenneth, my boy, I'd like to introduce you to Katelyn. My one and only heir." He put the emphasis on the last word.

Poe took her hand. "I'm honored to meet you, Ms. Rooney."

"Call her Katelyn," Lawrence ordered.

He noted the way Poe kept control of her hand for a little longer than necessary. The boy wouldn't let any grass grow under his feet. Poe kept his attention on Katelyn too. Smart. They chatted for several minutes, and Lawrence saw how Katelyn flirted. She liked him. And why not? Poe was certainly handsome enough. Their children would be good-looking too. And with any kind of luck, they would possess Lawrence's business acumen.

His wife called to Katelyn over by the food table. "I'll be right back," Katelyn said with a lingering glance at Poe.

Poe watched her leave. "Your daughter is lovely."

Lawrence put his hand on Poe's shoulder. "Feel free to call on her. I'd like nothing more than to have you for a son, my boy."

Poe's eyes widened and he smiled. "I'm honored, sir. Do you think your daughter would be agreeable?"

"I'm sure you could persuade her."

Poe's smile widened and his blue eyes were bright. "I'd like nothing better." He glanced toward where Katelyn stood talking to guests. "Before she comes back, I have some news to report."

"Oh?"

"The property is owned by someone other than Brent Mitchell."

Lawrence shrugged. "Shouldn't be a problem, should it? Offer the same deal to the real owners."

"I did. She was reluctant at first, but I think I can persuade her. It just may take a few weeks until I have her signed contract. The wrinkle is that Nicole Ingram is her business partner and friend."

"Nicole Ingram? That's no problem. She's in my employ."

For the first time, Poe appeared uncertain. "You know her?"

"She's part of the firm I hired to renovate some buildings. You know all about that."

"I know the firm's name. I didn't know the employees."

"What is this about?"

"She's the woman who found the cave."

It wasn't often that Lawrence was unable to speak. "What did you do with her?" Lawrence held up his hand. "Never mind. I don't want to know. This is getting more and more complicated. Just get the property signed and delivered. I want to break ground by the end of the summer."

Poe nodded. "My thoughts exactly. The thought of ten million dollars was quite an enticement to the owner."

"Just get it done," Lawrence snapped. He nodded toward his daughter, who was approaching with a smile. "You'll be part of my family soon if you get this deal settled."

Emotion flickered in Poe's eyes and his jaw hardened. "I'll do that, sir. You won't be sorry you trusted me with this."

Lawrence's good mood had evaporated. The property would be his no matter what he had to do.

———

The winds died by early afternoon. Alec stood surveying the storm damage in the heart of Hope Beach. Libby had insisted on coming with him and Zach when the sheriff called about all the

damage. Alec thought she was afraid Nicole's body was going to be discovered floating in the debris, but he prayed she wouldn't be assaulted with such a sight.

At the first glimpse of his house, he thought it had been spared. Then he drove closer, and water sloshed to the top of the truck tires. "I'm flooded," he said, unable to keep the dismay from his voice.

Zach pointed. "Both boats look to be all right though. They're both still attached to their moorings. Listen, can I take out the old boat?"

"The sea is still too rough," Alec said.

Libby grimaced. "It looks like the entire town is a mess." She was staring out the window at the still-turbulent water. "There's no sign o-of Nicole, is there?" Her voice quivered.

He reached over and squeezed her hand. "Tom would have told us if there was." He released her hand and stared at his house. "Guess I'd better see how bad it is inside. You can wait in the truck if you like."

"I'll come." She shoved open her door and stepped into the water.

He took her arm when they reached the front of the truck. He waved at some of his Coastie buddies, who were down the street carrying belongings from a house. The water filled his boots, and he shivered as the cold soaked his jeans. The flood covered Libby's flip-flops and reached nearly to her knees. His spirits sank lower as he pushed open the door and saw the flooded living room. "Gonna be a lot of damage," he said.

"There's plenty of room at the hotel," she said. "Let's gather some things. I'll help."

"It won't take long. You can wait here." Alec went into his bedroom and pulled some jeans and T-shirts off hangers, then scooped up underwear from the bureau. In the bathroom he grabbed toiletries, then met Libby in the hall again. "Let's toss this stuff in the truck and check on the rest of the town."

She nodded and followed him back outside. People were assessing the damage along Oyster Road. He wondered if she knew which house had been her father's. Taking her arm, he pointed down the street. "Your father lived there."

She stared at the two-story house and he tried to look at it through her eyes. Ray had always kept it in top repair, but it was in sorry shape now. The storm surge still lapped a foot up the gray clapboard siding. The sea had deposited debris around the porch and the yard swing. The wind had torn some shingles loose, and they flapped in the last of the wind.

"Aunt Pearl said Vanessa was at a friend's, but is that her?" She pointed down the street.

He followed her finger. "Yeah, that's Vanessa. How did you know?"

"She looks a lot like me."

He glanced at her. Same high cheekbones, same expressive dark eyes. They wore their hair differently, and Vanessa always covered her face with a ton of makeup. Libby was much more natural. "Guess you're right. You want to meet her?"

She shook her head, but about that time Vanessa caught sight of him. "Alec!" She waved to him and sloshed through the water toward them. She was dressed in shorts and a red tank top. The tips of her short hair were purple.

"Sorry," he said. "Should I introduce you?"

"I—I don't quite know what to say. Give me a minute." Libby sounded breathless.

Vanessa reached them. "Is Aunt Pearl all right? I heard you rescued her last night." She gave Libby a curious glance, then her gaze went back to him.

"She's fine. Where did you ride out the blow?"

"At the church. Brent too. He's there now helping clean up. It's a mess."

"Looks like your house is hit pretty hard too."

She shrugged. "I figured we'd join Aunt Pearl at the hotel. At least it's still ours until the dragon lady comes to claim it." She blew her bangs out of her eyes. "I still can't believe Dad would give our property to some daughter who has ignored him all these years. I want to be out of town when she comes. I want nothing to do with her. Ever."

He tried to interrupt her fierce flow of words, but she barreled over him.

"It's a good thing my *sister* wasn't in residence yesterday, or Aunt Pearl would have been out on the streets."

He could see Libby take a step back. "Uh, Vanessa, there's something you should know."

Libby put her hand on his arm and shot him a pleading glance. He closed his mouth.

Vanessa's face took on a rosy hue, and her voice rose with every word. "I can just see her arriving and trying to lord it over us. I'm going to put her in her place the very first thing. She didn't know Daddy. *She* certainly didn't love him, or she would have come to visit. I hope she just sells the place and stays away. No one here wants to meet her."

"She might not be so bad," he said.

Vanessa's brows arched. "You think the best of everyone, Alec. I'm sure she's some money-grubbing landlubber who doesn't know the first thing about island living. I hope she realizes that and doesn't bother us any longer than necessary. When we hear she's coming, I think I'll take a vacation."

Libby's face was getting pinker and pinker. Alec didn't think she'd take much more before she blew.

ELEVEN

As Libby listened to her newfound sister rant, her emotions veered between anger and hurt. Why had she thought her new family would be as happy to meet her as she was to meet them? Her aunt Pearl had been welcoming, but Libby was an outsider in this small community.

Vanessa's diatribe finally ended. She turned her attention from Alec and stared at Libby. "I feel like I should know you. Have we met? I'm Vanessa Mitchell."

Libby forced a pleasant smile to her face. "I think I seem familiar because we look alike. And we should. I'm your sister, Libby Holladay."

Vanessa went white. Her mouth opened but only a garbled word came out. Red washed up her face, and she closed her mouth before finally opening it with the strangled statement of "Half sister." Her mouth looked like she'd just bitten into a bad oyster.

"I don't blame you for being upset," Libby said. "Please understand though. I had no idea my father was living. My mother told me he died when I was five."

Vanessa's eyes narrowed, but there was a flicker of uncertainty in them. "I find that difficult to believe."

"It's true. I . . . I wish I'd known him." She held her hand

toward Vanessa. "You can't imagine how thrilled I was to find out I have a large family. It's something I've always longed for."

"No cousins or other family?"

Libby shook her head. "My mother never talked much about my father. All she ever said was that he died when I was five, and it was good riddance as far as she was concerned."

Vanessa glared. "Daddy was a wonderful man!"

"So I've heard since I got here to try to find Nicole."

"Nicole?" Vanessa glanced toward the water, then back. "The woman who was kidnapped? You know her?"

"Yes. We're in business together."

Vanessa's glare was still wary. "I met Nicole. I was sorry to hear about what happened to her."

"She told me about you. I was watching on the beach cam to catch a glimpse of you. I saw her taken."

"That must have been hard," Vanessa said, her voice warming for the first time. "I was going to meet her and show her the old lighthouse ruins. I got held up. When I got there, she was gone. I liked her a lot."

"Please don't talk like she's dead," Libby said, tears starting to her eyes. "She's not dead. She's *not!*"

Vanessa bit her lip. "I didn't mean to say she was. I hope you find her."

Alec put his hand on Libby's shoulder. "Don't give up hope," he said.

"I will *never* give up," she said. "She's not going to be another woman who disappears without a trace from an island." The thought of never knowing what had happened to Nicole haunted her.

"Maybe you should contact the media," Vanessa said. "They can get word out. Someone might have seen something."

"That's a good idea," Alec said. "I know a guy who works for the Richmond newspaper. I'm sure I could get him out here."

Libby recoiled at the thought. "Nicole would hate to be the

center of a media circus." But would she, really? She'd probably revel in the attention.

Alec nodded. "But if the coverage could help find her . . ."

"We're going to find her soon. I know it." But even as she proclaimed her belief, Libby's pulse skipped. "Maybe you're right," she said, her shoulders sagging. "Make the call."

Alec squeezed her shoulder, then dropped his hand back to his side. "Want us to help you gather some things, Vanessa? We're going back to Tidewater in a little while. Let me call my friend first, then we'll help you."

Libby forced a smile to her face. "I'd like you to come to the inn too. I'm eager to get to know you."

Vanessa's stormy eyes revealed how torn she was. Libby knew the woman wished she could throw the invitation back, but if she did, she'd have nowhere to stay. Pearl's house was damaged as well. It only made sense to join the rest of her family.

"What about Brent?" Vanessa asked. "Is there room for both of us?"

"Of course," Libby said.

"We can stop by and introduce him to Libby too," Alec said. "I need to talk to Zach. I'll be right back."

Libby's stomach plunged at the thought. Zach had already mentioned how upset Brent was about the news that she had inherited.

Vanessa shot a glance Libby's way. "He's not going to be welcoming, just FYI."

Libby kept her smile pinned in place. A soft answer turned away wrath. She had to remember that. "I understand you are both dismayed to find out that you have a sister. I'm not going to push you. I hope you find that I'm not such a bad sister to have."

Vanessa shrugged. "Whatever. Don't say I didn't warn you. He's liable to go off on you. That's all I've heard since Horace gave us the news. Brent had plans for that property."

"I've heard that too. What kind of plans?" Libby asked.

"What difference does it make now? Unless you plan to split it with us?" Hope tinged her words.

"Horace told me our father left you both plenty of money," Libby said, refusing to be goaded.

"But the property you have is what Brent needs." Vanessa turned and squinted. "Here he comes now. He must be done at the church."

Libby turned to look and saw a young man jogging toward them. He wore denim shorts low and loose around his waist in the style she hated. His blond hair fell across his forehead, and his expression was sulky. She wanted to love this new family, but they were making it difficult.

———

Nicole's muscles were cramped from the night on the roof. The hurricane had blown itself out hours ago, but she remained atop the roof. The surge had covered the island, and the water was still a couple of feet deep. The shack was off its foundation, and she feared it was going to float off to sea with her on top of it. The table and chair from inside bobbed in the flood below. Her cot with her food and water also floated in the debris under her feet.

Her eyes burned, and she told herself not to cry. Someone would be along. Surely someone would come. That boy knew she was out here. Nicole would give anything to be in her own tiny room, to look out and see the tired houses across the street, to hear the traffic that she hated. She would never complain again if she got the chance to be home.

The sun was getting hot on the back of Nicole's neck, and her thirst was mounting. She was going to have to get down off this building and see if seawater had leaked into her jug. Staring at the brown swirling water, her courage ebbed. Who knew what was below that

roiling surface? Poisonous snakes or spiders came to mind. Hugging her knees to her chest, she tried to talk herself down into the water. There were no snakes out here. Nothing that could hurt her. Though logically she knew that, she didn't want to test it. What if the storm had washed all manner of nasty creatures onto the island?

She licked her cracked lips. Dehydration would kill her if she didn't get down. There was no sense in staying up here out of fear. She rolled onto her stomach and scooted down until her legs hung off the edge of the roof. The plastic bucket was long gone. All she could do was lower herself as far as she could, take a deep breath, then let go.

Her bare feet splashed into cold water. The seawater rushed to enclose her legs up to her thighs. She forced herself not to look down into the swirling water as she slogged through it to her cot. She seized the jug of water. Still full. Hefting it to the light, she examined the cap. Tight. She exhaled with relief, then unscrewed the top and took a swig of water.

The moisture on her tongue revived her. She replaced the cap, then grabbed the cot and dragged it toward the shack. The door was cockeyed now and hung open. Practically swimming, she tugged the cot into the building and glanced around for some way to secure it. There was nothing, so she left it floating there in the water and grabbed her provisions. She would stay on the roof until the water receded.

TWELVE

When Alec crossed the street, Zach was sitting in the truck, thumping his hand on his leg in time with the blaring country music. He was oblivious to Alec's approach and jumped when his uncle touched his shoulder.

Zach bolted upright and turned down the radio. "I was about to go looking for you."

"Something wrong?"

Zach chewed on his lip. "I wanted to ask to take the boat out. I know you said no earlier, but the waves aren't all that bad. I have that job."

Alec lifted a brow. "It's still pretty rough out there, Zach. And it's getting late."

"I've been out in worse. In the dark too."

"True. Are the supplies that urgent?"

Zach's gaze cut away. "I need the money. And they're depending on me."

Alec fished in his pocket for the keys to the boat and handed them over. "Okay. Be careful. Wear your life vest."

Zach's smile was big as he jumped from the truck and jogged through the standing water to the pier. The sea had calmed considerably since they arrived. The flood from the storm surge had

gone down a bit too. Now the water barely covered the tops of Alec's boots. But recovery was going to take awhile.

Alec opened the door of his truck and slid inside to make his call.

Earl Franklin answered after two rings. "I was going to call you, Alec," he said, wasting no time with a greeting. "How's it look out there?"

"Rough. Storm surge did more damage than you'd expect from a cat-1. Most of the houses in town have sustained considerable damage."

"Sorry to hear that."

Alec could hear the speculation in Earl's voice. The reporter was probably already planning a feature. "Listen, there's a bigger story here. I think you need to get over to the island as soon as possible."

"What's up?"

"A young woman was kidnapped right off the beach. Her friend was watching via one of the beach cams. So far we've found no sign of her."

"I heard about that. After we left town, I realized we'd given the woman's friend a ride to the island. Tom called to ask me about her."

"I thought you might want to do an article about the abduction, get some publicity rolling. It might help the case."

"You think the Holladay woman killed her and made up the story?"

"Why would you say something like that?"

"She didn't say a word about her friend's kidnapping to us. Seems suspicious."

Alec opened his mouth, then shut it again. He didn't have a good answer to that other than a gut feeling. His fingers curled into the palms of his hands. Surely the crime couldn't be a hoax. But no, Nicole's car was there at the beach. And her cell phone. It

would show that a call had been connected to Libby's phone for several minutes.

Unless she had an accomplice.

"Alec? You there?"

"I'm here. All I can tell you is that we're investigating the kidnapping. If you give the case some attention, maybe someone will come forward with information."

"One way or another," Earl said, his voice deep with satisfaction, "it will be all over the national news. Maybe international. I'll head out there as soon as I can. Any chance you can come after me? My sailboat is being repaired. I heard quite a few charter boats were damaged. I might have trouble getting someone to bring me."

"Things are a mess here, and I need to work. If you don't find a charter, call me back and I'll have Zach fetch you after he delivers some supplies."

"Okay, I'll see what I can do first." Earl hesitated and didn't hang up. "Keep an eye on the friend, Alec."

"I will," Alec said. He ended the call. Libby couldn't be guilty of something like that. She was genuinely devastated by her friend's disappearance.

Maybe the hurricane had exposed new leads for Tom. Alec got out of the truck and headed toward the sheriff's office. His cousin was likely to be out helping the townspeople, but his receptionist would know where he was. He spotted Tom's SUV driving slowly away from the church and waved.

Tom stopped the vehicle beside him. The window came down, and he peered up at Alec. "Something wrong?"

Alec leaned on the side of the vehicle. "I got hold of Earl Franklin. He's coming out to do a piece on Nicole Ingram."

Tom uttered an expletive, and a frown wiped away his smile. "What'd you go and do that for? It will be a media circus. I was careful not to give him any information when I talked to him."

"Every hour that passes puts Nicole in more jeopardy, and you know it." He stared at the sheriff. "Listen, I have a question. Earl said something that got my attention. He seems to think Libby might be involved because she's close to Nicole. You don't suspect her anymore, do you?"

Tom shrugged. "Most homicides are crimes of passion. The murderer is usually someone known to the victim. And we still haven't seen the video of the kidnapping. The tech guy I hired can't find even a piece of that video. All we've got is what Libby told us."

"Well, you found Nicole's phone and car."

Tom nodded. "That's the only reason we're treating it as a real kidnapping." He stared at Alec. "You're in the perfect position to keep your eye on Libby. See if you notice anything suspicious."

"I don't believe she did anything to her friend."

"Well, you can be alert, can't you?"

"I guess so." Alec looked down the road, then back to his cousin. "Did you trace the call between the women?"

"Sure. It lasted four minutes. The only prints on the phone we found at the beach were Nicole's." Tom scowled again. "I wish you'd asked me before you called in the media. I've got enough on my plate with the hurricane damage."

"Sorry."

"I'm sending out a sketch artist to see if she remembers any details about the two men she saw. Let her know they're coming, will you?"

"Sure." Alec stepped back so his cousin could drive on. He watched the SUV's taillights come on, then wink out as Tom rounded the corner toward a group of people picking up the pieces that used to be the town library.

Could she be guilty of something unthinkable? He hoped not. Libby was the first woman who had intrigued him.

Libby's heart stuttered in her chest. She'd always wanted a brother, but Brent was not quite what she had in mind. He stared at her, then at his sister, as if he sensed the tension between them. Libby smiled at him, but he didn't return it.

"Hey, sis," he said to Vanessa. "You about ready to go out to the hotel?"

Vanessa sent her brother a warning glance. "I'd better introduce you, Brent. This is Libby. Dad's *other* daughter, Libby." She pressed her lips together as if the admission had pained her.

Brent took a step back. His glare pierced Libby, but she kept smiling in spite of the way her chest contracted. "I've been looking forward to meeting you, Brent." She held out her hand, but when he ignored it, she dropped it back to her side.

His gaze swept over her. "You look a lot like Vanessa."

His tone wasn't as hostile as his expression. Not yet anyway. Libby smiled. "I can see that. Vanessa is beautiful, so I take that as a compliment." Her statement didn't change Vanessa's scowl. "We must take after our father. You look more like your mother?"

He shrugged. "Are you staying at the hotel?"

"Yes."

"That woman who was kidnapped two days ago, Nicole? Libby is her business partner," Vanessa said.

His eyes widened. "I talked to her at the ice-cream shop. She didn't say anything about being connected to you. She just said she was looking to restore some of the downtown area for a client. And she asked about Tidewater Inn."

"You told her how disgusted you were about me inheriting, right? That's okay. I know it must have been a shock. I was surprised as well."

He frowned and crossed his arms over his chest. "Dad never mentioned that he was going to do this. So yeah, I was surprised."

"So you wanted to sell the land?" Libby asked.

"Sure. The inn doesn't even turn a profit."

"It doesn't matter now. It's not yours," Vanessa said. "Libby says her mom told her Daddy died when she was five."

"You never saw Dad all these years?" he asked.

"Not that I remember. I'm eager to hear more about him." She tried another smile on him. "I've always wanted a brother."

His eyes flickered. "This is a lot to take in."

He wasn't welcoming her with open arms yet, but she could live with guarded cordiality. "It's a lot for me too. Can I help you grab belongings from the house?"

He shrugged. "If you want." He pointed to the house just down the street. "We live there."

She followed him and Vanessa toward the large two-story, eager to see more than the cursory glance she'd had earlier. The shingle home had been allowed to go gray with the salt. It was newer than the hotel, built in the twenties. The home had been well taken care of and featured an expansive yard that had probably once been meticulously tended, but the floodwaters had left debris everywhere, and some of the shingles were missing. The shrubs and flowers would likely be dead by this time next week, killed by the seawater.

Brent held the door open. "It's a mess. The first floor was flooded. Bedrooms are upstairs."

They trooped through the small entry to the living room. The floor was still damp, and Libby feared the dark floors would warp soon. They were expensive teak, she guessed. One wall had a built-in oak bookcase filled with books. Libby winced to see how waterlogged the books on the bottom shelf were. She longed to examine the books and discover her father's reading tastes. The tables held a few pictures.

She picked up one of a man and a woman standing under a tree. The man had dark-brown eyes and light-brown hair like hers. She liked his open face and contented smile. The woman

was lovely with nearly black hair and deep blue eyes. "Our father?" she asked.

Vanessa took the picture from her. "And our mother." Her tone told Libby she didn't want to answer any questions.

Libby wanted to linger and look, but Brent went on through to the stairway, so she had no choice but to follow him up. There were four bedrooms on the second floor, and she started toward the back one.

"That's Daddy's room. You can't go in there," Vanessa said.

Libby stopped with her hand on the doorknob. "I'd love just a peek. I want to know more about him."

Vanessa set her jaw. "Not today. My room is here." It was as if she was willing to expose herself to prevent Libby from invading their father's space.

Not hiding her reluctance, Libby turned and went into her sister's room. The scent of perfume hit her when she entered. Something so strong and flowery that it made her sneeze. Vanessa was feverishly pulling shorts and tops from a bureau and tossing them onto the queen-size bed. The room's polished floors matched the downstairs wood.

"Love the floors," she said. She grabbed a suitcase from the shelf and began packing it.

Vanessa didn't look up. "Thanks." She went to the attached bathroom, then returned moments later with an electric toothbrush and toiletries. She dumped them on top of the clothes in the suitcase. With her hands on her hips, she stared at Libby. "What do you expect from us anyway? That we're all going to be a big happy family now that you've arrived? Forget it! You're not my big sister. You're not anything to me. I don't know you and I don't want to know you."

Libby dropped the top she'd been folding. *Be generous with grace.* "I want to know my family," she said. "Is that so hard to understand?"

"The family has to want to know you too. You can't just force your way in here and expect us to fall on your neck."

Libby rubbed her forehead. "I'm sorry if I've been presumptuous, Vanessa. That wasn't my intention. If I back off, would you agree to trying to be friends?" She held out her hand.

Vanessa stared at Libby's extended fingers and shook her head. "I'm not promising anything. I think the only reason you're here is for the money. There's been ample time to get to know us before now if that's what you really wanted."

Libby dropped her hand to her side and struggled to keep the tears at bay. "I'll see you at the hotel." She turned and plunged through the door and down the stairs to the fresh air outside, free of her sister's vitriol.

She'd tried to honor her father's request, but she'd failed.

THIRTEEN

Every inch of the island was damp and covered with flotsam when Nicole finally descended from the roof. Her face and arms were sunburned from her hours atop the shack, and her tummy rumbled and twisted in its desire for food. She'd eaten half of a peanut butter sandwich, but that was all she'd allowed herself. What if no one came back for days? She would conserve her food and water as much as possible.

Libby had always preached that she should have foresight, but Nicole wasn't sure any kind of wisdom would get her out of this predicament. She kicked a palm frond out of her way and resisted the urge to cry. Tears wouldn't get her rescued. Glancing at the fallen palm fronds, she decided to gather them up. Maybe she could make an outdoor shelter from the sun. She wouldn't be cooped up in the waterlogged shack that smelled of mold and fish.

Once her arms were full of fronds, she deposited them under the palm tree and went back for more. After she'd gathered every frond from the island, she sat down to rest under the tree. The wet ground dampened her shorts almost immediately. Glancing at the water jug, she resisted the urge to drink.

She thought she heard a motor in the distance. Leaping to her feet, she ran to the edge of the water, but at first she saw nothing.

Then in the trough of a wave, she saw a boat carrying one person. Shouting and waving, she jumped up and down. The boat was heading for the island like before, and as it neared, she realized it was the same craft as yesterday. The same young man dropped anchor offshore.

She had to convince him to take her off this cursed island. Standing with her hands at her sides, she waited for him to splash ashore. He carried more supplies, so the pain in her stomach would soon be eased. And fruit! She spied apples and oranges in his arms. She salivated at the thought of their sweet taste.

"You're okay," he said. "I was worried the storm surge would carry you off."

"It would have if I hadn't climbed on top of the building." She couldn't take her eyes off the apples. Pink Lady, her favorite variety. "Can I have an apple?"

"Sure." He handed her one.

She bit into it, relishing the sweet yet tart flavor that flooded her mouth. It was all she could do not to moan at the taste. And while she was eating, she didn't have to talk to her jailer. Though she *needed* to talk to him, needed to convince him to let her go.

Wiping her mouth with the back of her hand, she smiled at him. "Were the seas rough?"

"Not bad. I caught some mullets. You want some?"

"I would love some. But how do we light a fire?"

"I brought a lighter."

She watched him slosh back to the boat and return with a box. Inside she spotted fish, a lighter, a knife, and other food items. If she could get the filleting knife, she'd force him to take her to the mainland.

"We'll need firewood. I should have thought of that," he said.

"I have palm fronds. Will that work?"

"No." He glanced back toward the boat. "I can cook it on board,

though. There's a grill in the galley." He squatted and grabbed the knife, then began to clean the fish.

Nicole had never wanted anything as much as she wanted that knife. She wanted to leap on him and wrest it away, but he was muscular and she wouldn't have a chance. Even the lighter would do her no good without firewood to burn. She eyed the palm tree. Unless she could manage to set it on fire where it stood.

He finished cleaning the fish, then put the knife in his back pocket and picked up the fillets. "I'll be right back." As he walked toward the boat, the knife slipped to the sand.

She swooped down on the weapon. The handle felt substantial and deadly in her palm. Turning her back to the boat, she tried a few threatening swoops with it in her hand. Could she even bring herself to hurt him? He seemed to believe she was a danger to some imaginary brother. There was no malice in his treatment of her.

She glanced over her shoulder. He was intent on his task, and she caught a whiff of the fish beginning to cook. How could she get this to go down her way? After he returned to the beach, she could back out to the boat with the knife in front of her. He might be afraid to charge her for fear of getting cut. She would have to turn her attention away to get in the boat. Still, she should manage to get aboard before he could wade through the waves. But what if he boarded in spite of her efforts?

All she could do was try. Swallowing hard, she put the knife behind her back and turned when he approached with the cooked fish. "Smells good," she called.

"I'm not the cook my dad was," he said. "I hope it's done. And it's hot and filling."

"Was? Your dad is dead?"

His lips tightened and he nodded. "He died in a plane crash. He and my mom."

"I'm so sorry."

"Thanks." He set the tray of fish on a rock.

"Where do you live? In Hope Beach?"

He nodded. "With my uncle. He's a Coastie." His tone held pride. "I don't want to live anywhere else. I'm a commercial fisherman, like my dad. At least that's what I want to do, if my uncle will let me." He bent down to slide the fish onto a paper plate.

While he was bending over, she shoved him with her foot, and he toppled onto the sand. In a flash, she was running to the boat.

When her feet hit the water, she turned and brandished the knife. "Stay back!"

He'd gained his feet and already stood only five feet away. "You won't cut me."

"Try me!" She wagged the knife blade at him. "I've been kidnapped, half starved, left to rot during a hurricane, nearly drowned. I'm not someone you want to mess with."

She began to back through the waves toward the boat. He stood watching her with a scowl.

"You are just as crazy as they said," he called. "You don't even know which direction is land."

She stopped. "I'll figure it out."

"You don't have enough gas for exploring."

He was just trying to scare her. She continued to back toward the boat. Her bare foot moved and found nothing under it. The underwater hole made her lose her balance, and she fell back into the water. She came up brandishing the knife and sputtering, but he was already at her side.

He snatched the knife from her hand and grabbed her arm. "I was beginning to wonder about what I'd been told, but you just proved how dangerous you are. You tried to cut me like you did your brother." He dragged her back to the beach and left her there.

Brent and Vanessa were ensconced in rooms across the hall from Libby. After she'd helped to settle them, Alec called her to say a sketch artist was coming. Libby met the artist—a woman—in the parlor and did the best job she could. She could only pray the drawings helped find Nicole.

After the artist left, Libby went to see if she could help Delilah with dinner. The manager had a suite on the second floor and rarely left the property. Libby had the impression that Delilah had been here a long time and was content with her home. Maybe she could get some information out of the woman.

She found Delilah in the kitchen stirring something that smelled amazing. "Is that she-crab soup?"

Delilah smiled. "It is. This is a special recipe with whipping cream and butter. No flour to thicken it either. Want a taste?" Delilah held out a spoonful.

Libby sipped it and closed her eyes as the rich, buttery flavor hit her taste buds. "It's heavenly."

"I thought you'd like it."

"Can I help with anything? We have a lot of people to feed."

Delilah's eyes widened. "Really? You wouldn't mind? I let our cook take the day off to help with cleanup in town."

"I love to cook, actually. I don't get much opportunity since it's just me and Nicole. She's rarely around anyway. It's hard to cook for one." Libby lifted the CD player in her hand. "I need music though. That okay with you?"

"Of course. I sometimes listen to Beethoven."

"This isn't Beethoven." Libby plugged the player in and started the Counting Crows CD. The lyrics to "Big Yellow Taxi" made her pause. *Paved paradise.*

Delilah stared at her. "Is that what you want, Libby? To see this place become one big parking lot?"

Libby's smile faded. "I don't want that to happen any more than you do."

"So what are you going to do?"

"I don't know yet." She pulled the notebook out from under her arm. "Do you have a menu plan for the next week? I assume our guests will be here that long?"

"A few weeks, most of them," Delilah said. "It sounds like Ray's house is pretty bad, so your brother and sister might be here longer, maybe months."

Months. It would be expensive to feed all of them. Libby mentally counted up the residents. Eight. "Are they chipping in for food?"

"Alec was quick to give me some money for him and Zach. I doubt Vanessa and Brent will contribute. They consider the inn home." Delilah's glance held curiosity. "They know who you are, right?"

"They were less than pleased to meet me."

"Don't take it to heart, honey. It's just a shock. Especially to Vanessa. She's always been a daddy's girl, and she's just jealous."

"Jealous? I didn't even know him."

"But he loved you," Delilah said. "Vanessa realizes that. She never wanted to share Ray with anyone, not even her mother. She's been obsessive about him. So much so that Ray had her in counseling when she was fifteen or so. It got a little better, but this has got to send her reeling."

Was their mother anything like her own? Libby had noticed people often chose the same kind of mates when they remarried. "What about their mother?"

Delilah smiled. "Everyone loved Tina. Ray was nuts about her right up to the day she died." She pointed to the refrigerator. "If

you want to fix some salad, go right ahead. We're having grilled lobster, soup, and salad tonight."

Libby winced at how much that must cost. "For so many?"

Delilah stirred the soup. "Zach brought me the lobster and crab. I only had to buy veggies for salad. This is a cheap dinner."

"That was nice of him. Most young men wouldn't have thought of that."

"Alec's brother raised him right. Most folks in Hope Beach look out for one another. Zach's a little troubled right now, but he'll be all right. He's basically a good boy. Trying to find his place in the world."

Libby almost asked about the intriguing Coast Guard captain, but she didn't want to reveal her interest to Delilah. It was much safer to talk about her family.

"How long have you worked here?" She put the salad ingredients on the butcher block in the middle of the kitchen and found a chopping knife.

"Fifteen years. I came here when I was eighteen. I was in foster care and had nowhere to go when I got out of high school. Ray found me crying my eyes out on the pier. When he heard what I was going through, he offered me a job on the spot. At first I was a housekeeper, but I worked my way up. I've been manager ten years in October."

"How many employees are here?"

Delilah stopped and thought. "Three in housekeeping, a groundskeeper, and me."

"I wish I'd known my dad. He sounds like a really great man."

Delilah's eyes glistened. "He was the best."

"You sound a little in love with him."

"Maybe I was." Delilah put down the soup ladle. "I could never take Tina's place, but I would have been willing to try. He never looked at another woman though. Even though I let him know I was available."

"You're much younger."

"I'm thirty-three," Delilah admitted.

"He was in his fifties when he died?"

"Yes, he was fifty-two. But he looked much younger." Delilah shrugged. "The age difference never bothered me. A man like that doesn't come along often."

Libby mixed the greens and vegetables together. "So everyone says." She went back to the refrigerator. "No avocados?"

"There's one in that bag." Delilah pointed to a paper sack on the counter.

"We'll have to get more. I like avocado in everything. I'll make my special avocado dressing for tonight too."

"Sounds great. What about your mother?" Delilah asked. "Do you know much about their marriage?"

"Only that it lasted a short time. They were both young. My mother said he lit out when I was three. I was bitter about it when I was a teenager. Now I find out that my mother lied all those years. She told me he died when I was five. It's pretty devastating."

"I'm sure it is. One thing I know about Ray—he would never shirk his responsibility."

"My mother tried, but she was a kid at heart herself, even at fifty. I was more a parent than she was sometimes. We moved around a lot. I think I went to ten schools in twelve years."

Delilah winced. "Some of Ray's old letters and albums are in the basement. You might want to go through them."

"Oh, I would!" Libby began to chop the avocado.

The thought of learning more about her parents and their lives appealed to her. So much of the time she felt alone, as if a piece of herself was missing. She'd assumed the cause was some dim memory of her father. Even now that she knew he was an honorable man, his abandonment still hurt.

FOURTEEN

The huge living room table felt crowded with so many around it. Alec had never eaten here at the Tidewater Inn when there were so many guests. A white linen tablecloth covered the mammoth table, and fresh flowers made a bright centerpiece. Platters were heaped with steaming lobster, and a white tureen contained the soup he'd just tasted.

"Great meal, Delilah," he said. "No one can make she-crab soup like you."

Delilah smiled and ladled soup into a bowl for herself. "Libby helped. Wait until you taste the avocado-ranch dressing she made from scratch."

Libby was to his right, and she brightened at the praise. "I hope everyone likes avocados."

"Is there any store-bought dressing?" Vanessa started to rise from her seat directly across from the table.

Her aunt Pearl shot her a look that made her sink back into her chair. "I've bought too many avocados for you to think your tastes have suddenly changed, Vanessa."

A dull red crept up Vanessa's neck, and she tipped her chin up. "I'll try it, I guess." The glance she shot Libby was full of challenge.

Alec wanted to tell her to stop acting like a spoiled brat, but he

tucked his chin and took another sip of the soup. "I could live on this, Delilah. But I'm not going to. The lobster looks great."

Libby glanced at Zach. "I hear we have you to thank for this fabulous dinner."

Zach shrugged. "I had a good afternoon on the boat."

She smiled at him. "Modesty. I like that in a man." She turned to her other side to listen to Thomas Carter.

Alec suppressed a grin at the way Zach's shoulders squared when she called him a man. Libby had a way about her that made every man in the room want to impress her. Even old Thomas was busy telling her about the days when he built boats. She listened with the kind of attention that would make any person feel important. Why had she never married? But maybe that was a false assumption. She could be divorced.

Thomas finally ended his story. Libby glanced across the table at her siblings. "Brent, I met Kenneth Poe this morning. He told me about his client's interest in buying the inn."

Brent stiffened and looked up from his plate. "Did he make you an offer?"

"He did." Libby broke off a piece of French bread and dipped it in her soup. "I had no idea this place was worth so much money."

Everyone seemed to freeze. Alec shot her a quick glance. Was she trying to see what kind of reaction she would get? The strain in the room seemed to grow. How much money had she been offered? A million or two? That would be enough to tempt most people.

"You're not going to sell, are you, honey?" Pearl asked.

"Of course she is," Vanessa said. "She doesn't care about the family. She just wants the money."

"I don't know yet," Libby said. "I haven't had a chance to even think about what should be done. *You* were going to sell," she said, directing a level gaze at Brent before glancing at Vanessa again.

"Why is it all right for your brother to sell but not me? Why don't you characterize him as a money grubber?"

"Brent knows this island. He would have done what was best."

"The offer is from the same person," Libby said. "So there is nothing different except who is benefiting."

"Children, let's not argue," Pearl said. "Your father would be very displeased by your attitude to your sister, Vanessa. I'm disappointed myself. We are all family, but you're not acting like it."

"I haven't done anything," Brent said. "Libby, you can do whatever you want. It's your property. Dad seemed to want it that way."

Alec winced at the coldness in Brent's voice, but Libby just nodded.

"Thank you, Brent," she said. "I don't know what I'll do yet. It's a lovely old place. I wish I had the money to keep it. It needs a lot of repairs." She glanced at Alec. "What do you think about a resort going in here?"

He raised his brows. "Resort? We'll need ferry service or a very long bridge to draw in enough people to support it."

"The ferry service is coming," she said. "That's why Nicole was here. We had a client who wanted us to restore some of the more important buildings and make Hope Beach more attractive to tourists."

"It hasn't been announced if it is." He glanced at Brent. "You've heard this?"

Brent nodded. "From Poe. I doubt his investor would be spending that kind of money if he wasn't sure it was happening."

"The island will change," Alec said. "We'll be like Ocracoke. Which is better than Myrtle Beach at least. The tourists aren't overwhelming. It's still a fishing village. We'll survive, whatever you decide."

Delilah's spoon clattered into her bowl. "Easy enough for you to say! This place is my home. It's my *life*." She stared at Libby.

Seneca Falls Library
47 Cayuga Street
Seneca Falls, N.Y. 13148

"Don't think for a minute that they won't tear this place down. That's what he told you, isn't it?"

Libby nodded. "That's the only thing holding me back. I would have to compromise my passion for historic preservation if I let them do that."

Libby's soft answer defused Delilah's anger. The red faded from her cheeks, and she slumped back in her chair. "Don't do this. I can't bear to leave my home."

Libby bit her lip and looked down at her plate. "I can only promise that I'll consider everything, Delilah. I'm in a hard spot. I don't have the kind of money it would take to restore the inn. Without a major investment, it's going to fall down around your ears." She glanced at Brent. "Why did our father not keep it up? The house in the village is in great condition."

"I can answer that," Pearl said. "The place was due a paint job when Tina died three years ago. Ray had a small stroke, then started letting things slide. The sea is hard on buildings. They need constant maintenance. I told him he needed to spend some time here and make a project list, but he didn't do it. Then his illness turned chronic, and he decided to transfer all his liquid assets to the kids. He wanted to make sure everyone was taken care of."

"I can understand that," Libby said. "But he left me no money for upkeep. It was as if he wanted me to sell it."

"I'm not sure I believe that," Alec said.

"Then why leave me saddled with a house that's in need of so much?"

"Maybe he wanted to see what you were made of."

She absorbed his comment, then nodded. "I suppose we'll never know."

"What you're made of?" Alec raised his eyebrows.

"No. What he wanted me to do."

101

"If anyone can figure it out, it's you," he said.

Vanessa's head came up and she gave him a sharp glance. He realized he'd let too much of his admiration show. If Vanessa hated Libby before, it was going to be worse now.

———

The basement stairs creaked as Libby eased down them. The dank smell was nearly enough to make her turn tail and run, but the promise of the prize contained in the trunk below was stronger than the claustrophobia squeezing her lungs. The bare bulb in the ceiling put out enough light to see the old leather chest right where Delilah had told her it would be, against the wall beneath the shelves lined with jars of canned vegetables.

She was going to grab the albums and letters and run right back to her room with them. The place gave her the creeps. The distant sound of dripping water added to her unease, though the stone floor was dry. The place was free of cobwebs too, so Delilah must keep it swept out.

Libby hurried to the trunk and lifted the lid. The fabric-lined interior smelled of disuse. The trunk was packed with bundles of old letters and photo albums. Her pulse thumped in her throat. Would there be any mention of her or her mother in these old letters? Any photos of her?

A framed picture was in the very bottom of the trunk. Libby held it up to the light. She barely recognized the smiling young woman as her mother. Why had her father kept it all these years? His marriage to Tina seemed to have been ideal. Her mother looked like she was about twenty-five. Young and carefree. Her long, straight hair was on her shoulders, and she wore a buckskin dress covered with beads.

Her mother had been happy but never content with any situation or with any man. She was always striving for the next big thing. Everyday choices had molded her mother. Libby touched the beads at her neck. Her own choices could make her a better person if she chose wisely.

She sorted the contents, then lifted the pile of albums and letters and carried them back up the stairs and to her bedroom. There was no one around. The sun was setting, and she'd arranged to meet the reporter with Alec, so she dropped the mementos on the bed with a regretful glance and went to find him.

FIFTEEN

Libby and Alec sat on the expansive porch at Tidewater Inn after sunset and listened to the ocean. "I thought he'd be here by now," Alec said.

"I don't mind waiting," she said. "It's a beautiful night."

The stars were bright in the night sky, but the moon hadn't risen yet. He kept shooting glances Libby's way. She seemed so at home here.

"What?" she finally said. "Do I have soup on my nose?"

He grinned. "Sorry. I was staring, wasn't I? It's the offer for this place. Would you really sell it, or were you just trying to see what you could find out from Brent?"

"I don't want to sell," she said in a low voice. "But I don't see that I have any choice."

"There's always a choice."

She stiffened. "What would you do?"

"Turn over every rock to find a way to keep it."

"Well, I have another life. The place is gorgeous and historic, I give you that. But sometimes sacrifices have to be made. The money will change my life. And I have a stepbrother who needs help. He was hurt in Afghanistan and is on disability. I could do a lot of good there." If he would let her. She wasn't eager to have

a relationship with her. He'd been a teenager when their parents married, and he had no time for her.

"Life isn't all about money."

"Spoken by someone who has always had enough."

She wasn't going to listen. He peered at the dock as a boat approached. "Looks like Earl is finally here. You ready for this?"

"I'll do anything to help find Nicole."

"You can wait here." He rose and went to the dock. When the boat neared, he caught the rope and tied it to the pilings.

"I'll be back in about an hour," Earl told the captain.

The young man in shorts nodded. He plugged in earphones and settled back in his chair.

Earl was in his fifties with a paunch. His one pride was his thick head of red hair. It had faded with the years, but he still wore it over his ears like an aging Beatle. "She up there?" he asked, jerking his thumb toward the house.

"Yes. Go easy on her though. She's had a rough few days."

Earl chewed on his ever-present toothpick. "Sounds like you believe her story."

Alec shrugged. "I know what it's like to be accused of something you didn't do. I don't want us to assume she's guilty until proven innocent."

"Is Tom going to ask the state for help?"

"Yes. With the hurricane, I think he's overwhelmed." He fell into place beside Earl, who was walking up the boardwalk to the hotel.

"My story will get some action."

They reached the grand steps. Libby was standing on the porch waiting. Her expression was one of dread. This wouldn't be easy for her, airing her life to the world. Alec sent her a reassuring smile. "This is Earl Franklin," he said when they reached her.

The two exchanged a long look. "It's you." She glanced at Alec.

"Earl and his wife gave me a ride to the island," she said. "Naomi thought I was Vanessa."

"You never said a word about your friend having gone missing." Earl's voice held accusation.

She bit her lip. "There was just so much to explain. It seemed easier to say nothing."

Alec already had an uneasy feeling about the exchange. It did seem odd that she wouldn't have told Earl and Naomi anything. Especially Naomi. If any woman had the warm manner that invited confidence, it was Earl's sweet wife. And Libby hadn't made any secret of the incident to him. Alec could see the suspicion on Earl's face.

"There's iced tea," she said, pointing to the table with the refreshments. She resumed her seat in the swing. Tucking one leg under her, she sipped her tea and regarded them over the rim of her glass.

"Don't mind if I do." Earl poured himself a glass from the sweating pitcher. "Ah, nothing like sweet tea." He settled in the rocker and took out a pen. "Hope you don't mind if I record this? It's easier than trying to write it all down." He clicked a switch on the pen recorder without waiting for her to answer. "Can you take me through the events that led up to your friend's disappearance?"

She blinked. "Okay."

She plunged into the story about the client who wanted restoration estimates and ended with what she saw on the beach cam. She broke down again when she got to the part about the men taking her friend. Alec couldn't imagine how he'd feel if he saw someone he cared about being kidnapped and couldn't do anything to stop it.

Earl leaned forward. "Ms. Holladay, did you harm your friend?"

She sat upright, sloshing tea over the side of her glass onto her shorts. "Of course not!"

"You didn't kill Nicole, dump her body in the Atlantic, then call the sheriff with some far-fetched story about an abduction?"

"No, no! You can't possibly believe that." She stared wildly from Earl to Alec, then back again. "Nicole is my friend. I would do anything to find her. Anything!"

"Yet the website with the cam is blank during the time your partner was supposedly kidnapped."

How had he found that out? He must have talked to Tom. Alec wanted to interrupt, but he bit his tongue and let Earl continue his questioning. She'd survive. It *was* strange that the tape had been messed with.

Earl smiled. "I did a little research. You're a computer expert. A person at the historical society said you're their go-to person when they have any computer issues. It's not out of the realm of possibility that you hacked into the cam data and erased that portion of the tape."

"It was an accident." She gulped and held his gaze. "I was trying to save the video. It wouldn't let me, so I . . . I hacked into the system and tried to save it that way. Something happened, and the next thing I knew, the data was gone."

"I see. I must say I thought you'd come up with a more believable story than that," Earl said.

"It's the truth."

Alec watched her face, the way it crumpled, the way tears formed in her eyes.

"I think you've made enough accusations, Earl."

Her fingers inched toward him but stopped before she touched his hand. "I didn't hurt Nicole, Mr. Franklin. If you write a story suggesting that I did, you'll only aid whoever took her."

Earl turned off his tape recorder. "Let me know if you remember anything else." He tucked the recorder into his pocket and strode to the waiting boat.

—

The boat carrying Earl back to Kitty Hawk cruised away, and none too soon for Libby. She wanted to throw something, to scream about the injustice of anyone even thinking that she might have hurt Nicole. His blue eyes watching her somberly, Alec continued to sit on the porch with her. He probably still suspected she had done something criminal.

She set her iced tea on the table and paced the expansive porch. "You said you'd give me the benefit of the doubt."

His sip of tea seemed deliberate, as though he was fishing for extra time before answering. "I am. But it seems strange the data would be missing from the cam."

His doubt was written on his face, and she fought to keep her voice level. "I swear to you I didn't do it on purpose. Yes, I might have caused it. I don't know." She clasped her hands in front of her. "Did you talk to your cousin when we were in town? I want to *do something*! I have to find Nicole."

"With the hurricane, Tom's going to have his hands full. And to be honest, this kind of thing is much more serious than the domestic disputes and traffic tickets he normally deals with. He's my cousin, but I think this is way over his head."

"I'm going to have to find her myself. It's clear no one else is going to do it."

He raised a brow. "You? What do you know about looking for a missing person?"

"Nothing. But I can retrace her steps. Talk to everyone she spoke with. Surely I'll find a clue somewhere. I can't just sit here and wait!" Her voice broke, and she turned her back on him.

She was alone here, and it was time she faced it. The people in the inn shared only her blood. They cared nothing about her. Well, maybe Aunt Pearl cared a little, but her warmth might only

be curiosity. Libby refused to entertain the thought that Nicole might be dead.

She sensed rather than heard his approach. His hand came down on her bare arm, and its warmth made her shiver. She didn't turn to look at him. He had brought that reporter here.

"I'm sorry," he said. "Reporters and law enforcement are trained to look at the person closest to the victim."

She whirled, jerking away from his touch. "Don't call her that! She's not dead, she's not!"

His hand dropped to his side. The wind ruffled his dark hair. "I'm sorry. I didn't mean it that way. She's still a victim of violence. Kidnapping is a violent act."

She shuddered and moved farther away from him. "Earl is going to write a piece suggesting I hurt her, isn't he? He really thinks I killed her and dumped her body in the ocean."

"I'll talk to him. I think he'll be fair."

The breakers rolled over the beach in a hypnotic rhythm. She turned to stare at him again. "Is that what your cousin thinks too? Is he going to taint the state's investigation by implying that I'm guilty?"

"I don't know what Tom is thinking. Look, I'll help you, okay? I'll take some accrued leave. I know everyone in town. It's a good idea to trace Nicole's movements. Someone has to know what happened."

His words were so gentle. Even though she'd screamed at him, he stayed calm. "Why would you do that for me?"

He shrugged. "I was falsely accused once."

"What happened?"

He folded his arms across his chest and moved back a step. "My older brother drowned. We were mulletting with a neighbor. I was about Zach's age. My older brother was named Zach too. He was twenty."

She heard the pain in his voice and wanted to tell him he didn't have to describe what happened, but she found herself holding her breath and wanting to know more.

"Giles, our neighbor, was with us. He was supposed to have checked the fuel in the boat. We were pretty far out and the engine died. No gas. The ship-to-shore radio had broken the week before, and we couldn't call for help. My brother was the strongest swimmer, so he decided to swim for help."

"Oh no," she said softly.

He sighed. "His body was never found. A fishing trawler found us the next morning. As soon as we got to land, Giles started railing at me, saying it was all my fault. If I'd filled the tank, my brother would still be alive. Everyone believed him. The pain and disappointment in my parents' eyes haunted me for years. Still does. They believed Giles instead of me."

"Have you talked with them about it since you've been grown?"

He shrugged. "Pointless now. Even if they believed me, it wouldn't make up for their condemnation back then."

"That's so sad, Alec. It has to have been so hard for you to lose two brothers. And then your parents, in a way."

He went silent for a moment. "Mom keeps the house like a shrine. Everywhere I look I see pictures of my brothers from babyhood to the year they died. In Mom's eyes they are saints now. Something I'll never be."

"And your father?"

"He doesn't say much. Mom rules the household. Her hero worship eventually drove Beth away too. Beth is my younger sister. I don't think she's been home in three years."

"I'm so sorry." She touched his hand. "I've always felt a little unlovable since my father abandoned me. I *thought* that's what he did anyway. Now everything I believed is all jumbled."

He held her hand in an easy grip. "You'll figure it out."

"So will you. I'm already sure that you're a good man, Alec."

A tinge of color stained his face. "Hardly. I was a wild kid. I guess that's why I want to help Zach avoid my mistakes."

"Most of us have to learn the hard way."

Her skin was still warm from touching his hand. He knew what it was like to be misunderstood. She wasn't in this by herself.

Sixteen

The rest of the house slept, but Libby paced the rug in the parlor. The grandfather clock in the corner chimed two, but she wasn't a bit sleepy. She should have been. Her last full night's sleep had been before this nightmare started.

What was she going to do if everyone began to look at her as a suspect? How could she clear herself?

"Libby?" Pearl stood in the doorway. A pink nightgown covered her bulk, and her hair was in a long braid. "Are you all right?" She stepped into the room. "You've been tense ever since dinner."

"You'd be tense too if you were accused of harming Nicole."

"What? Who accused you of such a thing?"

"Earl."

"Oh, honey, he's just snooping for something sensational. The truth will come out. You'll see." She beckoned for Libby to come with her. "You're tall. I need some help in my room, if you don't mind."

Libby followed her up the stairs. Helping Pearl would give her something to focus on besides what other people thought of her. When they reached Pearl's room, she looked around. It was very different from the way it had been when Nicole's things were here. Now there were angels everywhere, spilling out of boxes, perched on the dresser top, and heaped on the bed.

She picked up one that held a child in its arms. "How many angels do you have?"

"Oh, I've lost count. Well over two hundred, I'm sure."

"Did you bring them all?"

Pearl picked up an angel still in its box, which was lying beside the bed. "I could hardly leave them in the house, now could I?"

Libby smiled. "Of course not. Why angels?"

"I've always loved stories about angels. I'm sure I saw one once."

Libby found she believed Pearl. "What did he look like? And how did you know?"

"I was ten." She gestured to the window. "It was right out there in the water. I wasn't a very strong swimmer and I got a cramp in my side."

"Oh no."

Pearl nodded. "The surf was high and I couldn't keep my head up. I finally decided I would give up and just go to heaven. My grandpa had died two months earlier and I missed him anyway. So I quit swimming. I said, 'I'm going to heaven now.'"

Libby sat on the edge of the bed with the angel in her hands. "What happened?"

"I felt a hand on my arm, and the next thing I knew I was on my knees in the sand vomiting seawater. I looked around and a teenage boy was walking away. I called out to him and he turned around and smiled." She paused and her eyes were moist. "I've never seen a smile like that before or since. He said, 'You'll be fine now. It's not your time.' Then he turned and jogged away."

"You'd never seen the boy?"

Pearl shook her head. "He wasn't a real boy. There was something special about him."

Libby wanted to believe her aunt. Even more, she wished she could have an experience like that. She touched the beads at her

neck. Somehow God felt more *real* here, on this island. Almost as if he could whisper in her ear at any moment.

Pearl smiled. "How'd we get on that subject? You need to get some rest and I'm blathering about something that happened fifty years ago."

"What can I help you with?"

Pearl pointed to the closet. "The disorder is driving me crazy. It's why I'm still awake at this crazy hour. I want to put some of the boxes of angels on the closet shelf, but I'm too short. There are some boxes in there that could go to the attic. That would leave me enough room. Can you reach?"

"I think so." Libby opened the closet door and eyed the boxes on the shelves. She stood on her tiptoes and pulled down the first box easily. "I think I need a chair for the one in the back."

Pearl brought her the desk chair, and Libby climbed onto it. "Can you flip on the closet light? It's dark in here." When the light came on, she peered to the back of the shelf. "What is this?" She reached in and brought out an envelope. "It's an old letter." She climbed down from the chair and sat on the edge of the bed where the light would allow her to read.

The bed sank as Pearl settled beside her. "It looks like it's addressed to Tina."

Libby opened it. "Did she ever stay in this room?"

Pearl shrugged. "Not that I know of."

Libby pulled out the letter inside the envelope. The writing was in a bold hand that suggested it had been penned by a man. The style was a little hard to read. She held it under the light and read aloud.

"'Tina, I will ruin Ray. You'll see what a huge mistake you've made.'"

Libby stared at her aunt. "Does this make any sense to you?"

Pearl gave a faint gasp. She snatched the note and crumpled it. "It's so old. I don't think we can possibly know what it means."

When Pearl fanned herself, Libby knew her aunt was hiding something. "What do you know?"

Pearl pulled her braid over one shoulder. "Ray had some financial problems a few years back. I never heard what went wrong. He lost about half of his money."

"He still had plenty to leave my siblings."

"He'd already put that money for them in trust funds."

"You suppose someone set out to harm him financially?"

"I can't imagine something so sordid."

"What wrong choice could Tina have made?" Libby wished she'd had the chance to look at the back of the sheet. "The letter is yellowed, like it's old. How long were Dad and Tina married?"

"Twenty-five years the month before Tina died."

"My father didn't wait long to replace my mother."

Pearl started to speak, then closed her mouth and shook her head.

"Was anyone else interested in Tina?"

Pearl rubbed her head. "I think there might have been, but it was so long ago. I just don't remember."

Libby sighed. It didn't matter anyway. This was old news and had nothing to do with finding Nicole.

Libby lay in the comfortable bed with her eyes open. She'd expected to sleep until at least eight, but something had awakened her. Birds sang outside her window, though the sun was not yet up. The air had the sense that sunrise was just around the corner. She rolled over and glanced at the alarm clock on the bedside table. Five thirty. The sun would be up in half an hour.

She listened again to the sleeping house. What had she heard? Or had it been a dream? She sat up. "Is someone there?"

The sound of running feet came from beyond the door. Her first inclination was to cower under the covers, but she wasn't going to give the person the satisfaction of thinking she was frightened. It was probably Vanessa. Or Brent. She forced herself out of bed and went to the door. There was a folded sheet of paper lying on the carpet. Something inside made it bulge.

Libby nudged it with her foot, and the paper opened to reveal a black blob. She leaped back until she realized it was a dead jellyfish. Why would someone leave this for her? Though she hated to get close, she lifted the paper and carried it into the attached bathroom, where she dumped the jellyfish into the trash. The paper was blank.

She balled up the paper and tossed it into the wastebasket, then pulled on shorts and a top. Whoever had left the creature couldn't make her cower in her room. The beach called, and she could watch the sun come up over the ocean.

The sky was lightening as she stepped onto the porch. A figure loomed to her left and she jumped, then realized it was Alec. "What are you doing up so early?" Mercy, he was handsome in his crisp white shirt and the khaki shorts that showed tanned, muscular legs.

He grinned. "I could ask you the same."

She told him about the jellyfish. "I'm not going to let her scare me."

He lifted a brow. "Her? You think it was Vanessa?"

"Probably. Does a jellyfish have any symbolism?"

He shrugged. "The obvious one is that she's calling you spineless. But that doesn't apply to you. It's clear to all of us that you've got backbone."

She had to smile at that. "I'll admit that it scared me this morning when I found it. But if you tell anyone, I'll deny it."

He grinned and made a zipping motion across his lips.

She pointed toward the whitecaps. "Want to take a walk?"

He pulled his hands from his pockets. "My thoughts exactly."

They jogged down the steps and down the slope to the beach. "I found an old letter last night in the room where Aunt Pearl is staying." She told him what the note contained.

"All that was before my time, but someone would probably know if Tina had another beau. I don't see how that matters now though," Alec said.

"It probably doesn't. I guess I'm just interested in all the history." She paused to peer at a black blob on the beach. "What's that?"

"A mermaid's purse," he said, steering her around it. "Technically known as a skate's egg sack."

She shuddered. "Looks creepy, like some kind of alien." She fell into step beside him again. The murmur of the sea was balm on her soul, and she ran into the gentle waves as far as her knees, letting the water wash away her worries.

"You look happy," Alec said, watching her.

She splashed him with water. "The water's warm!"

He grinned and jogged into the waves with her, then splashed her back. She licked the salt from her lips and smiled. "I'm not going to let Earl's suspicious nature rob me of my peace of mind. I know I'm innocent."

He sobered. "That's good. Because he could do a lot of damage."

"Maybe. But I have to believe the sheriff has enough integrity to look for the real criminals."

"I think he does, but sometimes it's tempting to take the easy way out."

"I'll keep pushing back until he finds the truth." Her high spirits began to sink. Alec's sober demeanor reminded her that she still faced many problems. She didn't even want to see Earl's article.

"What are the plans for today?" she asked. "I want to get started on finding Nicole."

"I thought we'd take the cutter out with my friends. I got permission to search for her, and I talked my boss into allowing you to be on the boat."

"I wish we would find her today." She stared out at the water, which shimmered with gold and orange as the sun lifted its head above the horizon.

He touched her arm. "Don't give up hope."

"I haven't." She rubbed her head. "What made you decide to join the Coast Guard?"

He smiled. "That's an easy answer. I'm happy when I'm on the sea. The Coast Guard rescued us when I was a kid, like I mentioned."

She sobered. "When your brother died."

He nodded. "Riding on that cutter back to land, I knew I wanted to snatch people from the jaws of death the way we'd been rescued. It seemed very noble."

"And is it?"

"Sometimes. When we're successful. Sometimes we're not though. We're not always in time to save lives. Then it's hard, and I feel like a failure."

"I don't think you could ever be a failure." She held his gaze for just a moment, then turned back toward the house. "I think I'll fix coconut pancakes for breakfast."

She couldn't think of a man she admired as much as she did Alec. He was quite a guy. The strain between them was gone this morning, and she prayed it meant he fully believed in her now.

SEVENTEEN

It was ten by the time Alec drove Libby to town to go searching. While Libby ducked into the store to buy some sunscreen, Alec walked across the street to step into the sheriff's office. He found Tom at his desk filling in paperwork.

"Got a minute?" Alec closed the door behind him.

Tom leaned back in his chair. "You bet. What's up?"

"You heard from the state boys on the search for Nicole?"

Tom pursed his lips. "Yeah. There are two detectives coming first of the week."

"Why so late?"

"The state is still reeling from the hurricane, I guess. And their best detective is in Saint Croix on vacation. They're sending him and his partner out when he gets back."

"I guess it will have to do."

"You find out anything by hanging around Libby?"

Alec shook his head. "I think you were right about Earl though. He came in with guns blazing for her last night. He found out about the missing video. Did you tell him?"

Tom frowned. "You know better than that. I wouldn't do anything to compromise the investigation."

"I wonder how he found out, then."

"He might have a contact in the Virginia Beach office. I guess it doesn't matter. It's going to come out sooner or later."

Alec fell silent as he tried to think of how he could convince his cousin to drop his suspicions about Libby. "This morning she said she was sure you had the integrity to dig for the truth. Don't make me think you're less of a man than we both know you are."

Tom flushed. "Come on, Alec, you're letting yourself be fooled by a pretty face. I admit she's a looker, but use your head. Stay neutral and consider that she might be implicated."

"I am. What other evidence have you found about the two men?"

Tom leaned back in his chair. "Two men in a small boat with an outboard motor were seen offshore."

"That reminds me of what Mr. McEwan said." He told Tom about the old man seeing a boat with two men and a sleeping woman.

"Might be our perps," Tom said.

"Did you get a description of the boat? Libby could say if it's the same one she saw. We might be able to track it."

"It was too far for my witness to make out the name or make. Did you ask McEwan?"

Alec nodded. "He said he thought it was a Sea Ray, but he wasn't sure. Said it had some wear and might be a charter boat."

"I'll check out the marinas on the mainland and at Kill Devil."

It sounded like Tom was going to stay objective. The tension eased out of Alec's neck. "Promise me one thing, okay? That you won't prejudice the state boys against her. Let them come in and look at the situation with fresh eyes."

Tom hesitated, then looked down at his desk. "They are already looking at her, Alec. She wiped out the video."

"I believe her story about doing it accidentally."

"I don't know what to believe yet. But we have to consider all possibilities. I need you to promise to keep an open mind and report anything suspicious you see about Libby."

"I know the meaning of duty," Alec said. "I'm not going to hide anything. But we need to find Nicole. Every hour that passes is bad news and you know it."

"I'm doing my best. We're looking too. You have to consider that we may never find her though, Alec."

"I don't want to give up too soon."

"Neither do I."

———

The Coast Guard boat rode the waves so well Libby barely felt the swells left from the storm. Nicole had been gone three days. Was she even still alive? Libby stood at the bow of the craft and scanned the sea for any sight of her partner. Alec stood shoulder to shoulder with her and lifted binoculars to his eyes. He'd stopped to change into his uniform.

"We've got the boat for three more hours," he said.

Libby moved restlessly. "I don't think she's out this way. There's nothing here." She'd seen nothing but gulls and whitecaps.

"I don't either."

"If it was the kidnappers the old man saw, could they have had a destination in mind?"

"There isn't much out here but open sea."

"No islands?"

He shrugged. "Just uninhabited bits of sand. Nothing that would withstand a hurricane or support life. Some people picnic on the small islands, but there's no food or water on most of them."

She held out her hand. "Can I borrow your binoculars?"

"Sure." He handed them over.

She adjusted them to suit her and studied the whitecaps. Nothing. Every hour that passed left her feeling more and more hopeless. Where could they turn for information?

She handed back the binoculars. "Could we check the little islands?"

He spoke to Curtis, and the boat veered toward a tiny spot of land to the west. "It will take days or weeks to search them all. It would be insanity to put her on one of them."

"I'm not going to give up. She has to be somewhere. What do you think they did with her?"

He pressed his lips together, then shrugged. "Hard to say. They could have veered toward land at any point and put ashore."

"You don't think they did though, do you? I hear it in your voice. You think they dumped her."

"Libby, we don't know what happened or why they even took her. Anything is possible."

She felt a rising tide of distress and clamped down on it.

"It's too early to give up," he said. "We're going to keep looking."

His tone held determination. She smiled at him. "Thank you."

The craft reached the tiny island. Alec ordered the anchor lowered and the raft readied. "Want to go ashore?"

She eyed the island. It looked deserted. "I'll go."

"It's likely full of bird offing," he warned. "The pelicans like this island."

"I'll manage. Are they nesting?"

"Yes. They breed from March to November. So we may see some fledglings." He helped her into the raft with the others, then rowed ashore. The raft touched bottom and he jumped out, then dragged it to the sand. "Stick with me, just in case." He asked his friends to go the other direction. Josh and Sara went east.

She and Alec went west toward a patch of spindly trees. "Oh look!" She pointed to the ground. "Is that a pelican nest?"

"Yes. There are two eggs. That's common. The parents take turns incubating the eggs." He grinned. "That's the way it should be. The mom shouldn't have to do it all."

122

"Nice of you to admit it," she said. She glanced at him out of the corner of her eye as she turned away. Did he feel that way about raising kids? He handled Zach well.

It took less than five minutes to meet up with the other two Coasties. Gulls scolded them as they searched, but the island held nothing.

Sara fell into step beside her. "You doing okay?"

Libby liked the other woman's manner. Calm and confident. "I'm fine. Alec says you're the EMT? Is it hard to work with mostly men?"

"I used to think I had to prove myself, but the guys are fair. They let me pull my own weight." She smiled. "Most of the time."

"Does anyone ever stay on these little islands?" Libby asked.

"Sometimes fishermen will camp out, or teens will party on one. Once in a while a foolhardy mainlander will get it in his head to build a house on one, but it never lasts. The isolation gets to them after a while. Nothing is convenient either. One accident and things can get hairy quickly."

The four of them walked to the center of the island, where Sara pointed out a stash of beer bottles, both empty and full. A cornhole game had been set up, and someone had carved the words *I love Carrie* onto a tree trunk.

"Kids," Josh said. He and Sara headed back to the boat.

"What's that?" Libby pointed to the ground. "Looks like someone built a fire here."

"Probably kids cooking fish," Alec said.

She prodded the ashes with her foot. Nothing but pieces of charred wood.

"Wait." He knelt and sifted with his fingers, then his hand came up holding a pocketknife. He stood, his mouth pinched.

"What's wrong?"

"It's Zach's."

"How do you know?"

He showed her the name carved into the side of it. "He told me he dropped it overboard. This must be a hangout. I'm going to have to have a talk with him."

"You sound discouraged. You're thinking of the beer, aren't you? Boys generally experiment with alcohol."

His mouth was pinched. "He knows better. And he's driving a boat, which makes it worse."

She wanted to ask more, but there was a wall up in his manner. "He seems to love you."

He shook his head. "He's been a handful since his parents died."

"I know they were killed in a small plane crash. Do you know the cause?"

"Dave was an amateur pilot. Their plane went down over a lake in Minnesota. The authorities think clouds rolled in. He wasn't certified for instrument flying."

"I'm sorry."

They boarded the boat and got under way again. She strained to see the next island. Maybe Nicole would be on that one.

"We'll check there too," he said. "But I don't think we're going to find her on an island."

She jutted out her chin. "We have to try."

He glanced at his watch. "Two hours. Then we have to go back. Zach is bringing in fish to feed the town. We'll all need to help."

She wanted to scream that finding her friend was more important than fish, but she swallowed hard and nodded. This man and his friends were helping her. She would be grateful.

EIGHTEEN

The cutter docked at the Coast Guard headquarters in the bay. Alec pointed Libby to the ladies' room, then he walked with his friends across the grassy field toward the parking lot.

"Buddy, you better watch out," Curtis said.

Josh grinned and moved his hand like a diving airplane. "Kaboom! You're about to crash and burn."

Alec stopped and stared at them. "What are you two idiots talking about?"

Josh poked Alec's arm. "We're talking about you, my friend. And that pretty lady. You're already halfway smitten."

"That's ridiculous. I've only known her a few days." He started walking away.

Josh exchanged a long look with Curtis. "We're too late, Curtis. He's gone past denial to defensiveness."

Alec wanted to scowl, but he couldn't hold back the bark of laughter. "I'm just helping her, guys."

"That's what they all say," Curtis said. "I get to be best man though, right?"

"No, I get to be best man," Josh said. He punched Curtis in the arm. "Just because you're a month older, you think you get to do everything."

"No one is best man," Alec said. "There's no wedding."

"You mean we get to come to your house and watch the Dodgers play forever?" Josh whooped. "Now you're talking."

Curtis was grinning as he watched Josh cavort along the lawn. "What do you really think of Libby?" he asked Alec. "Any news on the case at all?"

"Not that I know of." He told his best friend about the disastrous interview with Earl, and Libby's admission about erasing the video.

"That's bad, Alec," Sara said. "You're *sure* it was accidental?"

"I believe her. Why are you asking? Do you know something about hacking?"

Curtis gave an innocent smile. "Well, this is all hearsay, you understand. I've never actually done it myself."

Alec grinned. "Okay, spill it. When did you hack a website?"

"Well, in college, there was this girl I liked. She had a website and I thought it would be cute to hack it and put up a poem I'd written for her."

Sara punched him on the arm. "Get out! You didn't. Poetry? From *you*?"

Curtis grinned. "I did. But the next day I wished I didn't. She wouldn't speak to me. So much for that relationship."

"How'd you learn to do it?" Alec asked.

"I was taking website design. If you know a little, you can do a Google search and get the directions on how to do it. As long as the website doesn't have a good firewall. And many don't."

"What about the cams here? Do they have good firewalls?"

Curtis shrugged. "I'd think so, but with the budget cuts, it's hard to say."

"So maybe a college student could have done it. Or just anyone with a little knowledge."

"Maybe."

"Is IP tracing always accurate?"

Curtis shook his head. "A trace can be misdirected. So you need more evidence than a trace."

Alec gestured to the building. "Here comes Libby."

"When are you going to take her out on a real date?" Josh asked.

"Where would we go? Get a grip, Josh."

"You've got a boat. Take her for a nice, romantic dinner in Kill Devil Hills."

His friend had a point. Maybe Alec would do just that.

———

Zach's face was set and strained. Alec eyed his nephew's expression as they stood on the church lawn filleting fish with half a dozen men. Residents from all over the village had brought their gas grills and skillets. Griddles stood ready to cook the seafood, and news of the fish fry brought most of the townspeople to the church with dishes the women had prepared.

Curtis threw a mullet into the bowl. "You think that's enough? We're not going to clean *all* of these, are we? Where'd you get a haul like this, Zach?"

Zach shrugged. "Out past the sandbar. I knew the fishing would be good."

"I think that nephew of yours can read fish minds," Josh said to Alec. He pursed his lips like a fish. "Come catch me. I'll be good eating."

Zach's smile didn't reach his eyes. "Ha ha."

"When are you going to join us in the Coast Guard?" Curtis asked.

"Like, never," Zach said. "I just want to fish."

Josh poked a scale-covered finger at Alec. "Look at your uncle. He serves his country and fishes too. A perfect combination."

Alec wanted to tell them to lay off, but he was curious to see if their ribbing would get Zach to reveal why he was in such a rotten mood. He placed another fillet on the growing mound in the big stainless bowl. But Zach hunched his shoulders and continued to work on the fish. He didn't look at either of Alec's friends.

Pearl hurried across the lawn toward them. "We're going to start cooking the fish. This was wonderful of you to do, Zach. You're a thoughtful boy, just like your dad. He would have done this too."

Zach straightened and smiled. "Thanks, Mrs. Chilton."

She patted his cheek. "So polite."

Zach grinned and so did Alec. Pearl could change anyone's frown into a smile.

"I think we're ready to start cooking," Pearl said. "Zach, would you carry the bowl for me? It's about as big as I am."

Zach carried the big stainless bowl overflowing with fish fillets to the grilling station. A dozen men stood by, ready to start the cooking. The aroma of charcoal made Alec's stomach rumble. Side dishes covered the tables that had been hauled from the church basement.

He loved Hope Beach. It was a gift from God that he'd been able to live here all his life. Good people, good friends—what more did he need in his life? His contentment vanished when he caught a glimpse of Libby. Okay, so maybe he was a little lonely.

Josh nudged him with his elbow. "Look away. Resist the pull."

Alec grinned. "Maybe I don't want to resist."

"Be like me. A confirmed bachelor."

"Right. I've seen you looking at Sara."

Josh folded his arms across his chest. "I don't know what you're talking about."

"No?" Curtis knocked Josh's hat off. "I don't know why you don't ask her out, man."

Josh retrieved his Dodgers hat. "It would mess up the working relationship. What if it didn't work out but we still had to work

together? Besides, it's better to be alone. Then I can do whatever I want, when I want."

"In Genesis God says man was not meant to be alone," Alec said, "that a woman completes him. My mom always reminded Dad of that when he complained about something." Alec grinned at the memory.

"All my parents did was fight," Josh said. "Until my mother lit out for somewhere else with another guy. I never saw her again."

"Sara's not like that," Curtis said. "If you don't ask her out, I will."

Josh stiffened. "Oh, come on now, that's not playing fair. She wouldn't go with you anyway."

"Want me to ask and see?"

"No. Just lay off, okay?" Josh's good-natured grin was gone. "I'll ask her if I get good and ready."

Alec had never seen his friend so serious. Who knew Josh's joking hid so much pain? He put his hand on his friend's arm. "Okay, we'll lay off. But think about Sara, okay?"

"Someone mention my name?" Sara was smiling as she joined them. She looked different out of her uniform, happy and carefree with her honey-colored hair blowing in the wind.

Josh shot them a warning glare. "We were just wondering where you were."

She lifted the dish in her hands. "I made my famous sweet-potato casserole. It's about the only thing I know how to cook."

Josh's face was red and he didn't look at her. Alec decided to take pity on him. "Hey, Sara, would you make an effort to be a friend to Libby? I think she feels a little out of place. Her family has been less than welcoming."

"I'd be glad to." A smile hovered on Sara's lips. "We talked a little out on the island today. I'm glad you're interested in her. I like her."

He wanted to protest that he wasn't interested, but they'd all know he was lying.

NINETEEN

ibby stood slightly apart from the happy crowd populating the churchyard. She wanted to be part of the group, but so far no one had taken notice of her. What was it the Bible said about friends? *A man who has friends must himself be friendly.*

She pasted on a smile and approached the closest group of women. "Can I help? I have a really great coating recipe for fish." She targeted her question to the only familiar face, Sara, who'd been on the Coast Guard boat.

Sara smiled. "Hello, Libby. I'm glad you're here. I'm terrible at cooking. What do you need for your breading? I'm a good gofer and I can rustle up the ingredients."

"Cornmeal, flour, paprika, pepper, and onion powder."

Sara held up her hands. "Whoa, whoa, I need to write that down." She pulled a scrap of paper from the purse at her feet and jotted it down. "Be right back."

The other ladies smiled and spoke to Libby as she waited for Sara to return. Their friendliness was a balm to her, and several told her they'd been praying that Nicole would be found. Her pulse blipped when Alec came across the lawn toward her.

He smiled when he reached her. "You any good at cooking fish?"

"I can fix fish that will have you begging for more," she said.

"I have a special breading I use. Sara went after the ingredients for me."

"I can't wait to taste it."

Surely he hadn't come over to make small talk. She searched his expression. "Any news?"

"I've been thinking about that beach cam website. Can we retrace exactly what you did? Did you copy the video to start to save it?"

She shook her head. "I tried to save it to my laptop and it wouldn't work. So I decided to look at the coding and copy it that way. I had just gotten in when it blipped, and everything was gone."

"Maybe someone else was there too. And the trace got misdirected to you. Curtis says it's possible."

"I wish I could believe that. I hate that something I might have done has hindered finding her kidnappers. How can I prove my innocence to the sheriff and everyone else?"

"I don't think you can unless we find the men responsible."

"It feels impossible." She glanced around. "This might be a good time to question people, don't you think?"

"Good idea."

She nodded toward Horace's secretary. "I thought of a few other questions for Mindy."

Mindy was sitting on a lawn chair by herself with a glass of iced tea in one hand and a novel in the other. She seemed oblivious to the hubbub going on around her. Libby had to speak her name for the woman to look up from her book.

Though Mindy smiled, her gaze wandered back to her book, then up again. "I thought you two would be around here somewhere."

"Did your house have any damage?" Alec asked.

She shook her head. "Mine's on a hill. The storm surge didn't reach me."

Alec glanced around. "Is Horace here somewhere too?"

"He and his son both came. His wife is in Virginia Beach." She looked at the book in her hand again.

Libby took the hint. "I am trying to figure out what all Nicole did when she was here. Did she mention any of her activities when you talked to her?"

Mindy thought for a moment. "She went parasailing."

"Who took her out?" Alec asked.

"Brent. I think he was a little smitten."

Libby gasped, and Alec straightened. She stared up at him. "Don't you think Brent would have mentioned that to us? He only mentioned talking to her in the ice-cream shop."

"Yeah, that seems odd."

Libby glanced across the lawn to where Brent stood talking with friends. "I'm going to ask him about it. What day did she go out with him, do you remember?"

"I think it was last Saturday."

Libby started toward Brent, then saw Sara standing by the grills with a basket of items in her hands. "I'd better do my part with the fish first. Sara went to all the trouble to get me the ingredients."

"I think I want to watch this," Alec said. His lips twitched.

"You think I can't cook?" She tried to put indignation into her tone, but her smile gave her away. "You had plenty of my avocado dressing. Did *you* bring a dish?"

"I can make a mean bowl of microwave popcorn, but that's it," he said. "I don't think there's much demand for popcorn." He took her arm and steered her back to where Sara waited. "I think everyone wants something more substantial."

"I like popcorn," she said. The moment the words left her lips, she wanted to recall them. They sounded flirtatious, as though she was angling for an offer. His fingers seemed to warm as they tightened on her arm, but it had to be her imagination.

He cleared his throat. "Listen, I know your mind is on finding Nicole, but when this is all over, you want—"

"Alec, I need your help," Pearl said. "We need a few more tables hauled up from the church basement."

"Sure thing, Pearl."

Did he sound relieved? Libby watched them go and wished he'd finished his question. Had he been trying to ask her out?

———

Brent seemed to be deliberately avoiding him. Alec tried to catch him alone several times during the fish fry. Every time Alec neared him, Brent moved off to talk with another friend.

Libby's fish was a success. She stood talking recipes and food with several of the women from town. It warmed Alec to see how quickly she had made connections. Maybe she wouldn't sell out and leave. She gave a little wave when she saw him, and then spoke to a couple of women before joining him.

"Everyone liked my fish," she said, a trill in her voice.

"It was terrific." He took her arm and moved her out of the way of men carrying chairs back to their cars. "I've tried to talk to Brent, but he's jumping from place to place like a nervous cricket."

"Where is he now?" She glanced around. "There he is. Heading to the street. And he's alone."

"Let's get him." He grabbed her hand and they hurried after Brent. "Brent, wait up!"

Brent appeared not to hear, but he broke into a jog. Alec let go of Libby's hand and ran after him. He reached Brent as the younger man opened the car door. "Hang on there, Brent. We need to have a little chat."

"I'm in a hurry," Brent said. His gaze went past Alec to Libby, who was rushing toward them.

"This will only take a minute."

Her cheeks pink, Libby reached them. "Glad we caught you, Brent. We heard something today and wanted to ask you about it."

"Yes, I took Nicole parasailing, all right?" He shrugged. "It was no big deal."

"Mindy mentioned that she'd told us?" Alec wished he'd instructed her to keep a lid on it. He would have liked to gauge Brent's reaction to their discovery.

"Yeah. So what?"

The kid was cool. Too cool. Alec couldn't put his finger on why it bothered him. "It's odd you never mentioned it. Were you afraid you'd be implicated in her disappearance?"

"No. I was out of town the day she was kidnapped. Is that all?"

"No, that's not all!" Libby put her hands on her hips. "What is *with* you, Brent? You're oh-so-smooth. Can't you just say what you think for once? Every time I talk to you, I can tell there is so much going on in your head."

"I'm thinking of nothing but my future," Brent said. He pushed his car door open wider.

"I get that my coming derailed some plans. It derailed my life too, but you all seem to forget that. And the other thing you ignore is that none of this is my fault! If I had lobbied for our father to leave me that property, then I could see your attitude. But I didn't."

Brent started to get in the car, but Alec blocked him. "Why didn't you tell us you spent time with Nicole? You never answered that."

"It didn't seem important." For the first time, Brent looked uncertain.

"What are you hiding?" Alec stood in the way of the door shutting. "Come on, Brent. We're not letting you go until you tell us the truth. What did Nicole have to say that day?"

"We didn't spend that much time talking. We were parasailing."

"You traveled together. Did you know who she was?"

Brent's jaw tightened. "I didn't know she was Libby's business partner, if that's what you mean. She asked me about the property, said she had someone interested in buying it. I already had their offer on the table though, so that was no big news."

"Why do you want to sell it instead of keeping it in the family?" Libby asked. "Did you disagree with our father's goal of preserving Hope Beach's peace and quiet?"

"I want to get off this podunk island," Brent said. "With that kind of money, I could go anywhere, do anything."

"You have quite a large amount of money coming even without the inn," Libby said.

"A million dollars will be gone in a heartbeat," Brent said. "That's nothing in today's economy."

What planet was this kid living on? Aware his jaw was hanging open, Alec shut it. "You could go to Harvard, start a business. Buy a house just about anywhere. What do you want to do that would require more than a million?"

Brent's eyes flickered. "You wouldn't understand."

"Try me."

"I'd like to build ships. Cruise ships."

It was a goal Alec could admire. "So get a job doing that. You don't really know anything about building ships. Start at the bottom and work your way up. There's virtue in that. Starting a business when you're ignorant of how to go about it is sure to result in failure."

"It doesn't matter now, does it? I'll have to make do with my paltry million. But don't worry. I'll figure out a way to accomplish my goal." He gave Alec a cold stare. "If you'll move away, I'd like to go."

Alec shrugged and backed off. The guy wasn't going to tell them any more. They watched him leave.

"I think there was something more between him and Nicole," Libby said.

"Me too. Let's talk to Vanessa."

TWENTY

The TV blared in the rec room, where Brent had apparently been in a hurry to watch some kind of shoot-'em-up film starring Bruce Willis. Libby and Alec walked through the inn in search of Vanessa. When they failed to find her, Alec stopped to snag bottles of water from the kitchen. Delilah was whipping cake batter and handed over the spoon when Alec begged for it.

"Have you seen Vanessa?" Libby asked.

Delilah slid the cake pan into the oven. "She said something about going for a swim."

"It's after dark," Libby said. "Isn't that dangerous?"

Delilah shrugged. "She's done it for years."

"Sharks are out now." Libby shuddered at the thought.

"The most dangerous time is just as it's getting dark," Alec said. "That's when they go out to feed."

"Does she know this?" Libby asked.

"Sure. Anyone who lives here knows the danger. But Vanessa isn't one to let anything stand in the way of what she wants to do." The spoon was licked clean and he put it in the stainless dishwasher. "How are you doing for money, Delilah? There are a lot of us to feed."

She hesitated. "Okay."

He pulled out his wallet. "Here's another hundred." He pressed it into her hand.

Libby caught a glimpse of his wallet and realized he'd given her all the cash he had. It shamed her to realize she'd given nothing toward food. Yes, the place was hers, but still. Alec didn't owe them anything. No money had been requested, but he'd handed it over without being asked. More than once.

She had a hundred tucked back for emergencies. This wasn't an emergency, was it? But her fingers dived into her wallet and pulled out the folded bill tucked behind her driver's license. "Here, take this too, Delilah." She had to force herself to release it into the other woman's hand.

When Delilah smiled, Libby felt lighter somehow. Her chest was warm. So this was how it felt to give. When was the last time she'd given so freely? Had she ever done it?

Delilah blinked rapidly and bit her lip. "Thank you, both of you. You're very generous. Some of the folks can't afford to give anything. Old Mr. Carter, for instance. All his pension money is in the groceries that have spoiled in his refrigerator. He feels terrible about it too, poor guy. And Vanessa and Brent can eat me out of house and home. Especially Brent. He expects peanut M&M'S to be in constant supply."

"I'll tell them to kick in some money," Libby said.

"Oh no, don't do that! They'll know I said something."

"I'll just ask if they have," Libby said. "I'll be very diplomatic."

Delilah began to smile. "There's cocoa fudge in the fridge." She pulled open the refrigerator door and pulled out the pan.

"Is this from the box of Hershey's cocoa?" Libby asked. She took a piece and bit into it. The flavor took her back to a time when she'd stand at the stove on a chair and stir the fudge while her mother gave directions. "Oh my goodness, I haven't had this

kind of fudge since I was a little girl." She licked her fingers. "I'd better leave before I eat the whole pan."

"You could use a little fattening up," Delilah said.

"I think she looks pretty perfect," Alec said. His face reddened when Delilah laughed. "We could watch the movie with Brent while we wait. Maybe he'll say something more about Nicole."

Libby started to agree, then had another thought. "Which room was my father's when he stayed here? I'd like to look through it."

"Of course." Delilah wiped her hands on her apron. "He had a big suite on the third floor. In fact, his room was the only finished space on that floor." She grabbed a ring of keys hanging on a hook by the back door. "It's locked, so use the red key. It's clean. I make sure of that every week."

Libby's pulse skittered as she took the key ring. "Where are the stairs to the third floor?"

"At the end of the hall, down past my quarters. Take your time. Vanessa won't be in for another hour." Delilah pointed. "Use the back stairway."

Libby led the way up to the second-floor hall, then back to the third-floor stairs. "Why would he put his suite up there?"

"I think he wanted a retreat where he could play the piano without disturbing anyone," Alec said.

"Piano?"

"He played beautifully. There are some tapes of him playing. They must be around here somewhere."

"I would love to hear one. All of them, actually."

The attic stairs were steeper than the main flights. The stairwell was closed as well. Alec reached past her to flip on the light. The steps creaked as she mounted them to the landing in the attic. It had been beautifully restored to highlight the maple floors, exposed rafters, and large windows that let the starlight shine in.

"How nice," she said, taking in the decor. The chairs went well

with the camelback sofa and antique tables. "He had good taste. Chippendale chairs?"

"I think so. You would know better than I would."

There was a flat-screen television mounted on one wall. A bookcase filled with books was on the opposite wall. There was a small kitchenette with a microwave and coffeemaker beside it.

"Looks like his bedroom was through there." Alec pointed to a door on the other side of the cabinets. "Or do you want to look around here first?" He walked over and switched on the table lamps.

The warm glow illuminated the table. Libby frowned and went to inspect the purse. "That looks like Nicole's bag." She picked up the Brighton bag and opened it. Nicole's favorite lipstick, Burt's Bees Fig, was in the top pocket. She pulled out the wallet and glanced at the driver's license. Nicole's face smiled back. "It *is* Nicole's! What was she doing up here?"

———

The contents of the purse lay strewn on the coffee table. "Nothing out of order?" Alec asked Libby. The find had shaken her. Her high spirits vanished.

She picked up a piece of paper. "What's this about? It's a note from Mindy asking her to meet Brent for parasailing. Look, Mindy was going to go with them. She didn't mention that. I think we need to ask her how many times she saw Nicole. She hasn't been up front with us."

"I'm going to tell Tom about it too. Something isn't right about all of it. I think Mindy knows more than she's telling. Brent too." He stretched his arm across the back of the sofa. She was sitting close to him. Was it on purpose?

"I'm so tired of trying to figure this out."

Her hair tickled his arm. All he had to do was drop his arm

around her and pull her close. What would she do if he tried it? Slap him? He felt as though he'd known her forever. They'd spent more time together in the past four days than he'd spent with the last woman he'd dated for two months. The fragrance in her hair was wonderful. Vanilla maybe? Sweet and enticing. He leaned a fraction of an inch closer and inhaled.

She must have heard him, because she turned her head and lifted a brow. "Is something wrong?"

"I was just smelling your hair," he said, his voice soft.

She didn't slap him. In fact, she leaned a little closer. "Vanilla shampoo," she said.

Her breath whispered across his face. With his right hand, he reached out and twisted a curl around his finger. "Nice," he said. With the back of his hand, he caressed her jaw. His gaze was caught by the glimpse of a necklace under her collar. "Is that Ray's?"

"You recognize it?" She pulled it free of her shirt and held it up. "WWJD. I've been trying to figure out how Jesus would act if his siblings hated him."

"So that's how you've been keeping your cool so well." Ray's legacy continued, even now. The realization stunned Alec.

"I don't know that I've been doing a good job of it. It's hard. My dad's letter asked me to be generous with Vanessa and Brent. I think he meant more than money."

"I'm sure he did. Money never mattered much to him."

"He said to be generous in grace. It would be easier just to share the property with them. Neither of them make it easy. But I'm trying."

No wonder he was so drawn to her. She was remarkable. "Back at the fish fry, I was going to ask you if—"

"What are you doing up here?" Vanessa shouted from behind them. She stood at the top of the stairs.

Libby sprang to her feet. "I'm looking around. How was your swim?"

Nice way to keep her cool. Alec managed not to grin. Her soft answer did nothing to calm Vanessa, who stood with her hands on her hips. Her wet hair hung down her back, and she wore a blue cover-up.

"See any sharks?" he asked.

Her gaze skewered him, and she ignored the question. "This is my father's personal space. You have no business here."

"I own it," Libby said, a steel undercurrent in her voice.

Vanessa strode across the floor to stop two feet from Libby. "So you keep throwing in my face! You may own the property, but you don't own the personal contents."

"Oh, but I do," Libby said. "Ask Horace if you don't believe me."

Tears hung on Vanessa's lashes, and Alec realized she was genuinely hurt. It wasn't anger that drove her. She was covering her pain with outrage.

"You miss your dad, don't you?" he asked her. "Do you come up here often?"

Vanessa burst into tears and covered her face with her hands. "She didn't even know him or love him." She ran to the bedroom and twisted the knob, but it didn't open. She pounded on the door and shrieked, "It's not fair. It's not!"

Libby went to her and put her hand on her shoulder. "Vanessa, I'm sorry. I wish I'd known him. It's not my fault, you know."

Vanessa flinched away. "Don't touch me! It wasn't my fault either, but I'm paying the price."

Libby said nothing. Her hand fell to her side. She bit her lip and turned away.

"You two are sisters, Vanessa. You can build a relationship if you work on it."

Vanessa folded her arms across her chest. "It's too late. I don't want to." She rattled the doorknob. "Give me the key. I want to go in. By myself." Her eyes narrowed, and she stared at Libby's neck.

"That necklace. Where did you find it? Up here?" She swiped at Libby's throat.

Libby leaped back. "Our father left it to me."

Vanessa went even whiter. "That's impossible. He knew I wanted it."

"I'm sorry," Libby said. "I can show you the letter. He wanted me to think about the meaning of the necklace every day as I'm working to try to get to know you and Brent."

Vanessa's face worked and her eyes filled again. "That belongs to me. You have no right to it."

Alec winced when he realized what Ray had intended for good was causing more division between the sisters.

TWENTY-ONE

The beads were warm and smooth under Libby's fingers. *What would Jesus do?* The necklace was just a thing. Yes, her father had left it to her, had wanted her to have it. But did it mean even more to Vanessa? Her father had asked Libby to give mercy and grace to Vanessa and Brent. What exactly did that mean?

Libby studied her sister's face. Were those tears of pain or of anger?

Vanessa covered her face with her hands. "Don't look at me like that."

"Like what?" Libby asked. "I'm trying to understand."

"I don't want your understanding. Or anything else from you. I just want my daddy back!" Vanessa whirled and rushed out of the room.

Tears sprang to Libby's eyes too. Alec put his arms around her, and she buried her face in his chest. "What should I do?" she choked.

"What do you mean?"

She pulled away and touched the beads. "About this? Should I give it to her?"

"I don't think I can tell you the right thing to do. What does your heart say?"

"I think Jesus would give it to her." Her voice broke, and she swallowed hard. "It's only a thing. I think I may have already gotten out of the necklace what my father hoped I would. But he wore it for over twenty years. I feel close to him when I'm wearing it. It's all I have of him. So I want to keep it."

"No one is making you do anything. It's your choice."

She studied his kind eyes. "You think I should give it up, don't you?"

He shook his head. "I think Vanessa is acting like a spoiled brat, and I wouldn't give in to her. But she's not my sister. I'm not the one trying to be part of a family the way you are. I don't know what the right answer is."

"I don't either. Vanessa *is* acting like a brat. But I see her pain too. I think I'm going to have to pray about this and see if God will give me some clear direction."

"Let's pray together." His head touched hers.

She closed her eyes and listened to him pray for wisdom and discernment on how to best handle the family dynamics. No other person had ever prayed with her like this, about concerns that mattered so deeply to her. Her spirit bonded with his as they asked God for help.

"Amen," she said when he was finished. "Thank you, Alec. You're a good man."

He shook his head. "I've got lots of faults, believe me."

"I'm not seeing them," she said, holding his gaze. "Thank you for caring enough to pray. I don't know anyone else who would do that."

His fingers touched her chin and tipped her face up. He leaned forward and his lips touched hers. Warmth spread through her belly and up her neck. His lips were firm and tender. No kiss she'd ever experienced affected her like this one. In his arms she felt safe and treasured. She palmed his face, relishing the feel of the

stubble on his cheek. He was all man, yet the tender side of him was so godly, so strong.

She pulled away when Delilah called up the stairs. "Alec, phone call."

"Sorry," he said with obvious regret. "I'll be back." He went down the stairs.

Libby stared at the door to her father's inner sanctum. There was no reason not to go inside. Before she could talk herself out of it, she fitted the key into the door and unlocked it. Her hand shook when she twisted the knob, and her knees were weak. She pushed open the door.

There weren't many windows, so she flipped on the lights to illuminate the dim room. It contained a king-size bed with tan and blue linens. Pillows were heaped at the head of the bed. The walls were painted a creamy tan. The wood floors gleamed. Libby wandered around the room, picking up pictures and examining details. There were many photos of her father with Vanessa and Brent. Also ones of him on a big yacht with his wife.

If only she could have been part of his life. If only there was even one picture of her with her father. Libby turned back toward the door and spied a brown leather Bible on the bed stand. She picked it up and settled on the edge of the bed. The ribbon marked a passage in Hebrews 13. She skimmed it until she saw verse 16 highlighted in yellow.

But do not forget to do good and to share, for with such sacrifices God is well pleased.

She clutched the beads. God didn't mean the necklace. She could share other things with Vanessa. But even as she argued with herself, a sick roiling in her belly told her the truth. God had answered Alec's prayer with a clear message.

The question was whether she could make herself give up something so precious to her.

Debris still littered Oyster Road, and folks were out cleaning their yards. It was going to take a long time before Hope Beach looked like it did before the storm. Mud puddles were everywhere, and gulls swarmed the area, scavenging sea creatures that the waves had left behind. The air reeked of rotting fish and seaweed.

She sniffed the air. "Smells like the sea on a really bad day."

"Careful." Alec put out his hand to stop Libby from stepping in front of a kid on a motorbike.

The wind tugged strands of her shiny hair loose from the ponytail. She sure was pretty. He'd lain awake for hours last night reliving that kiss. Their attraction felt God-ordained to him.

He nodded toward a neat white bungalow that had been converted into a small café. "Mindy is usually getting an egg sandwich for her and Horace about now. Let's see what she has to say about the note in Nicole's purse."

They crossed the street to the courtyard. Live oak trees shaded tables draped with red-and-white cloths. Inside, several residents spoke and nodded greetings to them as they threaded their way to where Mindy sat with lunch in one hand and a novel in the other. Her attention was on the book as she absently took a bite of her egg sandwich.

She looked up when Alec cleared his throat. Her gaze went from him to Libby and back again. She finished chewing and swallowed, then dabbed her napkin to her lips. "You looking for Horace? He's not here."

"Nope. We wanted to talk to you. Mind if we join you?"

She put down her book with obvious reluctance. "I don't have long. Horace will be wanting his egg sandwich in another fifteen minutes."

"This won't take long." He pulled out a chair for Libby, then

settled into the one beside her. "We want to ask you a few more questions."

Mindy hunched her shoulders. "I already told you everything I know."

Alec brought out the note they'd found in Nicole's purse. "I don't think so."

Mindy's face went white. Her gaze darted from him to the note. "Why didn't you tell us you went parasailing with them?"

Mindy bit her lip and looked down at her hands. "It didn't seem important."

"Every detail is important. We have to retrace Nicole's tracks and find out what happened to her," he said.

Libby leaned forward in her chair. "What did you all talk about?"

Mindy took a sip of her pink lemonade. "Mostly business stuff. She talked to Brent about the sale of the inn."

Libby shook her head. "By then he would have known I owned the inn, not him. So why would Nicole discuss it with him?"

Mindy looked down at her lap. "He wanted to know if she could talk you into giving up your inheritance. He thought she might have enough influence."

"What did Nicole say?" Libby asked.

"That no one would be that stupid."

Knowing Brent the way he did, Alec could only imagine how well that went over. "I'll bet that ticked Brent off."

"Yes." Her admission was barely audible.

So that's why Brent brushed them off when questioned about the parasailing event. If they knew there'd been an argument, he would draw suspicion.

Mindy glanced at her watch. "I need to get back to work." She signaled to the server, who brought her the bill and a white lunch sack. She left money on the table and rose. "You aren't going to tell

Horace, are you? He wouldn't like it if he knew I'd gone out with them. She was a client."

"If Brent had anything to do with Nicole's disappearance, it's going to come out sooner or later," Alec said. "You should tell him yourself."

Mindy shook her head violently. "He'd fire me in a heartbeat. I know Brent had nothing to do with it, so I'm safe." She scooped up the bag and headed out through the dining room and into the courtyard.

Alec sat back in his chair. "I think we'd better talk to your brother. He knows more about this than I thought."

TWENTY-TWO

The last of the clouds had rolled away when Libby got out of Alec's truck in the circular drive by the old hotel. She was struck again at the structure's beauty. Someone moved on the expansive columned porch, and she saw Brent leaning on the balustrade. Vanessa was at a table with a coffee cup in her hand.

Libby's stomach tightened at the thought of the coming confrontation. She wanted to love her siblings. That they might be involved in Nicole's disappearance was too horrible to contemplate.

"Steady, let me handle this," Alec said when she drew in a deep breath.

She knew he would be calmer than she was, so she nodded and followed him up the sweeping steps to the grand porch. At the moment, she was glad she hadn't given the necklace to Vanessa.

Brent straightened when they drew near. Libby studied his handsome face. Vanessa was beautiful as well. Their adversarial situation showed no signs of changing. Libby touched her necklace. *What would Jesus do?*

Brent's smile melted away when he glanced at Alec's face. "Something wrong?"

"You tell us." Alec stared at him. "You tried to persuade Nicole to talk Libby into giving up her inheritance. And when

Nicole refused, you argued. Two days before she disappeared. That looks bad."

Vanessa joined them at the railing. "Who told you this?"

Alec folded his arms across his chest. "That's not important."

"It had to be Mindy. She was the only other person there," Brent said. "So what? It's no crime to try to convince Libby to do the right thing."

"The right thing." Libby shook her head. "It was the right thing for you. Not for anyone else."

His eyes were cold. "I didn't know you. I still don't. You're a stranger to us and to this town. You don't understand."

"So help me understand! I know it's too much to ask to be part of the family, but the least you could do is treat me with common courtesy."

Vanessa and Brent exchanged a glance. Was it Libby's imagination or did her sister look a little shamefaced?

Alec narrowed his eyes. "So why didn't you go meet her to show her the lighthouse, Vanessa? Because the two of you'd made plans to do away with her?"

"We had nothing to do with her disappearance," Brent said.

The screen door opened and Pearl stepped out. For someone so rotund, she was light on her feet. "What's going on out here?" she asked. "Your voices are carrying to our guests."

"Brent and Vanessa may know more about Nicole's disappearance than they've been willing to tell us," Alec said.

"Oh dear me, that's not true, is it?" Pearl's gaze went from her nephew to her niece. "What do you know about that girl's kidnapping? Tell the truth now."

Pearl's appearance took all the bravado out of Brent. "We didn't have anything to do with her disappearance, Aunt Pearl."

Pearl's gaze narrowed on him. "Did you ask some friends to put a scare into her?"

He flushed. "I wouldn't do that."

Pearl lifted a brow. "No? I think Jennifer Masters might disagree with that."

"That was different."

Libby didn't like the way he looked down, or the color that came and went in his face. "You've done this before?" If he'd played a prank, then maybe she would have Nicole safe and sound yet today.

He shrugged. "It was just a trick on an old girlfriend."

"Way I heard it, you had two friends grab her and take her to the mainland, where they left her to find her own way back home," Alec said. "I'd forgotten about that. Is that what you did with Nicole? Tell us the truth. We can have her picked up."

"I didn't do anything!"

"Quit harassing Brent," Vanessa snapped. "He had nothing to do with this. Neither did I."

"It still seems odd that you didn't meet her when you said you would," Libby said. "I was watching on the cam. When she was taken, you were already ten minutes late."

"Being late is not a crime." She glanced at her brother.

This was getting them nowhere. The two weren't budging, but Libby didn't get the sense that they were guilty of harming Nicole. "How do you get to the lighthouse ruins you were going to show her?" she asked. "Maybe that's a place to start looking."

"She wasn't taken there," Alec said. "She was on the boardwalk."

"True enough, but we don't know anywhere else to look." Libby wasn't about to let any of them dissuade her. If she had to go by herself, she would. "Can someone direct me to it?"

"I'll take you whenever you want," Alec said. "I think it's a waste of time though. The site is down the shore in an area where no one ever goes. The fastest way to get there is by boat."

"How was Nicole going to get there?" Libby asked. "Were you meeting her in a boat or what?"

They both stared at Vanessa, who put her cup down on the railing and stared out to sea without answering. Libby curled her fingers into her palms. "Vanessa, I've had enough of your attitude. My friend is *missing*. She's been kidnapped. Do you get that? I saw two men forcibly take her away. She was kicking and screaming. One of them poked a needle in her arm." Her voice broke and she took a deep breath. "You'll help me find her or you can get out of my house."

Vanessa's eyes widened. So did Pearl's. Brent just continued to look bored.

"We have no place to go," Vanessa said. "I've spent more time in this house than you can imagine. Dad would roll over in his grave if he heard you threaten us like this."

Her sister's words brought Libby up short. Extend grace, he'd asked. She hardened her jaw. "All that matters to me is finding Nicole. Conflict like this is fruitless."

Vanessa's lips tightened. "I'm not the one who declared war. You think you can breeze in here and take over, but as you pointed out, you didn't even know Daddy. You're no real daughter."

"Maybe not," Libby said evenly. "But I own this place and I say who goes and who stays. So you choose which side you're on and let me know." She slapped her hand to her head. "What's the use? I'm going to go do something useful."

As she walked into the house, she fingered her necklace. Would Jesus have been so harsh? Maybe. He did confront the money changers in the temple. Figuring out how to act in a godly manner was even harder than she thought it would be.

⌒

Libby changed her clothes. Heat gun in hand, she attacked the layers of chipped paint on the trim around the front door. There

152

were easily ten layers of paint on the wood. When it softened and melted, she scraped it off with a putty knife and deposited it in a metal coffee can the gardener had found for her.

"That almost looks fun," Alec said from behind her. "Want some help?"

"I only have one heat gun or I'd take you up on it."

A white SUV pulled into the driveway. A slim woman with auburn curls stepped out of the passenger side. Moments later a stocky man with dark hair was out also and opening the back door on his side. A young boy of about ten joined the woman in the drive.

Libby put down the heat gun. They must be new guests. "Hello," she said, smiling at the family. "Welcome to Tidewater Inn."

The woman was staring at the inn with clear admiration. "I always forget just how beautiful it is until I get here again." She transferred her attention to Libby and held out her hand. "I'm Bree Matthews. You're expecting us."

Delilah had mentioned the family's arrival. It was their third visit in as many years. "We've got your room ready," Libby said. "Can I help you with anything? Call one of the men to help with luggage?"

"I'll help them," Alec said.

Bree pulled the boy beside her. "This is Davy. He's ten now and my big boy. That's my husband, Kade."

Kade was lifting toddlers from car seats in the back. "Be ready," he called. "They've been cooped up and will want to run for the water." He set a little boy and girl on the ground.

"How old are they?" Libby asked.

"Almost two. They're named Hunter and Hannah." Bree smiled and scooped her daughter up as she ran past. "You don't have your swimsuit on yet, honey," she told the child.

"They're beautiful." But Libby's attention was caught by the gorgeous dog that hopped out of the hatch. "Nice dog." Did they allow dogs in the inn? Delilah had never mentioned their policy.

"This is Samson, my search dog."

Libby watched Alec pet the dog. "Search dog? He finds lost people, like on TV?"

"He's the best." Bree snapped her fingers and the dog rushed over to lick them. "Good boy," she crooned.

Libby stared at the dog. He looked like he had quite a bit of German shepherd in him. "I don't know if you've heard anything about it, but we have a missing woman here. She happens to be my business partner."

Bree's gaze sharpened. "What happened? I haven't watched the news. We've been driving from Michigan and have been playing videos for the children."

Libby told her about Nicole's abduction. "You think he can find her?" Libby petted him and he nosed her leg.

"We can let him try." There was a shadow in Bree's green eyes, but she held Libby's gaze. "A water search is always harder. I want you to understand that. But he has a good nose. We'll do what we can, okay?"

Libby had hoped for utter assurance, but she managed a smile. "I appreciate anything you can do."

Bree glanced around. "Any idea of where to start the search?"

"I can show you where she was taken, but I also know Nicole was down the beach a ways, at some old lighthouse ruins. We haven't searched there yet, and I thought we might look at the ruins too. But let's get you unpacked first. I'll show you to your room."

Delilah had arranged for them to have the only two-bedroom suite so the children would have plenty of space. Libby hadn't been around kids much, and as the men unloaded the back of the SUV, she found her gaze lingering on the twins. Their dark hair was soft and curly. The little girl had Bree's pointed chin and hairline. The little boy was stocky like his handsome father.

"I want to see the water," Davy announced.

154

Hannah ran to Alec's leg and tugged on his jeans. "Water," she said, pointing toward the waves.

"We're going, bug," Kade said, touching the boy's hair.

Libby liked Kade already. The way he looked at Bree made Libby glance at Alec from the corner of her eye. Alec was tossing little Hannah in the air while she giggled and screamed, "More!" He seemed to be a natural with the kids. And he'd willingly taken on the raising of his nephew. That couldn't have been easy. Only a rare man would be willing to alter his life that much.

The women corralled the children while the men took the luggage to the room. Bree's mouth curved in a smile. "I like your fellow."

Libby stopped petting Samson, then resumed. "He's not my fellow. I haven't known him very long."

"Sometimes it doesn't take long. He seems like a nice guy."

"He's a good man," Libby agreed.

The men came back out. Kade had a vest in his hand. The dog began to prance around Bree when she took it from him. "Hold still, Samson." She knelt and slipped the vest onto the dog. His tail came up and he looked even more alert. "Someone is ready to go searching."

Samson's ears pricked at the word *searching*. He whined and looked down the beach. "He knows what we're talking about?" Libby asked.

"Oh yes. He loves his job. He acts differently when he's working. Let's go to the location where she was taken. Can you get me something that Nicole has worn? Put it in double paper sacks." Bree handed her two bags. "Our best chance is to go out on a boat and see if Samson can get a scent. But, Libby, it's going to be a long shot, okay?"

Maybe so, but it was a better chance than any other Libby had. She ran inside to grab one of Nicole's shirts. Having another ally had given her new courage.

TWENTY-THREE

Alec stood on the boardwalk with his hands in the pockets of his shorts and watched the freshening wind blow Libby's hair in tangles. As soon as they let the dog out of the SUV, he ran in circles, then back to Bree, who held the bags containing Nicole's shirt. Alec had heard of search dogs, but he'd never seen one in action.

"Where was she when she was taken?" Bree asked. She stood looking around the area.

"Right there." Libby pointed out the camera and the spot where her friend had been standing.

They scanned the same sand dunes, the same rolling ocean that Alec had seen earlier in the week when he'd come here with Tom. The only new items were a crumpled cigarette pack, an empty potato chip bag, and a few Marlboro butts.

Bree knelt and opened the bag. Samson thrust his nose into the bag. "Search, Samson!"

The dog pulled his head from the bag and barked. He ran back and forth across the beach with his nose in the air. Alec's jaw dropped as he watched the dog work. Samson clearly seemed to know what he was doing. When the dog stiffened, so did Alec, though he didn't know what it meant.

"He's got a scent!" Bree ran after the dog.

Alec and Libby followed. Libby's expression was intent and hopeful, so he rushed ahead of her, just in case whatever Samson was smelling was something Alec didn't want her to find. Samson trailed the scent to the parking lot. He ran to a trash barrel and began to bark.

Alec's gut clenched, and he prayed they wouldn't find Nicole's body in it. "Stand back." He motioned for the women to move back a few feet. Once he got the top off the garbage pail, he put on plastic gloves and began poking through it in spite of the stench. It was only about half full, so he relaxed, sure he wasn't going to find anything at all. The dog had probably gotten sidetracked by the food smells.

"That's hers!" Libby's arm shot past him and grabbed a pink straw hat. She shook off the debris. "I told you I saw it fall off her in the struggle."

"You're sure?" Bree asked.

Libby nodded. "I bought it for her for her birthday. What's it doing in the trash?"

"You shouldn't have touched it." Alec took it in his gloved hands. "Maybe the killers handled it."

The animation on Libby's face ebbed. "It came off her head in the struggle. I don't think they touched it."

"You said they took her right to the boat and offshore," he pointed out. "You saw them throw her into the boat and move off? They didn't come back for the hat?"

"I saw them leave." Her mouth drooped. "So this means nothing."

"We know the dog can smell her," he said. "Pretty amazing. I guess they could have come back and just thrown it away so nothing looked out of place on the beach. Anyone could have tossed it."

Bree called the dog back to her and had him smell the sack again. "Search, Samson!"

Samson sniffed the air, then ran back to the beach. He barked and raced to a spot near the water, where he began to dig. Alec and the women ran to see what he'd found. Alec knelt to help Samson, but he woofed and nosed at a pair of sunglasses before Alec could dig his fingers into the sand.

Alec held them up. "Nicole's?"

Libby nodded. "I think so."

The dog whined and pressed his nose against Bree's hand. She went through the process of letting him smell the bag again. He ran back and forth on the sand for ten minutes before going back to Bree's side. He whined, then laid at her feet.

"I think this is all he's got," Bree said.

"It was worth a try." Libby glanced at Alec. "Could you take us out tomorrow in the boat?"

"Sure. You think he can find something in the ocean?" Watching the dog work was interesting, but Alec didn't see how Samson could possibly find Nicole in that ocean.

Bree shrugged. "I won't lie and say it's likely. There's a lot of ocean out there and we really don't know where to even look. But Samson has done many other amazing searches successfully, so I want to try."

He appreciated Bree's honesty. Alec nodded. "We'll take my boat out first thing in the morning."

———

Libby was too restless to watch the movie playing in the living room. Bree was bathing the children and getting them to bed, so Libby slipped away from the group and went to the third floor again. Her interest in finding out how Nicole's purse had ended up there had resurfaced.

She flipped on the light, then stood in the main living area of the third floor and glanced around. The stairs creaked behind her and she whirled to see Brent stepping into the space.

"What are you doing up here?" he demanded.

"Looking around." She decided against reminding him that she owned the property and could go anywhere she pleased. She'd written in her journal that she hadn't extended much grace after their last encounter.

He scowled at her. "These are Dad's private quarters."

"I know." She gestured to the table. "Nicole's bag is here. Do you have any idea how it got up here?"

"*She* was up here?"

"It appears so. Unless someone put her purse here."

"Have you asked Delilah about it?"

She should have thought of that. "No. But you didn't answer my question. Did *you* know about it?"

His gaze was steady. "You really think I had something to do with her disappearance, don't you?"

She'd had enough of his evasiveness. "Why do you always answer a question with another one? Just answer me, yes or no. Did you see Nicole's purse up here?"

"No. This is the first I've been up here since Dad died. Your turn. You think I'm guilty of something bad, don't you?"

He looked so innocent, so hurt. Was any of it real? Libby wanted to believe him. He was her brother, after all. "I honestly don't know. I'd like to believe you did nothing to hurt her, but you have to admit your lies look bad."

"I didn't do anything to her. It was an innocent outing."

Libby reminded herself how young he was. Maybe she was overreacting. "I know you weren't one of the men who took her. I saw them. But you could have hired the men."

"I could have, but I didn't."

She wanted to know this brother, but she couldn't seem to get through. "You're hard to read, Brent. I want to believe you." She decided that Jesus would lay it all out there, so she gathered her courage. "What do you want, Brent? Do you even care that you have another sister? We're family, you know. We share our father's blood. I want us to learn to love each other."

His eyes flickered when she mentioned love, but then he folded his arms over his chest. "I'm sure you're a very nice person, Libby, but I have one sister and that's enough. You don't belong here. I'm sorry to be so blunt, but you can't show up here and announce you're part of our family and expect it to be so. To us, you're just a stranger."

Though she agreed with the gist of what he'd said, his cold gaze cut her. Her eyes filled, and she turned away so he wouldn't see. "I see. Thank you for being honest." He was still standing there when she regained her composure, so she turned back toward him. "In Nicole's journal, she mentioned that someone whispered to her outside her door. Was that you?"

His jaw tightened. "You're determined to pin something on me, aren't you?"

"Who else would have access here? And it was a male. Be honest with me, Brent. I've learned enough about our father to know he valued honesty and integrity."

His lips flattened. "Fine. I tried to scare her off. Satisfied? But I had nothing to do with her disappearance."

"Why did you want to scare her off? She wasn't hurting you."

His sigh was heavy. "Look, she told me she wanted you to keep the property and develop it yourself. I felt the honorable thing for you to do was to bow out. I still feel that way."

"She wanted us to develop it? That's crazy. Where could we come up with enough money?" Maybe Nicole had been making a play to squeeze more money out of the buyer. Poe seemed determined to have the land.

She held Brent's gaze and found truth there. "I believe you."

His eyes flickered. "Really? Or will those doubts surface again?"

She shook her head. "We've gotten off to a really bad start. Friends?" She reached out her hand.

Brent stared at her extended hand, then quickly touched his fingers to hers and withdrew. "Let's say acquaintances for now."

It was a start.

The steps creaked behind them, then Delilah stepped into the room. She stopped short when she saw them. "I went to the storage shed to look for something and saw the light on up here. I thought someone had forgotten to turn it off. Is everything all right?"

Libby nodded. "I do have a question though." She picked up Nicole's bag. "Do you know how this got here?"

Delilah's lids flickered. "I assume Nicole left it."

"She was up here? Why?" Libby didn't like the thought that Nicole had been poking through her father's things. Maybe this was how Vanessa felt.

"She'd asked to explore the house. I didn't give her any keys and had no idea she would find her way up here, but I must have left the door unlocked when I cleaned the last time. I found her here and chased her out."

"Did she say what she was doing?"

Delilah shook her head. "I think she just wanted to see what was here. She didn't seem to have an agenda, if that's what you mean."

Nicole was as much of a history buff as she was. Libby could see her wanting to poke into every nook and cranny of the attic.

So the purse was a dead end. "I'd like to be alone for a while," she said.

Brent and Delilah exchanged a glance. Brent shrugged. "You're the boss." He went down the steps and Delilah followed.

Libby exhaled and sank onto the sofa. In this place she could sense her father. It would be the perfect spot to have her devotions every day too. His Bible was still on the table where she'd left it. She hadn't had a chance to go through it much. When she picked it up, she realized there was a folded paper, stiff with age, under it.

She unfolded it and discovered it was a map of the island. The old lighthouse site was marked on it. Holding it under the light, she saw someone had written the word *cellar* with an arrow on it near the house structure. Another X marked the wellhead. The place once had several outbuildings too. She was eager to see how much of it still stood. And whether it harbored any clues to Nicole's whereabouts.

Twenty-Four

The sun was barely up, and haze still hung over the waves. Sea spray stung Libby's cheeks and filled her nose with the salty scent of the ocean. She crouched behind the windshield of Alec's boat to avoid a large wave that threatened to wash over the bow. "The sea is strong today."

Bree and Samson rode up front. The dog had his nose in the wind and wore an ecstatic smile. "It's gorgeous out here," Bree called. "Not quite the same as Lake Superior where we live, but close enough. Where are we going?"

Alec pointed to the shore. "The lighthouse ruins. We'll land there. I'll drop anchor, and we'll have to wade to shore. It's got a sandy bottom though, so no danger of getting dunked."

"I'm not afraid of the water," Libby said. In fact, she couldn't think of anything she enjoyed more than being on the sea. Well, other than digging into the history of a gorgeous old house.

The spit of land was narrow, only about twenty feet across. Scrubby bushes and vegetation that had stood up to the salt clung to the sparse soil. The small peninsula widened at the base and joined the main part of the island, where heavier vegetation hid whatever ruins they'd come here to see. Libby scanned the area for a hint of the cover-up Nicole had been wearing. She wasn't sure

if she was relieved or sad to see no sign that her friend had ever been here.

The boat touched bottom, and Alec tossed the anchor overboard. Samson dived over the side and swam toward shore. Alec clambered into the shallows, then held out his hand to assist Libby and Bree. Kicking off her sandals, Libby slipped into the water with him. The sea was chillier than she'd expected. The storm must have stirred up the cold from the bottom. She held her shoes out of the water and waded to shore. The sand was firm and smooth under her bare feet. When she reached the beach, she slipped her feet back into her sandals, then looked around.

"Where are the ruins? I don't see anything," she said.

He pointed. "This way."

He led them north, away from the finger of barren peninsula, deeper into the vegetation. Samson barked and ran ahead. Sea oats waved in the breeze, and beach grass fought to hold on in the dunes. Skate cases littered the sand. The sand began to run out and was replaced by thin soil that supported a maritime forest of straggly live oaks pruned by the salt into wedge shapes. Palmettos and loblolly pines marched along the forest.

Libby spied the ruins before he said anything. "There," she said, pointing. The area was still flooded, and she could see only the tops of brick and mortar. "It was a lighthouse once? There's not much left of it. I expected a standing structure."

"It was knocked over in a big hurricane in the late eighteen hundreds. Legend has it that Blackbeard stormed the lighthouse and captured the keeper's daughter."

"What happened to her?" Bree asked, shuddering.

He shrugged. "No one really knows. Some say Blackbeard loved her and carried her off to his lair in the Bahamas. Others say she jumped overboard and drowned rather than face dishonor. But it's just a legend. There may be no truth to it at all. People have

come out here from Hope Beach for generations. Weddings have been held here, ashes have been committed to the sea from here, and babies have been dedicated on this spot. It's almost a shrine to the town."

Libby glanced around. "Why? The place seems so barren."

He propped one foot on the ruins. "Over the years it gained the reputation of bestowing good luck on residents. The first marriage here that I know of was at the turn of the century. That marriage lasted sixty years."

She lifted her chin and sniffed the sweet-smelling air. "It has a welcoming feel in spite of all the ruins."

Advancing to the base of the building, she examined the debris. "Nicole was wearing a pink cover-up over a brown bathing suit. She had on pink flip-flops too. And her hair was in a ponytail."

"I'll take Samson and we'll nose around," Bree said. She pulled a bag of pistachios from her pocket. "Want some?"

Libby grinned and shook her head. She dug into her pocket and held up her jalapeño jellybeans. "I have these."

Bree wrinkled her nose, then she and Samson headed toward the line of vegetation. The dog had his nose down.

Alec walked the perimeter of the ruins and back. "I don't see anything but a few Coke bottles. We'll come back again when the water recedes."

"I'd wondered if she came out here on her own, but I don't see any sign of her."

"How would she get here? It would take an hour to walk from the house," he said.

"She's an avid runner. I imagine she could run along the beach and get here in forty-five minutes. She's not the type to wait for someone else to show her something of interest. I thought she might have come out here the day before to scout it out before

coming with Vanessa." She turned and looked out to sea. "Would they have taken her to the mainland? I don't know where we should look."

"The state has put out a bulletin about her. If she's there, someone will see her. This is summer. The coastline is crawling with tourists. It would be hard to take her anywhere without being seen."

"But not impossible if they did it in the middle of the night," Libby said.

"She was taken late in the afternoon."

Libby felt so hopeless. "They could have holed up somewhere."

"True enough."

Libby realized she was grasping at straws. "What about farther out? Are there any uninhabited islands on this side of the island?"

He nodded. "Plenty of them. Some of them barely as big as a postage stamp. I thought we'd check out as many as we can. We can go out in the boat and ask fishermen if they've seen anything too."

"You think she's dead, don't you?" The question tore from Libby's throat.

He stared down at her. "We both know that the longer it goes since she's been spotted, the scarier it is. But I haven't given up hope yet. Someone has to have seen something."

She searched his expression. "You really believe that?"

"I do."

His certainty strengthened her. She glanced back at the ruins. "Are there any photos of the lighthouse before it was destroyed?"

He nodded. "Your dad has quite a library at the old hotel. He was a history buff, and the information about the island and Hope Beach that he has is more extensive than anything the town library has."

It appeared she had something in common with the father who left her.

⌐⌐

Alec led Libby across the street from the harbor to the Oyster Café. It was lunchtime and there would be plenty of townspeople around who might have met Nicole during her stay. Bree had taken Samson to meet Kade and the children for lunch at Captain's Pizza.

"This is such a darling village," Libby said when they stopped outside the café. "I love it. So quaint."

He pushed the door open. The waitress seated them by the window that looked out onto the street where bicyclers zipped past.

"Why do so many people ride bicycles here?" she asked.

He hadn't thought much about it. "Gas is high, and it costs to get a car over here. I guess progress hasn't caught up to us."

"I like it. I'd like to get a bike."

"Your dad has one in the basement of the inn. I'll show you where it is."

She brightened. "I'd like to use his." Her smile faded. "Though it's likely to be one more source of contention with Vanessa and Brent. They don't want me to have anything personal of my father's."

"They'll get over it." He watched her toy with the necklace. "You still have the necklace, I see. I wondered if you would give it to Vanessa last night."

"I think God is telling me to do it, but I'm fighting the idea."

"It's never a good idea to fight God."

"I know." She gave a heavy sigh. "I don't want to do it. I've been praying he makes me willing to obey."

"Good prayer." He looked at the menu. "I think I'll get shrimp grits."

"Crab linguine sounds good," she said, staring at the menu. "Have you had it?"

He nodded. "It's good."

167

She glanced around the crowded space. "Who might have talked to Nicole?"

He scanned the tables. "I guess anyone in here could have. This is a popular place to eat."

"Maybe the waitress will remember her."

"Maybe." He motioned to the waitress, a pretty woman who was about twenty-five. He should know her name, but he couldn't remember it. All he knew was that she'd moved here from Kill Devil Hills about six months ago.

"What can I get for you?"

He gave their orders. "Did you meet the young woman who was kidnapped earlier this week?"

"Sure did. She sat at that table right there." The waitress pointed to the corner table behind them. "I didn't know her name, but I recognized her face when I saw it in the paper."

"Did she eat alone?" Libby asked.

The waitress shook her head. "Some slick city guy was with her. Real dark hair. Kind of reminded me of Elvis."

"Poe," Libby said. She shot a glance at Alec.

"Could you hear what they talked about?" Alec asked.

"I overheard them arguing a little," the woman said. "She said she thought he wasn't paying enough."

"For what?" Alec asked.

"I don't know. I didn't hear that." The server stuck her pencil behind her ear. "I'd better get this order in."

When the woman walked away, Libby leaned forward. "So maybe she was negotiating for more money for my land."

"Looks like it. When are you supposed to hear from him again?"

"I told him to give me a week. But we didn't set a specific time."

"Did he give you his card?"

Her face lit. "He did. I forgot about it." She dug in her purse and came up with a card and her phone. "My cell doesn't have any bars."

"Neither does mine. We can go over to my house and call after lunch though." Alec's head came up when Tom walked in the door. "Hey, Tom," he called.

Tom had been starting toward a free table, but he changed directions and headed toward them. "Mind if I join you?"

Alec shoved a chair out with his foot. "Have a seat. We just ordered."

Tom motioned to the waitress and gave her his order. He stared at Libby. "I heard you got a search-and-rescue dog team helping. I would have appreciated it if you'd let me know what you were doing before you did it."

She flushed but didn't look away. "I have the right to try to find my friend. You don't seem to be looking."

His jaw tightened. "I'm doing things you don't see."

"No harm in looking on our own," Alec said.

Tom's eyes were dark when he glanced Alec's way. "If you found anything, you contaminated evidence. You know better than that. I would have sent a deputy along with you to retrieve anything you found."

"Fair enough." Though Alec was sure the items they'd found had been dropped by Nicole, what if he was wrong? "We found a couple of things last night, but I'm sure they aren't evidence."

Tom's mouth was pinched. "What?"

Alec told him about the discarded hat and sunglasses. "Someone threw them away. Could have been the kidnappers covering their tracks, or it could have been someone cleaning the beach."

"Where are they?"

"In my truck."

"Alec, that was just plain stupid. I hope you didn't destroy something that might have led us to Nicole."

Alec exchanged a long look with Libby. He had been suitably chastised.

TWENTY-FIVE

B ree and Kade took the kids to explore the town and harbor, and Alec went with Zach back to town to buy some jeans. Worry had drained Libby, and searching for Nicole left her feeling hopeless. What if she never found her friend? Though she tried to kill the thought, it refused to go away.

For days the box of letters from her father had been in her closet. Libby fingered his necklace and decided to gather her courage and read some. But not alone in this room. Maybe with Pearl. She lifted the shoe box from the shelf and stepped into the hall where she practically ran into Vanessa.

Vanessa's eyes narrowed. "What's in the box? That's my father's handwriting on top."

Libby had studied those words for days. *For My Oldest Daughter.* "They're letters he wrote to me."

Vanessa made a grab at the top and flipped it off. "Let me see."

Before Libby could pull away, Vanessa had one of the envelopes in her hand. She stepped out of reach. "I want to understand what this is all about. How could my father prefer you over me and Brent? Surely you can see how I need to figure this out."

Short of snatching the letter back as rudely as Vanessa had taken it, Libby watched as her sister pulled the sheet of paper from

the envelope. It took all her self-control to stay calm. "I haven't read it myself. Please give it back."

The other woman lifted a brow but made no move to return the note. She unfolded it.

"Vanessa, that's enough." Pearl stepped from the doorway of her room. "You're being incredibly bad mannered. That was not meant for your eyes. If your sister wants to share it, that's up to her, but the choice is hers, not yours." When Vanessa kept the letter, Pearl stepped closer, plucked it from her hand, and handed it to Libby. "I'm sorry for her rudeness, my dear."

Libby stared at the page. This was an experience she'd wanted to savor, but if she wanted to be part of this family, she was going to have to make an effort. *What would Jesus do?* "Would you both care to look at these with me? We can go back to my room."

The expression on her aunt's face warmed, and the approval Libby saw there convinced her she'd done the right thing. Libby glanced at Vanessa, who shrugged and followed her back into the bedroom. Vanessa glanced around and made a beeline for the four-poster bed that dominated the large room. She kicked off her flip-flops and climbed onto the bed, curling her feet under her.

"This used to be my room whenever we came here for the night." Her tone made it clear what she thought of Libby staying in the room.

Libby opened her mouth to offer to switch rooms, then closed it again. Vanessa was not going to manipulate her. "It's a nice room." She glanced at the space beside Vanessa, then glanced at Pearl.

Pearl shook her head. "You sit there, honey. It's too high for me." She took the Queen Anne armchair at the foot of the bed.

If not for the tension coming off Vanessa in waves, Libby could almost imagine they were really friends holed up on a rainy night. She looked at the letter in her hand. "This is the oldest one.

I would have been fifteen when this came. So he evidently didn't try to contact me before this." She continued to stare at it. Did she even want to know what it said? These communications from her father were a clear sign of how much her mother had lied to her.

"Want me to read it aloud?" Pearl asked.

Libby reached across the bed and handed it to her. "It seems appropriate."

There was something in Pearl's face that caught at her heart. It was as if she knew Libby was about to hear something life-changing. Then Pearl glanced at Vanessa, and that expression intensified. Vanessa's head was down as she traced the pattern in the quilt. Libby tried to summon sympathy for the young woman, but Vanessa's prickly manner made it difficult. It was hard to remember they were sisters.

Pearl unfolded the letter and cleared her throat. "'My dear Libby. I know I'm breaking the custody agreement by trying to contact you, but I miss you so much. As time has gone on, I've been more consumed by grief over what we have done to you girls. It was wrong. I should never have agreed to the custody split. At the time, it seemed the best for you and Vanessa, but I've regretted it every day of my life.'"

Libby caught her breath. "Vanessa? What does he mean that it's best for me *and* Vanessa?"

Pearl put down the letter. "At last, it's out in the open. I always thought it was the most terrible thing I'd ever heard, but it wasn't my decision."

"What wasn't your decision?"

Pearl glanced from Libby to Vanessa, who was staring at her with the same horror on her face that Libby felt. *Custody split.* Did he mean that she and Vanessa were full sisters? Surely no parent would be so cruel as to split up siblings.

Pearl sighed heavily. "Vanessa is your younger sister."

Libby rose to her knees on the bed. "No, you don't mean we're *sisters*! Full sisters? Not half?"

Pearl nodded. "Vanessa is a year younger than you."

Vanessa scrambled off the bed. "You're lying!" She shot a glance of utter dislike at Libby. "I don't know what you're trying to do here, but this is some kind of scam."

"Vanessa, sit down," Pearl said in a weary voice. "You too, Libby. I can't believe Ray left this for me to untangle. Do you honestly think I'd be part of something unsavory, Vanessa? You know me better than that."

"It's not true, it's not!" Vanessa sobbed. She ignored her aunt's outstretched hand and rushed from the room.

Her knees too weak to support her, Libby sank back onto the bed.

———

Several people darted across the street in front of Alec's pickup as he drove slowly through the debris-strewn streets toward the sheriff's office. While he and Zach were at Skipper's Store looking for jeans, a deputy had stopped in to ask Alec to come to the jail. His tone was somber, and he'd said not to tell Libby. Alec feared some new evidence implicated Libby even more than the missing video had.

His cousin was leaning against the doorjamb smoking a cigar when Alec parked and got out of his vehicle. Tom straightened and blew a puff of smoke Alec's way. "Thanks for coming right away."

Alec waved the smoke out of his face. "What's up?"

"I'll show you. Come with me." Tom yanked open the office door.

Alec followed him to the evidence room, down a green hallway. A table in the corner held items that made his heart sink. Bright-pink flip-flops and a cover-up in a matching color. "Those are Nicole's?"

"Seems likely. They washed up on shore a few minutes ago. That woman and her dog found them."

"Doesn't mean she's dead," Alec said quickly.

Tom lifted a brow. "Come on, Alec, you and I both know the odds aren't good. Yeah, she might have lost her shoes in the struggle, but her cover-up is a different matter."

Alec winced. "You call Libby yet?"

"No."

"Why not?"

Tom headed for the door, and Alec followed. His cousin's closed expression sent a prickle of unease up Alec's spine. Tom went directly to his desk and jiggled his mouse. After a few clicks, he motioned to Alec. Alec stepped around the desk and peered at the screen. It displayed the video of the boardwalk where Nicole had disappeared. It displayed only sand and surf at first, then abruptly went black.

Alec frowned. "This the recording of the time she disappeared?"

"Yeah. I checked when Libby arrived in Kitty Hawk. She went to the harbor and tried to rent a boat about nine in the evening. That means she didn't leave Virginia Beach until seven, two hours after she made the call to 9-1-1. Yet she said she rushed off so fast that she didn't talk to the police."

"She may have waited that long for the police, and when they didn't show, she finally took off."

"Maybe." Tom leaned back. "I think we have to consider her as a suspect. And with the items that washed up, we have to treat it as a homicide."

"I can ask Libby why she didn't leave for a couple of hours."

"Don't show your suspicion. Maybe you can trip her up in a lie."

"You really think she harmed her friend?" Alec shook his head. "I don't see it, Tom."

"You and I have both been around long enough to know the likeliest culprit is usually the most obvious one."

"But not always. I think we need to give Libby the benefit of the doubt." Alec could see by the closed expression on the sheriff's face that he was wasting his breath.

Tom stood. "Look, are you going to help me or not? Or are you too afraid to find out the truth?"

"The truth is never something to fear. But I'm not going to be part of any scheme to railroad Libby."

"I'm not asking you to. Just be on the lookout for anything suspicious."

"I already am."

Tom twirled a pencil in his fingers. "There's more, Alec. I talked to Earl Franklin a little while ago too. Libby's mother died under mysterious circumstances. Libby was held twenty hours for questioning."

Mysterious circumstances. "So? The police were doing their job. She was never charged or you'd have mentioned that first."

Tom banged his fist on the desk and swore. "You're being just as pigheaded as usual, Alec. There's a lot in her past that's questionable."

Alec leaned over the desk toward his cousin. "So investigate, but don't assume she's guilty without getting facts! Otherwise, you're letting a murderer walk."

Tom's face was red. "Let's go tell your lady friend what we've found and see what her reaction is. Maybe that will convince you."

"I'm not the one who needs convincing," Alec said. He hoped that was true.

TWENTY-SIX

Nicole paced the tiny island. Fifty steps to the left of the hut and thirty steps to the right. Then around the back. She was going to go stark raving mad out here. The boy had been here yesterday, so she doubted he would come today. Not when he left enough food and water to last her for several days. She was stuck here under the blazing sun by herself.

She had to get off this island. What would happen if the boy never came back? Or another storm came? She eyed the clouds drifting across the brilliant blue sky. Was there anything she could use for a raft? She darted across the island so fast that her bare feet kicked up sand. Inside the shack, she paused long enough to let her eyes adjust to the dim light filtering through the open doorway and single window. There was no flooring to pry up, only sand. The cot was metal, so it would sink immediately. There was a wooden table. Maybe it would work.

She curled her fingers under the edge and dragged it to the door. It was too wide to pull through the doorway so she turned it on its side and maneuvered it out onto the damp sand. With difficulty, she managed to drag it to where the surf broke on the beach. The waves crashed so hard she wondered if she would manage to get it out to sea. The legs would make it more difficult too. She

scoured the beach until she found a rock about eight inches in diameter. Once she got it back to the table, she lifted it over her head and brought it crashing down on the table leg closest to her. It took four whacks to dislodge the first leg. She rolled the table around and continued to batter at the legs until she had all of them free of the top.

Now she had the makings of a raft. And if she could tie the legs together, she might have something that would work as oars. She stared at the trees. There were no vines. She wandered the beach again but found only flotsam and seaweed. Nothing strong enough to take on the crashing waves. Returning to the table, she looked from it to the foaming water. Using single table legs was going to have to do. There was no choice. And she needed to bring water and food with her, but how did she keep it from tumbling overboard while she got the raft out past the breakers?

The sound of the sea rolled over her, powerful and frightening. But she couldn't let fear deter her. If she did nothing, her death was almost certain. If she died in the attempt, at least she was doing *something*. She turned back toward the shack and ducked inside to get peanut butter and water. The peanut butter jar fit in the bra of her bathing suit. She tucked one bottle of water in the front of the bottoms and one in the back, but she didn't have high hopes that they would stay put. If only she had some rope.

Sighing, she grabbed an edge of the tabletop and dragged it into the water, then seized two table legs and tried to hang on to them as she tugged the wood farther into the water. The sea foamed around her ankles, and she waited for the right moment to pull the table through the waves. When the crashing wave receded, she lunged through the water with her fingers gripping the makeshift raft. The waves tried furiously to rip the raft from her fingers, but she managed to hang on. When the water reached her waist, she flung herself atop the table. Tucking the table legs

under her, she paddled with her hands for all she was worth. It seemed for every foot she managed to propel herself forward, the surf flung her back toward the island two feet.

The breakers were crashing just ahead of her. She paused her paddling until the right moment, then tried again with all her strength. The waves lifted her, then flung her past the breakwater. The ride smoothed out and the waves didn't threaten to tip her into the sea at every moment. She sat up and examined her circumstances. One bottle of water had been pulled from her bathing suit. The peanut butter had survived the experience, but she had only one table leg. It would be useless by itself. She nearly tossed it overboard, then reconsidered. Her resources were limited out here. She might need it for something.

The island was receding. She flopped to her stomach again and began to paddle with her hands. A fin appeared in the water beside the boat, and she snatched her hands back, then smiled when she realized it was a dolphin. If only the dolphin realized her distress and could help her find land.

The dolphin nosed her makeshift raft. She reached out and touched the mammal's skin. It felt like a warm inner tube. "Can you help me?" she whispered.

The dolphin bumped at her raft again, then flicked its tail and shoved at her raft. The table floated back toward the island. "Hey, that's the wrong way," Nicole said.

The dolphin pushed the raft with its nose again, and Nicole sat up. "Cut that out!" She glanced back at the island. Surely it was much closer. Her chest tightened and she grabbed the table leg and hit the water with it. The splashing didn't deter the dolphin. It continued to shove her back toward the island. Nicole didn't have the heart to actually hit the animal with the table leg. All she could do was splash and scream as the dolphin moved the raft back to the island.

The waves were suddenly higher, and she flung herself to her belly and clutched the sides as the breakers grabbed the table-top and flung it toward the island. She heard a tearing, grinding sound and was suddenly in the water with salt water burning her nose and throat. She couldn't breathe as the waves rolled her over and over until she came to rest in a foot of water with her knees stinging from scraping the sand.

She sat up and cried out as the waves offered up the pieces of her raft, useless now.

———

Pearl carried a silver tray bearing delicate blue-and-white china into the bedroom. "Here you go, honey." She put the tray on the bedside table. "The tea will make you feel better."

"Thank you, Aunt Pearl. You're very thoughtful." Libby stared again at the letter in her hand.

Several hours had passed since Libby realized Vanessa was her sister, but the shock had not lessened. How could her parents have done such a heinous thing? To separate sisters until they were combative strangers was a crime that could not be forgiven. Libby found no charity in her heart toward her parents. God said to forgive seventy-times-seven times, but in this case, even one time was too many.

She fingered the necklace. *What would Jesus do?* Right now, Libby couldn't seem to summon the desire to care.

Pearl touched her head. "There are homemade cookies with M&M'S in them."

Libby flung a letter aside that had contained three pictures of Vanessa winning a swim competition. "Not even chocolate can heal this. We have missed so much of each other's lives. It's monstrous."

Pearl eased her bulk into the chair. "There's nothing you can do to change what is, Libby. All you can do is go forward from here."

"Have you talked to Vanessa?"

Pearl's expression clouded. "She won't open her bedroom door."

"She hates this as much as I do. Maybe more."

"Ray spoiled those children. He would be heartsick if he could see how she is treating you."

Libby rubbed her throbbing forehead. "I can't blame her."

"This is hardly your fault."

Libby stared at her aunt. "Did you try to talk him out of this?"

"Of course." Pearl sat heavily in the armchair. "When he arrived here on Hope Island with Vanessa in tow, I begged him to go back for you."

"Did you know my mother?"

Pearl's eyes filled and she nodded. "She was very naïve and childlike. Once she made up her mind, there was no talking her out of anything. Your mother had been adamant that she wanted no contact with Ray. The only way to do that was for each of them to take a child. She argued that it would only be difficult in the beginning. Once you both forgot, everyone could have a fresh start."

Libby's throat closed. "No wonder I've felt so abandoned. I lost a father and a sister in one blow."

"Your father mourned your loss all his life. Not a week went by but he spoke of you."

Where her aunt's pity had failed to move her, Pearl's words about Ray opened a flood of pain. Libby tried to compose herself. "I don't have any memories of him. What did he like to do?"

"Come with me. I'll show you his pride and joy."

Curious, Libby rose from the bed and followed her aunt into the hall and up a narrow flight of stairs to the third floor. It was a different staircase from the one that led to her father's suite. This space smelled of disuse and dampness.

Libby glanced around the stark space. "No one lives up here, do they?"

Pearl fiddled with a key in the lock of the first door to the right. "Oh no. Once upon a time it was the servants' quarters, but since it became an inn back in the sixties, it's been used only for storage." With a final click of the knob, she flung open the door.

Their feet had left prints on the dust in the halls, but not a speck of dust was in this chamber. Ceilings soared to fifteen feet. The walls were painted a pale lemon, and the wood floors were polished. "What is this place?" Libby asked, peering through the gloom.

"One moment." Pearl felt along the wall, then light filled the room.

Libby's eyes took a moment to adjust, then she gasped as the paintings came into view. "A-Are those real?" She moved close enough to see the brushstrokes. "They look like Washington Allston originals."

"They are. Ray loved the religious ones. He said Allston always chose obscure events in the Old Testament to illustrate how we should live out our faith."

Libby stared at the picture of a young woman sleeping at the feet of an older man. "Ruth and Boaz?" This one was hardly about an obscure event.

Pearl nodded. "He loved it, though it also reminded him that he had failed you. Boaz always did the right thing, in the right order. Ray felt he would never aspire to that high mark."

Libby glanced around the room. "How many did he collect?"

"Five in all."

"They're worth a fortune."

"They are indeed. I'm surprised you recognized them."

"I'm a huge Allston fan. I have a tiny print that's sat on my dresser ever since I can remember." She put her hand to her throat. "Did my father give that to me?"

"The one of *Moonlit Landscape*?" Pearl nodded. "It was his favorite. Though he could never own the original, he has some prints stored in another room."

"So that's why I love Allston," Libby said. "I inherited the love from him."

"He used to take you to art museums, starting when you were six months old. We laughed and told him you were too young, but he carried you from picture to picture, explaining what each painting was and why it was significant."

Libby wished she remembered. How much of her personality and passions had she absorbed from a father she never knew?

"Why did my parents divorce? Why did he leave me behind? Did he love Vanessa more?"

Pearl took her hand and squeezed. "Never think that, honey! Your mother flipped a coin. He got Vanessa, and she kept you."

Libby shuddered at the word picture her aunt's description evoked. "Why would he agree to that?"

"He wanted to take you both, but back then it would have been impossible to get custody of both of you without her agreement. He had no grounds. She told him she only had the energy for one child, that he could take one. It was the luck of the draw."

"So they flipped a coin and ripped a family apart."

Libby didn't want to be bitter. She didn't. But it was hard to come to grips with what had been done to her and Vanessa.

A dog barked. Bree and Samson must have come back. "I think I'll go for a swim and clear my head."

"I'll pray for you, honey. You need to forgive and let go of this."

Easier said than done.

TWENTY-SEVEN

The water beckoned like a lover. Libby dug her toes into the soft sand and watched the waves for a moment. Samson had wanted a walk, so she'd taken him with her. Bree had taken the children to get cleaned up for dinner.

A swim would clear Libby's head, though she knew she should march right back inside and demand Vanessa talk to her. In Libby's wildest dreams she'd never expected to find a sister who hated her. This could have been such a wonderful day. Instead it was a nightmare that she couldn't awaken from.

She pulled off her cover-up and tossed it on the sand. "Want to go for a swim, Samson?" The dog's ears perked at the word *swim*. He danced around her and barked wildly, then ran toward the waves and snapped at the foam.

"Moron," she said, laughing. The dog barked excitedly in answer.

She kicked off her flip-flops and ran into the waves. The shock of the cold water made her gasp, then giggle like she was ten. A breaker rolled toward her, and she waited until the right moment before diving into it. The force of the current rolled her along the bottom, but she relished its power. When she was in the water, she forgot all her troubles. She surfaced and tossed her hair out of her face. The sea didn't feel so cold now that she was fully immersed.

She broke into a breaststroke and crested the next wave. Samson kept up with her as she swam out.

When she turned to look back, she was a hundred yards out. There didn't seem to be a riptide, so she flipped onto her back and let the waves float her along. Sheer heaven. It would be sunset soon, so she wouldn't stay out too long. Sharks would be out.

When the first nudge came on her leg, she thought it was a fish. She straightened to a vertical position and looked around. Then something grabbed her leg and yanked her under the water. She managed to gasp oxygen into her lungs before her head was submerged. Though the salt water burned, she opened her eyes underwater and saw a diver in a black wetsuit. It was too dark to see much detail, but she could make out the person's masculine build and the air tank on his back.

She kicked out with her right foot and hit him in the chest, but the blow didn't make him turn her loose. His fingers squeezed her leg so tightly that it was beginning to go numb. Bubbles rose around her as he dragged her deeper under the waves. He reached the bottom and stood on the sand. She floated just above him with his hand still holding her fast.

He's trying to drown me. The shock of realizing his intention made her release a bit of her precious air into the water. Her lungs began to burn. She flailed to free herself, but he was stronger. Samson would not be able to dive down to help her. If she wanted to live, she had to escape this man. Panic drove all thought from her head for a few moments, then she forced herself to focus.

Think, Libby! Her only chance was to deprive him of oxygen. She lashed out with her foot, aiming for his face. Her heel struck his mouthpiece and it flipped out of his mouth. Bubbles escaped in a flurry. He let go of her legs and grabbed the mask. Lungs burning, Libby shot for the surface. He would be right behind her. She had to get to safety. Her feet pumped, and she rose toward the light.

She didn't think she could hold out much longer. Her vision began to dim, then her head broke the surface. She filled her lungs with air and shook her head to clear it. Shore was more than a hundred and twenty yards away. She struck out for the safety of the sand, vaguely aware that Samson was snarling. A hand grazed her ankle and she kicked hard, then swam to the right and then back toward shore. The diver had the advantage of seeing her from below. It would be a miracle if she escaped him.

Help, Lord! Her muscles were beginning to tire from the exertion, but she kept up the pace. Her starved lungs wanted her to pause and gather in more oxygen, but there was no time. Not if she wanted to live. She dared a glance back and saw a head pop up. The sight galvanized her into swimming even more frantically. The dog growled to her right. He left her side, but she didn't look back until the snarling reached a ferocious level. The dog had his teeth clamped on the man's arm. The diver struck at Samson, but the dog held on.

This was her chance to escape. She swam for all she was worth. The shore grew closer and closer until her knees scraped bottom. She staggered to her feet and practically fell onto the beach. There was no time to recover though. She sprang back up and turned to stare out to sea. Where was the dog?

"Samson!" She screamed his name into the wind. The harsh caw of a seagull was the only answer. She half turned to run to the inn for help, then she saw his head break the waves. He was swimming for shore. There was no sign of her attacker.

She ran a few feet into the water to greet the dog as he struggled to shore. Sinking to her knees, she threw her arms around his neck. He licked her cheek weakly and she half guided, half carried him the rest of the way. They both collapsed onto the sand. Panting, Samson crawled onto her lap.

"Good dog," she crooned. She'd wanted to see an angel, just as Aunt Pearl once had. Samson was that angel today.

The sun had colored the clouds with red and gold when Alec found Libby sitting on a piece of driftwood. Her face was turned toward the sunset. Her arm was around Bree's dog. They'd been for a swim. He could see that her hair wasn't quite dry and neither was the dog. Alec paused to shake sand from his sandals, and Tom nearly bowled him over in his haste to get to Libby.

"Ready?" Tom whispered.

"I guess we have to be. Libby," Alec called. She turned her pensive face toward them. He knew when she saw Tom because her eyes widened and she inhaled. "Tom has some news," he said.

Her lips tightened and she got up. "You've found her body?" The dog pressed against her leg as though he sensed she needed comfort.

Alec paused to reflect on her answer. He knew Tom would assume she'd asked because she knew for a fact that Nicole was dead. He didn't believe that. "Not her body but some of her clothing. Bree and Samson found it."

"Where? Why didn't she come to tell me?" She'd thought Bree had acted a little strange. She'd been quiet before rushing the children in to get cleaned up, then off to dinner in town without Samson.

Tom grunted. "I ordered Bree to let us tell you." He put his hands on his hips. "What we found were her sandals and cover-up, Miss Holladay. They match the description you gave us."

"Oh no," Libby whispered.

"You were quick to ask if we'd found her body. I suspect it's because you dumped her body out there."

She went white and her fingers stilled in the dog's fur. "That's a terrible accusation. You were both so somber that I assumed the worst."

"Her shoes and cover-up indicate that she's no longer alive," Tom said, his voice harsh.

"I don't believe it." Libby's lips trembled. Her gaze sought Alec's.

Alec saw no guilt in her face. "Tom needs you to identify the belongings he found."

"Pink flip-flops and cover-up?" she asked.

He nodded. "Shoe size matches."

"Where did Bree and Samson find them?"

Tom shot a fierce glance at Alec that warned him to be quiet. "They found one shoe in some rocks and the other twisted with seaweed a few feet away. The cover-up was fifty yards down the beach."

"Maybe the things aren't Nicole's." Libby's voice rose. "Pink is a common color for beach items."

"I want you to take a look," Tom said, gesturing back at his truck in the driveway.

Libby nodded and they trekked back to Tom's SUV. He stuck his head through the open window and withdrew a plastic evidence bag. Without speaking, he handed it to Libby.

The bag crackled when her fingers tightened around it. She loosened the top and pulled out the clothing and flip-flops. "They look like hers. I bought her the cover-up for Easter." Her voice quavered. She turned the shoes over. "See this nick out of the bottom? Her mom's dog chewed them the weekend she got them."

Alec nodded. "Looks like teeth marks."

She closed the top and handed it back. "I think I can say without any doubt that these belong to Nicole."

Tom tossed the bag into the SUV. "I think we have to assume we're investigating a murder, Miss Holladay."

She visibly wilted. "I don't want to believe she's dead." She turned a beseeching glance toward Alec.

He didn't want to give her false hope. "You have to face facts, Libby," he said, gentling his voice.

"If she's dead, where is her body?" she asked. "Wouldn't her body have washed ashore too?"

Tom shrugged. "I know it's hard to hear, but it's rare to find a body. Fish take care of the remains."

Her eyes filled and she backed away. Alec glanced at his cousin and saw Tom narrow his eyes. Did he think her distress was put on?

"I'd like to ask you some questions, Miss Holladay," Tom said. "What happened to your mother?"

She reeled as though she'd been slapped. "What do you mean?"

"How did she die?"

Libby wetted her lips. "She fell down the basement steps."

"Isn't it true that the police suspected you pushed her?"

"I didn't!" Libby blinked rapidly. "She was drunk."

"You were held for questioning," Tom said.

"They let me go." Her eyes pleaded for them to believe her. "I had nothing to do with it."

"But you were home?"

She sighed and leaned against the SUV. "I was home," she agreed heavily. "But I was upstairs working on some paperwork."

"You lived at home?"

"Someone had to take care of her. If I wasn't there, she wouldn't have bothered with food." She tipped her chin up. "I took care of her. I cared for her for years."

Tom took a step closer to her. "What happened?"

"I heard a clatter. I jumped up and ran downstairs calling for her. When I found the basement door open in the kitchen, I rushed down the steps and found her lying at the bottom of the stairs. Sh-She was lying there with her eyes open. I tried to help her up, but I knew as soon as I touched her that she was gone."

"The policeman I spoke with seemed to think your story was fishy," Tom said. "Why was that?"

Alec could tell Tom already knew the answer but wanted to see if she would tell him the truth. He prayed for Libby to be honest and put to rest any doubts his cousin might have.

She looked at her hands. "We'd had an argument in town earlier that someone overheard."

"And you threatened to kill her."

"It wasn't like that!" She lifted her head and stared at Tom. "I said, 'I could just kill you when you act like that.' That wasn't a threat. It was just a figure of speech. A really awful figure of speech."

"What had she done?" Alec asked gently.

"She insulted the grocery store owner, then threw tomatoes at him. It was an ugly scene. I tried to stop her, but she was like that when she'd been drinking. There was nothing anyone could do. She was the sweetest person when she was sober."

Alec heard the ring of truth in her voice. She'd loved her mother. He glanced at Tom and saw compassion. Tom could tell truth when he heard it.

TWENTY-EIGHT

Libby felt like she'd been tossed around by a tidal wave. Could the sheriff actually suspect that she'd killed her own mother—and that she'd disposed of Nicole? Couldn't he see her heart? She'd started to tell Tom that someone had just tried to drown her, but then she saw the suspicion in the sheriff's eyes. He would think she was making it up to divert suspicion. What a mess.

It was none too soon for her when Sheriff Bourne's vehicle left the driveway and headed back to town. Alec stood at the bottom of the porch steps with his hands in the pockets of his khaki shorts. She'd been hoping to tell him about what she'd discovered from Pearl, but now she didn't have it in her.

Her eyes burned, and she rushed up the steps before she could disgrace herself by showing how much the sheriff's accusations had hurt her. Samson whined and trotted after her.

"Libby, wait! Tom is just doing his job."

"His *job* is to find out who took my friend, not to railroad an innocent person!"

He mounted the steps to the porch and stopped in front of her. "Look at it from his point of view. Can't you see why he would have some suspicions?"

She was in no mood for his placating tone. "While he wastes his time investigating me, the real criminals are walking free. Don't you worry that the men might take another girl? Someone *you* know and love?"

That stopped him. She could see him processing her question.

"You're saying you don't think it was personal? That Nicole just might have been in the wrong place at the wrong time?" he asked.

"I don't know what to think. You hear of human trafficking though. Who knows but that's what these men intended? How did they know she would be there at that time? Maybe they just came ashore and saw a lone girl and decided to grab her."

He stared at her. "You didn't try to rent a boat until nine."

"What?" She didn't understand the sudden change of subject.

"The night Nicole disappeared. That means you didn't leave Virginia Beach until a good two hours after you called 9-1-1. Why?"

"No. I threw some clothes in a suitcase and left right away. Then I got stuck in a traffic jam from a jack-knifed truck." Her ire rose. "Do you want to check with the state patrol? I came as quickly as I could."

There would be no end to the suspicion and accusation. She was going to have to do this on her own. The realization made her pulse jump. But it wouldn't be impossible. She had years of experience uncovering the history of houses, interviewing previous owners, delving into the secrets of dusty pages. While this would be a different investigation, she had determination and love on her side.

"I can see I'm on my own now." She turned to leave.

"You're thinking about doing this yourself? You'll just make Tom and the state detectives mad," Alec said.

"What other choice do I have? The story Earl wrote is going to hit the papers soon, and we both know it's going to be slanted toward my guilt. The state isn't going to look any harder than the

sheriff is. If I want to stay out of jail, I'm going to have to do this myself and find those men. And quickly. Before everyone in town is convinced I'm some kind of killer."

"Let's start with a sketch of what you remember."

"Are you going to help me or accuse me, Alec? I'm having trouble keeping it straight." If he doubted her, she didn't think she could stand it. His opinion mattered way too much.

"I told you I'd help. We've already started. I haven't changed my mind."

She searched his face. "For my father's sake?"

He nodded. "And for the sake of truth. Truth matters."

She relented. Should she tell him about today's attack? "It doesn't seem to matter to anyone but us," she said.

"What do you mean by that? Has something happened today?"

He had an uncanny perception. Where did it come from? She pointed to the rockers on the porch. "Let's sit down. This is going to take a few minutes." What would he think when she told him what their parents had done to her and Vanessa? Would he still idolize her father? And would he believe a diver had really tried to drown her?

A breeze lifted the strands of Libby's light-brown hair, and the porch light glimmered on her tresses. A few bugs buzzed the lamp. Alec stretched out his legs in the rocker and petted Samson, who rested his head on Alec's knee. The dog huffed with pleasure. If only people were so easily pleased. Libby had her legs tucked under her on the swing. He waited for her to explain what was going through that beautiful head of hers.

He noticed red marks on her ankle. "What happened there?" he asked, pointing.

Her gaze searched his face. She rubbed her ankle. "A diver tried to drown me a little while ago." She studied the marks. "I didn't realize he'd left marks."

He sat forward. "What? Someone tried to *kill* you?"

She nodded. "Samson and I went for a swim. A diver in a black wetsuit dragged me to the bottom and tried to hold me there. I managed to get away, and Samson helped until I got to shore."

He clenched his fists. "Why didn't you say anything to Tom?"

She shrugged. "He has his mind made up."

He pointed to her ankle. "You have proof."

"I didn't realize he'd left marks. And the sheriff would say I scraped it on something anyway."

Alec leaned forward and studied the marks on her skin. "Looks like fingers. We need to show Tom."

She rubbed her ankle, then shook her head. "He'd say I did it myself."

"No, he won't." He grabbed the portable phone on the swing and called his cousin. When he explained what happened, Tom told him to take pictures and bring her into the office tomorrow.

She was watching him talk with shadowed eyes. "What did he say?"

"He believed me. He wants pictures tomorrow and said to take some tonight too. He wants to get to the bottom of this, Libby."

She bit her lip and her head went down. Alec pulled out his phone and snapped several shots of her injury.

The screen banged open and Vanessa stomped out onto the porch. Her hands were curled into fists and her mouth was pinched.

She glared at Libby through narrowed eyes. "Don't think this changes anything! You'll never be part of this family."

"This isn't my fault, Vanessa. Mom and Dad did this, not me."

"Don't call him that! He was Daddy, always."

Alec found their conversation impossible to decipher. "What's going on?"

Libby sighed and leaned back. "It appears Vanessa and I are full sisters."

"You've got to be kidding." He eyed them both. There was a definite resemblance. They'd look alike whenever Vanessa lost the petulant expression she usually wore.

Libby tucked her hair behind her ears. "When our parents divorced, they each took a child. Our mother wanted nothing to do with our father and insisted this was the way it had to be."

"That's nuts," Alec said. This situation gave credence to her story of an atypical mother. "And neither of you knew?"

She shook her head, then glanced up at Vanessa. "Sit down, Vanessa. Standing over me like that isn't going to solve anything."

"Neither will talking." But Vanessa took a hesitant step forward.

Alec left the chair and moved to sit beside Libby on the swing. Vanessa shot him a grateful look. He liked being this close to Libby. The vanilla fragrance on her skin was enticing. "Did you remember another sister at all? Weren't you three when your parents split?"

Vanessa knotted her hands together. "I remember an imaginary friend. Her name was Bee."

"Bee. Lib-BEE," Alec said. "Maybe that was your nickname for her."

Vanessa frowned and shook her head. "I'm sure she was imaginary. She had a monkey named Fred."

"I had a monkey named Fred," Libby said in a low voice. "I still have him. He was a sock monkey."

Vanessa straightened. "He had an eye missing."

Libby nodded. "And his ear had been chewed by the cat."

"I remember that," Vanessa said in a stunned voice. "Do you remember me at all?"

Libby frowned. "I don't have very many memories from

childhood. Things were so rocky and constantly in flux. I have only snippets of things, and most of them aren't pleasant."

Vanessa's face clouded and she looked down at her hands. "You'd think you would remember a sister!"

Alec could feel Libby tense beside him. "Stress can damage memories, Vanessa," he said. "Doesn't mean she didn't love you."

"I don't care if she did or didn't," Vanessa snapped.

The screen door opened again and Pearl came out. Her feet were bare under her housedress. "I thought I heard voices out here." She chewed on her lip as she glanced at Vanessa. "Everyone doing okay?"

"Don't tiptoe around it, Aunt Pearl," Vanessa snapped. "How could you keep this from me?"

"If you would have opened your door, I would have talked to you about it."

Alec got up to offer his seat to Pearl, but she waved him off so he sat back down. She leaned her bulk against the porch post. "I'm not staying. This is something the girls have to work out on their own." Her gaze stayed on Vanessa. "I just wanted to assure Vanessa that this is true. I was there. I tried to talk them out of it, but your mother was adamant."

"My mother," Vanessa said, her voice stunned. "I just realized. Tina wasn't my mother!" Her voice broke, and her eyes filled with horror.

"She loved you as much as she loved Brent," Pearl said. "You know she did."

"I can't believe this," Vanessa said. She turned to stare at Libby. "Tell me about our mother. And what was her name? I don't even know her name!"

"Her name was Ursula." Libby held her gaze. "My childhood wasn't like yours, Vanessa. We moved around a lot. Mom was always looking for the rainbow over the next hill. She married again and divorced, then we had a revolving door with men coming and

going. She was never happy. She always wanted more and more but never got it. Possessions were important to her, maybe because of her childhood. Still, she loved me more than her things, more than her men. But maybe not more than her beer. In spite of that, my childhood wasn't bad. Just constantly disrupted."

Vanessa winced and turned her attention back to Pearl. "Why did Tina agree to the deception?"

Pearl patted her shoulder. "You started calling her Mama as soon as they were engaged. It just gradually happened. I think your father thought you'd be happier if you didn't remember another mother and sister."

Alec had idolized Ray Mitchell forever. To find he had such feet of clay was indescribably shocking. This kind of tangle was going to be hard to unravel. Alec doubted the women would ever manage to be close. It would take a miracle from God's hand.

Vanessa jumped to her feet and rushed back into the house. Pearl followed, calling Vanessa's name. The seaside cicadas filled the silence as Alec and Libby were left alone on the porch.

Alec stretched his arm across the back of the swing, not quite daring to embrace her, though the thought strangely crossed his mind. "How are you dealing with this?"

She leaned back and her hair brushed his arm. "I don't quite know what to think. It's hard to realize I have a family but that I'm about as welcome as a bedbug. But I don't care about any of this, really. I'm finding it hard to care about anything since Bree found Nicole's belongings. I don't want to believe she's dead."

He hugged her. "I'm sorry, Libby. I wish I could change things."

She swallowed hard and sighed. "Thanks for being here, Alec."

"Does Brent know yet? About you and Vanessa?"

She shook her head. "He's been gone all day. I suppose Vanessa could have called him, but if she did, I don't know about it."

Headlamps pierced the darkness. "I think that's him now."

TWENTY-NINE

Libby could almost imagine they were friends, maybe more than friends, as she sat near Alec with his arm on the back of the swing. Did he feel the connection she felt? He'd offered to help her, and he'd kissed her. With a man like him, that had to mean something.

Brent would be here any minute, but she'd rather sit in the silence than endure more confrontation. Her brother was about to find out he was more alone than he'd thought. Would this change his relationship with Vanessa?

Brent's shadow loomed in the glow from the lamps along the walk, then he walked up the steps to the porch. "You're sitting here in the dark?"

"We have the porch light," Alec said, pulling his arm down.

Libby felt cold without his warmth radiating to her back. Or maybe it was the way Brent's lips pressed together at the sight of her.

"Have a seat, Brent. You've been gone all day and a lot has happened," Alec said.

Brent still stood in the shadows. "I'll stand, thanks. What's up?"

"Libby and Vanessa are sisters," Alec said.

"Sisters? That's not news."

"*Full* sisters. Not half."

Libby listened to Alec explain what they'd discovered today. The deep tones of his voice soothed her. She was still jumping at every sound. Was her attacker out there even now, watching and waiting for the next time? And why had he targeted her? She eyed her half brother. Could Brent want her out of the way so he could inherit? She didn't have a will in place, so by law he and Vanessa would inherit as her closest relatives.

She hated to suspect her own brother, but someone in this town wanted her dead. That someone had already killed her friend, it seemed. Tears welled in her eyes at the likelihood that she would never see Nicole again. She became aware that Alec had asked her something. "I'm sorry?"

"I wondered if you had anything to add?"

She stared at Brent's expressionless face. Though they had only been around each other a few times, she got the impression that he took in everything behind those calculating eyes.

He shifted and she saw what dangled from his hand. Tanks and a regulator. She caught her breath. "Where have you been, Brent?" she asked, noting his broad shoulders. Could he have attacked her himself?

"What's that got to do with anything?" he demanded.

"I see you dive," she said, pointing to his dive equipment.

He glanced down at his equipment. "Yeah, so what? It's the Graveyard of the Atlantic out there, remember? Diving mecca."

"Where were you diving today?"

He gestured. "Out at a wreck offshore. What difference does it make?"

"A diver tried to drown me. Right offshore here. He wore a black wetsuit."

If the thought of her being drowned bothered him, he didn't show it. "Most wetsuits are black."

She stared at him. "Do you hate me, Brent?"

"I don't know you well enough to like or dislike you."

"Did you try to kill me?"

"No." His face was expressionless.

"Can I see your arms?"

He frowned, then shrugged and held both arms out where she could see them under the porch light. The skin was smooth and unmarked. "Samson bit my attacker."

"As you can see, I have not been bitten."

He could have hired someone, but she might as well let it go. Even if he was guilty, she'd never be able to tell.

Tires crunched up the drive. Samson stretched and yawned, then bounded down the steps to meet his owners. Libby followed.

Bree held out her arms. "I'm so sorry, Libby," she murmured. "I wanted to tell you myself, but the sheriff wouldn't let me."

"She can't be dead," Libby moaned, burying her face in her new friend's shoulder.

"Samson and I will do what we can," Bree promised. "We'll help you get to the bottom of this."

Libby lifted her head. "Someone tried to drown me tonight, Bree. A diver grabbed me and took me under. I'm frightened."

Bree went still. "But what could be the motive?"

Libby pulled away. "Money, property? I don't know."

"Don't go anywhere alone until we solve this mystery," Bree said. "I'm afraid for you."

Libby nodded and lifted Hunter from his car seat. "I'm going to stay close to Alec from here on out."

———

Libby sat on the porch by herself. It was well past midnight, but she couldn't sleep. She'd seen light coming from under Vanessa's door as well, so she knew her sister was likely just as

199

conflicted. Libby rolled the bead necklace in her fingers. *What would Jesus do?*

God had made it clear what she was supposed to do, but she didn't want to. This necklace meant the world to her. Vanessa only wanted it because she didn't have it. *Be generous with Vanessa and Brent.* Why did her father have to ask that of her? Why hadn't he asked that of them? They were the ones being hurtful. Why should it rest on her shoulders?

Alec's figure loomed in the doorway as he stepped to the porch. "Can't sleep?"

"No. Too much to process today."

He joined her and put his arm on the back of the swing behind her. "Anything I can help you with?"

"It's my dad!" she burst out. "Why did he ask so much of me and nothing of Brent and Vanessa? Why am I the one who is supposed to be generous? Why do I have to extend grace? I'm being pummeled with more than they are."

"I wonder if he knew that you're a Christian? I'm not so sure about Vanessa and Brent. Of course, it's impossible to judge another man's heart, but I've seen no evidence in their lives."

"To whom much is given, much is required." She paraphrased the verse from the book of Luke with a sigh. "Sometimes doing the right thing is so hard."

"What's the right thing you're reluctant to do?"

She pulled the necklace away from her neck and held it to the moonlight. "I have to give this to Vanessa."

"Ah." Alec's arm came down around her shoulders and he hugged her. "One thing I've discovered in my own walk with the Lord is this: when something is really hard but we do it anyway, the rewards are equally great. So if you just suck it up and do what you feel God is telling you to do, you're going to be really glad in the end."

She leaned up and kissed his cheek. He smelled good with some kind of spicy cologne. "Thanks. You're right. I have to do it."

His hand tightened around her shoulders, and before she could pull away, he brushed his lips across hers. The contact sent a warm rush through her. Surely he felt something for her. A man with his integrity didn't go around kissing women willy-nilly.

He pulled back and rested his head on the top of her shoulder. "I'll pray for you."

"That means more than you know." She kissed him again, relishing the stubble on his cheek. "I'm going to go do it now before I talk myself out of it."

"I'll wait here and pray. Come back down when you're done and let me know how it went."

"You're a great guy, Alec," she said, squeezing his hand. "I'll be back."

Before she could lose her nerve, she hurried inside and up the stairs to her sister's room. The light was still shining under the door. She knocked, hoping her sister wasn't asleep. That would get things off to a terrible start. "Vanessa? Are you still up?"

"I'm up." The door swung open to reveal Vanessa in a red nightgown.

"Can I come in for a minute?" Libby asked.

Her sister shrugged. "Suit yourself." She retreated to the bed, where she flopped on the edge and picked up a bottle of red nail polish.

The room smelled of nail polish too. Libby shut the door behind her. "You're up late."

"So are you. I imagine we're thinking about the same thing."

Was that a hint of warmth in Vanessa's voice? Libby decided to believe it was. "We're real sisters. I can hardly wrap my mind around it."

"Me neither. You might want to see that." Vanessa pointed to an old photo album. "Aunt Pearl gave it to me."

Libby picked it up and flipped to the first page. It showed a young woman smiling into the camera. She had a baby in her arms, and a little girl held on to her leg. "That's Mom. I'm the little girl. You're the baby?"

"I assumed so."

Why hadn't Pearl shown this to her? Libby tried to shove away her jealousy, but it crouched in her chest. She flipped the page to see several other photos. A baby in a crib with an older girl propping a bottle in her mouth, another with the toddler holding the baby on her lap on the floor, and one of a young man holding them both and smiling proudly. She recognized him as their father.

"They look so happy," she said.

"Aunt Pearl says the reality was far different." Vanessa looked up from painting her toes. "I don't remember her at all. Our mother, I mean. You'd think I'd remember my own mother! Do you have any pictures?"

For the first time, Libby looked at the situation from Vanessa's point of view. She'd been abandoned by her mother. She'd even been deceived about *who* her mother was. At least Libby had known the identity of both parents, even though her mother had lied about her father's death.

She nodded. "I have some back in Virginia Beach. I'll have some copies made for you."

Vanessa's expression hardened again. "I guess it doesn't matter. Tina was a real mother to me. She was wonderful. I still miss her."

"I've heard nothing but good things about Tina."

This wasn't going as planned. Vanessa seemed almost unapproachable. Libby inhaled and squared her shoulders. "I came here to give you this, Vanessa." She unfastened the necklace and held it out.

Vanessa's eyes widened and she held out her hand. Libby dropped it into her palm, and Vanessa's fingers closed around it. "But I thought you loved it."

"I have to admit I didn't want to give it to you, but God told me to." Her voice broke and she cleared her throat.

Vanessa frowned. "And you did it just because you thought you were supposed to?"

"I'm trying to obey what the letters mean. What would Jesus do? Jesus didn't care about possessions. The necklace is just a possession. So it's yours."

Vanessa held the hand with the necklace to her chest. "Thank you." Her gaze searched Libby's face. "Do you think we can have a real relationship?"

"I'd like that more than anything," Libby said. "I'm willing if you are."

"I'm willing." Vanessa fastened the necklace around her neck. "It's going to take time though. We have a lot of catching up to do."

"I have all the time in the world," Libby said.

She couldn't wait to tell Alec that he'd been right.

THIRTY

Alec gave the swing a push with his foot. Libby had been gone half an hour. He'd been praying that she would find favor with Vanessa, that a door to a good relationship might be opened between the two women. He had a sense that God was answering that prayer.

He heard a car and straightened. His stomach tightened when he recognized his truck, driven by his nephew. He rose to confront Zach for breaking curfew. This wasn't going to go well, but it had to be done. He waited under the security light.

The interior light came on when Zach got out of the truck. His whistle died on his lips when he realized Alec was standing on the walk. "Hey, Uncle Alec."

"It's nearly one," Alec said. "Your curfew is midnight."

"I'm seventeen years old. I don't need a curfew."

"Well, you have one anyway. Nothing good happens after midnight. Just things like this." He held out Zach's pocketknife. "I found this on one of the little islands. Along with beer bottles."

Zach snatched the knife from his hand. "I didn't do anything."

"You're saying you didn't have a little beer, have a little fun?"

"There's nothing wrong with that. You telling me you've never had a beer?"

"You're underage."

"And you never drank when you were my age? Come on, Uncle Alec. I've heard the stories about you. You were no saint."

"Which is why I'm trying to keep you from making my mistakes."

The security light illuminated Zach's angry face. He clenched his fists. "I don't have to listen to this."

Alec grabbed his arm as he started past. "You will listen. The next time you're not here at midnight, I'll come looking for you. I imagine it would be embarrassing to be hauled home in front of your friends."

"You wouldn't do that."

"I would and I will. This is a small island. I know every nook and cranny. You won't be able to hide from me."

Zach's eyes narrowed. "I'll run away."

"And you'll end up in a boys' home. Is that what you want? Look, Zach, I'm trying to help you. I know it hurts that your parents are gone. How do you think your dad feels when he looks down from heaven and sees how you're acting?"

Zach took a step back. "I'm trying to make sense of it, okay? I always wanted to be the kind of man my dad was. I idolized him. But what good did it do Dad to try to please God if he was just going to kill him?"

Alec tried to embrace the boy but Zach shook him off, so he dropped his arms back to his sides. "Integrity has rewards that are more valuable than how many days we spend on the earth."

The boy's face worked to restrain emotion. "If God cared, he wouldn't have taken both my parents. That's just plain cruel. Mom and Dad always told me that God loves me. I wish I could still believe it."

"I can see why you think he doesn't. Psalms says, 'Blessed in the eyes of the Lord is the death of his saints.' I know we miss

them, but now they are alive like never before. God doesn't view death in this life the same way we do." Alec thought he saw a sheen of tears in Zach's eyes.

"Is that supposed to make me feel better? It doesn't. I want my dad. I want to come home and hear Mom's voice. No one could make peanut-butter cookies like her. And she *cared*. So did Dad." Zach's shoulders slumped. "I don't have anyone anymore."

Alec put his hand on the boy's shoulder. "You have me. And your grandparents. Plenty of us love you, Zach. Don't shut us out. We're all in this together. We're all hurting."

He opened his arms, fully expecting Zach to turn away. Instead, the boy buried his face in Alec's chest.

"I miss them," Zach said.

Alec hugged him. He struggled to speak past the lump shutting off his throat. "I do too. But we're still family. We will get through this."

Zach pulled away, looking a little embarrassed by his outburst. "I'll try to be home on time tomorrow."

"I'll wait up." He wanted Zach to know the rules still stood. "Time for bed, bud. We have church in just a few hours."

Zach made a face but said nothing as they walked to the porch. When Zach went inside, Alec settled back on the swing to wait for Libby. The front door creaked, and she burst through the opening with a smile on her face. He rose as she rushed toward him. She launched herself at him, and he caught her and hugged her. The scent of her vanilla shampoo filled his head. "I guess it went well?" He had to grin at her exuberance.

Her arms went around his waist and she hugged him. "It went super, Alec. You were so right."

He didn't want to let her go, but when she pulled away, he released her and led her to the swing. "So tell me about it."

Her face beamed as she told him about the pictures and

Vanessa's reaction to the necklace. "It was hard. Really hard. But you were right—my sacrifice opened a door between us. We may never be as close as typical sisters, but we're on the right path. We have a lot to get caught up on. She's going to tell me about Dad, and I'm going to tell her about Mom."

Her voice was full of excitement, and he smiled. "God always comes through."

"I think I've learned more about God this week than I have my entire life," she said. "And it's all thanks to you."

He hugged her. It was a habit he could get used to. "I'm not the Holy Spirit. He was telling you the right thing to do, and you obeyed."

He'd never been able to talk to another woman about God so freely. That had to mean something.

———

People of every age and description crowded the pews at church. Fishermen, stay-at-home moms, and shop owners mingled as friends and neighbors. Libby squeezed past Alec to stand in the aisle and shake hands. People eyed her curiously but were a little more standoffish than the last time she'd been in town.

If she were alone for a few minutes, she would slip up to the front and sit in the first pew. Not that God would answer her question of *why*. Libby wasn't ready to accept that Nicole was dead. Not yet. She didn't feel any sense of closure.

Alec touched her shoulder, and she realized most of the people had cleared out. She smiled at him. "Sorry, I was woolgathering."

"You okay?"

She nodded, her throat too full to speak. "I love this church. It was built in about 1890?"

He nodded. "You're good."

"Comes with the job."

His eyes were grave. "I wanted to wait until church was over to tell you. The article in the paper came out today. It's on the front page."

She examined his expression. "It's bad?"

"Yeah." He took her elbow and guided her down the aisle to the front where they settled on the pew. He opened his Bible and pulled out a clipping. "He basically implies you're another Susan Smith."

The woman who drowned her children. Numb, she took the clipping and scanned it. "He talks about my mother's death too, even though I was never charged with that. He's painted me as some kind of monster."

She was stunned. This was even worse than she'd expected. Why would Earl do something so vicious? She'd liked him on the trip from Kitty Hawk. Was this his revenge for her not telling him about Nicole's disappearance sooner?

Alec's expression was pained. "I'm sorry, Libby. This is my fault. I thought he'd help us, not hurt us."

He'd said *us* as though they were one unit. The realization that he sided with her was a comfort she could cling to. "What can we do about this?"

"Not much. Suing him for libel would just draw more attention to it. All we can do is try to find out who grabbed Nicole. And make him look stupid."

"Why are you doing this?" she asked, searching his face for clues.

"Doing what?"

"Helping me. Standing by me. Your own cousin thinks I might be guilty."

He was silent a moment. "You're Ray's daughter. He would expect me to help you."

Not quite what she'd wanted to hear. She'd hoped he'd tell her he liked her. That he believed in her. "You've never said why you idolized my father so much."

He closed his Bible. "Ray was my father's best friend. He was like a second dad to me. More than that, like a real dad. My father was often busy with his fishing boats. Dawn to dusk, he was out hauling in seafood. Lobster, crab, fish. He never had time to pitch me a ball or take me to the mainland for a game."

"He was working, providing for his family."

He nodded. "Sure. But Ray made time. And when I got into trouble when I was in high school, he turned me around. Forced his way through my rebellion with love and strength. It's because of him that I'm a Christian today."

"Why would he do that? Care about a kid that wasn't his own?"

"I honestly think he was trying to be Jesus in the flesh to me. To do what he could to share his faith through his actions." His gaze searched hers. "And maybe he was trying to atone for what he did to you. I know that's what you're wondering. Why did he help me and not you? Trust me though, Libby. Your dad was a good man."

"So he was a model Christian." She'd been more of a lax one. When was the last time she helped someone out just to bring praise to Jesus? Never. She wanted to do better, though, to shine like Alec did. Her hand went to her neck, but it was bare. No WWJD necklace anymore. Its impact hadn't faded though. She prayed it never would.

His smile was gentle. "Ray was more than a model Christian. He was a conduit for God's love to most everyone he met. I often saw him take bags of food to widows and give money to those in need."

She remembered turning away that woman who was collecting money for the house-fire victims. "He had plenty to give."

"Not in the early days. He always said God would provide for his needs. He just had to be faithful." He smiled. "Tina used to get so aggravated when he'd raid her larder and leave them without food. They couldn't always afford to buy more, so he'd trudge off to the store to buy peanut butter and bread. They always made it though. He would tell her that you can't out-give God."

She couldn't imagine that kind of generosity. If only she'd had a chance to know him.

THIRTY-ONE

N o, no, not that!" Libby stopped the workers from hauling the walnut wainscoting out of the lifesaving station. "I can restore it. It's native walnut."

The man made a face. "Looks ruined to me."

"Trust me, I can fix it."

She directed him to lean it against the far wall, then glanced at her watch. Alec was going to take her and Bree out searching on the boat this afternoon, but she had to get this project started. Once the renovations were complete, she was going to donate it to the town. Just being back to work in some way lifted her spirits. She might not be able to find Nicole, but she could help the town.

Libby wandered through the station. It practically boasted of its previous life. The boats that had carried rescuers to the seas were propped against one wall. One had holes in it, but two were in good shape. The bunks that housed the men were rusty and falling apart, but she could see in her mind's eye an exhibit that would explain the courageous work done here through the decades. The building was good and solid. It deserved to be saved, and her work would bring in visitors.

She climbed the old circular stairs, the iron clanging under her feet, until she stood in the widow's watch and stared out to

COLLEEN COBLE

sea. The lookout's job would have been monotonous until that moment when a ship broke to pieces on the shoals.

So much history here.

"Libby, someone here to see you," one of the workers called.

She turned her gaze from the sea to the parking lot. The sheriff's SUV was parked by the door. She gulped. The state authorities were supposed to arrive today. Sheriff Bourne had probably escorted them himself so he could watch her squirm. She prayed for strength as she clanged down the steps and found three men in the main room watching the activity.

"You're putting this place on the national registry?" the sheriff asked.

"Yes. It shouldn't be hard. There's so much important history here." She held out her hand to the two agents. "Libby Holladay."

The first man was in his fifties, skinny and wiry with a thin mustache and pale blue eyes. "Detective Monroe," he said, shaking her hand.

The other one also took her hand. His brown eyes were cold and judgmental. He was in his thirties and had an eager-hunter look about him. "Detective Pagett," he said. "We're here to find out what happened to your business partner."

"I'll do whatever I can to help you find her."

"Would you like to step outside so we can discuss this in private?" Monroe asked, glancing at the workers who were watching them.

"Whatever you say." She would not show any fear.

"After you." Pagett held open the door for her.

The hot sunshine on her face gave her strength. She heard the church bells ring out the time, as if God was telling her to take courage. There was a bench outside by the walk, so she headed for it and settled on it. "I've been working all morning, so I hope you don't mind if I sit down."

212

"Not at all," Monroe said. "Now, about your partner. We particularly want to talk to you about the day she disappeared. Where were you?"

"I was documenting a house for the national historic registry." She told them where it was located. "The new owner wanted us to do the restoration."

"Did anyone see you there?" Pagett asked.

She started to shake her head, then stopped. "There was a lady in the neighborhood collecting money for a family who had suffered a house fire. I don't know her name, but if you talk to the people who had the fire, they will likely know. I think the woman will remember that I was there."

Pagett's mouth grew pinched. "We'd like your permission to examine your bank account."

"That's fine."

His brows rose at her quick agreement. "You haven't withdrawn a large amount of money?"

She laughed. "Do you have any idea what I make? There was never a large amount of money to spend. It's all I can do to pay my expenses."

Monroe took out a notebook. "Let's talk about the call from your partner."

"She called while I was at the old house. She told me I had a sister here, and that if I could log on to my computer, I could have the chance to see her."

"There was an open wireless at your site?" the sheriff asked.

She shook her head, trying not to show her impatience. "No, but I have a card to tether my computer to my cell phone."

"I thought you didn't make much money. That would be an expensive gadget," Pagett said.

"It's part of my work and not that expensive. I get leads on the road all the time and I need to be able to pull up the maps. They're

too small to see on my phone." She crossed her legs and clasped her hands over her knee. "Look, detectives, I can tell you think I did away with Nicole, but you couldn't be further from the truth. Find out who took her. It wasn't me. I saw two men."

The older agent had an expression in his eyes that made her hope he was listening, so she targeted her gaze at him. She described the kidnappers and everything she saw. As she talked, she remembered more about the boat and gave them details on color.

Monroe put his notebook away. "We'll get on it, Ms. Holladay. Thank you for your time."

"But don't make any plans to leave Hope Island," Pagett said.

"Trust me, I'm clinging to hope for dear life," she called after them.

⸺

With the sea spray in his face and the sun on his arms, Alec steered his boat toward a small cove down the shore from where Nicole's belongings had been discovered. He cut the engine. "I checked tide and current charts. I think there's a good chance the killers could have been out here when they threw her overboard. The currents would have carried anything placed in the water here to the shore where her shoes and cover-up were found."

Libby's face was pink with the sun, and she had her long hair back in a ponytail. The style made her look about eighteen. "She's not dead, Alec. I know it. We'll find her."

Alec smiled and said nothing. The day stretched out in front of them, and Alec found himself wanting to hang on to every minute. What did that mean? She was becoming way too important to him too quickly. He glanced at Bree and Samson in the front of the boat. The dog was enjoying the ocean breeze but didn't seem to have caught any kind of scent yet.

Libby lifted a pair of binoculars to her eyes and scanned the horizon. "There's nothing out here but ocean. I'm a little disoriented."

The disappointment in her voice struck a chord with him. He'd hoped for more too. He pointed. "The lighthouse ruins are there." He moved his finger to the north. "The lifesaving station where she was taken is there."

"So that's why we're here?"

"I suspect whoever took her brought her out here right away. I suspect they killed her almost as soon as they grabbed her. That's why Bree found her things where she did." When she stiffened, he touched her shoulder. "Whatever happened, her things went over-board out here. The shoes and clothing washed ashore too quickly for them to have let much time elapse."

Her expression grew somber as she stared out at the sea, and he wished he could carry some of her pain. Was she imagining Nicole's last moments here, struggling for survival? No, she was seeing a different scenario. One where Nicole was alive and awaiting rescue.

She let the binoculars hang down from her neck. "Now what?"

He pulled out a currents chart he'd brought. "The only other place where her body might have washed ashore is here." He stabbed a finger to the north of the lighthouse ruins.

"We were there the other day. We walked right past."

"It was flooded then, but the water has gone down now. I'm going to anchor offshore and see if we can find anything." He avoided saying the word *body*.

She swallowed hard. "Okay."

He squeezed her hand. "I won't leave you." He saw Bree turn her back as though to give them more privacy.

Libby stared at him. "Are you for real?"

"What do you mean?"

"I didn't think men like you existed. Strong, steady, spiritual. I think I must have dreamed you."

Her admiring amber eyes brought heat to his cheeks. "I'm just an ordinary guy."

"You're anything but," she said softly. She looked past him to the shore. "Do you think Brent is behind this, Alec?"

He'd hoped she wouldn't ask. Not until he poked around a little more. "It's possible," he admitted. "The money he was promised for the land could corrupt anyone."

"Ten million."

"How'd you know that?"

"Poe offered me the same thing after I arrived."

"What did you tell Poe?" He couldn't keep the dislike from his voice.

"You've met him?"

"Once."

"You don't like him."

He pressed his lips together. "He's out for his own interests."

She sighed. "Isn't everyone?"

"The Bible teaches God first, then others, then self."

"I don't think I've met anyone who followed that."

"Your dad did."

"We're not talking about my dad but about Poe."

He shrugged. "He makes money brokering deals for investors in New York. You could probably get more money if you asked for it."

"Would you sell it?" There was only curiosity in her voice.

"No way. Your dad was adamant about preserving Hope Beach. He owned enough property to keep out most investors. And his influence swayed those who might have sold out. He also snapped up houses for sale, then gave them to deserving families."

Her eyes widened. "You're kidding! He gave away *houses*?"

"Property is cheap here. He wanted to keep the town for the fishermen, the little guy. If he let a market boom start, the only

216

people who could afford to live here would be rich tourists who come for the summer."

She fell silent, her gaze still on the shore. "Poe said I didn't have long to decide. That if I waited too long, his investor would just move on to another property."

"There *is* no other property of its size with beachfront. The state owns much of the shoreline. They'll have your property, or the resort idea is toast."

"That does make it more valuable. How much more do you think I could get?"

She obviously hadn't listened to a thing he'd said. He wasn't sure he had the words or the inclination to dissuade her. If she couldn't see the ramifications of her actions, then she had more of a mercenary heart than he'd thought. "Another five million. Maybe ten."

"You're mad at me," she said. "I'm sorry, but I have to think of my future too. If I keep the inn, how will I even afford the upkeep? There's no money to do the repairs that it needs."

"Some of the men from town would help. I can swing a pretty good hammer." But when he remembered how much needed to be done, he knew his offer wouldn't make much difference.

He motored toward shore. Change was coming to his small island whether he liked it or not.

THIRTY-TWO

A crane swooped low over the water and caught up a wriggling fish. Gulls screeched overhead as Libby waded ashore. "I love this place," she said. "It's so peaceful here."

Bree and Samson had already disappeared from sight. There was no one around but Libby and Alec, and she found herself walking closer than necessary to Alec. If she had the courage, she'd hold his hand. Her gaze went to the lighthouse ruins. The maritime forest beckoned but not as much as the ruins did.

"You're a historian," Alec said, smiling. "If there's a ruin around, you're content."

"Exactly right." She stepped close to the lighthouse foundation. "What secrets are hidden here? Wouldn't you like to know? The men who manned this lighthouse saved lives, but I'm sure they had hidden heartaches too."

She would rather daydream about lives gone by than face why they were here. What if they found Nicole's body in this place? Glancing at Alec, she saw he understood. Words seemed unnecessary between them. She'd never been with anyone who was so in tune with her.

The wind ruffled his hair. "Can't you just imagine Blackbeard coming ashore where we did?"

"I'd like to live out here," she said. "Maybe I could have the inn moved to this spot."

"Way I hear it, this spot is right where Poe's New York investor wants to build his resort."

She frowned. "Here? I thought it was going to be where Tidewater Inn is standing."

"Who knows. Rumors are floating all around. Ask him." He nodded toward the water.

While they'd been talking, another boat had anchored and sent a dinghy ashore. Poe stepped out of the rubber raft. He shook sand from his shoes, then headed toward them with a set smile.

Libby suppressed a sigh. They didn't have time for this.

"I was told you might be out here," Poe said, stopping when he reached them.

His face was pink with sun, but it only enhanced his good looks. Libby was sure he knew it too. "You came all this way to find us?"

His smile never faltered. "It's a lovely day."

"I haven't had a chance to think about your offer," she said. "I do have some questions though. Where exactly will the resort be built?"

"He has plans for this entire stretch of coastline."

"Even here? This is almost sacred ground," she said.

"Oh yes, most certainly here. With all the legends about Blackbeard, he'll want to capitalize on that. Maybe a wedding chapel." He dismissed the topic with a shrug. "That's not our concern though. We simply need to come to an agreement. I realize you're still looking for your friend, but my client is growing quite insistent. I suspect he'll move on to another idea if you don't make up your mind."

"Nicole is dead," Alec said.

Libby opened her mouth, then closed it again. Protesting wasn't going to change anyone's mind.

He blinked. "Y-You're sure? I haven't heard anything about that. Where was her body found?" Tugging at his tie, he shifted his feet in the sand.

Why would he be so agitated? Was his client that eager to get her land?

"Her belongings were found," Alec put in.

The tenseness seemed to go out of Poe in a rush. "I'm so sorry."

The words seemed sincere, so she decided to accept them at face value. "You understand that selling this property has been the last thing on my mind."

"Of course. But as I said, my client is growing impatient."

"There is no other land for him to buy here, so quit harassing the lady," Alec said. "You and I both know this is his only shot."

Poe's lips flattened and his nostrils flared. "Her father was the one opposed to selling. I'm sure others in town would be willing to let their property go for the right price. Her brother was quick to agree."

"This is the only stretch of beach that can be purchased. The rest is state land."

Poe shrugged. "My client has connections. If he wants state land, I suspect he could get it." He turned to Libby. "I'm prepared to make an offer of twelve million. But we must sign the deal this week."

"What's the rush?" she asked. "I told you I need to think about it."

"These things take time, and my client wants to start construction this fall."

"I'm sorry, I'm just not prepared to make a decision." If only he would just leave. They had an unpleasant search to make and he was in their way.

"Very well. I'll check back with you in a few days."

She watched him walk stiffly away, then clamber back into the rubber raft. She turned to study the peaceful setting. "So this place will be gone. That makes me sad."

"You have the power to stop it," he said.

"Not really. That's a lot of money to walk away from. I don't think I can do it. I see it upsets you, but I suspect you've never been poor. I think of all the good I could do with that money. And the pantry will always be full."

"My family wasn't wealthy, Libby," he said. "But I don't believe money solves everything. If you don't have money problems, you have health issues or personal problems. God uses whatever means at his disposal to mold and shape us." He took her arm and turned her back toward the ruins.

She'd never thought of it that way before. But she still couldn't see letting go of such an unbelievable sum of money.

They poked through the ruins for an hour without seeing anything of import. On their way back to the boat, she heard a shout. Bree was jumping up and down and waving. Libby broke into a jog.

"Look at this," Bree said, pointing to the ground. "Have you been down there?"

"What is it?" Libby asked, stooping to lift away some bricks. "It looks like a door to the cellar."

"This area used to have a lot of brick heaped up. The storm surge must have moved enough of the debris to reveal the trapdoor," Alec said.

"You didn't know it was here?" Libby asked. She shoved several bricks out of the way. "We might see things that haven't seen the light of day in decades. Can we take a look?"

He began to help her and Bree move bricks. "Probably nothing important, but if you want to explore, we can."

———

The flashlight in Bree's hand pushed back the shadows and showed water in the bottom of the hole. A rickety ladder descended into the darkness. "Musty," Libby said, wrinkling her nose.

"You can hold the light," Bree said, handing it to her.

Libby peered past her. "Wonder what's down there? When do you suppose the last people were in here?"

Alec flipped on his flashlight. "Late eighteen hundreds maybe. That's when the whole place came down."

Her pulse sped up. No telling what she might find down there.

"There might be rats or spiders," he warned.

She stopped. "I'm not afraid." But her quivering voice told a different story, so she cleared her throat and forced strength into her tone. "They'll run from us."

He gave her a skeptical glance, then shrugged. "I'll go first and make sure it's safe."

He put the handle of the flashlight in his teeth and began to climb down the ladder. Libby heard the ladder groan several times and held her breath, but the rungs held. His feet splashed into the water, and she trained her light on him to see how deep it was. The water came to his calves.

"It's not too bad," he called up. "I'll hold the ladder if you're sure you want to come down."

"I'm sure," she said. She tucked her flashlight into the waistband of her shorts and began to step down.

Even the ladder felt damp. The musty odor filled her head. She climbed down until she was standing in knee-high water that made her shiver. It was colder than she expected. She plucked her flashlight out and flipped it on. With a little more light, she felt more confident.

"Stay," Bree told Samson. She joined them in the cellar.

Alec swept his light around the room. "Looks like it was a root cellar. There are old jars of canned food down here." He moved to a shelf that held Ball jars. "Looks like pickles."

Libby followed him and peered at the contents. "I think they're still good."

"I wouldn't eat them," he said, his voice laced with disgust.

"Me neither." She followed him, sloshing through the water to explore the rest of the cellar. Bree was examining the walls.

Old barrels, tools, and items from yesteryear floated in the water or hung on the walls from rusty hooks. She didn't recognize some of the tools and glanced at Alec.

"One of the keepers was a doctor," he said.

Whale-oil casks bobbed in the water. She paused at an over-turned case of shelves. There was less water here. Her foot struck something and she looked down to see what it was. Horror froze her in place when she realized a human skeleton lay partially submerged at her feet. Uttering mewling noises, she grabbed Alec's arm. Her muscles finally obeyed her, and she turned and ran for the ladder. She thought Alec called her name, but she didn't stop until she was crouching in the sand and heaving. Samson whined by her ear as if to commiserate with her distress.

A few moments later Alec's hand was on her shoulder. "It's okay," he said, his voice soothing in her ear.

She shuddered. "That was a person." Details she hadn't noticed at the time came back to her. "A woman. I saw a blue sundress." She sat back and swallowed hard, then allowed Alec to help her to her feet.

"I think I know who it is," he said, his voice grim.

Bree clambered up the ladder and stood beside her. "Are you okay?"

"Did you see the skeleton?"

Bree nodded. "It's not Nicole."

"No, no, of course not." She stared into Alec's face, noting his pallor. This hadn't been easy for him either. "Who was she?"

"I think she was Ray's wife, Tina," Alec said.

Libby stared back at the opening. "Tina? I don't understand. She was murdered? I just heard she died."

Alec turned to look at the cellar hole too. "She went out on a boat ride and never came back. Her skiff was found broken up and half submerged, but her body was never found. So it was assumed she hit a rock and drowned."

"What does this mean?" she asked, trying to take it all in. "How do you know it's Tina?"

"She always wore a dress. And there was a picture of this dress all over town."

She looked at the yawning hole in the ground and shuddered. "D-Do you think someone killed her and threw her down there?"

"That was my first thought. I suppose it's possible she went exploring and got trapped."

"But the boat . . ."

He nodded. "Exactly. Someone would have had to deliberately scuttle the boat."

She hugged herself. "I don't like this."

"Neither do I."

She looked away from the dank hole. "When did she die?"

"Three years ago. The news caused Ray's first stroke, a small one. He loved her very much."

Pity stirred for her father. "I'm glad he's not alive to see this. If she was murdered . . ."

"The press is going to have a heyday with this." He took her arm and turned her toward the boat. "One good thing is that it might deflect attention from your friend's death for a while."

She stopped and clutched his arm. "I want attention to stay on her. That's the only chance we have of finding out who killed her."

"You don't suppose there could be any connection between Tina's death and Nicole's, do you?" Bree asked.

He frowned. "I don't see how."

"Nicole came out here," Bree said. "What if she saw something? Something that put her in danger?"

"Maybe. But she didn't get into the cellar. It was covered over until the storm surge." He stared back at the cellar. "I need to let Tom know about this. I saw a passageway when we were down there. It looked like it went toward those rocks." He pointed to a rocky point of land jutting into the sea. "I've seen a cave there, but I always thought it was shallow and not very big."

He took Libby's arm and led them all to the cave. They waded into the water and out to the rocks, where he pointed out a small opening.

Stooping, she peered into it. "It's bigger than it looks."

Bree glanced into the cave, then glanced at Libby. "Any chance Nicole would have gone exploring?"

Libby nodded. "Oh yes. She explores caves every chance she gets. Last summer she went on a spelunking vacation with some friends. She mentioned finding one here on the island."

Alec's lips tightened. "We might have a connection, then."

THIRTY-THREE

The palm tree provided a little shade. Nicole had been out since morning watching for a boat, any boat, but the sea remained empty. Her stomach growled, and she worked on ignoring it as best she could. The bread was soggy, and the thought of plain peanut butter wasn't appealing. Besides, she had no idea if the boy would even come back. Her eyes grew heavy, so she propped up her head with her arms and closed her eyes for a few minutes.

A gull cawed and she sat back up, rubbing her eyes. When she stared back out to sea, she saw the reason for the gull's displeasure. A boat skimmed the tops of the waves as it headed for her tiny beach.

Scrambling to her feet, she dusted the sand from her legs and hands and went down to meet the boy. He was wary as he dropped anchor and splashed ashore. It was going to take all her persuasion to convince him she wasn't crazy.

"Got your supplies," he said, dropping a sack onto the sand. "See ya."

"Wait!" She ran to catch him.

When he held out his hands to shove her back, she stopped. "I won't touch you. Just talk to me for a minute, okay? It's lonely out here by myself." Tears sprang to her eyes and she sniffled.

Concern replaced the wariness on his face. "Hey, don't cry. I can stay a minute. Just don't try anything, okay?"

She nodded. "Okay. I'm sorry about before. I was just scared." She searched his gaze. "Is anyone back on Hope Island looking for me?"

"Why would anyone there be looking for you? You're from Raleigh."

She shook her head and decided to go ahead with her plan. The truth. "I live in Virginia Beach. My partner and I have a restoration business. We were hired to restore some buildings in the downtown. My partner's name is Libby Holladay. I'm Nicole Ingram."

He gasped and took a step back. "How'd you hear about that? Did you talk to the Ingram girl sometime?"

"I *am* the Ingram girl. My birthday is July 4. I'm twenty-five. Libby is Ray Mitchell's daughter, but no one on Hope Island knew about her."

His eyes narrowed. "You're lying."

"I'm not." She reached out toward him, but he flinched and stepped back. "Please, check it out. Ask to see a picture of me. You'll see I'm telling the truth. I don't know what all those men told you, but it wasn't true. I was at the boardwalk by Tidewater Inn, and two men kidnapped me. Is Libby in town?"

She was sure of the answer to that. Libby would leave no stone unturned until she stood on this beach and rescued her.

"You don't know anything," he said. "Nicole Ingram is dead. They found her belongings on the beach."

The revelation made her take a step back and gasp. "I fought them. My pink cover-up came off in the struggle. One of them tossed it. And I lost my flip-flops when I jumped overboard. That's all they found, right?"

"I don't know what they found. Just that Nicole's clothes were on the beach."

"Libby didn't believe it, did she? She's still on the island?"

"She's still there. Poking around to try to find out who kidnapped her partner. But I'm not convinced you're the one she's looking for. Your brother told me you were wily and not to believe any story you concocted."

She managed a smile. Even if she didn't get off the island today, he would go back and investigate. He'd find out she was telling the truth. "So don't believe it. Check it out for yourself. Then tell Libby where I am. I'll make sure the police know you were duped, that you weren't an accomplice."

As soon as she said the word *duped,* she knew she'd made a mistake. No guy liked to look foolish.

"I'm not stupid," he said. "You're the stupid one. Trying to snow me with a crazy story like this."

"Look, I know it sounds crazy. But it's even crazier that someone would kidnap me and stick me here in this place. Think! What would be the motive? Locking up a crazy sister? There are places for that. His story makes no sense, and you'd know it if you had any brains at all!" She was past caring if he was mad. Past worrying about hurting his feelings. "You've got to see the truth."

"I'm out of here," he said, turning on his heel. He stomped off toward the boat.

Nicole ran after him and grabbed his arm. "Check it out," she said desperately. "That's all I ask. My picture has to be in the paper. Or online. You'll see I'm telling the truth."

He brushed her hand off. "I'll check it out, and then I'll let you know how crazy you are."

She tried on a winning smile. "What's your name?"

"Zach," he said.

"You have a nice boat."

"Yeah. My uncle likes to fish."

"He's a commercial fisherman?"

He shook his head. "Works for the Coast Guard mostly. Fishes in his spare time."

"And your parents?"

"Dead."

A common bond. "I'm sorry. My dad has cancer, and I'm afraid he won't make it. It's hard."

"What about your brothers?"

She saw where he was going with that. "No brothers. Only two sisters, and they both live in California."

He stepped into the waves. "I gotta go. I'm going to be late."

She wanted to scream and beg him to take her with him, but she forced herself to smile and wave. "Thanks for the supplies, Zach. Don't forget to look up my picture."

———

Alec held the door to the sheriff's office open for Libby. He knew by her expression that she dreaded being interrogated by his cousin. "I'll do the talking," he whispered, guiding her toward Tom's office with his hand at the small of her back.

She held her head high as several workers glanced at her curiously. Her courage impressed him. Not many women would have gone into that cellar hole with him. Not many women would hold up under the suspicion she'd been under.

They found Tom at his desk scowling at the computer. He straightened when he saw them. "Hey, what's up?"

"We found something out at the old lighthouse ruins." He pointed to the first chair. "Have a seat, honey." He nearly bit his tongue off when he realized he'd called Libby *honey*. She smiled and didn't seem to take offense, though, so that was good. He sank into the chair beside her. "We could both use something to drink. Got any bottled water?"

"Yep." Tom reached into a small refrigerator behind his desk and extracted two bottles. "You both look pretty puny. I don't think I've ever seen you so white."

"Thanks." Alec uncapped his bottle and took a swig of water. "It was a rough day. The storm surge uncovered a cellar out at the ruins."

"A cellar?" Tom frowned. "I didn't know about a cellar."

"It's been there all along. Remember that pile of bricks toward the back? It was under there. The force of the water moved the bricks and uncovered the trapdoor. Libby, Bree, and I went down to explore."

"And?"

In answer, Alec pulled out his smartphone and pulled up the picture he'd taken. "We found this." He handed the phone to his cousin.

Tom studied it in silence. "No telling how long that's been down there."

"I'd say about three years."

Tom looked up sharply. "Three years? Why would you say that?"

"Take another look. Recognize anything?" When Tom's face stayed blank, Alec leaned forward and poked his finger on the blue dress. "That's Tina's dress."

Realization dawned on Tom's face. "Tina Mitchell?"

"Yeah. A picture of her in that dress was plastered all over the state for a month."

"You're right. Holy cow." Tom sat back in his chair. "How did she get there?"

"We've been wondering the same thing." Alec told him about going back into the cellar and finding the other entrance.

"So anyone who knew about that could have gone in there. How did Tina know? And did she get trapped in there by the tide

or something?" His face changed. "No, that's impossible. Her boat was clear down the coast. It had to have been deliberate."

"That's what I thought too. Someone put her body there, probably after they killed her, then scuttled her boat to make it look like an accident. Forensics can maybe tell what happened."

"Or maybe not," Tom said. "Doesn't look like there's much left."

"Nicole was an avid cave explorer," Libby put in. "What if she found the cave leading to the cellar? What if she found the body and the murderer saw her?"

Tom stroked his chin. "Maybe." But he glanced at her with a hard expression.

"It makes sense," Alec said. "Whoever took Nicole didn't keep her long. It was like they grabbed her and disposed of her right away. I'm guessing they didn't want her to tell anyone about the cellar and what it contained."

"Seems a little far-fetched to me," Tom said. "She wouldn't know who anyone was, killer or victim."

"But the minute she reported it, you would have known as soon as you saw Tina. I think there's evidence in that cellar that will lead us to the killers."

"I'll call the state detectives. They have more resources than we do. I don't want to muck up this investigation. Holy cow," Tom said again. "Tina Mitchell was murdered. But why?"

"When we know that, we might know who."

"Ray maybe? No relationship is perfect."

Alec bristled. "Don't even go there. Ray was a good man. The best."

"Even good men snap," Tom said. "You know it's usually the person closest to the victim." His gaze slid again to Libby.

"Not this time," Alec said.

"One of the kids?" Tom suggested. "I remember hearing they were having some battles about Brent's lack of a job. He

expected his parents to hand out money, and they wanted him to work."

Alec glanced at Libby. She should tell Tom about the attack and how Brent had a wetsuit, but he knew she wouldn't want to get her brother in trouble.

Libby leaned forward with her hands clasped. "Please, Sheriff Bourne, I didn't kill Nicole. Or my mother. I'm not some kind of monster."

Tom tapped his fingers on the desk. "Can we place Nicole at the cellar?"

"I know she'd been out to a nearby cave. She told me in the call."

But then Tom's face hardened and he stood. "Good work, Alec. Staying close to her has paid off, hasn't it?"

Alec went hot, then cold. He leaped to his feet with his fists clenched. "Let's go, Libby." He held out his hand.

She took it, glancing from him to his cousin and back again. "What do you mean 'staying close to her'?"

Tom was white. "You didn't think he was hanging around because he liked you, did you? I asked him to keep an eye on you."

Alec stared at Tom. Why was he doing this? Libby stared at him with eyes filled with pain. "Libby," he began.

Without a word she turned and rushed for the door. He started to go after her, then turned back to Tom. "Why did you do that?"

"I thought if she was shook up, she might reveal something."

"She's a good woman, Tom," Alec said. "I'd better leave before I bust your face in and you have to throw me in jail for attacking an officer."

He stormed from the office. Libby was nowhere in sight.

THIRTY-FOUR

It was a long hike back to Tidewater Inn, but Libby needed the time to compose herself. She vacillated between anger and hurt. So Alec's support had all been a ploy. She should have known he couldn't be the superstar he seemed. She paused to sniffle and wipe her eyes.

An old Buick slowed and she saw Pearl behind the wheel. The window came down, and her aunt beckoned her to get in the car. Libby went around to the passenger seat.

"What are you doing walking alone?" her aunt scolded. "Especially after what happened to your friend?" She studied Libby's face. "You've been crying. Have a spat with Alec?"

"He tricked me," Libby burst out. "He was just pretending to help me. All the time he was trying to see if I killed Nicole."

"And who told you this?"

"The sheriff." Libby glanced around the car. "You've got a block on the pedals."

"So I can reach them." Her aunt pressed her shoe against the block on the accelerator and the car jerked into motion. "Let me tell you something about our sheriff. Tom idolizes his cousin. But he's also jealous of Alec. Tom knows he'll never be the man Alec is. So he tries to bring Alec down to his own level every chance he gets. I've seen it over and over again."

"But he didn't deny Tom had asked him to find out what he could."

"I'm sure Tom *did* ask him. He likely saw the way Alec looks at you. Tom wouldn't have liked it."

Libby's cheeks heated. "Alec looks at me? What do you mean?"

Pearl laughed. "Oh, honey, a blind woman could see that besotted expression. The guy fell hard right from the start."

"I don't think so." But Libby's heart sped up at the possibility. Could it be true?

"He took vacation to help you. He's been underfoot every moment since you arrived. The man is smitten." Pearl's sideways glance was sly. "I believe he feels as strongly about you as you do about him."

"He's just a friend." Fresh tears blurred her vision. "At least I thought he was a friend."

"Uh-huh. A friend. You can talk to your old aunt. You feel way more for him than friendship."

"We haven't known each other all that long."

"Long enough to recognize the attraction."

"Well, yes. He's unlike anyone I've ever known. I *thought* he was, anyway. Now I don't know."

"You know." Her aunt turned the old car into the drive. "Huh. Looks like we have company."

Libby stared through the windshield. "It's Horace."

The attorney was getting out of his big Cadillac with a folder in his hand. He mopped his brow as he waited for Libby to step from the car.

"Horace. I wasn't expecting you," Libby said, shutting the car door behind her. She smiled at the older man. "I could use some sweet tea. How about you?"

"Sounds mighty fine, Miss Libby, mighty fine." He held up his

folder. "I took the liberty of coming out to bring you the first draft of your will."

"I'd forgotten about it." It was the last thing she wanted to worry about right now, but the man had gone out of his way, so she smiled to hide her disinterest.

"A good attorney never forgets a client's needs," Horace said.

They went up the steps to the porch. "If you want to have a seat on the swing, I'll bring out the tea," Pearl said. "That way you can talk in private. We have a lot of visitors at the moment."

Horace settled on the chair with the cushions. Libby took the swing and tucked her feet under her. They ached from walking. Would Alec come after her? Maybe she should have waited around to talk to him. She was still hurt, but maybe Pearl was right, and Tom was trying to wreck their relationship before it had a chance to start.

"Miss Libby?"

With a start, she realized Horace was speaking to her. "Sorry, what was that?"

He tapped the paper he'd slid toward her on the table. "You want to read over this will?"

She took the paper and began to skim it, though the chore was the last thing she wanted to do. When she got to the part about her beneficiaries, she stopped. "I want to leave half the money to Vanessa."

"And the historic preservation foundation?"

"The other half." She glanced at him. "What happens if I die before this is executed?"

"The laws of the state will prevail. In this case, your next of kin would inherit. That would be Brent and Vanessa."

So Brent would have had motive for drowning her the other night. But was it motive enough to believe that he would hurt her? She hated to think her own brother could be so cold and calculating.

She slid the will back to Horace. "How long before this is ready?"

He pursed his lips. "Just a few days. My secretary is on

235

vacation, and I'm quite hopeless with a computer. As soon as she gets back, I'll have her amend this and draw up the final papers. Is there anything else you'd like to add?"

She toyed with the idea of leaving Alec something. After her near drowning the other day, she'd been thinking about death. No one knew when their time would come. But it was too soon to think that something permanent might develop between her and Alec.

She shook her head. "I think that's it. Thanks for getting to this so quickly. I'd like to wrap it up as soon as possible."

"We'll do that, Miss Libby."

Her aunt bustled through the door with a tray. "Here we go, Horace. I took the liberty of bringing you some cookies as well."

Libby saw Alec's truck kicking up dust behind it on the road. Her pulse jumped, and she rose to excuse herself from Horace.

———

Alec waved to Horace as he drove off. Libby vanished inside the house as he started up the porch steps. Clenching his jaw, he followed.

Pearl saw him and pointed. "She went into the greenhouse."

He thanked her and went down the hall to the back of the house. Ray had built the greenhouse for Tina twenty years ago. When she was alive, she grew orchids. They still bloomed in the large, sunny space, though Delilah didn't have the green thumb that Tina had possessed.

"Hey, Libby," he began.

She was standing in front of a particularly beautiful white orchid. She didn't turn when he spoke.

"Look, don't freeze me out, okay? Turn around and talk to me."

"There's nothing much to say," she said, still bending over the flower.

"Tom was out of line."

"Was he? It seems he asked you to keep an eye on me. Or is that not true?" She finally turned and stared at him, her hands behind her back. "Did you suspect that I killed Nicole?"

He didn't want to answer that, but with her somber gaze on him, he couldn't lie. "I had to consider the possibility."

"Is that the real reason you asked Earl to do an article? So he'd dig and find out what you couldn't ask?"

"I wanted to find Nicole. At the time that's all I was thinking about."

"So you agreed to stay close to me and see if I was a murderer?"

"Yes. But I quickly realized you would never hurt anyone."

"I thought we were friends," she said, her voice soft. "I thought you were my only true ally here in town. Now I find out that you were just helping out your cousin. And that hurts."

"We *are* friends." It was much too soon to tell her that he was developing feelings for her that were stronger than friendship. "Please don't let what Tom said derail our friendship."

The hurt in her eyes didn't lessen, but she nodded. "I'll try. I'd like to talk about Tina. Do you have any idea what might have happened to her? Did she have any enemies?"

He'd been trying not to think about her. "It's a puzzle. She was as well liked as your father. He was devastated when she died. Walked the beach for weeks hoping to find her."

"If we figure out who killed her, it may lead us to who kidnapped Nicole. I think it's very possible she found Tina's remains."

"I agree. The first thing we might do is talk to Pearl. She knows more about the town than anyone. And she knew Tina better than anyone else except Brent and Vanessa. I suppose we'd better tell them too."

"It's going to be a hard day for Vanessa. First she finds out how our father lied to her, then she discovers the woman she thought was her mother was murdered."

"You sound sympathetic."

"Of course I am. She's my sister. I'm going to work hard to build a relationship with her."

Pearl stood in the doorway with a tray in her hands. "Anyone want coffee and cookies?"

Her eyes were bright and curious. She was probably dying to know what was going on. "I'll take some," Alec said. "We need to talk to you anyway."

Pearl set the tray on the table. "Libby, I hope you accepted his apology."

"I did," Libby said.

He should have known that Pearl would sniff out any news. "Did Libby tell you we found Tina's remains?"

Pearl's smile vanished. "Tina Mitchell?"

Alec nodded. "There's a cellar at the lighthouse ruins. The storm surge revealed it. She was there." He explained how they'd found the cellar and the other entrance.

Pearl was pale. "So you're thinking Nicole was killed because she found Tina?"

Libby nodded. "Alec says you knew her better than anyone, except maybe the kids. Did she have any enemies? Did she seem worried in the weeks before she died?"

The chair groaned when Pearl settled into it. She frowned as she took a sip of her beverage, which was more cream than coffee. "I told Tom that something was wrong back when she came up missing. He dismissed me. So I was right."

Alec frowned. "What do you mean? What did you see?"

"She was withdrawn, sad. I thought maybe she was suffering from depression and spoke to Ray about it."

"Had he noticed?" Alec asked.

Pearl shook her head. "He'd been gone on a trip. I called him while he was in California. He said she'd been quiet on the phone,

but he assumed it was because she was tired from taking care of things while he was gone. He promised to talk to her about it when he got home. He arrived on an afternoon. She went missing that evening."

"So he didn't talk to her about it?"

"I didn't want to bring it up. I was afraid she . . ."

"Drowned herself?" Libby asked. She clasped her arms around herself as if she were cold.

Pearl shivered. "Exactly. I didn't want Ray to blame himself if that's what happened."

Alec tried to remember that time when they were all searching for Tina. "Did you see her with anyone during that time?"

Pearl looked away. "Some rich investor from New York named Lawrence Rooney. He'd come to see Ray but spoke to Tina. He hung around a few days." Her tone was careful.

"What did he want?" Libby asked.

Pearl pressed her lips together. "Tina never said."

"And that upset you because she usually told you everything?" Libby guessed.

"I didn't want to think she would be interested in another man." Her chin jutted. "I still don't think Tina was interested in him."

"Maybe I'll see what I can find out about the guy. There might be a link." This long after Tina disappeared, he feared there would be little evidence left. "Maybe."

Pearl rose. "You realize we need to tell Brent and Vanessa?"

"I know," Libby said.

Pearl sighed. "What a terrible day. I'll send them down to speak with you." She hurried away as if she couldn't wait to leave them behind.

Alec's gut tightened. From Libby's tight expression, he knew she was dreading it too.

THIRTY-FIVE

Vanessa's eyes were red as though she'd been crying. "What's going on?" she asked when she came into the greenhouse, glancing at Alec, then over to Libby.

Vanessa was wearing her father's necklace. Libby hoped it would help her sister through this. "Have a seat."

Brent slouched in with his hands in his pockets. He sank into a white wicker chair by a large geranium. "More drama?" he asked in a bored tone.

Libby pressed her lips together. "There's something you need to know, and we didn't want you to hear this from anyone else. And your perspectives may help Tom's investigation as well."

Vanessa straightened where she sat on the wicker sofa. "What's wrong? You're all so serious."

"There's news about Tina, Vanessa," Libby said.

Vanessa frowned and glanced at her brother. "I don't understand. She's been gone for three years. Why are we talking about her now?"

Libby wished she didn't have to tell them. "Yes, yes, I know. But her remains were found today."

Vanessa's eyes grew wide. Brent inhaled sharply. Libby tried to put herself in her siblings' shoes. No matter how much they distrusted her, they were bound by blood. She needed to help them through this if she could. They were all grieving something.

"Where was she found?" Brent asked.

Libby reached toward him, then dropped her hand. "Out at the lighthouse ruins. In the cellar."

Brent frowned. "There's no cellar."

"It's been hidden all this time. The storm surge knocked debris out of the way. But there's another way in." Libby glanced at Alec. "Would you explain, Alec?"

Vanessa and Brent listened in silence. Their expressions changed to incredulity, then to shock as they realized their mother had been murdered.

"But maybe she just found that cave," Brent said.

Vanessa shook her head. "The boat, Brent. The boat had to have been deliberately scuttled. Otherwise, it would have been found nearby on the shore. Even if she pulled it ashore and then found the cave and the tide dragged it back to sea, it would have been found closer to the ruins. Not where it was."

Tears slid down her cheeks, and she kept her head down. Libby wished she knew the best way to comfort her.

"Exactly," Alec said. "We also have to wonder about Nicole now."

If only Libby had had more time to talk to Nicole that day. So many regrets. "Nicole loved caves. The last time I talked to her, she said she'd found a new cave with something exciting in it. Before she could tell me what that was, the men appeared."

"Did you happen to hear Mr. Rooney talking to your mother?" Alec asked.

"Mr. Rooney? You mean that investor guy?" Vanessa asked. "He took us to dinner in Duck one night. You should have seen his yacht!"

"He was trying to impress Mom," Brent said. "Kept telling her that she and Dad could travel the world, have a house wherever they wanted."

"You didn't like him?" Libby asked.

He shrugged. "Not so much. Mom didn't either. When he tried to pressure her to talk to Dad, she told him to take her home."

"Why did she agree to go to dinner in the first place?" Alec asked.

"You know how Mom was. She didn't like to hurt anyone's feelings. And he'd come all that way to talk to Dad."

"Why didn't he call first and make sure D-Dad was home?" It still felt strange to say *Dad*.

"He did," Vanessa said, her tone implying that she didn't appreciate any criticism of her father. "But Daddy got called out at the last minute. One of his businesses in California burned, and he went to make sure the employees were taken care of."

"So your mother tried to placate the guy by talking to him herself." Alec put his hands in his pockets and paced. "Did you hear what he wanted?"

Brent shrugged. "What they always want. This strip of land on the ocean. I think this is the guy that Poe represents. He offered ten mil."

Libby bit her lip to keep from telling him the offer had gone up.

"Did your mother seem tempted?" Alec asked.

Vanessa shook her head. "Mom never wanted to leave the island. She didn't care about yachts and travel. It was all Daddy could do to get her to go to Virginia Beach from time to time."

"She was a homebody," Brent agreed.

"And it's not like Daddy was hurting for money," Vanessa added. "He gave her anything she wanted."

"Did they know the state was talking about putting in a ferry system?" Libby asked.

"Oh yes," Vanessa said. "Daddy made several trips to try to talk down the proposal. He was determined not to let them ruin our island."

"How did you feel about that?" Libby asked, glancing at Brent so he would know she wanted to know what he thought as well.

Brent shrugged. "Dad didn't care much for progress, but lots of younger men like me would like to see more jobs. Even tourism would pay a steadier wage than fishing does at times. And what is there here except fishing?"

"Is that why you were going to sell this place?"

"Maybe. If I could have sold it and started a shipbuilding business here, it would have brought in jobs." His grin was cold. "And it was a lot of money."

Just when she thought she could warm up to the guy, he turned everything around again. Libby had no idea how to read Brent.

———

"Come along, Poe," Lawrence said. He glanced at his daughter. That color dress made Katelyn's skin look like a pumpkin. An unfortunate following after fashion.

Poe rose from the Rooneys' dinner table. "I'll join you in the game room in a few minutes," he said to Katelyn. "All right?"

"I'll be waiting." Her flirtatious glance lingered on him.

Lawrence led the boy to his office. Closing the door behind him, he approached the desk. "I can tell something is on your mind. Has something gone wrong?"

Poe sat in the chair across from the desk. "There's a rumor that Nicole Ingram is dead."

"What? Did you do something to her?"

Poe shook his head. "It wasn't me. Her shoes and cover-up were found, and the authorities are presuming her dead."

"That's not catastrophic, then. They can't blame us for something we didn't do." He eyed Poe. "We didn't have anything to do with this, correct?"

Poe shook his head. "Libby doesn't believe it. She's tenacious. She's got a search-and-rescue dog team there."

Lawrence dismissed the concern with a wave of his hand. "The dog can't tie us to something we didn't do."

"True enough." Poe inhaled and leaned forward. "That's not all though. The cellar has been found. And Tina's remains."

Lawrence bolted out of his chair. "You said no one would ever find her. We should have dumped her body in the ocean." His scowl darkened. "This is your fault."

Poe spread out his hands. "I agree I should have just hauled her body from the cellar when I found it there. But at the time, I was afraid the discovery of her body would heat up the investigation and derail our plan. If they thought she drowned, the hunt would die down. And that's what happened."

"Is there anything you aren't telling me? You didn't kill her, did you?"

"Absolutely not. She must have fallen and hit her head. She was dead when I found her."

"You'd better not be lying."

Poe held his gaze. "I'm telling you the truth. If you have doubts about me, now is the time to say so."

Lawrence looked away and shook his head. He didn't want to alienate Poe when things were going so well with Katelyn. "The problem now is what do we do? Investigators will be poring over that cellar."

"They may not find the cache."

"I'd rather not take the chance," Lawrence said.

"What do you propose?"

"I don't know yet. I'll have to think about it."

Poe relaxed in the chair. "I have an idea."

THIRTY-SIX

When Delilah served the Tidewater Inn guests after-dinner coffee, Alec gestured to Zach and they stepped outside. Over the meal, Alec had caught Zach staring at Libby quite often. Did his nephew see the attraction between them?

"School will be starting soon," Alec said, stooping to pick up an unbroken conch.

Zach folded his arms across his chest. "I'm not going back to school, Uncle Alec."

"Now, Zach," Alec began.

"Don't try to talk me into it. You know I just want to be a fisher-man. It's an honest profession. I don't need college to catch fish. I already know the ocean like the back of my hand."

"I know you do. But the world is changing. What happens if the fishing falls off? It's a hard life, Zach. I'd like to see you have something else to rely on. There's plenty of time to try different things. You don't have to set your course right now. At least go to two years of college."

Zach's chin jutted out. "I don't want to. And you can't make me."

The boy—no, Zach was a man now—was in charge of his own destiny. Much as Alec wanted to insist on college, how could

245

he know what was best for Zach? How could any man know what was best for another man? There was no denying that Zach was a natural-born waterman. He was in his element when he rode the seas. His dad, Alec's brother, had been the same way. It was probably why he'd been so hard for their father to handle. Zack, like Darrell, just wanted to be back in Hope Beach.

Alec made one final attempt. "What about online classes? Just a couple to keep learning."

Zach hesitated. "I'll think about it."

"That's all I ask."

"I don't know what classes I'd even take though."

"What about something like marine biology? You'd be good at that, and you'd be helping the ecology." A flicker of interest in Zach's eyes encouraged him. "The Banks have some challenges to face. Maybe you could be part of finding help."

Zach had quit listening. His gaze went past Alec, and Alec turned to see Libby heading toward them with a newspaper in her hand. She looked pale and upset.

"Something wrong?" he asked when she reached them.

She held out the newspaper and he saw it was a New York paper. "The story has been picked up. Front page." She opened the paper to reveal a picture of Nicole.

"I'm sorry," Alec said. It had been a total miscalculation to get Earl involved. The reporter was probably rejoicing at all the interest and might even follow up with more damaging articles.

"I should have expected it," Libby said.

"Can I see it?" Zach asked, holding out his hand. Libby handed it over and he studied the article. Zach handed back the paper. "I'm sorry."

"Thanks, Zach." Her eyes narrowed as she stared at him. His Adam's apple was bobbing, and he didn't meet her gaze. "You are on the water a lot. Would you keep an eye out for anyone

suspicious? There were two men. One was in his forties with a cap pulled low over his eyes. He had a beard. The other was in his late twenties. He had blond hair and it looked like he hadn't shaved in a couple of days. He might not always look so scruffy though."

"We did a police sketch. That might help," Alec said. He gave a curious glance at his nephew, who seemed unusually still. "Stop by Tom's office and take a look. Keep your eye out for the men."

"You're sure she's dead?" Zach asked.

Alec shot a glance at Libby. She seemed to be holding together all right. "As sure as we can be without a body," Alec said. "I think I know where the men dumped her." He told Zach about the spot offshore from the old ruins.

"I don't want to accept it," Libby said, her voice quiet. "One minute I'm resigned to it and the next I'm sure she's still out there waiting for me to find her."

"I get out there some. I'll keep an eye out," Zach said. "You think the men were local?"

Alec frowned. "I don't, no. I would vouch for every resident male on the island. This isn't the kind of thing our people would do."

Zach put his hands in the pockets of his denim shorts. "I guess people can hide their true natures sometimes."

An uncommonly perceptive comment from his nephew. Alec sometimes despaired at how little progress he felt he was making in shaping Zach. But hadn't he been the same way when he was Zach's age?

"One of my friends is having a party on the beach," Zach said. "I thought I'd go."

"Be careful." Alec wanted to add *don't drink*, but he knew Zach would hear the implied admonition in his voice. Not that it would matter what he said. Zach would do what he wanted to do. All Alec could do was pray.

Zach nodded and jogged to his old pickup.

"Zach is a good boy," Libby said. "You need to trust him a little."

"I *do* trust him."

"Your tone didn't indicate much trust." She turned to stare out to sea. "I keep thinking that there's something I could have done to stop them from taking her."

"It wasn't your fault," he said gently.

She turned back toward him with a pained expression.

"God is in control of life and death and everything in between, Libby. We can drive ourselves crazy by thinking of all the what-ifs in life."

Her eyes were luminous with tears. "I just feel helpless."

Did he make the first move or did she? He wasn't sure, but the next thing he knew, he was holding her with her face buried in his chest. It was the most natural thing in the world to press his lips against her fragrant hair.

———

Libby could feel Alec's heart thudding under her ear. She wanted to preserve this moment and stay in the safe circle of his arms. Right now it felt as though no harm could come to her. She'd stood on her own for so many years that she hardly knew what to make of this desire to be protected and nurtured.

His hand moved in a caressing motion down her hair, and he pressed his lips against her forehead. "You're a special person, Libby," he whispered. "I love how fiercely you treasure family. You even care about Vanessa and Brent when they've been nothing but cold to you."

"Vanessa is warming up."

The scent of man and sea was an intoxicating mix. She burrowed closer to the solid warmth of his chest. If she lifted her

head, he might kiss her again. Part of her wanted that, but the fearful side kept her cheek firmly pressed against his shirt. If he kissed her again, she might lose her heart completely. Right now, if she walked away from this place, she might survive. If she gave too much of herself away, it might destroy her. And she didn't know what the future held.

His arms gripped her shoulders and he created a small space between them. His fingers tipped her chin up. She closed her eyes and held her breath. His lips were warm and persuasive, and she dropped any pretense of holding on to her dignity. It was too late to hang on to her heart. She kissed him back with all the depth of feeling she didn't know she possessed. The beat of his heart sped up under her right palm, trapped under her. She exulted that she moved him as much as he moved her. Whatever was developing between them was something they both felt.

He pulled away. "Want to go for a walk along the beach?"

She nodded. That was safer than being pelted by feelings she had to resist. They strolled along the dense sand, hand in hand. The companionable silence lulled her. She didn't feel the need to fill it with chatter.

He stopped by a fallen tree, pulling her down with him to sit. The moon glimmered on the water and the salty breeze from the ocean lifted her hair in a sultry caress. "I haven't kissed a woman in a long time. I didn't want you to think I was some kind of Lothario."

She had to smile at the anxiety in his voice. She hadn't even considered that he might worry about that. "Thanks for telling me. I don't even know the last time I went out with a man. I've been too focused on my career."

A smile tugged at his lips. "Glad to hear it."

"What about Zach?" she asked, hoping he wasn't offended by the question. "I got the impression I interrupted an argument."

His smile faded. "You did."

"I'm sure he's still hurting from his parents' death."

"Dave was a fisherman too. He had a charter boat based in Hatteras. Zach was with him all the time until he died. That's all the kid has wanted to do—be on the water. He wants to be a commercial fisherman. My parents couldn't control him. I think he wants everyone to know how miserable he is."

"So you took him?"

"He landed in jail for vandalizing the school the day before you showed up. So yeah, you could say he's been a handful."

"You were doing your duty," she said.

"It's more than duty. I love the kid. He and I have always been close. Right now, he's pushing me away, but I think that's starting to change."

"He's a good kid."

His glance was warm and tender. "I think so. When he first got here, he was sullen and distant, but he's coming around. He loves the sea. Being a waterman is therapeutic."

"Waterman?" She liked the romantic sound of the word.

"It's what we call men out here who make their living off the water. Fishermen, ferry workers, charter-boat owners."

"So you're a waterman too?"

"We all were. Me, Darrell, even my sister, Beth, works with the sea. She's a marine biologist," he said. "Guess I shouldn't come down too hard on Zach. It's in our blood. He can't help it."

"You don't want him to be a waterman?"

"I want him to have something to fall back on. Fishermen have a hard life fighting weather and tides all the time. They're at the whim of the capricious ocean. When you came out, I was trying to talk him into taking some online classes. He doesn't want to go away to college."

"Maybe he feels safe here. And closer to his parents."

Alec slipped his arm around her waist. "Yeah, I guess so." His lips grazed her forehead. "Why aren't you married? A girl as beautiful as you is usually taken early on."

He thinks I'm beautiful. "I've never been close to marriage. I guess I've been afraid to trust anyone. Dealing with my mom's instability has made me cautious. I've never even had a steady boyfriend. We moved around so much that there was never a chance to develop any kind of relationship."

"You think you can trust me?"

She stared into his face. "Can I?"

"I'm a man of my word, Libby. I'd like for us to see where this relationship might go. Are you game?"

"I think so," she whispered.

His lips found hers again and she turned off the warning in her head.

Thirty-Seven

"W e generally don't allow guests in the library," Delilah said, unlocking the glass-paned door. "You're hardly a guest, of course, but I wanted you to be aware that there are many valuable books in here."

Libby stepped into the room and inhaled the aroma of old books. Her aunt, Alec, and Bree were right behind her. Their presence would make the job easier, though she would have gladly spent hours here alone. There was nothing she liked better than to delve into history. She slid her glance to Alec and back again. Their earlier walk on the beach still lingered in her heart.

"Do you need me to show you around?" Delilah asked, her tone indicating she hoped to be released.

"No, I'm sure we'll figure it out."

Libby glanced around the large room. There were floor-to-ceiling oak shelves on two walls, a desk on the wall with the window, and a library table against the other wall. The floors were polished oak. The wood hadn't been stained, and the naturally light color was attractive.

"I haven't been in here in years," Pearl said, walking to the nearest bookshelf. "What do you want to see first?"

"I want to take a look at the history of the lighthouse." Libby's

attention was distracted by a picture on the desk of a woman in her fifties with auburn hair and hazel eyes. She was on the bow of a boat with a man and they were both laughing. Her father and Tina looked so happy and carefree.

Libby moved past the picture to study the books. The ones on architecture caught her eye but she forced herself to skim by them. A large book on the Outer Banks looked interesting. She took it to the library table.

"I found it," Pearl said, turning toward her. "This is the oldest one. Ray found it twenty years ago. There aren't many copies in existence, and it's in pretty bad shape."

"What do you hope to find in the book?" Bree asked.

Alec pulled a chair out for Libby. She settled into the chair and gently opened the book. "No one knew about the cellar, but I thought there might be pictures of its history in the book I'd heard about."

"What can I be searching for?" Bree asked, turning back to the shelves. "Any other books we need to study?"

"See if there are any on the history of the island. I know it's unlikely, but what if there are more tunnels that lead to where Nicole might have been taken?" And searching through what had happened in the past might provide a clue to the present.

The paper of the book Libby examined was brittle and yellow. She checked the front of the book. Published in 1923. "When did the lighthouse cease operation? You mentioned the late eighteen hundreds. Can you be more specific?"

"I believe it was in the hurricane of 1899," Pearl said. "It was known as the Great Hurricane, and we lost many lives. I wasn't born yet, of course, but my grandparents used to talk about it."

The pictures Libby thumbed through were faded but legible. She paused to read some of the text, then continued to skim the book. "Hey, wait a minute," she said. She picked up a piece of

paper stuck in the middle of the book. "This is a light bill. In Nicole's name. She was reading this book." She stared at the page marked by the paper. "This shows a cellar door. So it wasn't a secret back in its heyday."

"And it proves she knew about the cellar," Bree said.

Alec stepped behind Libby and leaned over her shoulder to look at it more closely. His breath whispered past her cheek, and she fought the attraction his close presence generated.

He flipped the page and began to read aloud. "'The lighthouse was self-contained. The keeper and his family grew vegetables on a small plot of cleared land and stored the harvest in the cellar.'"

"Just like every other family," Libby said. "That doesn't tell us anything."

She couldn't read, couldn't think, with him so close. His neck was close enough that if she leaned over, she could press her lips against his warm skin. She needed to concentrate on figuring this out, so she shifted away.

"There's more," he said. "Listen to this. 'Blackbeard was said to have escaped through one of the secret passageways from the cellar to the rocky cliffs at the water's edge.'"

"So it mentions the passage you found," Libby said. "And Nicole would have seen this. Knowing her, she was sure to have looked for the cave." She leaned over to read the book. "Passageways, plural. So there is more than one."

"There *were*," he corrected. "No telling if they're still there."

Bree was staring at the book. "The name Blackbeard conjures up all kinds of images of treasure."

"People have searched for his treasures in the Outer Banks for years," Pearl said.

"Could Nicole have heard the legends and decided to look herself? Maybe she decided to hunt by herself?"

"It sounds like something she would do," Libby said.

"We can go back there and take a look for other tunnels," Alec said. "Though the tide is wrong right now. We can take a look tomorrow afternoon though."

Libby shut the book. "I want to see if we can find any sign of Nicole."

He looked away and nodded. She knew he was thinking that the kidnappers likely killed Nicole. Libby could only pray he was wrong.

———

Libby had an hour before she and Bree were supposed to meet Alec at his boat. Libby stepped over the warped floorboards in the living room of her father's house. "I was afraid they were ruined," she told her sister.

"Insurance will replace them," Vanessa said. She still wore the necklace Libby had given her. "Daddy was adamant about keeping up on the insurance." She started for the stairs. "I'm not sure what you're hoping to find in his bedroom."

"I don't know either." Libby followed her up to the second floor. "But someone harmed Tina. Maybe there's a clue in her things to what happened. I appreciate you allowing me to investigate."

Vanessa shrugged and opened the bedroom door. "Here you go. I'll help if you tell me what to look for."

Libby glanced around the room. "Anything out of the ordinary."

The blue comforter on the king bed was smooth. Assorted pillows were heaped at the head. Libby paused at the dresser and studied the pictures. One showed her father and Tina with Vanessa and Brent. They were dressed in red and stood by a Christmas tree.

"That was our last Christmas together," Vanessa said. "Six months later and Mom was gone."

Libby put the picture back. There was a jewelry box beside it. "May I?"

Vanessa nodded. "I used to love to go through Mom's jewelry box when I was a little girl. There's a secret drawer in the bottom." She reached past Libby and lifted out two trays full of necklaces and earrings. The bottom showed no sign of having any compartment.

"Is this the same jewelry box?"

Vanessa nodded. "There's a switch here." She pressed a spot on the bottom and one edge sprang up. "Mom used to hide notes in it telling me she loved me."

"That's so sweet."

"I still have some." Vanessa lifted the fake bottom from the drawer.

Libby expected to see an empty space, but it contained several folded papers. "Letters or bills?"

Vanessa unfolded one. "This one's a letter."

Libby wanted to read it, but she didn't want to offend her sister. Vanessa had been warming up so dramatically. She could wait until Vanessa offered the information. The letter might be very personal.

Vanessa's frown darkened as she read. She finally handed it to Libby and selected another letter. "This doesn't make any sense. It almost sounds as if . . ."

The paper was stiff in Libby's hand. "As if?"

Vanessa pressed her lips together. "As if Mom had a lover. But that's impossible. She loved Daddy."

Libby held the letter in the light of the window.

Tina,

Seeing you again brought back all the love I thought I'd torn up by the roots. Even now I would leave my family if you would agree to do the same. It's not too late for us. Think about it and give me a call if you want to talk.

Yours, L

"L. Who could that be? First name, last name? Any idea?" Libby asked.

"Not a clue," Vanessa said, still reading another letter.

"Anything in that one?"

"This one sounds angry." Vanessa handed it over.

"Angry? Like in murderous?"

Vanessa's expression was troubled. "Maybe."

Tina,

I can only assume by your actions yesterday that you intend us to be at odds. So be it. You'll find me a cold adversary. I will take what I want and you'll only have yourself to blame for the consequences. Your rejection only strengthens my determination. Your life is about to change.

L

Libby glanced up. "Wow, very ominous."

Vanessa hugged herself. "The tone of the letter gives me the creeps."

"Is that all?" Libby glanced into the jewelry box and saw nothing more.

"Just this." Vanessa held out her hand, palm up. A charm was on her palm.

Libby held it up to the light. "Looks like a stingray or something."

"It's a skate. Mom had a charm bracelet with sea creatures on it. She loved it. The skate was lost a few weeks before she died. She wasn't sure where she lost it."

Libby handed it back. "She obviously found it." Now was the time to ask, but she still hesitated.

Vanessa frowned. "She never mentioned that she'd found it. Mom loved the skates but shuddered when she saw their egg

sacks. She couldn't understand why they had a pretty name like mermaid's purse when they were so ugly. Daddy used to take early walks and pick them all up so she didn't have to see them on her morning run."

"Did you put a dead jellyfish under my door?"

Vanessa's hand closed in a fist. Her lips flattened, then she shrugged. "So what if I did?"

"Were you trying to scare me off or what?"

Vanessa leaned against the dresser. "I'm sorry I did that. I was angry. I thought you'd take the warning and leave. Were you frightened?"

Libby opened a drawer. "More mad than anything."

Vanessa opened her fist and fingered the charm. "It's odd this was in her secret drawer and not back on the bracelet." She turned it over and squinted. "I never realized it was engraved." She walked to the window and held it to the light. "*Love, L.* I know the original wasn't engraved."

"The man who wrote the notes gave it to her."

Vanessa turned back toward her. "And she refused to wear it."

"Which might have added to his anger with her. Let's go see the sheriff."

———

Alec took a gulp of stale coffee and shuddered. "Anything from the coroner on Tina's remains?"

The circles around Tom's eyes were pronounced, and his clothes were rumpled. "He couldn't determine cause of death."

"So no clue to what happened to her."

"Nope. And it being three years ago, I'm having trouble piecing together what happened the day she disappeared. I have the old notes, but we thought her boat hit a rock and she drowned.

We didn't treat it as foul play, so there's very little in the file. A statement from a fisherman who saw her speeding toward the old lighthouse ruins is all we have. And he's dead now."

"What about the cellar itself? Anything there?"

"One interesting detail. There was a rope tied around Tina's left ankle. We have no idea if it was put there before or after death though."

The door opened behind Alec, and he turned to see Libby and Vanessa enter the sheriff's office. Neither was smiling.

Libby shot a quick glance his way, then held out two pieces of paper to Tom. "We found these in Tina's belongings."

Tom took the papers and began to read. Alec looked over his shoulder. "Looks like Tina had a secret admirer," Alec said.

"There's this too." Vanessa held out a charm. "Look on the back."

Alec took it and squinted at the tiny lettering, then handed it to Tom. They listened to Vanessa tell them about a lost charm and how this apparent replacement had been in the secret compartment.

"Who is this L person?" Tom asked. "Any ideas?"

"Not a clue," Vanessa said. "Sheriff, you have to find out who did this to Mom."

"I'm working on it, Vanessa."

Alec studied his cousin's expression. He didn't seem to be staring at Libby with suspicion. Maybe he was finally beginning to look elsewhere.

"Ready?" Alec asked. "Bree and Samson should be at the boat by now."

———

Bree held the clothing Libby had given her under Samson's nose. The breeze on the water ruffled the dog's thick fur. He sniffed the

shirt and whined, then lifted his nose above the bow of the boat. "Search, Samson," she said.

Libby watched in awe. "Can he really find a person by sniffing the air? I thought dogs sniffed the ground."

"Samson is an air tracker. A person gives off skin rafts that float in the air. A trained dog can detect them."

"But it's been almost ten days since Nicole was taken," Alec said.

"He may still get a scent." Bree looked away.

Libby stared at Bree. Hadn't she said something about Samson finding someone after two years? Then the memory clicked into place and she remembered that dogs could smell dead bodies for a very long time. A lump formed in her throat, and she prayed the dog would find a live scent. Something to lead them to Nicole.

The boat accelerated across the tops of the waves. It was calm and beautiful today, though humidity hung in the air. Bree's curls were a little frizzy from the moisture. Sea spray struck Libby's bare arms and felt good on her heated skin. She prayed for a sign from God today, anything that would allow her to hope that her friend was still alive.

"How can you tell if he smells something?" she asked Bree.

"He'll bark. I'll be able to tell," Bree assured her. "Alec, run the boat in a crisscross fashion across the bay so he gets more exposure."

It seemed they looped back and forth across the water for ages, but glancing at her watch, Libby realized they'd only been at this for two hours. She was beginning to lose hope that they'd find something today.

The dog continued to sniff the air as Alec guided the boat back and forth across the gleaming water. The village of Hope Beach beckoned in the distance. A few people on the pier waved as they scouted the area. Libby waved back, suddenly feeling part of the community.

Samson's ears pricked. He stiffened and barked, straining toward the harbor. "Go that way!" Bree shouted, pointing toward the pier.

Libby's heart pounded. She stood, then nearly fell when the boat accelerated.

"Hang on!" Alec seated his hat more firmly on his head and the boat surged.

Samson was barking frantically. The next instant, he leaped over the side and swam toward a boat. He reached it and tried to paw his way onto it, but it was too high for him.

"That's my old boat," Alec said, frowning. "I don't use it much, but Zach had it out this morning."

His boat? Libby stared at him. Surely he wouldn't have had anything to do with this?

He cut the engine and the craft slowed, then stopped near the dog. He tossed the anchor overboard, then reached down and helped Samson clamber up the ladder. The dog shook himself, spraying water over everyone. He rushed to Bree's side and whined. He strained toward the old boat, a Chris-Craft.

Libby stared at Alec. "What does this mean? The dog is saying he smells Nicole on your boat. Right, Bree?"

"That's right," Bree said, rubbing Samson's ears. "Let's board the boat and let him sniff around."

Alec took an oar and maneuvered the two boats close enough together that they could step from one deck to the other. Samson leaped onto the boat and began to bark. He ran to the side of the boat and his barking grew more frenzied. Bree stepped aboard the old boat, and Libby followed her.

"What's he trying to tell you?" Libby asked.

"It looks like Nicole was here or something of hers is here. He's indicating that area there," Bree said, pointing to the starboard side.

Alec joined them. "That's impossible. She would have had to swim out here and board it. What would be the point?"

"You never use this?" Bree asked.

He shook his head. "Zach uses it sometimes, but he's never met Nicole."

"That we know of," Libby said. She'd rather believe Zach had a hand in this than the alternative—that Alec was guilty.

"What are you saying?" he asked.

"Is it possible Zach was involved in her kidnapping?" She didn't want to accuse the boy, especially to his own uncle, but the dog's reaction meant something.

"No," Alec said, his voice clipped. "I can't believe you'd even think that."

No one would want to think his nephew would be involved in something so heinous, but Libby couldn't ignore this. "I need to talk to him, Alec. Right away."

"I won't have you accusing him," Alec said. "And based on the reaction of a dog? That's ridiculous."

"Is it? You've admitted that he's been in some trouble."

"Alec, Samson is definitely reacting here," Bree said. "This isn't just some mistake. Nicole was either on this boat, or at the very least, she touched it. He doesn't give false positives."

"Look around," Alec said. "Let's see if there's any other evidence. I can't accuse the boy without tangible evidence."

Her lips tight, Libby opened doors and peered under seats. Under the cushion where Samson stood, her hand touched something soft, and she pulled up a ponytail holder. It still held strands of blond hair. "I have to talk to Zach."

Alec paled. "Don't accuse him of anything," he said. "There has to be some explanation."

"That's all we want," Libby said. "Where is he now?" Zach had left the inn before nine this morning.

"He said he was delivering the supplies for his job and then was going to help do some cleanup around town," Alec said. "There's a group in the square washing the mud off the stores."

He started the engine and guided the boat to the dock. Libby grabbed a post as they neared, then threw the rope around it. She was the first to leap to the boardwalk. Maybe they would find Nicole today.

THIRTY-EIGHT

The townspeople were out in force today. Great strides had been made in the cleanup over the past week. Paint shone clean and free of the mud and mildew. Alec spoke to several neighbors as he searched for his nephew. No one had seen Zach, and Alec began to wonder if the boy had lied about where he was going today.

The business district, such as it was, ended at the juncture of Oyster Road and Bar Harbor Street. A few residents were on Bar Harbor, but Oyster Road just led to the fish house. "Let's check the fish house," he said.

"What's a fish house?" Libby asked, falling into step beside him.

"It's where the fishermen gather and sell their day's catch. Zach likes hanging out there," he said. "I think he feels close to Dave there. I know I do. My brother was always laughing with the other fishermen in there, swapping fishing stories."

The low-slung white building was at the end of a pier where rowboats and water jets docked. He stepped over nets and crab pots on the way to the door of the fish house. The scent of fish was strong.

He nodded to the few men outside the door. "Anyone seen Zach?"

"He's out back helping Rolly unload," one of the men said.

Skirting the building, Alec continued on down the pier, where he found his nephew lifting crab pots off a friend's boat.

When Zach saw him, he frowned. "What's up, Uncle Alec?"

"We need to talk to you. In private." Alec jerked his thumb back toward the street, away from listening ears. Getting a rumor going was all they needed. Zach was getting enough of a reputation as a troublemaker.

Zach wiped his wet hands on his shorts, then slipped on his flip-flops to follow them. He glanced at Libby, who was studying him. "What? Did I suddenly grow horns?" he demanded.

She looked away. "Sorry. We just need to ask you some questions."

They reached the road. There was no one in earshot. Alec put his hands in his pockets. "You know Samson is here to look for Nicole?"

Zach glanced back at the fish house with a longing expression. "Yeah. So?"

"He picked up a scent for her."

That got Zach's attention. "That's good, right?"

Alec nodded. "But the scent is on my old boat. According to the dog, Nicole was on there. So we searched and Libby found something." He glanced at her.

She held out her hand, palm up to expose the ponytail holder. "This is Nicole's."

Zach went white. He took a step back, then whirled to walk away, but Alec grabbed his arm. He had a sick feeling in the pit of his stomach. "Zach, what did you do?" he whispered.

Zach looked at Alec's hand on his arm. "I didn't do anything. You're always willing to think the worst about me, aren't you?"

"Then how did that hair thing get on my boat?"

Zach bit his lip. "I was going to talk to you about it." His face

265

worked. Then his shoulders slumped. "I just take her supplies," he said. "I didn't know who she was until I saw her picture in the paper last night. Then I didn't know what to do about it."

Libby's face lit. "She's alive? Really, Zach?"

He nodded. "I saw her a couple of days ago. Took her some water and food."

"Where?" Alec asked. He'd figure out what to do about punishing Zach later.

"A little island northwest of here. I have the coordinates."

"Who put her there?"

He shrugged. "I was taking the old boat out to fish. Two guys stopped me and asked if I was looking to make some money. The older man told me that he'd had to stash his crazy sister on an island until he could get her into the hospital he wanted. Said she'd tried to knife him and to be careful because she was dangerous. I was only supposed to drop off supplies every couple of days, then leave."

"That sounds like a fishy story," Alec said.

Zach's lids flickered and he made a face. "He made it sound plausible. I know now it was stupid for me to believe him, but he gave me all these details and I swallowed his story. And they were paying well."

"Why didn't you tell us when you figured out who she was?"

Zach looked down at the ground. "It was just last night. I wanted to tell you, but I was afraid you'd think I had something to do with it."

"Have they paid you every time you've gone?"

Zach shook his head. "They gave me a thousand dollars to buy food and to pay for my services. They told me what to take her too. I just did what they said."

"I wish you would have trusted me," Alec said. "Come with us. We have to get her."

Libby could hardly sit still as the boat skimmed the waves. They were so far out to sea that she couldn't see land. Where was that island? She prayed that Nicole was holding on to life, that she would be well and whole when Libby found her.

"Where is it?" Alec asked Zach.

The boy pointed to the horizon, and Libby saw a faint speck that might have been land. They drew closer, and she realized it was a tiny island barely twenty or thirty feet in diameter. How had Nicole survived the hurricane? Libby strained to catch a glimpse of Nicole, but all she saw was a hovel of a building. The place appeared deserted.

"Where is she?" she demanded.

"Maybe in the shack," Zach said. "Though she's usually out as soon as she hears the motor."

Alec took the boat in as close to shore as he could and shut off the engine. Zach tossed the anchor overboard, but by the time it splashed into the water, Libby was already knee-deep in the waves and barreling toward the tiny beach. Bree and Samson were right behind her.

"Nicole!" she shouted.

She rushed to the door of the building and yanked open the door. It took a moment for her eyes to adjust enough to see that the one room held nothing but a few pieces of broken furniture.

"She's not here!" she told Bree, who came in behind her. "Where could she be?" Zach and Alec entered the building.

Zach glanced around. "Her food and water aren't here," he said.

"What does that mean?" Libby asked.

"I brought her a jug of water, peanut butter, canned stuff. None of it is here."

"Has someone else come after her?" Alec asked.

Zach shrugged. "Beats me."

"Who were the men who hired you?" Alec asked. "Didn't you get their names?"

"I didn't know them. One said his name was Oscar Jacobson. The other never told me his name. All I cared about was that they were paying me cash."

"Sounds like a fake name," Alec said.

Bree took Nicole's clothing out of the paper bag and held it under Samson's nose. "Search, boy!"

The dog nosed around the shack, his tail wagging. He barked at the bed, then ran to the door and around the side of the shack. "He smells her," Bree said.

Libby and Bree followed with the men rushing after them. The dog darted around the island with his nose in the air, then went back to the beach and stood with his tail drooping. He whined when Bree reached him.

"She's not here," Bree said.

"She couldn't have gotten off the island without help," Zach said.

"Look here," Alec said, staring at marks in the sand. "Looks like a raft or something was dragged here."

Bree knelt and touched the indentations. "Could she have built a raft and tried to escape that way?"

"She tried that once before and I found it torn apart on the beach," Zach said. He glanced toward the shack. "Whoa, looks like some of the roof is missing."

"Might she have used the roof for a raft?" Libby asked.

"It would be foolhardy," Alec said. "The ocean is treacherous around here. They don't call it the Graveyard of the Atlantic for no reason. Shoals, rocks—all kinds of things can tear a boat or a raft to pieces in a heartbeat. Would she be foolish enough to try that, Libby?"

She tried not to take offense at his question. "It's not foolhardy to try to escape kidnappers," she said. "Who knows when they might come back?" She turned to Bree. "Could Samson help us find her?"

"Maybe. It's a big ocean out there. He's lost her scent right now, but we could go out and see if he smells anything."

"That's our only option," Libby said. Her voice broke and she swallowed hard. What if Nicole was already capsized and drowning, crying out for help? The thought sent her rushing to the boat. "Come on! We have to find Nicole."

The rest of the crew ran after her, and in moments they were cruising the waves again. Bree gave Samson another refresher sniff, and the dog had his nose in the air. He strained at the bow of the boat. Alec crossed back and forth in front of the area where they'd seen the markings in the sand. Then Samson's tail began to wag. He barked furiously and strained out over the water until Libby thought he might fall in.

"He's got a scent!" Bree called. "Good boy," she crooned. His tail drooped as the boat headed west. "Wrong direction," Bree said. "Try north."

Alec corrected his course, and the dog's countenance perked again. Libby went up to sit by her friend.

Bree saw her and squeezed her hand. "We'll find Nicole."

"I just hope we're not too late."

"I'm praying and I'm sure you are too."

"I am," Libby admitted. "Constantly. But I'm so afraid."

"Put it in God's hands. He loves Nicole. He's out there in the big ocean with her."

The thought comforted Libby. Nicole wasn't alone. No matter what happened, God held her securely.

Thirty-Nine

The sun beat down on Nicole's head as she sat on her raft. Her skin was tight and hot, and she knew she was going to be hurting from a sunburn later. There was still no land in sight, and she wasn't even sure if she was floating farther out into the Atlantic or nearer to the mainland. All she could do was cling to the boards and hope. How long had she been here? She slanted a glance at the sky. Three hours.

Her food had made the trip past the breakers all right, but though her tummy rumbled, she wanted to save what she had since there was no telling how long she might be adrift. She wiped her forehead and stared at the horizon. Nothing. Her lids grew heavy, and she decided to sleep if she could. On her stomach with her head pillowed in her arms, she listened to the lapping of the waves and felt the gentle rise of the swells under her raft.

Where was Libby now? Her eyes grew heavy and she let them close. Sleep was good.

She wasn't sure what awakened her. Sitting up, she rubbed her eyes. The sun was lower in the sky. It must be nearly four or five. Then she heard it. The sound of an engine. She turned toward the *putt-putt* and saw a boat growing closer in the distance. Leaping to her feet, she screamed and waved her hands.

An answering shout came from the boat. Was that Libby? Nicole strained to see. It was!

"Libby, I'm here, I'm here!" Jumping up and down, she could barely breathe for joy.

Nicole recognized only Zach and Libby in the boat. Another man drove, and a woman with a dog stood in the bow. Zach must have realized she was telling the truth and gotten help. She would have to thank him.

The boat reached her raft. The man's strong grip clasped her arm and helped her climb the ladder to the deck, where she collapsed.

Libby sank down beside her and grabbed her in an almost painful grip. "Nicole, I thought they killed you." Her voice was choked.

Tears poured down Nicole's face, and she clung to Libby. "I knew you'd find me. I just knew it."

The two remained locked in an embrace for several seconds, then Libby pulled away and stared at Nicole. "Who did this to you?"

"I don't know. I can't remember anything. I woke up on the island and I've been there ever since. Alone, except when Zach brought supplies."

Libby hugged her again. "I'm so glad to see you. We found your flip-flops and cover-up. Everyone told me you were dead, but I didn't believe it."

"I knew you'd never give up on me," Nicole whispered. "You've always been a rock."

"Let's get you home," Libby said. "We'll get a doctor and make sure you're all right."

Nicole rubbed her belly. "And real food. I'd love a chicken quesadilla."

"I think we can find one of those," the handsome man said.

Nicole glanced at Libby, who was blushing. She was going to have to question her friend about her relationship with the guy.

After Nicole's checkup at the doctor's office, Tom asked her questions until Libby insisted her friend needed some food and rest. Libby took Nicole to the restaurant while Alec and Bree stayed behind to talk to Tom. Libby was filled with gratitude as she watched Nicole eat. It was a true miracle that they'd found her. Libby filled her in on the events of the nine days.

"Who's the guy?" Nicole asked.

Libby hated the way her cheeks heated at the mention of Alec. "Alec Bourne, Zach's uncle."

"You like him?"

How did she answer that? *Like* wasn't the most accurate word. "Well, he's been a big help. He's been right on the front lines helping to look for you."

"Even though his nephew kept me confined to that island?"

"He didn't know anything about it."

"Are you sure?" Nicole put down her fork. "Wouldn't Zach have been gone? Wouldn't he have taken the boat? Surely Alec would have asked what he was doing with the boat."

How would she make her friend see? "He's a good man, Nicole. I think you'll like him."

Nicole's eyes flashed. "I don't want to know him, that's for sure. I want to get out of this place and back to Virginia Beach now."

Libby opened her mouth to agree, then shut it again. The thought of leaving this island left a pit in her belly. "We have work to do here. I've started work on the lifesaving station. And have you seen those lighthouse ruins? I love it out there."

Nicole rubbed her forehead. "There's something about those ruins. When I think of them, I get a funny feeling in my stomach."

"Fear?"

Nicole shook her head. "Not fear exactly. Excitement maybe. Oh, why can't I remember?"

Libby reached across the table to squeeze Nicole's hand. "The doctor said you might not ever remember. He doesn't know what drug they used on you, but it might have wiped out that time period permanently. So don't stress about it. If you remember, great. But right now all I care about is that you're here and well."

"I'd like to see the lighthouse ruins. Maybe seeing them will help me remember."

Libby released her hand and signaled for the check. "Do you remember talking to me in front of the beach cam?"

"No." Her eyes widened. "Have you been working any of our projects besides the station? And have you heard from Rooney?"

"Your investor?" Libby shook her head. "I've been out of the office looking for you."

"You've been checking in, of course?"

"Of course. But no messages from him have come in."

"How strange. He's been pushing so hard for me to get the deal sewed up here."

"He's been trying to buy that property for years, from what I understand."

"I never had a chance to tell him that you own the property he wants and not your brother."

Something about the reference to Rooney nudged at her. Then it hit her. "His first name is Lawrence, isn't it?"

Nicole nodded. "And don't call him Larry. He hates that. It has to be Lawrence. Why?"

Libby told her about the notes she found in Tina's room. "L could stand for Lawrence."

"Or Laban, Lance, Levi, Lloyd, or any number of other names," Nicole said. "Even Libby! That's a stretch to think that Lawrence might be implicated in Tina's death."

"Maybe not. Vanessa and Brent said he was with Tina not long before she disappeared."

"He's going to want to talk to you. You own that property, Libby! You're rich."

"Only if I sell it."

"Of course you're going to sell it. Think of what it would mean. We could expand the business. Or rather I could. You'd never have to work a lick again."

The two of them were worlds apart now, even though they'd only been separated for a couple of weeks. "I've been learning there are more important things than money," Libby said.

"You've changed. It's that guy, right?"

Libby shook her head. "It's my dad." She began to tell her friend about the kind of man Ray had been and all that she'd learned, but Nicole's expression only grew more incredulous.

Explaining a sea change to someone was impossible. Nicole would just have to learn about it by watching her.

———

Though she should have been exhausted, Libby couldn't sleep. She finally gave up and went up the steps to her father's third-floor retreat at the Tidewater Inn. The light in the room was already on. Brent was sitting on the sofa with their father's Bible in his hand.

Her first impulse was to demand it back, but she restrained herself and smiled and joined him on the sofa. "Couldn't sleep either?"

He shook his head. "I like to come up here. I feel closer to Dad."

"Me too." Had he been reading Scripture? She hoped so. "I'm sorry I suspected you of hurting Nicole, Brent. I hope you can forgive me."

His brows rose. "It was understandable."

"Will you forgive me?"

"I'm not even sure I know what that means." He rubbed his forehead. "I quit going to church with Dad when I was fifteen. I thought I was too old and wise to swallow all that stuff." He stared at her. "But I've been watching you, Libby. You're different, just like he was. Maybe I'll go back to church."

Her throat closed. If only she could believe she'd had an eternal impact on this brother she longed to love. Her gaze fell on the Bible. *Give it to him.* She resisted the internal nudge. Did she have to give up everything dear to her?

Give it to him.

Her shoulders sagged. How could she resist God? "Would you like to have Dad's Bible?"

His eyes widened. "I know how much you love it. You come up here and read it all the time."

"I know. But there are special passages he's marked that might mean even more to you than they do to me." She leaned toward him and flipped to a highlighted verse in the worn book. "This is my favorite. Psalm 37:25. 'I have been young, and now am old; Yet I have not seen the righteous forsaken, Nor his descendants begging bread.' I know I'm not old yet, but I believe we are blessed because our father was a righteous man."

Brent's Adam's apple bobbed. "I know that's true." He clutched the Bible to his chest. "Thank you, Libby. I'll never forget this."

⌣

The sun was just coming up, casting a glorious display over the water. Alec sat on the porch railing and inhaled the scent of the sea. The door opened behind him, and he turned to see Libby stepping out dressed in hot-pink sweats with her hair up in a ponytail.

"Couldn't sleep?" he asked. "It's only six."

She shook her head. "It seems incredible that we found Nicole. Thank you for all you did for us."

"I'm glad it turned out so well." He averted his gaze. She was way too pretty this morning. Her eyes shone with excitement. "What's on the agenda for the day?"

"I'm going to go out to the lighthouse ruins with Nicole if she feels up to it. I'm hoping being out there will jog her memory in some way."

"I'll come with you."

She smiled and nodded. "We won't be gone long. I want to show her what I've gotten done on the lifesaving station too. We have a business to run, and it's been neglected for almost two weeks."

She would be leaving soon. He saw it in her expression. "Have you decided what you're going to do about the inn?"

She settled beside him on the rail. "Not yet. I don't want to sell it, but I don't see that I have a choice."

He wanted to protest again, but it wasn't his call. "Uh, could I take you to dinner tonight at Kill Devil Hills? We could take the boat and go to Port O' Call. They've got great crab legs and she-crab soup."

Her smile came immediately. "I'd like that."

The door opened again. Vanessa and Pearl joined them. "I thought we were the only ones up early," Vanessa said.

"You got in late last night. I heard your door after I'd gone to bed for the second time," Libby said. "I wanted to talk to you, but I was too sleepy to get up again."

"Oh?" Vanessa sat on the top step. Pearl pulled a rocker closer.

Libby leaned against the post. "I wanted to ask you about Tina's meeting with Lawrence Rooney. Did she ever tell our dad what he wanted?"

"You knew about that meeting?" Pearl asked Vanessa. Her voice was high and strained.

Vanessa nodded. "We were there with Mom and Mr. Rooney."

"His first name is Lawrence," Libby said.

Vanessa gasped and straightened. "They talked outside for a minute, and I heard her tell him to leave her alone. I thought it was because he was pestering her about selling the inn. But do you think . . . ?"

Pearl sighed. "He was engaged to Tina when Ray first met her," she said.

Vanessa gasped. "Mom was engaged to another man?"

Pearl nodded. "It was quite the scandal for a while. Tina came to town for a two-week visit with her grandmother and met Ray. It was love at first sight for them both. She broke off her engagement to Lawrence and was married to Ray three months later."

"I imagine Rooney didn't take that very well," Libby said.

"I think Tina was actually a little afraid of him. He threatened to ruin Ray."

Libby leaned forward. "He wrote that note I found in your closet!"

"Who can say for sure, Libby? But yes. It was likely his doing. He's always been powerful, even back then. His family owns a lot of properties. Ray tried to meet with him about Tina, but Lawrence refused. Over the years he's been a thorn in Ray's side on occasion. He's wanted the Tidewater Inn for all this time. I wouldn't be surprised if he thought he could get Tina back too, at some point along the way. He was an annoyance, of course. But I never thought he would harm your mother."

"I bet he wrote those notes we found in Tina's jewelry box," Libby said to her sister.

Alec shifted on his perch. "Tom needs to know about this. I

bet he's going to want to talk to Nicole about Rooney. I'll run into town and talk to him. I'll meet you out at the ruins later, Libby."

Libby flopped on the sand beside her friend and drew in a deep breath. The long run to the lighthouse had tuckered her out. She turned her head and smiled at Nicole. Her heart overflowed with thankfulness. Nicole was alive! What a wonderful miracle and blessing from God. Nicole had begun to remember what happened to her too, but the men who kidnapped her weren't familiar.

She sat up and inhaled the clear air. "What happened here?"

Nicole stood, dusting the sand from her palms. "I came here the morning before I was kidnapped. Vanessa was going to bring me to see the ruins, but I was too eager to wait on her. I figured I'd let her show me around like I hadn't seen it. There's more here than you know though."

"The cave?"

Nicole nodded. "You know about it?"

Libby pointed toward the cellar opening. "We found it after we saw the cellar."

"Then you know about the treasure?"

"Treasure? All we found was poor Tina."

Nicole smiled. "Want to see? You're going to be excited."

"You're being very mysterious," Libby said, following her friend. "Where is it?"

"In the caves. Just outside the entrance to the cellar. You're going to love this."

"You know about the cellar?" Libby asked.

Nicole nodded. "I found a map in your dad's Bible."

Libby followed Nicole back into the water. They waded through a shallow pool to the base of the rocks.

"You have to dive here to see the opening," Nicole said. She took off her shorts and top to reveal her bikini. "I was snorkeling here and just happened to find it. It's not hard though. Follow me." She held her breath and ducked under the water.

Libby stripped to her one-piece suit and followed. The opening was barely big enough to wiggle through. Nicole disappeared through the hole and Libby went right behind her, determined not to let her friend out of sight. They surfaced in a cave about twenty feet in diameter. The ceiling was ten feet from the surface of the water. Several holes in the rocks illuminated the space, though Libby had to squint to see.

"Bet it gets tight in here during high tide," Libby said.

Nicole nodded. "I wouldn't want to be here then." She swam to the other side and hefted herself onto a flat rock. "This way."

"I can't believe you came in here."

"I had a flashlight with me that day," Nicole said. "Wait until you see this though." She rose and went to the curving wall. "Someone put everything we need right here."

Libby heard a rasp, then light flared from a match. Moments later a light was flickering. "What on earth?" She heaved herself out of the water and went to where Nicole stood. "Someone has put candles and matches in here?"

"Look how old the candlesticks are," Nicole said.

Libby examined it. "It's bronze. Looks late sixteen hundreds maybe."

"It goes with the other things I found. Follow me."

Nicole led her down a long narrow passageway. The sound of dripping became stronger. The floor was damp and slippery under Libby's feet. At one juncture her inclination was to go right, but Nicole led her left.

"Where are we going?"

"The other room is this way. Almost there."

The candle cast flickering shadows onto the wall. Libby wanted to be back in the sunlight instead of this dark, dank place.

Nicole dropped to her knees. "Now we have to crawl."

"How on earth did you find this?"

"I dropped something right here. It rolled under this ledge and I found the opening." Nicole and the light disappeared under the rocky ledge.

Panicked at being left in the dark, Libby hurried after her and emerged into a larger cave. The candle did little to illuminate what felt like a vast space. A moment later another candle flared to life.

"Look around," Nicole said, smiling. She handed Libby another candle.

This candlestick was also old. Libby held it high and turned toward some objects on the wall to her right. Artifacts leaped out at her: a ship's bell, candlesticks, tin plates and cups, several portholes and helm items. Several cannons were in a jumble. There were many objects she didn't recognize.

She stepped closer. "What is this room?"

"I think it was a headquarters for Edward Teach."

"Blackbeard? Come on, Nicole."

"Look." Nicole stepped to the jumble and held her candle close to the ship's bell. The words *Queen Anne's Revenge* were engraved on the brass.

"Blackbeard's pride and joy," Libby said.

"I found a ship's log too. It says it's Teach's. But I don't see it now. Funny—the stash is smaller than I remember. This stuff is probably worth a fortune to museums. There's no gold or jewels but a wealth of information."

This rich history was more exciting to Libby than gold coins. "I bet the government will want to make this a protected area. Either a state park or a federal one."

"Probably. Archaeologists will have to confirm the artifacts' authenticity, but it all looks real to me."

"But the ship sank offshore somewhere around here. Wouldn't the bell have gone down with it?"

Nicole turned. "You're right. I hadn't thought about that. Did someone find the wreck and bring these things up?"

"Maybe. But this place might be more than a storage room. There are wooden bunks and old blankets. What's left of them anyway." Libby turned to stare at her friend. "It's going to take some professionals to figure this out. Did anyone know you found this? Maybe finding this was why someone wanted to shut you up."

"I don't think so. I only told Horace."

"I think we won't tell the professionals," a man said from behind them. "We won't tell anyone."

Both women whirled. Horace stood with a gun held casually in his hand.

"Horace?" Libby's gaze went to the gun in his hand. "What's this all about?"

"I can't let you ruin all my plans," Horace said. "I'm sorry. I didn't want it to come to this, but you leave me no choice."

Libby saw the determination on his face. "Nicole, the lights!" she screamed as she snuffed hers out between her forefinger and thumb. At the same time she threw herself atop her friend, and Nicole's light went out too. The cave was plunged into darkness. Then a bright light flashed from the gun.

FORTY

Alec told his cousin what he'd discovered about Lawrence Rooney. Tom called the state police in New York, and they agreed to pick up Rooney and question him about Tina's death. Alec thanked Tom and returned to the inn. The visit had taken longer than he'd expected, so he thought the women would be back from their outing to the lighthouse ruins.

He found Bree on the beach with Samson. "Is Libby back yet?"

She shook her head. "I haven't seen them. How long have they been gone?"

"A couple of hours."

"I cried just watching their reunion," Bree said. She rubbed Samson's head. "Reminds me of when I found Davy after thinking for a year that he was dead."

Alec had heard the story. "I have to admit, I thought Nicole was dead. Libby never gave up hope though."

Bree's smile held amusement. "It shows, you know."

"What shows?"

"How you feel about Libby."

His face warmed. "She's a friend."

Bree laughed. "She's more than that and you know it."

"Maybe she *could* be. We'll see where our relationship goes."

Kade and the children came to join them on the beach.

Samson rushed to them and licked Hannah's face. The little girl giggled and threw her arms around his neck. The older boy, Davy, ran ahead and splashed into the waves up to his knees. Alec's gaze lingered on the children. He'd always wanted a houseful of kids. What did Libby think about children?

He glanced at his watch. Where were they? Though they could just be lingering at the ruins, he felt a sense of unease. "I think I'll walk toward the lighthouse and intercept them. Lunch will be ready soon, so I'm sure they must be heading this way."

Bree's green eyes crinkled with amusement. "Have fun. I think I'll take the kids to build a sand castle." She put her arm around Kade's waist. "I haven't seen this big guy in days."

He hugged her back. "The twins have been asking for Mommy."

Alec went the other direction. The sand was soft, and he kicked off his sandals. When he still hadn't seen the women after ten minutes, he began to quicken his pace. Some unexplainable anxiety gnawed at his belly.

Someone had put Nicole on that island for a purpose. What if the women had stumbled into more danger? He broke into a run and was breathing heavily by the time he reached the ruins. There was no movement but the rustle of leaves in the maritime forest. The place was deserted, though he saw Libby's and Nicole's clothes on the beach.

He cupped his hands around his mouth. "Libby, Nicole!" His voice rose above the murmur of the waves. He listened, but there was no answering shout.

He walked to the water. The tide was going out, so their footprints were still intact in the sand. The footprints went into the water and didn't come out. What had happened here? Did they swim out to board a boat? If so, why weren't they back at the inn? And why did they leave their clothes? Not for the first time, he wished his cell phone would work on the island.

"Libby!" he shouted again. Where could she be?

He waded a few feet into the water. The waves were gentle today. He glanced at the rocks. The cave. Could the women have gone into it? Libby had said Nicole was an avid spelunker. Maybe she'd coaxed Libby into going in. It would explain the footprints leading back to the water. Could they have gotten trapped in there?

He sloshed through the waves to the mouth of the cave. He peered in but saw nothing. He shouted for Libby. His voice echoed off the stone walls, but he heard nothing. He exited the cave and waded to shore. The cellar door was closed. He opened it and descended as far into the darkness as he could, then shouted again. Still no answer.

Adrenaline gave Alec the energy he needed to make the run back to the inn. He was going to need Samson to help find the women.

The sound of water dripping penetrated the woozy feeling in Libby's head. She opened her eyes and blinked. A couple of candles flickered in the darkness. "Nicole?" she called out. Where was her friend?

"I'm here," a small voice said to her right.

Libby turned her head and saw Nicole against the wall. Her hands were tied in front of her. "Are you all right?"

"Yes. How do you feel?"

Libby's wrists were bound together. She raised them and touched her throbbing head. Her fingers came away sticky. "I'm bleeding. I think I hit my head."

"He shot you. Horace shot you." Nicole's voice rose.

Libby touched her head again and discovered a furrow. "The bullet just grazed me. I'm okay. The bleeding is stopping."

Clang. The noise across the room drew her attention, and she focused her bleary eyes as Horace used a sledgehammer on the wall.

He paused to wipe his brow. "Sorry about this, girls. I didn't want to hurt Nicole, and I really liked you, Libby. So I'm going to let the sea have you."

"I don't understand," she said, struggling to think through the roaring in her head.

"When I get this hole through, the tide will fill this cave. All evidence will be drowned. And no one will ever discover this cave full of secrets."

"But why? What harm could it do to let the world know about these artifacts?"

When he shrugged and began to pound again, she tried to think of what might happen if the world knew about this place. It would be an attraction to tourists. Knowing what she did about historical preservation, she was sure the government would take it over and run it as well. The state would want to preserve it, likely as a park. How could that be worth murder?

Kenneth Poe. She thought of what he'd said. *This* would be the spot of the new resort. But not if the state had the land. In fact, there would have to be access to the area. There would be no room for a huge resort complex on this side of the island. Poe's investor would not be allowed to purchase it.

Horace was an attorney. Had he been hired to help make sure the deal went through? Was he a partner with Lawrence Rooney? It made sense.

She waited until he stopped pounding again. "You're helping Poe? There's no crime in helping to close a sale."

"You think that's what he wants me to do?" Horace barked a laugh.

Libby weighed this revelation. And then the truth clicked.

"He knows you're a diver. He's paying you to get this stuff out of the cave before the state learns about it and steps in."

He stepped closer. "I don't expect you to sympathize, but I'm nearly bankrupt. Everything was sliding out of my fingers. The money I can get for this loot will save me. I'll be able to keep my boy at Harvard. I won't lose my house in Saint Croix. If this deal goes south, I'm finished. I'll have nothing left. I can't let that happen."

"And an old ship's bell is worth murdering two people?" Libby couldn't wrap her head around that kind of thinking. "Then why even tell me about the inheritance? You could have destroyed that will and let Brent and Vanessa inherit. They were going to sell to Lawrence."

His eyes narrowed. "That was my intention."

Libby caught her breath. "But Mindy mentioned it to Nicole."

"Stupid woman can't keep her mouth shut. I should have fired her long ago."

Libby struggled to get up and couldn't. "You can always start over somewhere else. Life isn't over just because your money is gone."

He seemed to be listening for a moment, then he shook his head. "It's gone too far now. If you live, you'll turn me in. I'll go to prison. My boy will have to quit college. My wife will have no support. Her family is all gone and I'm all she has. I'm sorry, but it has to be this way."

"We won't say a word, will we, Nicole?" Libby managed a smile. "I like you, Horace. Don't do something you'll never be able to live with."

His eyes filled with confusion, then he stepped back. "We both know you're just trying to save yourself. The minute you got home, you'd be calling Tom. I'm sorry. I really liked your father, you know. I'm glad he's not alive to know about this."

"He's watching from heaven," Libby said. "You think you're

doing this in secret? The Bible says we are surrounded by a great cloud of witnesses. And God sees everything."

Horace swallowed. "Don't you understand? I have no choice."

"There is always a choice to do right."

"Not this time. I'm boxed into a corner." He turned back to his task and began to whack at the wall again.

"Wait! You'll destroy all this treasure!"

He paused and turned back toward her again. "I got out what I could, but what's left is nothing compared to my family. And if you hadn't been snooping, I would have had time to transfer all of it to my basement. All but the cannons. So you have no one to blame but yourself." He lifted the sledgehammer again.

Thwack! Thwack! Two strikes from his sledgehammer and the wall began to crumble. He continued to pound until the hole was about three feet in diameter.

"I made it as large as I could so the end is quicker," he said. He dropped the sledgehammer. "Do you want the candles extinguished, or do you want to watch the water pour in? I want this to be as easy for you both as possible."

"Leave them lit, please," Libby said, trying to keep the panic from her voice.

Nicole began to struggle. "Please don't leave us here!"

Regret showed in Horace's eyes. "I'm so sorry," he said. "If I had any other option, I'd take it. God forgive me." He plunged through the door that led to the lighthouse cellar. Moments later the door shuddered and a deadbolt slammed home.

Though her ankles were bound, Libby began to struggle again and finally managed to get to her feet. "We've got to find a way to cut these ropes!" She jumped her way to the wall of artifacts. Surely there was a knife here somewhere. Or an ax. "Help me, Nicole!"

Nicole was crying, but she got on all fours, then managed to get upright. "We can't die here. I don't want to drown!"

"Stay calm," Libby said. "And pray." With her wrists tied together, all she could manage was an awkward sorting through of the artifacts. Bowls, cups, nothing sharp. "There's nothing here," she said.

She glanced toward the door. But no, she'd heard it lock. "Maybe we can hop out through the cave."

"We won't be able to swim."

"Alec will come looking for us. I know he'll look there."

As they moved toward the passage, water began to rush through the opening, faster and faster until the water was swirling around their ankles.

"Libby!" Nicole screamed.

FORTY-ONE

His lungs burning from his run, Alec stopped to catch his breath. He saw Bree and Kade still down the beach a ways. Brent was with them too. "Bree!" He broke into a run again.

She leaped to her feet when she saw him coming. "What's wrong? Where are the girls?"

"Missing." His breath heaving, Alec told her and Kade what he'd found. "Can we take Samson back to search?"

She snapped her fingers for the dog. "Right away." She glanced at Kade with an appeal on her face.

"Go, hon, I've got the kids. I'll be praying."

Relief flooded Bree's face. "You're the best. I'll grab Samson's vest from the SUV." She rushed up the hill to the drive.

"Bring flashlights," Kade called after her.

Brent's eyes were shadowed. "Libby's all right, isn't she?"

"I hope so."

Brent turned and looked out to sea, then back at Alec. "I need to tell you something. I wasn't sure before, but remember that diver who tried to drown Libby?"

"Yes."

"I saw what looked like a bite on Horace's arm the other day.

I saw him out at the lighthouse yesterday too. He was in his diving gear. I watched him through the binoculars, but I couldn't tell what he was doing. But he disappeared for a while under the rocks. I think there's a cave there."

Alec couldn't imagine that the jolly, absentminded attorney could be dangerous. "Maybe it just looked like a bite. Horace wouldn't hurt Libby or Nicole. I know about the cave, but I looked in there too."

"I suspect there's more there than you know. He was in there a long time and came out carrying a bag of something."

Bree returned with the flashlights and Samson's vest. "Ready?"

Alec took the flashlights. "Let's go. Thanks for the information, Brent. Tell Tom what you know. Come on, Bree. We'll take the boat." He turned and ran for the dinghy bobbing at the dock. He told himself Libby and Nicole were probably fine, but he didn't really believe his own reassurances. Something was wrong. Libby wouldn't worry them intentionally.

When they finally reached the ruins, he pointed to the cave. "There. The entrance to the cave is there." The boat scraped bottom. He leaped over the side and dragged it onto the sand, then handed Bree one of the flashlights. "Will Samson go in a cave?"

"Sure." She snapped her fingers. "He can sniff their clothes." Kneeling, she pointed to the pile of clothing without touching it. His tail wagging, Samson sniffed the clothing. "Search, boy!"

Samson whined, then his nose went up. He crisscrossed the beach, then barked and splashed into the water toward the rocks. "He's got a scent," Bree said.

Alec ran after him. "I had a feeling they were in there. But I called and they didn't answer." His gut clenched. What if someone had killed and dumped them? He pushed away the unspeakable thought.

The dog had reached the cave opening but seemed unsure

about how to enter. Alec ducked down, then clambered onto the ledge. He was dripping wet and realized he'd lost his flip-flops. "Come on, boy. Here, Samson."

Whining, Samson looked back toward Bree. "I'm going too," she told him. She splashed through the opening, then joined Alec on the ledge. "Come on, Samson."

The dog barked, then ducked his head and was inside. Bree helped the dog onto the ledge. Alec switched on the flashlight. The beam pushed back the shadows. "Libby, Nicole!" His shout rebounded off the walls and back at him. The cave floor was cold under his bare feet.

"Search, boy," Bree urged. She flipped on her flashlight as well and joined Alec. After a few minutes of walking, Samson's tail drooped. "Samson seems to have lost the scent," she said.

Alec pointed with his light down the passage. "The cellar is that way, but I checked the cellar."

"Let's check again anyway."

"Okay, this way." He illuminated their path with the light and led her toward the cellar. A few minutes later, they stood at the door. "Nothing," he said.

"I noticed what looked like a narrow passageway deeper into the rock a ways back. Let's check it out," Bree said.

"I didn't see it." He followed her back until she stopped and shone her light.

"There," she said. "It's narrow, but I think we can get through."

The passage seemed more a crack in the rock. He'd be able to get through, but just barely. "Would they have gone down there? They had no light."

"They might have seen it anyway."

He nodded. "I'll go first." He squeezed through the opening and found that the passageway widened to an even bigger space than the path that led to the cellar. "It's okay!"

Bree came through with Samson on her heels. "Search, Samson."

The dog wagged his tail and trotted forward, but it was clear that he hadn't picked up the scent again. Alec was beginning to feel discouraged. "This is leading through the rock to the ocean on the other side. I doubt we can go much farther." He tipped his head. "Hear that?"

Bree listened too. "Sounds like rushing water. You're probably right. We're going to find an opening into the sea up ahead. We might as well go back." She half turned, then Samson barked. He shot forward. "He's got a scent!"

Alec jerked forward into a run. The dog disappeared around the corner. Alec caught up with him in front of a locked door. There was a padlock on it, and water was pouring from under it. He pounded on it. "Libby!"

Samson's barking was frenzied. "She's close," Bree said. "Libby! Nicole!"

The roar of the water that they had heard was beyond this door. He had to get it open. There was nothing to use to bust off the lock. He heard a woman scream and he tensed. "Libby!" He jerked on the lock, but though it was rusty, it held. He didn't even have a shoe to help.

The flashlight! It was metal. "Hold your light on it," he ordered Bree. She shined the light onto the lock. He battered it with the flashlight that was in his hand, but the lock didn't budge. Moments later, his flashlight was in pieces.

Someone pounded on the other side of the door. Libby cried out, "We're here, Alec! The room is flooding. We're going to drown!"

"There's a lock on the door. I can't get it off. Hang on!" He turned around, looking for a rock, angry with himself that he hadn't thought of that before now.

Bree grabbed his hand. "There's no time! Look!" She pointed and he realized water was seeping out the sides of the door.

He clenched his hands. How was he going to save her?

———

Water was pouring through the opening Horace had made. It was now up to Libby's calves. She pounded on the door. "Help us, Alec!" Panic threatened to steal her power to reason. *Breathe.* She took a deep breath, then another. There had to be a way out of here.

Nicole had hopped along the cave floor to join Libby at the door. Her face was grim in the light of the flickering candle. The water was only a few inches from where the candle sat on a chest. When it was gone, Libby wouldn't be able to see Nicole's face.

"Lord, help us," she prayed.

"Are we going to die?" Nicole whispered. "I'm not like you. I never go to church. I haven't given God a thought through most of my life. I'm not ready to die, especially not with all I've done."

Peace seeped into Libby's soul. Whatever happened, God saw them. He held them close in his arms. "All you have to do is ask him to forgive you, Nicole. He's here with us. No matter what happens."

Nicole was sobbing. "I can't. I don't know how." She leaned against Libby.

The weight of her friend's body pressed against her, and Libby lurched to the side. When she did, she heard something splash into the water. Horace's sledgehammer. Had he left it behind? It could knock loose the lock. Would it fit under the door?

She pressed her lips to the crack in the door. "Alec, are you there?"

"I'm here. We're looking for a rock."

"I'm going to try to slide a sledgehammer under the door. Hang on." She knelt and grabbed the tool with her bound hands. The water was to her neck. She tried to slip it under the door. It stuck. "It won't fit!"

"Try turning it the other way," Nicole said. "Or slide it to a different spot. The bottom of the door isn't even."

Libby did as Nicole suggested. The water was rising fast. It was to her lips and the salt burned the cracks in her skin. She had to submerge to get enough leverage to push the tool. The sledge-hammer moved under the door's edge. Almost there. She jiggled it and slid it a few inches the other way. She felt a tug, then Alec pulled it away.

Gasping, she surfaced and sucked in air, but she had to float on her back to get it. The water was above her nose if she stayed on her knees. How could she regain her feet?

"Got it!" Alec yelled. "Step away from the door."

Libby tried to struggle back, but she was only able to move a few inches at a time with the water swirling around her bound hands and feet. "Move away, Nicole," she said as the door shuddered and rebounded with pounding on the other side.

The water was to Nicole's chest. She hopped away, managing to stay on her feet. Hanging on to Nicole's leg, Libby tried to get to her feet but couldn't. The candles sputtered and went out. The darkness wasn't quite complete because a little light came in from the hole where the water poured through. She released Nicole's leg and tried to float. The water seemed to be roaring into the cave now. The sound filled her ears, blocking out all thought. It was like floating in eternity, and she suspected she was about to die. She felt no fear though.

She reached her bound arms over her head, and her fingers touched Nicole's arm. Feeling her way to her friend's hand, she realized the water was nearly to Nicole's neck. The end would be

soon. "Please make it painless for Nicole, Lord," she whispered. "Receive us into your arms. Pray, Nicole."

She inhaled what she thought would be her last air, then a strong hand grabbed her around the waist. Alec's lips were against her ear.

"I've got you," he said.

"Nicole!"

"Bree has her. Let's get out of here." He propelled her through the water. "Hold your breath," he said. "We have to dive."

The roof of the cave was just above her. She sucked in as much air as she could manage, then nodded. With his arm around her waist, they dived. She opened her eyes, ignoring the stinging saltiness of the water. The dim light from the opening was just ahead. She saw Bree go through it with Nicole. *Thank you, God.*

Her head bumped the side of the opening, then Alec maneuvered them both through. The current caught them as they exited into open water. Her lungs began to burn with the need for oxygen. She cast her gaze upward. The top of the waves seemed so far away. She wasn't sure she could make it. Her panicked glance at Alec caused him to propel them faster.

Just when she thought she would have to inhale water, her head broke the surface. She dragged in air, then choked when a wave splashed her in the face. Alec still had his arm around her, and they floated in the waves.

He cupped her face with his hands as they floated. "I thought I'd lost you." He kissed her.

She clutched him and kissed him back, relishing the heat that swept through her veins, exulting in the fact that she was very much alive. When he lifted his head, she was even more breathless. "Where are Nicole and Bree?"

"On shore. I can see them." He turned her in the water so

she could see her friend waving. Bree and Samson were with her. Libby's limbs went weak.

"Let me see if I can loosen these ropes." He tore at the knots, then shook his head. "They'll have to be cut off. I'll help you." With his arm around her, they began to swim toward the shore.

It was slow going with only one of them able to propel them. She tried to pretend her bound legs were the fin of a mermaid, but it was awkward. Her muscles burned by the time her foot touched sand. Alec lifted her in his arms and staggered to shore with her, where they collapsed in a heap on the beach.

Samson licked her face and barked. "Good boy," she crooned. Nicole dropped to her knees beside her and burst into tears. "It's all right," Libby said. "We're safe."

FORTY-TWO

Tidewater Inn was even more beautiful after Libby's brush with death. It was home already. But what was she going to do about the mansion? She loved it so, but she couldn't afford to keep it up. As Alec guided the boat to the pier, she soaked in the sight of the lovely old Georgian house. She'd never own something so wonderful again.

"Libby!" Vanessa waved from the porch and ran down the curving steps.

Libby nearly fell off the pier when her sister grabbed her and held on as though she'd never let go. "Vanessa?"

"You're okay! I was so afraid when I heard you'd disappeared."

Libby hugged her back. "We're both fine."

Alec hovered at her side as though he feared letting her out of his sight.

"I'll talk to you later," Bree said. "I need to check on the children." Smiling, she went toward the house with Samson at her heels.

Libby followed with Alec close beside her. She wished she dared to reach out and take his hand.

Vanessa was still smiling. "Everyone is inside. The pastor came over to lead us in prayer for your safety."

Libby's gaze went to the necklace around Vanessa's neck. Maybe she'd really begun to think about what it meant. "We needed the prayers more than you know." She told Vanessa what had happened as they walked to the house.

Vanessa stopped at the base of the steps. "I know I've been nasty to you, Libby. I'm ashamed of myself when I remember all the terrible things I said. I'm sorry."

"You were in pain," Libby said. "I understand."

Vanessa shook her head. "I don't deserve for you to let me off the hook so easily. I know we have a long way to go, Libby, but I realized today when I thought you might be dead that I wanted you around. I want to learn what makes you laugh and cry. I want to try to learn to like reggae."

Libby smiled. "I'm not promising anything about oysters, but I'll try."

"It's a deal. You're not leaving, are you? You're staying here?"

Libby's smile faded. "I think I have to sell this place, Vanessa. There's no money for repairs." She gestured to the roof. "Look at the rot going on around the eaves. It's going to take a lot of money to fix it. But I'll split the sale price with you and Brent."

Alec tensed beside her. She wanted to explain her decision, but there was no way to make him understand.

Vanessa shook her head. "I realized today that if this place goes, everything will change. Brent argues that it will be change for the better, but I don't think so. There would be no more long walks on a nearly empty beach. No more pure sound of the waves and wind." Her voice broke. "There has to be another way. How much would it cost to fix it? I have an inheritance. I'll help."

Though the offer touched her, Libby shook her head. "It would be a hundred thousand dollars, I think. I couldn't let you do that. I'll pray about it. Maybe God will show us a way to save it."

Brent opened the door and came toward them. "I brought

Tom up to speed. He left to go arrest Horace. It took some talking to convince him I was telling him the truth. Horace has been part of this village forever. He was born and raised here. One of our own."

"I really liked him," Libby said. "I still can't believe it."

"The state police are going to come out and get a statement this evening. Are you up to that?" Brent asked. "You look wiped out."

"Yes. I just want it over with."

"I'll be inside," Vanessa said. "I want to talk to Brent." She joined her brother and they went inside.

Alec slipped his arm around Libby's waist, and they walked up the stairs together. "It's all over. Hard to believe. Now what?" he asked when they reached the porch.

"I'm going to make the biggest mess of chicken fajitas you ever saw and slather it with guacamole."

He grinned. "I'll even eat the hot sauce with you." His fingers traced the outline of her jaw. "You haven't answered my question."

She couldn't think with his touch igniting feelings she didn't know existed. "I don't know. I have to sell this place, Alec. You know I do."

"Don't decide too quickly. Are you willing to see what door God might open?"

"When you put it that way, how can I refuse?"

Laugh lines crinkled around his eyes. He bent his head and kissed her, then pulled back. "I think I can sweeten the pot a little. I don't want you to go. I want you to live here where I can take you out to dinner and to the movies."

Her heart was full to bursting. "You mean to see year-old movies?"

His breath stirred her hair. "I want to neck with you in the balcony and I don't care how old the movie is."

Her blood warmed at the expression in his eyes. "I'd like that too."

"I think we have something special, Libby. Something that will last. But you have to stay here to find out. You game?"

"I'm game," she said, suddenly breathless.

———

Her family. Libby's gaze lingered on every person around the large dining room table. Mr. McEwan, with his rheumy eyes and sparse hair. Delilah and her no-nonsense love for this place and for Ray. Bree and her family. Old Mr. Carter, who had already grabbed the homemade bread in the middle of the table. Her siblings Brent and Vanessa, already so dear. And Aunt Pearl, whom Libby loved so very much already. Only Nicole was absent. She'd given her statement to the state investigators, then gone back to Virginia Beach to attend to business. At least she wasn't pressuring Libby to sell the property.

Libby locked gazes with Alec, who was sitting across the table from her. Whatever happened, she wanted to live here on Hope Island, even if it wasn't in the beautiful old inn. This was home now.

Horace was sitting in jail awaiting trial, and everything he'd schemed to avoid would happen to him and his family anyway. Though he deserved his punishment, she grieved for his wife and children. He wasn't leaving a legacy of generosity like her father had. The police had checked out his computer and confirmed he had erased the video of the men he'd hired to get Nicole out of the way. With Horace's information, they'd been arrested too.

The police had discovered that Rooney and his goons hadn't actually killed Tina. She'd fallen and drowned in the cellar's standing water. When Poe found her, he'd panicked and left her there, then scuttled her boat to make it appear she'd been lost at sea. He was also in jail.

"I need your advice," Libby said during a lull in the conversation. "I don't want to sell this lovely old house. But I have no idea how to keep it." Libby listened to the hubbub around her as folks argued against selling the property.

She held out her hands. "Nothing would please me more than to keep Tidewater Inn, but I need some suggestions on *how* to make that possible. I got some quotes on restoration. Material alone is going to be seventy-five thousand dollars."

The group fell silent, and the dismay she saw on various faces made her heart plunge. But she could do a lot with the money from the sale of the property. Help her stepbrother and his family. Fix up the lifesaving station and other historic buildings in town. Help people recover from the hurricane. Buy Alec a new boat. There would be compensations for the blow to her soul if she had to give up Tidewater Inn.

Old Mr. Carter in his straw hat pointed a tobacco-stained finger at her. "I'd like to donate the money you need, young lady." He reached down to the old suitcase beside his chair, the same case he'd asked Alec to rescue during the hurricane evacuation, and it opened to reveal stacks of money. "There's plenty in here for materials if the townsfolk will donate the labor."

There was a group gasp around the table. "I couldn't. It might be years before I can pay you back, Mr. Carter," Libby said. She didn't want charity—she wanted a viable solution.

"Oh good grief, Libby," Vanessa said. "I've been looking at Daddy's art. There's our answer. Sell them."

The Allston paintings. Such an easy answer. Why hadn't she thought of it? "You're right," she said. "They are worth more than I need." She glanced at the dear faces around her. "But what about the town? Is selling better for the town, for progress? We need to be realistic."

"The ferry is still coming," Delilah said. "Tourists will need a

place to stay. Why not here? The rest of the town needs to think about what kinds of businesses are lacking and fill the need. We could end up with the best of both worlds. Like Ocracoke."

The ideas began to flow quickly. Libby couldn't stop smiling. She took notes in between bites of chicken fajitas, then later, after the table had been cleared, carried the dessert of flan out to the swing with Alec.

"Hey." He put his flan on his knee and slipped his arm around her. "I told you it would work out. You ready to accept the answer?"

"It's more than I'd hoped for." She touched his cheek with her fingers. "*You're* more than I hoped for."

His gaze held her rooted in place. "I look forward to exploring the future with you. Want to go to a movie tonight? I hear *An Officer and a Gentleman* is playing."

"Now that's *really* old," she said. "But I always sigh when Richard Gere sweeps her into his arms and carries her out of the factory."

"Would you settle for a moonlit ride in my fishing boat?" His smile was teasing.

"Will there be kissing involved?"

"Most certainly," he said.

"Then I accept." She didn't wait for the promised kiss, though, and lifted her face toward his in the moonlight.

ACKNOWLEDGMENTS

This book is a little bittersweet for me. It's my twenty-first project with Thomas Nelson, and Erin Healy has edited all but three of those stories. She's a fabulous writer in her own right, and *Tidewater Inn* is her last book to edit before plunging full time into her own wonderful novels. Thank you, Erin, for all the things you've taught me in the nine years we've worked together. We have been partners from that first Rock Harbor novel, *Without a Trace*. I treasure your friendship and your wisdom, and I'm so grateful for all the time you've spent on my novels. Love you, girl! I will be screaming from the sidelines for you louder than anyone else as you soar to the heights!

My Thomas Nelson team is my family and I love them and thank God for them every day. They helped me brainstorm this particular book too, and it was so fun to write because of that! Publisher Allen Arnold is loved by everyone in the industry—including me! He's a rock star! Senior Acquisitions Editor Ami McConnell (my dear friend and cheerleader) has an eye for character and theme like no one I know. I crave her analytical eye and love her heart. She's truly like a daughter to me. Marketing Manager Eric Mullett brings fabulous ideas to the table. Publicist Katie Bond is always willing to listen to my harebrained ideas. Extraordinary cover guru

Kristen Vasgaard (you so rock!) works hard to create the perfect cover—and does it. And, of course, I can't forget my other friends who are all part of my amazing fiction family: Natalie Hanemann, Amanda Bostic, Becky Monds, Ashley Schneider, Ruthie Dean, Jodi Hughes, Heather McCulloch, Dean Arvidson, and Megan Leedle. I wish I could name all the great folks who work on selling my books through different venues at Thomas Nelson. Hearing "well done" from you all is my motivation every day.

My agent, Karen Solem, has helped shape my career in many ways, and that includes kicking an idea to the curb when necessary. Thanks, Karen, you're the best!

Writing can be a lonely business, but God has blessed me with great writing friends and critique partners. Hannah Alexander (Cheryl Hodde), Kristin Billerbeck, Diann Hunt, and Denise Hunter make up the Girls Write Out squad (www.GirlsWriteOut .blogspot.com). I couldn't make it through a day without my peeps! Thanks to all of you for the work you do on my behalf, and for your friendship. I had great brainstorming help for this book from Robin Caroll. Thank you, friends!

I'm so grateful for my husband, Dave, who carts me around from city to city, washes towels, and chases down dinner without complaint. Thanks, honey! I couldn't do anything without you. My kids—Dave and Kara (and now Donna and Mark)—and my grandsons, James and Jorden Packer, love and support me in every way possible. Love you guys! Donna and Dave brought me the delight of my life—our little granddaughter, Alexa! I hope she understands soon what her Mimi does for a living as I'm about to embark on a children's book project for her.

Most importantly, I give my thanks to God, who has opened such amazing doors for me and makes the journey a golden one.

DEAR READER,

I'm so thrilled to share *Tidewater Inn* with you! The theme of the story—greed versus generosity—is one that resonates so much with me personally. If you're like me, you struggle to find the balance. No matter what resources God has blessed us with, he expects us to use them to help other people. Money isn't our only resource. Time, talents, and other gifts are to be given generously.

I also wanted to share the personal background of a character in the novel who is very special to me. Pearl is my grandma in the flesh, though the name Pearl is my first teacher in Sunday School. My grandma helped shape me in so many ways. She's been gone over twenty years, but I still hear her voice in my head. I strive every day to be more like her. I learned about Jesus at her knee. She taught me about generosity and loving other people. I owe her so much, and I wanted to share her with you. I hope you love Pearl as much as I loved my grandma! People say I'm just like her, and it's the highest compliment I could have. ☺

I so love to hear from you! Email me at colleen@colleencoble.com and let me know what you thought of the story.

Love,

Colleen

READING GROUP GUIDE

1. Libby had struggled to survive monetarily for years so the thought of having no worries about money was appealing. Money is not evil in itself. What do you think about wealth's influence on our spiritual lives?

2. It often seems our culture doesn't honor the older generation. Why don't we and what are we missing?

3. Vanessa and Brent didn't welcome Libby's intrusion into their lives. How would you feel if you found out you had a sibling you didn't know about?

4. Pearl is based on my grandma, and I smiled just writing her into the story. Her love for me and others was always unconditional. Do you have a person in your life who loves you that way?

5. Ray's biggest legacy wasn't money but a spiritual heritage. What do you hope to leave behind for your family?

6. Libby's struggle between greed and generosity is basically a struggle between selfishness and selflessness. What are some other common things we struggle with?

RETURN TO
HOPE BEACH IN

Rosemary Cottage

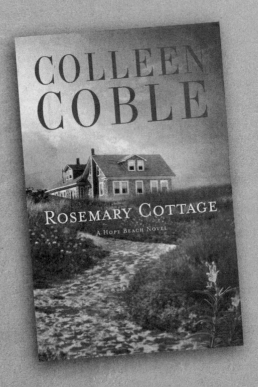

AVAILABLE JULY 2013

BLUE MOON PROMISE

is a story of hope, romance, and suspense . . .
immersing the reader in a rich historical tale
set under Texas stars.

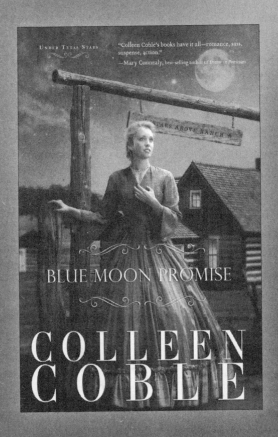

AVAILABLE IN PRINT AND E-BOOK

"*The Lightkeeper's Bride* is a wonderful story filled with mystery, intrigue, and romance. I loved every minute of it."

— CINDY WOODSMALL,
New York Times best-selling author of *The Hope of Refuge*

THE BEST-SELLING MERCY FALLS SERIES.

AVAILABLE IN PRINT AND E-BOOK

THOMAS NELSON
Since 1798

ESCAPE TO BLUEBIRD RANCH

AVAILABLE IN PRINT AND E-BOOK

THOMAS NELSON
Since 1798

Four friends devise a plan to turn Smitten, Vermont, into the country's premier romantic getaway—while each searches for her own true love along the way.

Colleen Coble,
Kristin Billerbeck,
Diann Hunt
& Denise Hunter

Smitten

Love is on the way

ALSO AVAILABLE IN E-BOOK FORMAT

THOMAS NELSON
Since 1798

ABOUT THE AUTHOR

Photo by Joe Saxton

RITA finalist Colleen Coble is the author of several best-selling romantic suspense series, including the Mercy Falls series, the Lonestar series, and the Rock Harbor series. She lives with her husband, Dave, in Indiana.